A Departure

Tom Ward

"a shockingly good debut novel about what happens when one world brutally ends and a new world begins. At its black heart, hope, humanity and a dream of escape. It will stay with you for long after you have read the final page.

Ward is a prize-winning journalist, an accomplished novelist and quite possibly the best young writer in the country. The smart move would be to read everything with his name on."

Tony Parsons,
Bestselling Author of Man and Boy

Printed for Crooked Cat by Createspace

First Green Line Edition, Crooked Cat Publishing Ltd. 2014

Discover us online:
www.crookedcatpublishing.com

Join us on facebook:
www.facebook.com/crookedcatpublishing

Tweet a photo of yourself holding
this book to **@crookedcatbooks**
and something nice will happen.

For Sue and Andy

About the Author:

Tom Ward is a 24 year-old British writer, and recipient of the 2012 GQ Norman Mailer Award. He has had short stories published on various websites and writes journalism for GQ, Marie Claire, Vice UK, Sabotage Times, Shortlist and Glamour.

Tom is represented by the Johnson & Alcock Literary Agency and can be found on Twitter at @TomWardWrites.

Acknowledgements:

Laurence Patterson - for taking a chance
George A. Romero - for making me long for a world without people
Danny Boyle -for showing me what this world looks like
Cormac McCarthy - for setting the standard
The O.B.B - for being all round good-eggs
Tony Parsons - for the advice and encouragement
Lance Kidney - for telling me I have a sick imagination

Tom Ward
March 2014

A Departure

Prologue

The sun covered them in its rays and made them golden. He held her hand up to the window, a slender silhouette against the glare from outside. Dust motes danced down her wrist and along her fragile arm. He sat up from the bed and gazed outside. A sycamore swayed lazily, the sky was a vibrant blue; a brilliant June day. The empty sky stretched before him like the empty days. College had become a hazy memory and now there were no obligations, except to each other.

She sat up beside him and slowly stroked his arm. The radio droned in the background, snatches of the news interlaced with their conversation.

"What are you thinking?"

"*...A major volcanic eruption inside the Arctic Circle...*"

He smiled. "I'm wondering why you always ask me that. As soon as you ask me I start trying to think about what I am thinking and then..."

"*...first time this volcano has erupted in almost 4,000 years...*"

Her fingers brushed his hand and his hairs stood on end. "Ok, what *were* you thinking?"

"*...no way near as catastrophic as the Novarupta eruption of 1912, but nevertheless has raised concerns due to f...*"

"I was thinking how everything is perfect. College is over, no more exams, I can drive..."

"*...perts say this change in activity could be to do with global warming and the rising temperatures which the Arctic is enduring as a consequence, howev...*"

"Yeah," she smiled. "Well done. I'm so relieved, we're finally free; as soon as we leave this bloody town we will be anyway.

Do you think... do you promise we'll still see each other?"

He looked into her eyes, staring up at him from under long lashes as sunlight burnt her cheek.

"*...inclement weather, cold winds over the next few days coming down from the north, unusual weather for this time of year. Ha! And I thought it was summer, what a shame...*"

"Of course we will. Durham is right next to Newcastle. Half an hour away. Not even that. I'll be able to come up and see you all the time and you can come down and see me, it'll be fine. It'll be great when we're both at uni, without our parents around...without your bloody mum..."

"*...avy rain, no surprise there! Well who...*"

"Hey, what has she done to you? She's always been nice. She cooks for you..."

"I know, I know. I'm sorry. You always slag her off though."

He felt her fingertips stand still on the back of his hand.

"Anyway, let's not talk about that. You asked me what I was thinking, and I was thinking that everything is perfect at the moment... and I think the main reason for that is... is being with you."

Something caught in his throat and his tongue felt too large for his mouth. "I love you."

Her nails pressed into his skin and her eyelashes became thick and wet. A pair of tears fell from blue wells and slid like a slow avalanche down her cheeks.

"Hey, don't cry..."

"I'm not... it's because I'm happy." She took his hand in hers and blinked her tears away. "I love you too."

He could feel her smile in his chest.

"I'm so happy. We're going to be together forever, aren't we?" she asked.

Outside, blue skies stretched as far as he could see.

"Yeah, we are. Forever."

Chapter One

Three days later

The car was smoother than his; quicker. He was going eighty-five but didn't notice. A mixture of sweat and blood stung his eyes and turned his vision red. A car stood abandoned in the middle of the road and he swerved around it, just in time. There was no driver to honk the horn. A body appeared on the road and he swerved again, but didn't quite manage to avoid the obstacle. The wheels bounced over the macabre speed bump.

His house appeared suddenly to his left and he pushed the clutch down and hit the brake hard. He was hardly aware of what he was doing. Too fast for his own driveway, he hit the fence that separated the two properties. The wood buckled and splintered, the windscreen cracked and the car stopped, half buried in the wreckage of the fence.

The seatbelt would not come off. He began to panic, his hands slippery and not his own. Finally, he unclipped the seatbelt and pushed the door open. He lurched from the car, clambering into the splintered fence and grazing his ribs. "Fuck!"

The boy grasped his side as he stumbled over the snapped matchsticks that used to be the fence. He stood a moment with his chin in his chest and sucked air between his teeth. He took a deep breath and straightened up.

Cornfields stretched away across the far side of the road. There had always been a stillness, a peaceful presence in the air when he looked into those fields. The corn swayed lazily on a summer's day and was calm in the cold nights. Now, in the evening dusk, the corn was serene, there was no wind to trouble it. In the distance, behind the field, the sun burnt low in the sky, a fiery smudge in the dusk light. The boy wiped something warm from the corner of his eye.

As he separated himself from the fence shards, he became aware of a jingling in the silence. He looked around. There it was, the man from *somewhere* on his street, riding his bicycle through the emptiness towards him. The man had a ruddy face that was a permanent shade of red, perhaps from sunburn through constantly being out riding his bicycle, or perhaps from the broken capillaries that formed an alcoholic's web across his cheeks and scabbed nose.

The swaying of the bike indicated that today at least, the latter was the cause of the man's complexion. The man approached the boy, the sky behind him mixed from a melancholy palette; deep blue stretched away from either side of the setting sun, the sun itself canvassed in crimson as though it was bleeding the last of its warmth into the western sky.

The man was almost there now. All the boy could do was wait to meet him. The only other option would be to run into an empty house. And the boy did not want to be alone, not yet.

The man's mood seemed juxtaposed against the darkness of the sky behind him as strains of a song echoed down the street. "Run, rabbit run, rabbit, run run."

The man was fat. A trilby hat just managed to balance on his head, and a dirty white vest held in his beer-bloated stomach. His face was decorated with white mutton-chops and a moustache bristled above his top lip. He looked like a Jim. The boy decided this was his name. He could call him whatever he wanted to, what did it matter now?

With, "He'll get by without his rabbit pie," Jim reached the boy.

The boy expected him to draw level and stop his bike, but instead Jim seemed to suddenly stop still; one minute he was sitting on the bike, the next he was standing there with his legs apart as the bike continued, wavered momentarily, then crashed into a lamppost.

"Never mind, eh?" Jim said. He drew close to the boy, his eyes darting quickly over the wounds on his face.

"How are ya? Fine night for it, hey?" With this, Jim half pirouetted, half spun around, gesturing behind him and towards the setting sun. He completed his dizzy circle, swayed, and then regained his balance. The air between them had turned to alcohol.

"How are ya then lad? How's yer dad? Where are they all?"

The boy ignored this. He did not offer any conversation to the man. He was not so sure his name was Jim now and he realised he only knew the man by sight. Now, especially, he had no reason to be polite. He waited for Jim to answer his own question.

"Who cares, eh? We have the place to ourselves! I've just been down to the pub, there's no one there! Empty! You want to join me fer a drink?"

"No, thank you."

"Fine. Hey, you know what we need? A car like that!" Jim jabbed a swollen finger in the direction of the car that was half buried in the remains of the fence.

"We could go anywhere in a car like that, what do you think? I don't know that my bike is much good anymore, do you?" Jim gestured past the boy to his bike, the boy followed his nod, but before he'd even had half a second to turn his head, Jim started up again.

He drew closer to the boy and lowered his voice to show he was serious. "It's our world now mate. Let's take your car."

"Erm, no, you're all right. I'm going to stay here for a while, see what happens."

"Then I'll take it! I'll have a ride round, then bring it back."

Jim's eyes bulged as he laid a fat hand on the boot of the car.

The boy wanted him to leave, but he couldn't let him have his father's car.

"No. This is my car, get your own. There are loads on the roads, all the way back from Hull. There's no one to drive them and no one cares about them."

Jim laughed. "I don't want one that's all smashed up; I want a nice new one."

"This one *is* all smashed up! Can't you see the windscreen or these broken shards of fucking wood all over it?"

Jim patted him on the shoulder again. "Calm down son, just give me the keys and I'll be off, don't worry."

The boy's eyes began to water. He took a deep breath, attempting to stay calm after the trials of the past few days. He mustered his last reserves of energy for a final show of defiance, hoping that after this, the man would piss off.

"Look, this is my car, not yours; there are plenty of cars abandoned on the road, with no one to drive them, so go get one of those. This one is mine, I'm sorry."

Jim seemed to suddenly sober up. The mist in his eyes cleared and he coughed up a ball of black phlegm that he spat to the ground, leaving a black string hanging from his mouth.

"I don't think you understand lad, give me your car!"

Wild eyes now and a flash of silver. A six-inch knife appeared in Jim's hand. The boy was too tired to be scared and was almost ready to give up to death, to go meet everyone he cared about, but he knew he could not give up that easily.

Jim lunged. The boy ducked to the side and found a broken fence post in his hand. He swung it into Jim's skull and the trilby spun away as the wood cracked. A fat fist hit the boy's cheek and he landed on his back. Jim launched himself on top of him and the boy rolled out of the way at the last second.

His fingers touched a stone and he closed his hand around it desperately, striking Jim a blow across the side of his fat face. They were sprawled side by side on the ground now. Jim lay face down, groaning into the concrete and then slowly, he began to rise. The boy saw this and threw his weight on top of the man and stayed there for some time, staring out across the fields. His eyes stung, his lungs were burning and he was hardly able to breathe through the pain.

Jim did not move and the boy remained on top of him, adrenaline shaking through his veins. Sweat weighed his T-shirt and his hands were clammy. After what seemed like a lifetime, he found the strength to get up.

He knew Jim was dead; that he had killed him, but it had been in self-defence. He couldn't get in trouble for it and, besides, who was there around to arrest him? Who was there *alive* to arrest him?

The boy was calm as he turned the body over and did not flinch when he was met by Jim's stony eyes, no longer full of drunken mirth. The white vest was tie-dyed red and the knife stuck out from Jim's gut. The boy wondered whether to take the knife. What should he do with the body? There was no one around to see it, but supposing someone did? Suddenly, he was scared. He was eighteen but felt like a helpless child. He stood up on shaking legs and walked away from the corpse lying in his driveway.

He had imagined what it would be like to kill someone: video games, action films. He had never been sure how he would feel if he were ever in that situation, but he hadn't imagined this feeling of emptiness, almost impartialness. Was killing that easy? Without warning, he doubled up and let forth a great green-black splurge of vomit that coated his jeans, leaving a long wet trail hanging from his mouth. He slid to the ground, kneeled in the puddle formed there, and vomited again.

With what felt like his last reserves of strength the boy pulled himself to his feet, using the still-standing shards of next-door's fence as a purchase for his slick hands. The splinters did not register.

The boy half-ran, half-limped around the side of his house and dug in his pocket for his key. Seeing the keyring felt like someone had punched his heart with a defibrillator. It was a small bear holding a heart, inscribed with the words '*Ti amo.*' His girlfriend had brought if for him as a souvenir from her holiday in Sicily. It was the last thing she had ever given him, a relic from an ancient time.

He stood motionless for a moment until a noise startled him into action. A dove taking flight. The key clattered in the lock and fell to the ground; the bear brushed his sick splattered jeans.

"Fuck!" His curse was a desolate and lonely noise that soon became swallowed by the empty evening. There was a certain heaviness in the air, as though the grief of the past three days was a tangible weight, asphyxiating the familiar stillness. The boy shivered and tried the lock again. This time the key found its place and the door opened.

Once inside, he slammed the door shut, locked it, drew the bolt and threw down the blind. His first thought was to put the lights on, but he was afraid someone would notice from outside. Maybe there was someone who had seen what had happened to Jim; or even another Jim, wanting to kill him and take his car. However, if he left the lights off, he would not be able to see if someone lurked in the shadows of his home, waiting with equally hostile intent.

"Get hold of yourself."

The boy took a breath and waited for his heart to calm itself. He knew that no one was in the house; they had locked it when they left that morning and it had still been locked when he had returned.

Try the lights. He hit the kitchen switch and the lights surged and then fell back into darkness with a crack that told him the fuse had gone. It was the same in the hallway. He opened a cupboard. Where were those bloody candles? Matches. Of course the first didn't work, nor the second. He let the snapped sticks fall to the floor and managed to light a candle with the third.

The light bobbed and cast shadows around the room. They were more pleasant than eerie, reminding him of bygone Halloweens, dressed up as a bin-bag witch with the house lit by candles. He would never see his family again. He forced these thoughts to the back of his mind, he had to overcome the feelings which ripened in his stomach; he had to keep busy.

He shook these thoughts from his mind, then dashed around the empty house and closed all the windows, drew the curtains and checked all the locks.

Moonlight shining through the window illuminated the bathroom mirror. The moon was fat and lit the room like a lunar floodlight borrowed from an empty football pitch. The boy studied the face staring out at him from the cold mirror. Deep lines of black shadow marked his features whilst the moon picked out his cheek and eyebrow along one side of his face. He seemed to have aged years, decades even.

His face was smeared with blood, dust, dirt, sweat and tears, a patchwork of grief detailing the hardships of the past three days. The face staring back at him was not his; the reflection did not even seem real. The boy reached out a hand and touched the reflection in the mirror, expecting it to dissipate like a ghostly fog, but it did not, and when he retracted his hand and touched his actual face, the reflection did the same.

He closed the blind and brought the candle in from the hallway. He had left it outside, afraid to leave unguarded darkness behind him. The candle added warmth to his reflection and seemed to banish the ghostly imitation created by the moonlight, which was now safely shut outside.

The boy paced about the bathroom and decided to try to wash, but only a thin gurgle of tepid water escaped the tap and all he succeeded in doing was spreading the dirt around his face. He stood in front of the mirror, not knowing what to do next and realised that he was alone in this house. Completely and utterly alone. There might not even be anyone left in any of the houses on the street. Was that a good thing? This was his home; he should not feel afraid, except now, in darkness and candle light, everything seemed foreign and unfamiliar. His life in this house seemed like a distant memory, only half recalled. Now there was no life to make it his home; it was simply an empty house.

Practicality took hold and he went downstairs into the kitchen once again, the candle sending shadows racing ahead. He was reluctant to take the knife from the drawer. He knew he should feel repulsed after what had happened with Jim, and he also thought that some sort of attack was unlikely, but a few days ago he had thought it unlikely that England, that the World, could be plunged into such catastrophe. Tucking the kitchen knife into his belt, he headed back upstairs and into his bedroom.

He did not recognise that room either. Clothes lay across the floor and his desk drawers had been flung open. It seemed more than fifteen hours ago that he had hastily packed as many of his belongings as he could fit into his old college bag and loaded it into the car, saying his goodbyes to this place, for what he thought was going to be forever. It was a mournful occasion, being reunited with his belongings again, his books strewn across his desk, his guitar resting against the windowsill; even the sight of his bed filled him with a sense of loss. It was like seeing an old friend again, but not having enough time to talk with them, and knowing that you'd never see them again, not in your entire life. He felt stupid, ashamed. People had died. He had lost his family and his friends and now he was upset about leaving his belongings behind.

Grief over the loss of his family re-surfaced in his mind but he pushed it back, saving it to deal with at a later date. Keep busy. He tore the quilt and pillow from the bed and trailed them through to the bathroom. It was the only room with a lock. After he had shut and bolted the door he felt safer, hidden away in this stronghold. It was the same feeling he had felt as a child, making dens; in here his solitude was almost impenetrable.

The thought of sleeping in the bath crossed his mind, but he dismissed the notion almost as soon as it appeared, he would be safe enough sleeping on the floor. No one would be attacking him with mortars or heavy artillery, if anyone attacked him at all. It was probable that no one even knew he was in there, and even more probable that whoever did notice would have their own problems to deal with. However, the boy did not entirely believe this, and he blew out the candle as a precaution against a tell-tale glow being seen from outside. The candle had offered him warmth and had bolstered his morale, but it had to be sacrificed to ensure his safety.

He arranged his pillow and quilt and laid down, wondering what to do with the knife. Should he keep it tucked into his jeans, or take it out and lay it nearby, perhaps under the pillow? Comfort won and he took the knife out and laid it next to the pillow, within arm's reach.

As recently as three days ago he had always gone to sleep with the knowledge that he would be safe in the night and would wake up again in the morning. Now, as he closed his eyes, Jim's stained vest appeared before him and the bruise on his face began to throb incessantly.

The boy shook his head as though chilled by a sudden draft and turned onto his back. He tried to keep his mind busy, tossing and turning and thinking happy thoughts. He remembered how he had tried to sleep in the bathroom once when he was younger, the idea seemed stupid to him now, but then it was an adventure. His father had almost tripped over him as he came in in the middle of the night and he'd shouted and told him he was an idiot for sleeping there. After that he had abandoned his camp and gone back into his own room.

Thoughts of his family continued to linger in the forefront of his mind, and he continued pushing them away, playing tennis with his memories. He did his best to keep his mind occupied and resist the thoughts he did not wish to entertain. But it was impossible to fight against his exhaustion and, as he began to surrender to sleep, his emotions crept over him.

Before, he had been a wind-up car, running without any thought and on limited energy, an empty vessel, but now he felt a crushing weight as everything came surging back. Before now he had not had chance to properly accept what had happened over the past three days. It was impossible that it could have happened: that over two thirds of the country could just drop dead. His friends, his family, almost all of them, had died. He had watched some of them die.

The boy remembered walking through town with his friends on Saturday, three days, and yet a lifetime ago. Families shopped, mothers pushed prams, college girls in short skirts giggled, a tramp busked and a couple hurled insults at each other from opposite ends of the street. Rubbish blew lazily and the sun painted over the dismal grey of the town with fresh warmth. The college girls shrieked and held their skirts down as the breeze blustered about them and the tramp began to shout in their direction, his vodka bottle outstretched in offering. A crowd of pigeons hobbled about a woman on a bench, scattering into the air as a young man in a tracksuit ran past, glancing over his shoulder.

The wind picked up and rubbish flew now, given life and wings by the wind. Skirts blew freely around the waists of the girls and the pigeons ducked and weaved in the air. Glass shook in the windows of the shop fronts in a rattling melee and a baby began to cry.

The gust became a gale. The tramp, resplendent in a suit jacket and jogging bottoms, had the cap blown from his grime-caked scalp. The wind grew to a crescendo, rubbish

14

forming an almost solid wall as it churned and flew in the air and then, as suddenly as it had started, the wind abated and the day was calm, rubbish dropping from the air as if someone had suddenly pulled the plug.

Along the street, people stood for a moment as though frozen. Then they began to fall. They did not trip, putting their arms out for protection; they fell lifelessly, straight down, like trees being felled. Some fell like dominos, knocking over those next to them. Some fell into shop doorways and confused the automatic doors, which opened for them and then shut, and then opened again, the bodies awful doorstops.

A teenage girl screamed at the still forms of what had, minutes ago, been a squabble of her friends.

The baby's cry had been replaced by her mother's. "My daughter! My daughter, someone help my daughter, please, she's not moving!"

The tramp glanced around in bewilderment. He took a gulp of vodka and limped off down the street after his hat, moving as fast as he could go. The boy was left standing there, surrounded by unmoving bodies, surrounded by the still forms of his friends as a few people milled about the street in shock, not knowing what to do, like dazed survivors on a battlefield. An old Indian woman cradled her husband's head in her arms, begging him to get up.

***

"Michael, Michael!" His mother's voice. "Come on, we have to go. We're leaving today. We're going to a safe place. Come on, you can sleep on the boat."

"Ok," he said aloud, half opening his eyes.

Of course, it was a dream. That was how his mother had woken him that morning. He lay there on his bathroom floor and the fog of the dream hung over him.

Slowly, he began to realise where he was, to remember what

had happened. He was alone in the night. As a child he used to wake up in the night, scared, but it would be all right because his mum would come, and then the morning would come, and he would be fine. Now his mother would never come to him again and the morning would offer no protection. The morning would only shine a new light on the horror of the past days.

Tears flooded Michael's eyes and ran down his cheeks. He felt no shame in his tears and there was no one around to judge him, anyway.

He lay there desperately alone and let out a meek cry in the night. "Mum."

But he knew she would not come. There were times when he had hated his family. He had spent long hours hating how mundane their lives were, how depressing and how stifling this town had been. He hated their choice to have children there and to live there instead of seeking somewhere exciting, exotic. He had been jealous of his friends, whose parents were richer and could afford holidays abroad, and he felt guilty now for condemning his parents for their complacency in life.

Michael realised now that none of that mattered. There had been so many stupid arguments and disagreements that he could never apologise for. He knew his resentment had been normal, but that did not alter how he felt now. His family were gone and he would never get a chance to tell them how much he loved them.

He fell asleep thinking of his sister when she was eight. Of how her mouth was full of toothless gaps and of how she had cried because she was scared of monsters. And he thought of how he had told her there were only monsters on the other side of the world, trying to cheer her up, but had only managed to upset her more.

Chapter Two

The next day was a scorching example of what June should be. The sun burnt the dry earth and birds flapped drunkenly from tree to tree. Light slanted in through the closed bathroom blind and cut Michael's face into alternate strips of shadow and light. The previous night's tears had left his cheeks streaked with the sweat, blood and mud that marked his face.

He awoke slowly as the light crept over him. His eyes burned and there was a steady throbbing behind his forehead. His mouth was dry as he staggered to the sink. Still no water. He tried the bath taps. Clear liquid splurged forward as pipes creaked inside the walls and Michael hurriedly gulped mouthfuls of the warm water from his cupped hands. The water ran for a few seconds before spluttering and gurgling into brown, watery mud, which splashed back at him and over his face and T-shirt.

Michael took the T-shirt off, wiped his face with it, and stood studying himself in the mirror. He felt and looked hung over. The lines he'd noticed in the mirror last night were now clearly pronounced in the daylight and the corners of his eyes looked red and sore. Stubble had grown around his chin; the only place he could grow it. A few days ago he would have been checking the rest of his face for new black hairs, but he did not think of that today. His skin felt greasy and he tried to think of a way to get clean. There was plenty of shower gel and shampoo in the cupboard, but without water, they were useless.

He scanned the room for something of use or an indication of what he should do now. The knife glinted at him from beside his pillow and he remembered the previous night's fears. In daylight, the knife seemed an unnecessary precaution and Michael was almost able to convince himself that the past few days had been nothing more than a bad dream. The lurching of his guts told him it had not and the image of Jim lying dead flashed across his mind. He slid the knife into his belt, taking no chances.

He made his way downstairs through the dormant house, past his sister's bedroom where goldfish floated at the top of their tank. Downstairs, the house was bathed in shadows, as if waiting for everyone to wake up. Light crept in at the edges of the curtains and the letterbox hung still. No post today.

A layer of dust had settled over everything in the kitchen and flies buzzed over unwashed pots in the sink. Michael opened the fridge and was met by darkness. The smell told him it must have turned itself off sometime after they had left the previous day. Cooked sausages on a plate looked edible enough and he salvaged them along with a bottle of Coke, which he hurriedly opened and held to his dry lips, the brown liquid spilling over his chin and making his eyes water.

Michael almost finished the whole bottle, then put it down on the counter and burped loudly. He began to laugh, but stopped himself as his eyes met a photograph of his sister on the kitchen counter. He would never be able to laugh at anything again.

He continued his search for food and found bread and Coco Pops in the cupboard. The bread was fine but when he took the milk from the fridge it was sour, so he left it on the side and put the Coco Pops back. Toast and sausages for breakfast, then. The toaster didn't work; neither did the cooker, nor the lights, nor the TV in the next room when he tried them. The electricity had finally run out. His father had said it would, acting like he had been in this situation before. Now it looked as though the power stations had either finally shut down or the electricity was being siphoned off elsewhere.

Michael pulled out a chair from the kitchen table. The chair legs scraped loudly across the stone floor and set his teeth on edge. He sat down and began eating his dry bread and sausages and washing them down with the warm coke. It wasn't the best breakfast he had eaten.

He thought of his girlfriend and how they had laid in her room four days ago. Then, the world was perfect. Now, he would never see her again. She was another person to add to the list of those who had left him. Who did he know now? His friends had all died or left town, but left for where? He didn't know. They had left into the unknown, just as his own family had tried and failed to do yesterday.

Michael chewed the dry bread slowly and thought suddenly of his mother's face, the eyes unmoving. How could it have happened? They were *soldiers, British soldiers;* not some rag-tag group of African rebels, drunk and stoned, but professional British soldiers.

The telephone rang and he came back to the present, except it wasn't the telephone but a dove warbling outside, perhaps the same one that had scared him last night.

"Fuck off," he said under his breath.

He glanced sideways without turning his head as though trying to direct his curse at the dove through his eyes.

"Cooo." The dove was not troubled by the boy's response; it was only a bird and the troubles of humans were not its own.

"Fuck off!" Michael yelled, and with this, he stood and upturned the kitchen table, sending his plate skimming through the air to smash against a cupboard. Outside, the dove had departed and silence had descended.

Michael stood on weak legs and brought a hand to his forehead. His headache had worsened. He raided the cupboard and tins and packets spilled forth until he found some paracetamol, two of which he washed down with the warm coke. What the hell was he going to do now? He had no one, nowhere to go. Yesterday, driving back from Hull, the radio had said that United Nations had ordered Britain be quarantined. All channels. An emergency national broadcast. After repeating the message for an hour, the radio had ebbed into silence and there had been no more voices on any channel.

The few days after Michael had been witness to his friends suddenly dropping like wilted flowers to lie at his feet had been pandemonium. On that first day he had stood in the middle of the high street for what had seemed like hours, trying to comprehend what had happened, the situation too surreal to understand. There had been the sound of a ringing phone then as well, and after a while he had realised it was his phone, and suddenly, he was holding it to his ear as his mother's voice brought him out of his daydream.

"Michael, Michael...are you there? Answer me...Answer m..."

"I'm here...what, what's happening?" he said, hesitating, stammering.

"I don't know love, are you okay? We're all fine. We're all fine. Dad's just gone to get your sister; she's been at Natalie's house... she's so upset."

"Mum...what's happened?" he asked, and he tried not to look at the bodies lying in the street like fallen leaves.

"I...I don't know love. I don't know. Come home... please." As she said these last words, her voice had cracked and wavered and then there was silence for a moment.

Michael wiped his eyes with the back of his hand. "I will, don't worry... I love you mum."

"I love you too son, come home." More sobs, and then he had hung up, embarrassed and alone in the street.

Michael did not know what to do now either. For a long while he stared out into the garden and was not even aware he was staring. His mind was blank, subconsciously absorbing the beautiful day outside. Small, quick movements captured his attention like a ripple spreading outwards on the lake of his consciousness. A bird alighted from a tree, excreting a trail of black faeces that hung in the air momentarily, before falling earthwards and landing in the centre of the trampoline in the garden.

The impact brought Michael back to reality. His head cleared as he moved away from the window. He knew what he had to do. He could not stay there, it would be pointless. There was nothing in this place for him anymore. He was not waiting for someone; no one was coming, certainly not his family. He did not want to stay there on his own either, what sort of life would that be? He did not want to live like some sort of vagrant in a dead town, scavenging for food like a feral dog.

The only option was to take a car and leave. His own car would never last and his parents' was not in the best condition. He would have to take an abandoned car from the streets and just drive away and never come back. He did not have an exact plan, but he thought perhaps if he got to Dover there might still be a ferry across to Calais, or some soldiers to help. He shook his head. No, not soldiers, he should avoid them at all costs.

It was decided. For the first time in four days, Michael felt good about something; he had a plan and a direction to take. Surely there would be a boat at Dover, perhaps not a ferry, but maybe something small. Something. Perhaps the French were helping survivors to escape. 'Survivors'. He hated that word, as far as he was concerned he had not survived anything, he just wasn't dead. Perhaps the French would be helping the 'Not-dead' to safety. They had said Britain was being quarantined, but surely they would help him; he wasn't infectious. There must be thousands of 'Not-dead' all over the country, all wanting to escape. 'Not-dead'. That wasn't much better than 'Survivors'. It was too close to 'Un-dead'. Perhaps 'People' was the only title he could use and he wondered why he had not thought of that before.

For the second time in as many days, Michael found himself rushing around his house collecting his belongings for the last time. Much of what he would have wanted to take, he had already packed the previous day and taken to Hull, leaving it behind in the commotion after the panic had started, abandoning his belongings to their fate beside the river.

***

The loft hatch opened with a creak. The ladder swung down and hit the floor with a bang, narrowly missing Michael's feet. He climbed up and gingerly plugged in the light, trying not to touch the exposed wires which looked like they had been gnawed at by a rat. He flicked the switch, forgetting there was no electricity. Of course the light did not come on and Michael was left feeling foolish as he stood half in, half out of the black hatch.

The meek daylight, which crept into the house from around the edges of the landing curtains, just about penetrated the darkness of the loft space, providing enough light for Michael to look around. The air was more dust than oxygen and he coughed as he pulled himself into the ceiling space, then crouched for a moment, wheezing in the semi-darkness. The air was warm and thick and he felt his skin prickle in the stuffy heat. After a few moments, his lungs became accustomed to the loft space and he set about his search. He quickly found what he was looking for, an old holdall that no one had used for years, covered in dust behind the Christmas lights. It was the only bag left in the house after his entire family had packed away all of their belongings the previous day.

Michael dragged the bag out from behind the lights and dusted it off with his hands, the rising cloud of dust sending him into another coughing spree.

He was about to climb back down when he noticed a box of photo albums resting on the floor just inside the loft hatch. He took one out and began to flick through its yellowed pages. His childhood filled his eyes and brought a tear to each.

He paused on one picture; his family and his grandparents on holiday in Cornwall. Remembering that holiday now, he felt like it was only two or three years ago, but realised it must have been more like seven or eight. In the picture, the sky was blue and they all stood huddled together against a stone wall behind which lay the beach. His grandmother's hair was still an auburn brown, his father looked slimmer, his mother had fewer wrinkles and his grandfather looked strong as he lifted Michael's sister in his arms. Michael saw himself, standing at the corner of the image, frowning.

The photograph shook something from the corners of his mind. His grandfather was supposed to have come with them the day before... Michael remembered standing in the living room, waiting with his bags beside him, his mother on the telephone, the muscles of her jaw quivering as she listened to her father's voice. Slowly, she had replaced the receiver and picked up her bags. "He's not coming."

That had been the end of the matter. How could Michael have forgotten him? Michael had lost his grandmother with everyone else, but his grandfather had refused to come and stay with them whilst they waited for the government to help them, and he had refused again when they realised there would be no help and decided to leave. Michael would not leave him a third time. He would go and see him now. Michael would make him come with him, and together they would leave.

He ran downstairs and picked up the telephone. No dial tone. No electricity. Did phones need electricity? Even if they didn't, Michael knew that, by now, the networks would all be down with no one to man them. Even if they were still capable of operating, surely the phone companies would have shut them down, rather than waste money and energy supplying a country where two-thirds of the population were not able to pay their bills. Michael put the phone down. His visit to his grandfather would have to be a surprise.

Michael dashed about with renewed vigour and began packing his holdall. He had packed most of his clothes the previous day and now he had only one pair of boxer shorts left. They would have to do. He changed the ones he had on for the fresh pair. He put his jeans back on and pulled on a new T-shirt. He knew it was too hot for his jacket, but he thought he just might need one along the way and he put it on. He had the Converse shoes he had been wearing, a hole appearing now in the heel, but they were his only pair and would have to do. Hopefully, he would not be doing much walking.

Michael looked around his room and wondered what else he might need. Not his digital camera, guitar or mobile phone charger. He tore a picture from the wall, of his girlfriend smiling in his arms, and folded it up, putting it into his jacket pocket along with the photo he had taken from the album in the loft.

Michael had his house key in his pocket and wondered if he would ever need it again. It felt wrong to leave it behind, a memory of this place where he had spent his childhood and it was attached to the key ring his girlfriend had bought him, still covered in black and green sick. He tried to wipe off as much as he could on an old jumper, and then put the keys back into his pocket.

His car keys were on his desk but he knew he would not need them. He glanced out the window at the ancient blue grey car that stood there rusting and decaying like an elephant gone to the elephant's graveyard to lie its bulk down and begin decomposing. He would definitely need a new car, or at least one in working condition.

Satisfied there was nothing else he could take from his

bedroom, Michael headed downstairs to gather other essentials. Food was paramount. He would not get far without it. He crammed as many tins and packets as he could into his holdall, and then filled carrier bags with what remained. He only left a tin of mincemeat, a festive relic out of place in the summer season.

The fridge was a write-off and there was nothing that could be salvaged, save the Coke, which he had already drank most of. He took the remaining bread from the side where he had left it and put it in one of the bags along with the Coke. He found matches, candles, and a torch hidden at the back of the cupboard, along with a few batteries and assorted pills, which went into a side pocket of the holdall. There was nothing else he would need; plastic cups and empty vases would not come in handy.

Michael zipped up the holdall and gathered the bunch of carrier bags. He had everything he might need. He looked around the kitchen. Was this really going to be the last time he would ever see this house? The last time he would ever set foot in it? Four days ago all he had wanted was to leave, to get out of this town. He had been looking forward to going to university, to making something of himself, so he did not have to live in a place like this, but now his house was bathed in melancholy.

Michael realised then that this house had not been the source of his frustration; it had been more of a safe haven from the banal town which rested close by like some grey animal of oppression. He would not miss the town, only some of the people who had lived in it.

So, farewell to this house, his home of eighteen years. Without his family to make them real, his memories of the place were dead, and if they were dead, they existed only in his head, where they would remain for ever. He need not feel guilty about leaving this place.

Michael decided to leave the curtains drawn as a sign of

respect, keeping the house covered up, preserved in case he ever came back. He swung the holdall over one shoulder, gathered up the carrier bags and made his way to the backdoor.

He was about to leave when he remembered he had not packed a map book, something which he thought might be somewhat essential, and so he raced back upstairs, anticlimactically passing the empty rooms he had just said a sentimental goodbye to. Eventually, he was ready and he gathered up his bags once more and stepped out into the daylight.

As he shut the door and turned the key in the lock, he felt like a curator closing up a museum, a capsule for the future, one that anticipated a time when explorers of the future would come across it and open it up. They would wonder who had lived there and how they had lived.

***

Michael placed the key beneath a plant pot, leaving the tiny bear to guard his home as a sort of promise that he would one day return. He walked down the drive and looked over his parents' car, which he had expertly parked in the neighbour's fence. It did not look so bad, just a few scratches. He could always drive it for a little while, and then swap it for another one abandoned on some road.

Michael circled the car, checking its condition. His eyes saw a crumpled and bloody heap on the ground, and he swept them away to his neighbour's driveway, where he caught a flash of silver half-hidden behind the wooden ruins of the fence. It was a brand new Jaguar and it looked to be in fine condition.

An old Bengali woman lived next door and the car was her son's. Michael did not know what her son did to be able to afford a Jaguar, but it was the nicest car anyone living on his

26

street had ever owned. He couldn't just take it though, could he? No, he couldn't; it belonged to someone, someone he knew, or at least someone he had occasionally nodded at over the fence.

Michael put down his bags and clambered over the ruins of the fence. He walked down the neighbour's driveway and around to the back door. The door stood ajar and it was dark inside the house.

He rapped lightly on the open door and whispered, more than called, "Hello?"

No one answered and Michael tried to pretend there was a possibility they might just be sleeping.

"Hello," he called again, louder this time. "It's Michael, from, next door...I just wondered if..."

He cut himself short. He knew they were dead. He had not *seen* them die, but if they were alive, there was no reason why they would still be there. If there were alive, why hadn't they taken their car and left?

Michael stood on the threshold and he knew there was nothing for it but to be a man and go inside to look for the car keys.

Gingerly, he placed first one foot and then the other inside the doorway. He hesitated on the threshold for a second before passing inside into the darkness.

The house had exactly the same layout as his, but in reverse, and so he stood once again in a dark kitchen. He felt as though he was trespassing and, even though he knew there would be no answer, he decided to call out one last time. "Hello!"

What was intended as a loud and assertive shout escaped as a hoarse whisper. He was half-glad when no one replied, embarrassed by this feeble attempt.

The living room too was shrouded in darkness, but an odd green light seemed intertwined with the gloom, as though it were both a part of it and a separate colour all at once.

Michael stepped further into the room. Heavy green curtains were drawn across the windows. He took another step into the room and all other thoughts were beaten from his mind by a stale odour which he could taste in his mouth and feel on his skin. It battered his nostrils and burned his eyes. It was the smell of rotting meat or eggs, but he knew the cause was neither.

Tears brimmed in Michael's eyes, a combination of the stench and fear. He gagged and cupped both hands to his face, protecting his mouth and nose. He imagined breathing in small particles of dead flesh floating in the air and it was all he could do to stop himself gagging.

Michael did not know what the right thing to do would be, should he leave now, or continue into the room and possibly find the car keys? He felt like a thief now as he realised he would be stealing from a grave. Maybe they would not mind though, maybe they would want him to take their car, after all, they were dead and did not need it, and it would be a huge help to him.

He was tired of thinking about making decisions and decided to just make one. He stepped inside, his hands still cupped around his mouth. The room was L-shaped like his own living room and he had to round the corner before he found the source of the smell. Why had he come in here? He had known they were dead and there they were, mother and son together.

The old woman and her son were sitting in front of a blank TV; both slumped in their chairs, as if asleep. Their skin looked drawn over their sallow faces and their cheeks were sunken pits. The smell was even worse here and Michael watched as small flies rose from the corpses, buzzing angrily at the disturbance. He looked away and out of the corner of his eyes he caught an insect of some nature crawling over the son's shoe.

Michael steadied himself against the back of a chair. He had come this far, he had to think about this logically; they had the car keys he needed. They did not need them and couldn't use them now. They were dead, they did not care what he did, and they would not have minded anyway. It was simple.

Michael took a step nearer the bodies and vomited. A small puddle of yellow splashed onto the carpet to be absorbed and rot there, and then he was only retching; he had nothing else left.

Wiping his mouth on the back of his sleeve, Michael tiptoed towards the bodies. He felt guilty that he was there, interrupting their peaceful sleep, as though he were reading the names on other people's gravestones. He remembered zombie films and vampire films and expected the bodies to rise at any moment and sink their teeth into his neck.

The son was dressed smartly in a shirt and black trousers: surely he would have the keys. The shirt pockets did not look like they had anything in them, so Michael moved his attention to the trouser pockets. The man's stomach was bloated and the pockets looked tight against the flesh of the thigh. Michael would not have fancied searching around in the pockets near a man's crotch if the man had been alive, but now the situation was a thousand times worse.

He was going to have to do it quickly; count to three and then plunge his hand in there. He stood panting as his heart hammered in his chest, one arm outstretched, ready to dart forward like someone trying to catch a dangerous animal.

Michael counted out loud. "Ok...one...two... one, two, three..."

He lurched forward an inch, then rocked on his feet like a stalled car.

"Come on, don't be a coward," he said to himself.

He began his countdown again. "Come on, one, two, come on, say three, say three... one, two, three!"

His hand was in the dead man's right pocket and then the left. He fished around thoroughly, not wishing to miss

29

anything, and only wanting to have to do this once. He could feel nothing but a wallet and a rectangular shape, which he guessed, was a packet of chewing gum. No luck there.

Michael looked around in the half-gloom of the room and his attention came to rest on the man's suit jacket laid over the back of his chair. The jacket was pinned to the chair by the dead man's weight. Michael was hesitant to touch it; was it right to touch a dead man's suit jacket? He decided it was no more impolite than rummaging through his trouser pockets. He reached out and gave the jacket a slight tug, but it remained wedged where it was.

Michael did not want to have to move the body, but whatever he was going to do he would have to do it quickly; he did not think he could stand the smell for much longer.

"Fuck it."

He grabbed the jacket and dragged it out in a single sharp movement, like a magician pulling out a table cloth from under a dinner set. The body rocked forward in one stiff motion, then slipped to the side so that it rested half on and half off the chair. Until a few days ago it would have been the most unnatural thing Michael had ever seen; now it was just one of many.

Michael quickly checked the pockets, not forgetting the inside one, and found them all to be empty. Frustrated now and wanting to leave, Michael put his hands inside the jacket so that they were covered, like someone using a plastic bag as a glove to pick up something unsavoury, and pushed the man's body back into its previous position. It felt like touching stone through goalkeeper's gloves. He left the jacket draped over the head. That was the respectful thing to do, was it not?

The old woman sat there staring at him with open eyes behind half-moon glasses and a gawking mouth that housed a blackening tongue. Michael gagged and glanced around, ready to abandon the search for the keys. It was not worth looking through dead people's pockets for car keys.

He stumbled backwards away from the dead woman and banged his leg on the corner of the coffee table behind him. "Shit!"

Michael hobbled around to better see where he was going and saw, there on the table, almost laughing at him, a set of keys with a Jaguar key ring laid beside an empty saucer. He laughed bitterly, snatched up the keys, and limped to the door.

He paused involuntarily when he noticed the dinner table, covered by a yellow cloth. Michael ripped the cloth from the table in a single movement, sending flowers crashing to the floor, then dragged the cloth across to the woman's corpse in a daze. There was no disgust now, only sympathy for this woman. She had not been a friend of his; Michael had not made the effort to get to know her, but he was sure she did not deserve to be left exposed to the world, looking like a hideous and gawking caricature of the woman she had once been. He threw the cloth over her, then turned and limped from the house, leaving the scent of death behind.

***

Michael unlocked the Jaguar and stuffed his shopping bags into the backseat. He turned the key in the ignition and the engine roared into life. The gears were strange and he put the car into fifth instead of reverse, before correcting his mistake and reversing at speed out of the driveway, bumping over the path and into the empty road where he found first gear and sped away, tin cans spilling from the bags into the back foot wells.

He did not glance out the window as he left his home behind; it was a place that existed only in his memory now. He sped away, swerving past abandoned cars, headed for his grandparents' house.

Chapter Three

Michael's grandparents lived in a quiet retirement estate filled with garish mobile homes painted mint green and salmon pink. When he was younger, Michael had not noticed how repulsive these homes were, and remembered asking his mother if they could get some gnomes for their front garden too, to which she had replied with a simple "No."

The estate was like a little town of its own, with enough winding streets to get lost for days. Michael had often wondered how the oldest residents survived in there. He had always imagined that some of them must have got lost trying to find their way home after a Tuesday afternoon trip to Asda. They would have been forced to live as vagrants, forever wandering in search of their homes. The handouts of the passing families with their screaming children would be all they had to sustain them.

Now, as Michael rolled over speed bumps and drove slowly past the gaudy mobile homes, this imagined situation appeared to have been realised. Here and there an elderly resident wandered, some dressed in only a gown and slippers, almost all of them clutching a Zimmer Frame or walking stick. They wandered on their own, each a lost and solitary figure, rambling aimlessly. Their faces displayed no emotion and they made no reaction to Michael as he passed.

An old woman in a sky blue dress stepped out into the road and Michael had to slam on the brakes to avoid hitting her. The car stopped inches away from the woman and she looked up from the road with vacant eyes before continuing on her way.

Michael shook his head slowly in disbelief as the residents milled about the streets like zombies. He wondered if some of them had retreated into their memories, into brittle minds too fragile to deal with the catastrophe at hand. After a life of ups and downs, hardships and happiness had these people had enough and finally given up?

A sense of melancholia descended upon Michael as he drove along. He began to think about what their lives may have been like. Some of these old shells might have been great people, or they may have had the potential to be great and never really accomplished what they wanted to. The spark had dimmed over the years, dimmed into incompetence and garish houses. Now, more than ever, these people were beyond help.

Michael drove slowly, turning these thoughts over in his head, and suddenly, he found himself outside a white pebble-dashed mobile home that after a second he recognised as his grandparents'. It was bigger than most on the estate and bricks had been laid around the bottom of it to make it seem like a real house instead of a temporary one.

Familiarity had always made it feel less garish than the other homes, but the plant pots on the gravel lawn went some way towards making up for this. Behind this house and the others on the row was a small wood and a smaller lake. Teenagers used to burn cars in the woods and Michael remembered a fire engine appearing once as smoke drifted towards the heavens from somewhere amongst the trees.

He parked the car and without bothering to lock it, he strode purposefully up to the front door. Michael knocked loudly to no response.

When no one had answered after the fourth knock, Michael began to panic, there had to be somebody he loved left. A noise from around the back of the house caught his attention and Michael left the front door and walked around to the side gate.

As he was fiddling with the gate that led onto the back

patio, his grandfather appeared from a gateway opposite, which was partly concealed by a rose bush and led out on to the bank of the lake. He was a big man, somewhere in his seventies. When he was younger, Michael had always thought of him as Sean Connery's Bond, possibly due to his Scottish roots or Naval past, and whenever Michael thought of him, he always saw Connery in his mind's eye instead.

A faded tattoo of a Naval motif was still visible on his grandfather's permanently-tanned right forearm which, today, protruded from a white short-sleeved shirt. The shirt was tucked neatly into grey chinos and a white fishing hat rested above his elephantine ears, protecting his bald head from the glare of the sun. In one hand he carried a large bag of stale bread. As he came through the gate he looked up and noticed his grandson standing there.

"Mike! You all right lad? I didn't know you were coming. I've just been feeding the ducks. Hungry little buggers, lots of cygnets this year too, don't know where they're all coming from, terrapins will get most of 'em though," he said, swinging the bread bag in the direction of the lake.

He frowned and turned back to Michael, scratching an ear with his free hand.

"I thought you'd left?" he asked, and before Michael had a chance to reply he was being ushered inside. "Come in, come on."

His grandfather led him towards the back door and up the steps. Michael walked after him in silence, unsure how to react to his surprisingly upbeat mood.

Michael's grandfather dropped the bread bag in a pile in the hall and they sat down in the living room, a comfortable room lined with maroon wallpaper and filled with crimson furniture and cherry cabinets, all of which did not quite fit together, but combined to achieve an eccentric palette of warmth that filled the room. Michael's grandfather sat opposite him and leaned forward in his chair, taking his fishing hat off as he did so, revealing the white bald patch beneath.

"What have you up to then lad, eh? Your grandma's asleep at the moment. She goes swimming every other morning you see, so she's knackered. What have you been up to?" he asked, rubbing his liver-spotted hands together in anticipation.

Michael hesitated to reply. What could he say to this? Did his grandfather really think his grandmother was still alive and was only sleeping? He must know what was happening, he was an intelligent man. Michael would not believe that he had finally lost it, become one of the zombies that aimlessly roamed the streets outside.

Michael studied his grandfather. He had had a triple heart bypass a few years ago, and only now did Michael realise the toll it had taken on him. His grandfather, once large and intimidating, looked shrunken and huddled. His giant's frame was hung with excess skin, where once it had been filled out and hard with muscle. Michael could not believe that those were the arms that used to lift him upside down, carry him outside and threaten to throw him in the lake, only half in jest, in Michael's young mind. The eyes too appeared older and a mist obscured their cobalt gaze.

He was the only grandfather Michael had ever known and his wife was the only grandmother Michael had known over the past six years, and Michael did not want to lose the very last one of his grandparents, the very last member of his family.

"Granddad," he said; it felt strange, the word an alien sound. He repeated the unfamiliar and fragile word. "Granddad...you...know what is going on...right? What's happening? What has been happening over the past few days? All of the people, well they're dead. Mum and dad, they're... gone..."

Something sank in Michael's chest as his bottom lip began to quiver. Suddenly, he was a young boy again, crying at his grandparents' house after falling over, but this time a plaster and some Germolene would not make things better.

He took a few deep breaths and bit his lip to hold it still. The rest of his story came rushing out like water over a fall.

"We went to Hull, to escape, like we told you. But the crowds... they were all pushing. And the soldiers, they started firing. And it..."

He stared at the pattern of the carpet and did not know what he was going to say next. Suddenly, he felt a large hand on his shoulder and he looked up from the crimson carpet. His grandfather leaned forward in his chair, two slow tears rolling over the cracked leather of his skin, like the first rains in a desert. It was the only time Michael had ever seen him cry.

The cold eyes behind the tears stared into Michael and without saying anything, told him that he would be ok. Michael believed it for a second and tried to jump to his feet, to do something, anything positive. His grandfather's hand on his shoulder pushed him back into his seat and he began to speak.

"Me and your grandma, we would have been married sixty years this August. Those sixty years are almost my whole life, and I could not have asked for a happier life. I remember when we were courting, she used to go away for the weekend, every now and then, with this girl she worked with. It was devastating, not being near her. She would only be a few hours away, Bridlington or Scarborough, but still, at those times it felt like I might never see her again. I used to send her letters, all embarrassing stuff I'm sure you don't want to hear. Anyway, when she was away, I thought, *At least she'll be home in a few days*. And then she was, she came back and my life was better than it had been when she was away."

Michael sniffed and wiped something from his eyes as thoughts of a girl and a sun-filled bedroom came to him. His grandfather patted him on the shoulder as he continued. "Then we got married, had your mum..."

The man sitting opposite Michael hesitated for a second and his eyes swept the room, trying to pick up the thread of his story. He scratched his bald head, a smile creased his face, and then he continued.

"Your grandma and I, we settled down. Even when we moved to this estate we were happy. We had everything we needed, a nice house, a bit of a lake outside and a bloody good family. This place isn't much, and most of the other old buggers around here are going dotty, but me and your grandma, we were at home here, wherever we were together, that was our home. Being together is the only thing we had known for most of our lives. That's why I couldn't come with you yesterday. I love you and your sister, your mum, even your dad. But Isabelle has my heart. A man has to stay close to his heart. I couldn't leave. I know you youngsters don't like living here, but everywhere is the same. You will never find a place where everything is perfect. If you tried, you'd be looking for something that you would never find, not that it matters now, I suppose. The closest I ever came to it was finding Belle, and when I found her, nothing else mattered. Home could be anywhere with her."

He paused again and ran a hand across his scalp as though he still had hair. His blue eyes stared at something over Michael's shoulder.

"Belle had a good life, she really did. I don't think she had ever been unhappy for more than a few hours, and her time came, as does everyone's. I was scared, in all honesty; I was scared to be alone, but I could not leave her. I put her in the bedroom and I've been sleeping in the spare. I'm not crazy. I know she's gone. I just didn't know what to do, how to act." He paused and smiled at Michael, and the boy felt his own spirits rising.

"It seems to me like you have some idea, which is a credit to you, because I'm clueless. They teach you all sorts in the Navy, but this... this sort of thing is unheard of. I'm too old for this; the problems of this world belong to a new generation now. Your Gran and I, we've had our share of trouble, but losing Belle and trying to live without her has been my greatest challenge. To be honest, now that she's gone, there isn't anything for me to live for anymore."

Michael's heart jumped into his throat. He was about to protest, but his grandfather continued before he could speak.

"No, don't say anything Michael. It's terrible that your mum's gone, she... she was such an angel when she was a young girl." A smile creased his face. "Your sister too, she was just the same, spitting image, but, and it sounds terrible to say, it doesn't make much of a difference to me now. I haven't got much time left, and I said my goodbyes before you all left yesterday. You coming back today, it was a nice surprise, but a sad one too. I had told myself I would never see any of you again, and I'm sorry if you've come here wanting my help. I'll give you anything you want, I'm not going to need much now, but I am an old man and soon I will die too."

He held up a hand to pre-empt Michael's response. "Yes Michael, I will, but you are young, lad, you've got to make your own way, especially now, in these times."

He paused and looked to be chewing on something, and then he said, "I'm sorry Mike. There is nothing I can do, except tell you that I believe in you..."

Tears flowed freely down both faces now. Michael stared at his grandfather, trying to hold his gaze as if that would somehow suddenly return everything to normal. His grandfather's misted eyes continued to stare over Michael's shoulder, as though over Michael's shoulder lay the past and a young and carefree Isabelle. Michael thought again of his own girlfriend. He needed to be with her again. He had to get out of there and he had to take his grandfather with him.

He stood up suddenly. "We have to leave here together. We can get to Dover, then to..."

The old man shook his head and with that one gesture

Michael was silenced. "No. No Michael, I'm not leaving. I am going to live out my final days with Belle here, at least in spirit."

Michael knew then that there was no way to change his grandfather's mind and defeat was an iron weight in his chest.

"What will you do now?" he asked.

His grandfather smiled. "I'll live, it won't be for long though, I don't think. It's ok, it's all right. I've known my time was coming for a while and now it's almost here. It's a happy time. I'm not religious, but I know I have taken as much as I can from this life and maybe there is another waiting, who knows? A life full of all the mates who have died over the years, a place where everyone is waiting for me: my parents, my family, your mum, Belle. Don't worry about me. Things can only get better for me. It's you I'm worried about, surviving alone here. Dover, eh? You best take some supplies. I assume you've got a car?"

With this, he rose, ambled across to the window and looked out at the car parked outside.

"A Jaguar. Ha, a bit better than the old AX, hey? Well, come on through to the kitchen and we'll see what I don't need."

Michael rose and followed him through to the kitchen. He stood in silence whilst his grandfather filled shopping bags from the cupboard for him, chattering away as he worked, normality temporarily restored.

"Yeah, they were selling these cheap, you get all sorts from that bargain shop, it's perfectly good quality too. I know we used to get a bit for your mum. Do you like peaches?"

Michael shook his head.

"No? Well more for me then."

**

After half an hour of raiding the cupboards, Michael stood

in the doorway, carrying three new carrier bags laden with food. His grandfather had given him almost everything in the house and had insisted he take it all, despite Michael's protests.

"You'll need it more than I do, lad."

Now there was nothing more to do and they stood, awkward in the silence, a little boy and his mountain of a grandfather, once again. Michael studied the patterns of the kitchen wallpaper and his grandfather put on his fishing hat and then took it off again.

The only thing left for Michael to do was leave and he reluctantly broke the silence. "Thank you for all of this. I'm sorry about Grandma. I hope that you will be ok...I love you."

His grandfather looked right into Michael's eyes now, the clouding mist no longer there. He nodded to the bags in Michael's hands. "Don't worry about all that stuff, I don't need it. Take it all out of my way, it's yours. It's a shame everything has gone tits up the way it has. We were going to leave you a little bit of money, your Gran and me. So I suppose this food can be your inheritance. Don't thank me too much."

He waved Michael out onto the front steps. "Now, go to Dover. Get out of here and live your life. Promise me one thing though? Don't stay in France when you get there. They're awful buggers, worked with a few in Egypt." He winked at Michael and for a brief second the beginnings of a smile flickered across his face.

Michael smiled. It was a natural reaction that he could not help, and this time he did not feel guilty. His grandfather returned the smile for a moment, then nodded. "I love you too Mike. Be careful; don't be too sad, it does no good to dwell. Remember you cannot change anything. Now, go," he said finally. He held the door open and Michael gathered up the bags and walked down the steps into the summer heat.

"Oh, wait!" One last thing from his grandfather who turned and disappeared back into the house. Michael could hear the sound of drawers opening and the contents being rummaged through. Strains of, "Where the hell is it?" carried back to him.

As he waited, Michael looked back into the house. He remembered playing dominoes at that table, making biscuit cake in the kitchen, picking his nose until it bled in that chair, being bored on Boxing Day afternoons. His grandfather emerged to fill the doorway again, this time carrying a Swiss army knife.

"You and your sister got me this for one of my birthdays; I don't know if you remember? I use it a lot; I just couldn't remember where I had put it. Anyway, I want you to have it. It might be of some use. It has a knife, a screwdriver, a bit for fishing with...lots of useful things."

Michael took the knife, and for a second he saw Jim's body outside his house. He swallowed and forced out the words, "Thanks, Granddad."

They embraced; his grandfather's arms once again powerful.

When the time came for them to part, neither shed a tear, and his grandfather stood watching from the doorway as Michael reversed the car back down the narrow streets to where he could turn around. Then his grandfather was a small figure in the doorway, then he vanished back into the house and Michael was gone, sliding past the zombies, as noticeable to them as smoke in the night.

Chapter Four

By now it was mid-afternoon and the sun had edged past the midpoint of the horizon and the heat had become more bearable. As he drove, Michael thought it strange that the sun should shine so inappropriately, but then the skies did not know or care about what happened below them, it made no difference to them whether there were seven billion people on Earth, or none. The sun and the other stars, the planets and distant universes, would be there long after the last human had vanished into obscurity.

To Michael, this town had only seemed habitable in the summer time, when parks were lit with green and trees cast shadows, instead of harbouring more cold or merely a small dry patch beneath their naked boughs. He knew the weather did not make a place what it was; it only helped to change people's moods and sometimes to make things more bearable. In the end, it was all just mood lighting, painting over the grey truths of this dreary canvas of a town.

Michael drove onwards, thinking of his grandfather and his whole family. He thought not of their deaths, but of their lives. He thought of his twenty-year old grandfather, sending love letters to his young grandmother whilst she was away on holiday. Why could people not stay young forever? What was the point of age, except to create memories and longing for what had been?

Michael drove past a park, practically the only sizeable one in town, the only one unspoilt, where you could go on a warm day and perhaps get lost and pretend you weren't in this town at all, but were visiting a forest somewhere.

Despite all of this, it was as though he was passing by in the middle of the night. The park was empty, devoid of all life. There were no joggers, no footballers, no children on the swings, nobody walking dogs, no girls in skirts, just empty fields of grass and trees. Michael decided it looked more peaceful that way, tranquil even.

Then he noticed something grotesque; a true act of betrayal. A small, but muscular, black dog snarled and slobbered as it sank its teeth into a dead man's leg, tearing into the limb, trying to devour both flesh and bone, the body shaking like a scarecrow as the dog pulled against it.

Michael could not watch anymore and he turned his attention back to the road. He imagined the dog's owners had died and the dog had been left starving for days. Perhaps the man in the park had been its owner and they had been out walking together when the wind came, and now his faithful hound had forgotten all allegiance, except to his own survival.

Michael drove along. The roads were littered with cars, now literally discarded rubbish; abandoned and unwanted, useless to the drivers who lay slumped at the wheel. Many had crashed into trees, or the car in front, when their drivers had suddenly lost their lives at the wheel, and this made the roads a dangerous and difficult place to traverse.

Michael did not know exactly where he was going; he only knew he needed to get out of town and head south. It would be impossible to leave via the motorway; he had travelled that way with his family the previous day and it was virtually blocked by the abandoned cars of people attempting to flee the town, like spiders washing down the drain. He would have to go through the villages that skirted the town, and then try to find the motorway again, in a place where it would be easier to join it. It was either that, or travel down A-roads all the way to Dover, he did not know which just yet. Right now Michael's only priority was to leave this town for good.

He checked the petrol gauge and found the tank was nearly

empty, so he steered the car in the direction of the nearest garage. Over the past few days, people had fought over what fuel was left at the petrol stations, taking as much as they could. It didn't worry Michael too much. There hadn't been that many people left with cars, and most of them would have left town over the past few days. There had to be petrol left somewhere.

***

Michael drove up to the garage slowly, approaching with caution. It was a twenty-four hour petrol station, which backed onto an old housing estate. From a few hundred feet away, Michael could make out only a few cars in the forecourt, certainly less than six, and there were no signs of anyone fighting.

For a moment, Michael panicked as he remembered he had not brought any money with him, but then he smiled dryly as he remembered there was not likely to be anyone there to ask him for money, nor was there anyone to arrest him, even if someone did ask him to pay. The thought lingered as he drove past the fast food restaurant he used to work at after long days at college. He could park now and smash all of the windows, and there was nothing the Colonel or anyone else could do about it. He knew it would not do any good though, if ever it would have, and he tightened his grip on the steering wheel and drove past.

As he pulled into the petrol station, Michael found himself amazed by the absurdity of it all. Over the previous few days, people had fought and nearly killed each other over fuel but today, they queued patiently in their cars as if they were on their way out for a nice Sunday afternoon drive. There was no hint of fighting or even impatience. Michael could not decide which was more absurd: people fighting for petrol, or people not fighting when there was no one to stop them and they could take what they wanted.

However, it looked like petrol was the only thing people were prepared to queue for. The kiosk window had been smashed, and the shop raided. A man in shorts walked across the forecourt to the window and leaned in through the broken glass, his upper body disappearing into the shop for a moment, before re-appearing with a bottle of water. He strode casually back to his car, swigging from the bottle.

When it was Michael's turn to fill up, he got out of the car quickly, wanting to get out of there as soon as he could. The calmness of the petrol station seemed to be inviting trouble. He fumbled with the nozzle and the petrol cap, the Jaguar unfamiliar to him. Eventually, he worked it out and began to fill the tank. Out of the corner of his eye he could see a man coming towards him, and he urged the petrol to go faster under his breath, so that he might avoid unwanted attention and conversation.

The man was making a beeline for Michael and did not appear to be about to stop. Michael looked up; it was clear that whoever he was, he was not going to leave him alone. The man was dressed in a suit, but was missing the jacket and had a wide grin spread across his face that looked like it was held there artificially and maintained with a degree of effort.

"Hello! Hello there!" the man called as he made his way towards Michael.

The man attempted a wave, but the movement caused him to come off balance and slip on spilt petrol.

He regained his balance and straightened out his tie as he came trotting over to stand beside Michael. He was skinny, of average height, with a beer gut that was prominent beneath his tucked-in shirt and at odds with his slim frame. He wore black round-framed glasses that matched his black curly hair and on his shirt he wore a name badge which informed anyone who cared that his name was Steve.

"Hi, my name's Steve," he said, offering a hand for Michael

to shake.

It was obvious to Michael that this man was not a threat, but there was still a possibility that he might be some sort of hanger-on, possibly looking for a ride in Michael's (borrowed) car.

Michael ignored the hand and Steve held it there for a second before letting it drop to his side in defeat.

"Yes. I'm Steve. Are you all right? Of course you're not, no one is are they, eh? Strange times we're living in. Now, what, what the *hell* do you think happened four days ago, eh? People just dropping dead, for no reason. It just doesn't happen, or it didn't. I heard on the radio, on the second day, that there was no explanation. You know, after the ambulances and police and firemen, well what was left of them, you know when they came and took some of the bodies away from the streets and everywhere else? Well apparently they ran tests, down in London, I suppose, and they said, experts it was, they said they could not determine the cause of death. No medical evidence, no clue as to what had killed all of these people. Isn't that weird?"

It was nothing Michael had not heard days ago.

"Yes, Steve. Yeah, it...it's weird. Now excuse me, I have to go." Michael struggled with the nozzle, distracted by Steve's further attempts to make conversation. In the end, he gave up and let it hang beside the pump.

Steve followed him around the car after he had refitted the fuel cap.

"Ok sure. Where are you going then? Out of town, eh? My parents are out of town, I'm not quite sure where, I haven't heard from them in a while..." Steve paused and fiddled with his tie again.

"Hey, I don't suppose I could come with you, get a lift outta here? We could all do with a friend right now, and I have loads of money, if you need it?"

Steve began to rummage in his trouser pockets, but

46

Michael quickly cut him off, "No thanks, Steve. I don't need money and this is my car, I'm not taking anyone with me. Sorry."

"Oh no, I don't need your car, I have one over there." Steve pointed to a shiny black Audi parked at another pump. "I was just wondering if you would like some company?"

"Well...thanks Steve, but I think it would really be for the best if I just went on my own. I've got some stuff to do, you know, kind of...personal stuff, so...no offence but..."

At that moment there came a crash of breaking glass, as flames erupted from behind the fence that separated the petrol station from the housing estate. Michael glanced over in surprise as a low murmur swept through the assembled customers.

The fire burnt fiercely, the peaks of the flames dancing visibly above the six-foot fence. Michael could feel the heat from where he stood. The fence was wooden, and it was only a matter of time before the fire caught on to it and devoured the wood, and then there would be no barrier between flame and fuel.

Steve's forehead creased in confusion. He began shuffling uneasily from one foot to the other. An expression which might have meant, "What the *hell* was that?" appeared on his face.

"I don't know," Michael said, in answer to the imagined question.

"What?" Steve asked, afraid he had missed something.

"Nothing."

Michael turned his attention back to the fence, knowing he should leave immediately, but curious as to what had caused the fire. A second passed before three pairs of hands, followed by three heads, then three bodies, appeared at the top of the fence. The three youths clambered over, trying to balance their cigarettes in their mouths and their beer cans in their hands as they jumped down onto the petrol station forecourt. They were dressed in a uniform of cheap, smoke-blackened tracksuits.

A fourth youth appeared at the top of the fence, and began to pass over a number of bottles filled with a clear liquid, with dirty rags stuffed into the necks. Michael had seen enough films to recognise a petrol bomb.

"Steve, we need to leave. Steve."

But Steve was distracted. He stared quizzically at the youths, like a naturalist observing a new species of animal for the first time. He wondered why these four boys were smeared in black ash, not linking them to the fire which was beginning to creep up and along the fence. As stood observing them, one of the youths took out a lighter, held the flame to the rag of one of the glass bottles, then hurled the petrol bomb back over the fence like a flaming baton.

A split second later, there came a crash of glass and a whoosh of flames from the far side of the fence. The boy turned and grinned at the others. "Fucking hell man, did you see that? Fucking Pakis; you're welcome to our estate now, hahaha."

Steve grabbed hold of Michael's arm.

"Oh my God, do you...do you think they...*burned* someone's home? An Asian's person's house? Oh my God."

"We need to get out of here," Michael said as he shook his arm free of Steve's grip. Michael was calmer than he thought he should be; Steve's anxiety irritated him and he resisted the urge to act in the same manner.

Steve ran towards his own car, fumbling in his pocket for his keys, but his escape was cut short when one of the boys noticed him, as a hound spots a rabbit that has just hopped from cover.

"What's this dickhead doing?"

They moved as one towards their new target. One of the boys began lighting a fresh petrol bomb, flaming scraps of rag floating in the fume-heavy air.

"Hey, all right mate, you got a pound?" one of the group called towards Steve.

Steve dropped his keys and jerked around in confusion.

"What? Why, what do you want a pound for?"

The boys were beside him now. The tallest of the four laughed, then punched Steve squarely in the face, breaking his glasses in two and causing blood to rupture from his nostrils.

Steve sank to the floor and curled into a ball, covering his head with his arms and trying to remain as inconspicuous as possible, not realising it was already too late. A woman screamed somewhere behind Michael and he turned to see her flee to her car, before screeching off and colliding with an abandoned four-wheel drive.

Michael was back in the playground. What could he do? Should he try and help Steve, try and save this stranger from the bullies, and in doing so, put himself at risk? He knew the right thing to do was to try, but it was easier watching a hero on screen than trying to be one. The boys kicked at the form huddled on the floor, jostling each other out of the way to get closer.

"See mate, we can do what we want. Where are the fucking police now, eh?" the tall one asked, directing the question towards no one in particular.

"Yeah, those Paki fucks didn't deserve to live, and now we're having a bit of fucking justice!" another chimed in.

"Fucking terrorists probably caused this thing!" a third spat.

Steve stammered meek oppositions from behind his skinny arms, which he still managed to hold over his face. "Please leave me alone...I have money. You can take what you want, just please leave me alone!"

"Shut up," spat the shortest of the group, a beer can in hand, its contents sloshing over the immobile prey.

"Where are the fucking pigs? Where are they now, eh? They're dead. They stop us doing what we like, and now the pricks are dead, just like those bastards next door."

Steve tried to raise his head clear of the melee, and one of the youths upended a can of beer over him, plastering down his hair in a sticky mess of blood and beer. A blood splattered St. George's flag flexed with the movement of the boy's arm.

The boy tilted back his head to scream at the sky and words erupted from the hole in his face like sewage from a burst pipe. "You pricks! This is our fucking town, this is our fucking country. We own this land, you bastards, and we'll do what we like."

Michael could stand no more. He wished he had something to throw at the gang of yobs, something to smash into their faces until they were incapable of making sounds. He had the penknife his grandfather had given him and the knife from his kitchen still tucked into his belt, but the thought of a cold blade and warm blood sent a shiver down his spine.

The words '*Run rabbit run, rabbit run run run*' began playing through Michael's mind. He shook his head but the song continued. He did not want to kill anyone else.

Michael unlocked the Jaguar, slid into the driver's seat and started the engine on the second attempt. He got out again, leaving the car running, and walked calmly over to the crowd of yobs, before punching the nearest one in the face. It was a bad punch, but it connected with the chin of the tall, skinny boy who reeled backwards in surprise.

Michael stood motionless for a second, in shock himself at what he had just done. A fist made contact with his face and brought him back to reality, and he flailed his arm in the direction of the punch without looking, lightly grazing something.

He knew he could not fight them all, and he grabbed Steve under the arm, dragged him out from the midst of the crowd and towards the waiting car. Steve was heavy and hung limply as Michael pulled him along, and when they reached the car, Michael had to push him into the passenger seat. Steve slouched there, sobbing inconsolably as blood seeped from the multitude of cuts that marked his face. Michael ran around to the driver's side, thrust the car into first gear, and then they set off at speed, almost crashing into a car that had been left abandoned in the bay in front of them when the yobs had appeared.

The boys set off after the car like greyhounds, all four of them sprinting beside the vehicle, one with blood shining down his face, another one with a flaming baton held high.

Steve was sticky with his own blood. He sobbed gently, then stuck his head out of the open window and screamed at the pursuers, "You mother fuckers! You fucks!"

Steve glanced around the car for something, squinting through his broken glasses. His eyes caught on the glint of the penknife in Michael's belt. Before Michael could stop him, Steve had snatched the penknife and half jumped, half fallen out of the car, the open door flapping behind him as he launched himself into the pursuing arsonists.

"Steve!" Michael yelled as he snatched at the empty space where, up until a few seconds ago, Steve had been. But now he was not there, and there was nothing Michael could do but watch the scene unfold behind him. He had tried.

A flash of orange in the rear-view mirror reminded Michael of the fire bomb still held by one of the yobs. He pulled Steve's door shut, put his foot down and sped away from the garage, swerving past a car which stood abandoned, partly blocking the road.

He was afraid to look back, but forced his eyes to the rear-view mirror. Steve was wielding the knife and one of the yobs lay on the ground, holding his stomach in a pool of blood. Two of the boys were trying to restrain Steve so that the tallest one could get in a clean punch, and that was when it happened.

The yob holding the petrol bomb released his grip on the bottle of fire as Steve's elbow connected with his face. It fell in slow motion, a perfectly rounded bottle, its contents swaying gently inside, as a crown of fire burned above, the liquid and fire protected from meeting each other only as long as the glass remained intact. Then, shattered glass, a detonation of shards and the liquid fire spreading like the contents of a dropped egg, engulfing the fighting men, leaping up their legs to entomb them in its bright shroud, rendering them screaming, scorching masses.

A pump exploded, sending an arrow of fire into the middle of the group of thrashing figures, causing one (Michael could not tell which) to be propelled backwards through the air into the windscreen of Steve's car.

The pumps exploded one by one, at their leisure, fashionably late to the party, making an entrance with a bang. Flames licked at cars momentarily before devouring them whole in new explosions. There was one final explosion as flames rocketed into the sky and consumed the petrol station, gorging themselves on the stored fuel; plumes and plumes of black smoke drifting to inhabit the air like a sinister flare.

The blast shook the Jaguar and it was thrust forward like a child's toy as the rear windscreen cracked with the force of the explosion. It felt like the car itself was on fire. Inside, the air was thick and hard to breathe, as though Michael was trapped in a capsule of burning gases. He imagined thrashing black human shapes dancing in the flames in the rear-view mirror, and he wrenched the mirror desperately to the side so that he could only see the carnage behind him in his mind.

All this happened slower than anything had ever happened in Michael's life, yet it had occurred faster than the blinking of an eye. The smell of burning seeped, through the open window, into the car. Michael closed the window quickly, and then closed all the vents desperately, almost violently, trying to beat back the smell of fire and burning bodies. He wanted to pull over and be sick and cry and he screamed into the steering wheel until his voice was hoarse and he sobbed empty tears.

He sped on and on, nearly hitting seventy miles an hour,

and almost crashing every second of the way as he swerved to avoid cars and bodies in the road. He passed a sign that told him he was now leaving this town and relief washed over him, and he vowed never to go back there again, not for anything. His house could rot into the ground, for all he cared now, it was infected by the noxious town and he would never again consider it a safe heaven. His grandfather too would soon be gone. He *was* gone now, choosing to live out his final days there alone.

There was nothing for Michael in that town, and there never had been. He did not belong amongst the scum who hassled people in the street and the cowards stuck in boring jobs and lives, who were too scared to change. He had hated it since he was old enough to hate and he hoped the petrol fire would spread and destroy the whole town.

Chapter Five

The hours slipped by as Michael drove onwards, every second taking him further from the town. He drove through dreary villages and past lonely fields, thinking of his family, his friends, of Jim and Steve, of bodies in the road, bodies next door and sour milk in the fridge. After a while, his mind became numb and he thought of nothing except the road ahead. He had only the vague destination of Dover to guide him, but he had taken no steps to ensure he was heading in the right direction, and in his desperation to distance himself from his town, Michael ploughed onwards and onwards along winding country roads, out into the unknown. For long stretches of time, the only vehicles he encountered were tractors, the bodies of farmers slumped at the wheels.

At first the sun held in the sky, but after a while, fog set in and heavy drops of ominous rain began to pattern the windscreen. Michael did not know how to work the windscreen wipers and struggled with buttons and switches until they came on. He had no idea what time it was and, checking his watch, he discovered it to be nine forty-one. Had it really only been that morning that he had woken up alone on his bathroom floor? So much had happened since then that it now felt like a long time ago. He wondered how many corpses had he seen that day. Too many for any eighteen year-old, that was for certain. Too many for anyone.

Michael felt a degree of resolve beginning to build inside of him. It had only been a single day, but he had survived so far; perhaps there was a chance of him surviving to become an old man and giving his grandson the same sense of determination his grandfather had given him.

The car crept onwards through the outlying villages. One village Michael passed through was home to a group of sobbing women, all kneeling at the foot of a tree, from the boughs of which hung two dead bodies, one a middle-aged man, one a small girl, her face pale and a noose around her neck. A ladder lay discarded at the foot of the tree beside the women. Michael looked away quickly and drove on.

The mist had thickened now and was pressing in around the car. He put the lights on, more to light his own way than to warn anyone of his presence, he doubted there *was* anyone else on the roads to warn, anyway.

The villages he passed through became ramshackle. Way out here in the country they had fallen into disrepair and local customs. Homemade signs proclaimed the speed limit as twenty miles an hour, but Michael was only doing ten. Old farming equipment was strewn along the roadsides, overflowing from fields, rusting in his path as he swerved through it.

He saw only one other car on this road, the first car in an hour. It was piled high with suitcases, rugs, blankets, boxes and bags. The car's burden was reflected a thousand times in the faces of the driver and her companion, who stared ahead with furrowed brows and vacant eyes.

Michael had begun to tire as the fog closed in around him, impeding his progress. If he stopped now it would have to be for the night. He doubted that out here in the sticks there would be any yobs like those from the estate, but he did not want to risk it. Who knew how many angry, shotgun-toting farmers patrolled the area? He decided if he was going to sleep, it would have to be in a field, away from the road and away from a village, somewhere where he would be hidden and safe. The area he was travelling through at that moment was ideal; an open stretch of road bordered on both sides by fields, with no villages that he could make out in the distance. He was certain no one would find him if he were to stop there, especially with the fog closing in every second.

Michael took the next turning down a bumpy lane that ended abruptly after only a few hundred yards. He had misjudged the turning in the fog and he reversed the car back onto the road, not bothering to look out for traffic, and continued onwards. A few miles along he came across a grassy field, cornered by a patch of trees in a far niche. A small track led down and, after following it for a while, Michael turned off and drove through the moisture laden tall grass, leaving a trail like that of a giant snake behind him in the failing light.

The trees were a mixture of sycamore and elder and they bunched together to create a shady copse, just large enough to accommodate the car as it forced its way in, the wet tires rolling over nettles and shrubs. Michael stopped the car, got out, stood and looked around in the failing light, he was almost certain the car could not be seen from the road. The spitting sky had increased its barrage and now heavy tears of rain were thumping down onto the car roof. The rain, along with the mist, had made it almost impossible to see more than a few metres.

Michael hurried back inside the car, out of the rain and was suddenly overcome with a wave of hunger. He held his growling stomach and realised he had not eaten since his dry bread that morning. There was a plentiful supply of food in the backseat, perhaps even too much for one person, especially as much of what his grandfather had given him would not last long without refrigeration.

With this in mind, Michael decided to go for the perishables first, and began to rummage through the bags like a stray dog searching through bins. He pulled out a packet of mackerel and tore it open, ripping away pieces of fish and swallowing them whole, ignoring the bones and wiping his oily hands on his jeans. He finished the fish, but it was not enough, and he opened another pack and ate nearly a quarter of a loaf of bread with it, before throwing the rubbish out into the rain that harassed the car and washed over the sides like a curtain, closing him in from the outside world.

Daylight was fading rapidly now and Michael wanted to finish his meal before it was dark. He did not want to have to use the light in the car and risk someone noticing it. He finished off the few apples he had, and was finally full. Now all he needed was something to wash it down. The flat Coke would have to go first. Michael's grandfather had given him some bottles of water, but the thought of drinking warm flat Coke made his stomach churn and he decided to get it out of the way.

As he lay there in the back of the car, Michael had an idea to collect rainwater to supplement his supplies. He would try to slice the empty Coke bottle in half and stand the two halves outside to collect rainwater that he could drink in the morning. This was easier said than done, and with his kitchen knife he eventually succeeded in cutting the bottle into two ragged edged shapes, which in no way resembled two halves. After doing this, Michael ran out into the rain and pushed the bottle halves mouth upwards into the ground, making sure to replace the lid so that dirt did not get into the top half.

Back in the car he was feeling pleased with himself and what he thought was an excellent idea. Outside the rain pattered incessantly against leaves and the metal of the car. There was nothing left to do but sleep. Michael's arms ached; there was a dull throbbing along his veins and his eyes felt dry and crusted. The front seat was no place to sleep; the backseat was the only choice. He had forgotten about the bags of food that sat in the back and he got out of the car and struggled with the keys to open the boot, and then ran around to the back door and grabbed as many bags as he could, trying to get the task done as quickly as possible in the downpour.

Michael threw the bags and his holdall into the boot, one bag splitting, sending cans and tins bouncing off into the

57

mud.

"Fuck," he hissed. It was not a problem; he could retrieve them in the morning. He slammed the boot down quickly and got into the backseat, shutting the door and locking the car from the inside.

With difficulty, and many banged limbs, Michael stripped down to just a T-shirt and jeans. Then he folded his wet jacket inside out and tucked it under his head as a pillow, then lay down with the knife beneath the jacket, as he had done the previous night. His cheek throbbed from the blows it had received, but before he had begun to think about the day's events, or feel sorry for himself, he was asleep.

***

His dreams were a montage of explosions, stabbings, punching and kicking. Fiery violence played through his mind like a Greek tragedy: act one; uncountable deaths, act two; deaths in flame and violence, and act three? He tossed and turned and sweated and muttered under his breath as he cried in his sleep and reached out to protect himself from people who were not there.

Michael awoke, still half asleep, carrying the demons of his dreams into reality. He searched frantically for the knife, before remembering where it was. He reached a hand under the jacket and felt the cool metal, and for the first time in four days he felt safe, hidden away there in the corner of this field in the middle of nowhere.

He sat upright in the backseat and rubbed the palms of his hands into his sleep-crusted eyes. His muscles ached and were twisted with cramp, and he tried to stretch as best he could in the back of the cramped car. Rain washed down the windows in steady streams, dripping in slowly through the crack in the rear-window. Alone in the dark car, Michael could not help but remember the journey to Hull with his family.

"Don't drive so fast, you'll crash. Watch out for that car!" his mother had cried from the passenger seat, as Michael's father focused on the road ahead.

"Will you shut up? For God's sake, I'm trying to get us away from here and all you can do is..."

"John, it's all very well trying to get us away, but if we die now we may as well have died days ago!"

"Will you shut up, both of you! You just moan and argue all the time. People are dead!" his sister had screamed from the backseat.

She had been brooding silently for the entire journey, and now, she could take their arguing no longer.

Their mother had turned around in her seat to face her. "Oh shut up Sarah, you aren't the only one who is upset. You don't have to be a bitch just because your boyfriend is missing."

At any other time, Michael would have tried to provoke his sister by saying something like, 'Yeah, he was a prick anyway,' but now was definitely not the time. He too had tried to ignore the arguing, but after a few minutes he had had enough.

"Oh for God's sake, shut up!"

His father had cut in.

"Mike..."

"Shut up! Shut up! You two are always arguing about nothing! There's nothing any of us can do except get to Hull and get a fucking boat or something. Arguing isn't going to change that, is it?"

"Yeah exactly, that's...," his sister said, but Michael had cut her off as well.

"You shut up too! You're always fucking moody. You think you're so cool because you're fifteen; well, being cool doesn't matter anymore, your mates aren't around, everyone's fucking dead!"

His anger had fizzled out and his voice came out high and

broken on the word "dead".

Michael's father had also had enough. "Will everyone please shut the hell up? I'm sick to death of it. All three of you just going on and on, let me drive in peace!"

Michael's mother had tried to cut in with a final word, as she always did, but Michael's father had silenced her with the sternest look Michael had ever seen him give her. In that moment, Michael had gained a new respect for his father.

That had been years ago, no, only days. Had it even been more than one day? What time was it? Was it tomorrow yet? What would he do when it was tomorrow? Maybe it was tomorrow now. Had it stopped raining? Yes, he could hear the silence. It was still night-time, he could see the darkness.

***

Michael woke early the next morning, feeling twisted and uncomfortable. His back ached and his face and hair felt greasy. He crawled out of the car on his stomach, head and arms first, like a snake. The grass was soaked from the night's rain and he wiped his wet hands on his jeans. The fog had cleared considerably some time during the night, but ghostly wisps still lingered around the wet tree trunks.

Michael looked out from between the trees and could not see the road, only clouds where the edge of the field met the horizon, as though the end of the field reached all the way up to the sky, or dropped off the earth like a waterfall. Above the fog and cloud were the beginnings of a sun.

Michael stumbled about, stretching his arms above his head, his knotted muscles cracking as the muscles in his legs come back to life after their uncomfortable night's rest. He felt something hit his shoe and looked down to see one of the coke bottle halves he had set up to catch rainwater lying on its side. The collected rainwater escaped across the grass where it was held momentarily, before becoming a smaller and smaller puddle as it was drank down into the earth, pieces of grass and small flies floating in this temporary lagoon. The other bottle was still upright and was full of water; muddy water with bits of dirt and dead flies floating in it, along with a leaf or two.

Michael decided not to drink the rainwater after all. However, he thought it would be a shame to waste it, especially as his plan had worked so well, and so he stripped off and stood naked as he poured the remaining water over his head. What little water there was ran down the groove of his back and felt better than any shower he had ever taken. He would never have imagined that he would be happy to shower with cold muddy water, but after two days without washing, it felt as refreshing as diving into an icy stream. Drying himself on his towel, Michael felt like he had a fighting chance of surviving.

He dressed and forced down more stale bread. He washed it down with bottled water that tasted much better than he imagined the rainwater would have done. Maybe he could get some iodine from somewhere. Wasn't that what you used to purify water? It still did not sound appealing; yellow water instead of brown, but at least it would be clean. The only problem was that he had no idea where he could get iodine. Michael was sure it would not come to that, there would be thousands, millions of bottles of water in shops everywhere, and water never went off, either. He would be fine; besides, it would only take him a few more days of travelling before he reached Dover.

Michael walked around the small copse, gathering up the cans he had spilt the night before. It was quiet beneath the trees and, as twigs snapped underfoot, Michael realised the small noises of animals were absent.

Once he had collected all the tins he could find and had put them into the boot, Michael wandered off into the trees to urinate. He passed a small dead bird, lying rigid in the grass, its body torn to pulpy shreds by what may have been a bullet wound. There was another bird, and then another, and littered between the bodies, were little gold cylinders like nuggets of gold, resting half-hidden in the grassy blades. Bullet casings. Then, the carcasses grew in size. A dog, shot through the head, lay in a clump of bushes, flies and puddles of blood and lumps of brain surrounding it.

Michael turned away in disgust, a hand over his nose to keep out the smell of rotting flesh. He changed direction and walked off into the bushes, but after a few steps, he froze in his tracks. A pair of black boots at the end of long, green-trousered legs stuck out from behind a bramble bush.

Michael could not see any more of the body and did not want to. He staggered drunkenly backwards, away from the body. As he did so, a thick, black, cloud of flies arose from where they had been feasting and swarmed and buzzed angrily at him for disturbing their meal.

On the ground beside the man, at an odd angle as though dropped, not placed, was a green canvas satchel, from which had split a cascade of bullets, that now nestled in the wet grass. As far as Michael was able to tell, the bullets were encased in the same shells as those discarded around the birds and the dog. Another empty shell case lay on the floor beside dead the man's boots.

On the other side of the body lay a gun. Michael was intrigued and, unable to help himself, he took a step closer to the body. It was a hunting rifle, the sort used to hunt deer in America, or Scotland; the great frontiers of wilderness. It was a bolt-action rifle with a stock of deep brown wood. A thick leather strap was attached at the wooden butt and just below the barrel. The end of the brazen barrel was marked by splatters of a dull crimson red and Michael knew at once what this was. Along the top of the barrel were a series of raised ridges for aiming the rifle. Michael had a feeling the previous owner had not needed to be so accurate when he had last pulled the trigger.

The gun lay there seductively, slender and lethal. Michael had always imagined that at some point he might own a gun. He had imagined himself as James Bond, or some war hero, and now it seemed there might be a chance for these fantasies to come true. He could become a hero in this new land, devoid of any authority. He might have to; he had already tried to save Steve.

Michael shook his head, shaking away his childish ideas. This was not the Wild West, and many had already died needlessly, it would be foolish to invite further violence. Then again, the gun might be useful. He would never use it, not on a *person*, but it might be a useful deterrent, or it might be useful for hunting. Wasn't it better to have a gun and not need it, than to not have one and want one? It would be stupid not to take the gun; he had to be protected. What would happen if he found himself at another petrol station without a weapon?

Michael decided the gun would be useful and bent to retrieve it, pausing as he stood stooped across the dead man's legs, flies buzzing beneath his nose. He felt suddenly faint and he knelt in the fresh mud. What was he doing? He could not take this gun, it belonged to someone; it belonged to those legs, which belonged to a man.

Michael knelt there and wondered what must have been going through the man's mind when he had decided to come out here and do this; decided to shoot all of those birds, his dog, himself. Why had this thing; this disease, this attack, this infection, whatever the hell it was, come to England and killed so many people? What the hell were people supposed to do now to survive?

Michael battered the mud with his fists and sobbed his frustration into his jacket. His family were gone and he was alone. After a while, his eyes had dried and he picked up the rifle with hands that were not his and slung it over his shoulder, then stooped again to gather up the satchel and loose bullets which had been scattered when the previous owner had let the bag drop to the ground.

**

The gun was heavier than he had expected and the satchel heavier still. The weight assured him that the rifle was real. Michael had held guns before, when he had worked collecting dead birds for the shooting parties in the fields and villages that bordered his town. He had always had BB guns and pellet guns as a teenager and, occasionally, aimed half-heartedly at birds with his friends, always reluctant to kill. The most recent gun he had seen had been two days ago. It had fallen from a holster on a soldier's hip, as the soldier fell from above to his death in the crowd below. In the midst of the melee, Michael had stood staring at the pistol, entranced. It lay there black and metallic, holding his gaze whilst the riot roared around him. Michael had wondered then, for half a second, if he should pick the gun up, but before he had had chance to decide, he had been swept away in the surge of the crowd.

He had not thought about this detail since it had happened, and he thought it funny that it should come back to him now. He supposed it had been buried under everything else that had happened in the past few days. Maybe, he thought now, if he had picked up that gun, he could have done something to help his family. Maybe they would be with him now.

Michael pushed these thoughts to the back of his mind where a store of guilt and grief was rising, waiting to be sifted through once he had gotten away from here and life had returned to some semblance of normality.

Wanting to get away from the body, Michael pushed through the trees and bushes to the opposite side of the small copse and sat down in a patch of wet grass, overlooking the golden corn fields with the body and the road to his back. He turned the gun over in his hands, admiring each individual detail of it. It was a relic of someone's life, and years ago it had been used by its last owner to shoot deer in Canada, and it had once killed four deer in one day. However, Michael was to know none of this.

He wanted to load it and test a shot, but he could see nothing in the distance to aim at. He was also afraid that a shot would ring out for miles in this empty place, devoid of all sound from traffic and TVs. It also might be possible that the unfamiliar sound may lead someone to him, perhaps someone who might be prepared to fight the rifle away from him.

The blood on the barrel was a grisly reminder of the death the gun could bring. Michael wiped it off as best he could with a wet dock leaf, trying not to touch the stain with his bare skin. After this, he played with the rifle for a while, testing the sights, clicking the bolt into place and pulling the trigger, at first hesitantly, fearful of a bang, despite knowing the gun was not loaded.

After a while, he began to feel guilty about wasting time sitting around playing with the gun, and he fought his way back through the bushes to the car. There he took a bullet from the satchel and rubbed it dry on his jeans. He took the rifle, pulled back the bolt, inserted the round into the breech, and then slid the bolt forwards again. He found the safety and clicked it on. He did all of this almost automatically, trained by video games and films. The rifle was ready to fire if Michael ever needed it, although he hoped that day would never come.

Michael opened the boot and wrapped the rifle in a T-shirt so that it would be protected and not clatter about, and then he hid the gun and satchel underneath the rest of his bags. His watch told him it was already ten o'clock. A few days ago ten o'clock would have been like the crack of dawn to him, but now he knew he had wasted almost all of the morning, and he would have to decide what he was going to do to make the most of the rest of the day. The atlas told him he had headed in the wrong direction when he had left town yesterday. He was still in the northeast and, instead of heading south to Dover, he had driven in circles out into the countryside.

Michael traced the general direction he had taken from the few place names he remembered from the previous day's driving, places with such cheer-inducing names as Whitgift, Ousefleet and Saltmarshe. From what he could deduce from the map, he was not far from a small village called Potsdon, and he decided this would be his next port of call before heading south.

Yesterday, all he had wanted to do was to make a rough plan and escape his town as quickly as possible, but now, in the light of morning, he was calmer and feeling more open to suggestion. Maybe someone in Potsdon could help him, if there *were* any people left in Potsdon. At the very least, he decided, he might find some food there that someone had conveniently left for him.

Chapter Six

Twenty minutes later, Michael drove into Potsdon. It was an unremarkable little settlement that no one knew or cared about outside of the surrounding villages and fields. As with the previous village and the one before that, and the one before that, Potsdon seemed to be made of grey. Grey streets, grey walls, grey houses, grey signs and probably grey people. It was a tiny village, so small that Michael wondered how anyone had even come to live there.

The streets were deserted. Overturned bins spilled their moulding contents across the paths. As with everywhere else Michael had passed through, abandoned cars were scattered sporadically across the roads and paths. A few cars rested as crumpled messes at the feet of trees, and Michael spotted a Mini half submerged inside the shattered wall of what was once a bungalow. It was clear that this village had not been exempt from whatever catastrophe had befallen England however many days ago, but strangely, there were no bodies to be seen.

Michael drove slowly, by now almost an expert at avoiding the debris that littered the roads. After half a mile he came upon a newsagent's. The shutters were down over the windows, but the front door was open. A red and gold sign above the doorway informed him that this was Marashi Stores. Movement by the door distracted him and three boys, who must all have been younger than twelve, appeared from inside, laden with bags that they placed on the pavement outside the door, before heading back into the shop.

Michael parked the car as best he could behind a small

coach that had ploughed into a lamppost. He tried not to look at the bodies inside as he passed, but morbid curiosity got the better of him and he jumped in surprise; the coach was empty; there were no bodies to be seen.

The shop lay in darkness. As with everywhere else, there was no electricity, and the shutters prevented the daylight seeping in farther than the rectangle of light which the open doorway cut into the blackness. Michael stood hesitantly in the doorway; it felt strange stepping into a shop in the dark. He knew it was only a newsagent's, the same as all the other newsagent's he had been in, but now in darkness and out of context, the shop felt eerie and foreboding.

While Michael was lingering on the threshold, making up his mind, one of the young boys pushed past him, another bag in hand. Michael noticed the bag was full of chocolate and porn magazines. He reasoned to himself that if they were taking things, then the owner couldn't be there, so it wouldn't matter if he took a few things as well.

Michael stepped into the gloomy shop, took a bag from the counter, and threw in a handful of packets of chewing gum that lay next to the till. He did not need cigarettes as he had never taken up the habit, and lottery tickets and scratch cards were surely redundant now. It was possible that one of those cards had £500,000 on it. Michael deliberated whether to take one or not, he could even scratch them all now and just take a winning one and then, when the country was sorted out again, he would be rich. That was if the country was ever sorted out.

Michael thought about it and reasoned that all of the scratch cards were sure to be void now. Once the government was re-established, they would never let anyone keep the money, there must be people robbing banks all over the country, by now. In a heartbeat, Michael had become rich and in another, it had all been swept away by reality.

Nothing else on the counter caught his eye. Maybe a lighter. You never knew when you might need fire. Michael took one and threw it into the bag. The petrol station flashed through his mind, a fiery snapshot, and then it was gone, pushed back into the depths of his mind, out of the way. Keep busy.

He moved through the shop and found the three boys at the back, trying to jump up to reach the magazines on the top shelf. Two of them looked older than the third, who must have only been about nine. The older two looked around eleven or twelve and one could have been the brother of the smaller one. All had filthy clothes and dirty faces. The smaller boy's nose was encrusted with snot.

Michael reached up and took a few magazines down for them, handing them over with a grin. "There you are lads. Do your mums and dads know you're in here?"

The boys looked at him with vacant eyes and Michael knew he was looking into empty basins that had not held emotion for days.

He began to mumble apologies, realising now that these children's parents were probably dead. "I'm sorry...are you..." Michael did not know what he was going to say, but it did not matter because at that moment a crash resonated from the other side of the shop, and all four of them almost jumped out of their skins. There was another crash and the sound of jars smashing as tins rolled down an empty aisle towards them.

The three boys took off as fast as they could, leaving the magazines behind. The older two made it to the door but, just as the smaller one was almost there, a long and sinewy arm appeared from behind one of the aisles and caught him by the scruff of the neck, lifting him from the ground.

The arm belonged to a wiry Persian man who held the boy pinned up against a shelf of bread. The man was somewhere between fifty and seventy but it was hard to tell where as his face was distorted by heavy lines and a deep scowl. He was dressed in a long crimson bathrobe that hung open to reveal a body withered and folded like an ancient and knotted tree, the branches twisted together at odd angles to form ribs and arms. Under the robe he wore only a pair of stained white y-fronts.

The man had the boy pinned by the neck with one hand and in the other he held a sharp bread knife. He jabbered incomprehensible words at the crying boy, his grey beard stroking the child's face with each word.

Michael crept closer and was able to make out what the man was saying.

"What are you doing in my shop? It's *my* shop you little thief! I will cut your hands off! There is no one to stop me anymore. No police, no parents! You think you can steal from me, you brat? I have told you kids before, but you come back. You come back to steal! You steal my magazines, you filthy little bastards? You and your brother! If your mother was still alive I would make her chop your hands off!" The boy's face had turned a dark shade of red. He squirmed beneath the man's grip, but was unable to escape.

"That's enough!" Michael stammered from the shadows. He had stood transfixed by the old man's tirade, not believing that a grown man could be threatening a young boy in this way, holding a knife to his neck as the child struggled and cried.

"That's enough," Michael repeated, managing to hold his voice steady this time.

The old man spun around. "Who the hell are you? Another thief? Do you know who I am? I am Marashi and that is *my* name above the door, not yours!"

Distracted by the materialisation of Michael, Marashi had absent-mindedly dropped the young boy, who ran as fast as he could towards the door. Marashi shouted after him.

"Where are you going boy? Come back here so I can chop your hands off!"

Seeing his attention distracted, Michael began to edge towards the door. As though suddenly remembering him again, the old man spun around to face him once more, thrusting the tip of the knife at Michael's neck, the point nicking his Adam's apple. Michael swallowed nervously and tried to suck his throat in and as far away from the blade as possible.

"I'm sorry," he said, and he felt the tip of the knife scratch against his throat as he spoke. "I thought it was an empty shop, you can keep your things, I..."

"Too right I can keep my things, you son of a bitch, it's my shop! This is *Marashi* Stores, and I am Marashi!"

Michael was about to nod but thought better of it. "I know. I'm sorry, I didn't mean to steal. I didn't know anyone was here. I have money, I can pay you..."

"Money? Ha, why would I want money? What can I buy with it, eh? Who is there to buy things from? Money is worthless, take a look around at this world! Where are all the shopkeepers, where are all the bankers? Where are the big business men? The economy is over! Nobody wants these pounds anymore, they are worthless! They're a dead currency, just like this country is dead and just like thieves like you are dead!"

Michael had been staring down at the knife pressed against his throat, trying to keep his body rigid, whilst also balancing on his toes in order not to not slip forwards and accidentally impale his neck. He looked up now and chanced a glimpse into the old man's eyes. They looked blood-shot and crazy. Would this old bastard really kill him, he wondered? He did not want to find out and knew he had to get out of there as quickly as possible.

Michael realised then that he was still holding the carrier bag full of stolen goods and swung it up into Marashi's face. There was hardly anything in it and it was not heavy enough to cause any damage, but it was a useful distraction, nonetheless.

The old man let out a yelp of surprise and flailed wildly at the bag, skewering it on the knife as it flapped in front of his face, half wrapped around his arm. Michael did not waste a second, and ducked out from under Marashi's flailing arms and ran for his life out of the shop, the old man screaming after him.

Michael inserted the key in the ignition with shaking hands, sweat dripping from his brow.

"Shit! Bloody hell! What is wrong with him? Bloody hell!" He managed to start the car and glanced up quickly at the shop doorway. The old man was not in the doorway, waving the knife at him, as Michael had expected, but Michael did not want to wait around to see whether he might re-appear, and he put the car into quickly gear and took off down the street.

As he drove along, Michael kept a look out for the three boys, but they had long since vanished. As he scanned the streets, Michael noticed a thick plume of black smoke rising steadily from behind a cluster of trees. He crept along slowly, houses peeling back on either side of him, until eventually, a park was revealed to his left. He saw there the source of the smoke. Hidden at first by trees, and then revealed as they too slipped away behind him, was a great mound of burning corpses, rising twenty feet into the air.

Now Michael understood why he had seen no bodies. From his position in the car, Michael saw that the bodies at the bottom of the pile had already been cremated. They had been reduced to little more than black charred limbs and faces with grey stained teeth and black eye sockets gaping out from the pyre.

A crowd had gathered around the macabre bonfire as though it were November 5th. Two men stooped and picked up a small bundle. It was the body of a little girl and they swung it into the flames. The girl rolled down the sloping mound of corpses, her clothing catching fire on the way, before she bounced away from the mound and onto the grass, coming to rest no more than two feet away with flames simmering on her dress and hair. The men saw this and rolled the body back towards the fire with long wooden sticks.

The men were covered from head to toe in ash, and they wore long marigold gloves and had dishcloths wrapped around their noses and mouths to stop them breathing in the smoke. The others gathered around the mound were dressed normally, in dresses, suits, jeans and jumpers, and they watched the fire as if watching an attraction at a summer fair.

Michael stopped the car and stumbled out of the vehicle, feeling suddenly faint. He stood for a moment; one hand resting on the bonnet as his stomach twisted itself into knots. He stood hunched over the bonnet, soaked in cold sweat and trying to calm himself.

Morbid curiosity drew him towards the fire, and without knowing why, Michael began to walk across the road to the park. As he approached, he noticed the smell; that of a barbeque where the meat has been on the heat for too long, mixed with the smell of charred cloth. He clasped a hand over his mouth and it was all he could do to stop himself gagging again.

The people gathered around the fire seemed to be the only ones left in the village, except for the old shopkeeper. There were men and women and pensioners and children, all gathered close to the flames. Michael could see a prudish looking woman, middle aged and thin, arguing with one of the oddly garbed men.

"You cannot do this! They are people! They are part of our village! We must bury them properly at the church. A person has the right to a choice of funeral. You cannot just cremate them. We must look at their wills, their last testaments and find out what they wanted. This is inhumane. It its barbaric! We must give them a proper service at the church, the vicar can..."

One of the men she was addressing cut in. He had pulled the cloth down from his face, to reveal a thick growth of stubble, and his cheeks appeared creased from the ash collected there. "You stupid bitch! Bury them? Who's going to do that, eh? We'll all rot! They are decomposing, do you not understand that? I'm not going near a rotting, contagious body, not even with these bloody marigolds on!" He attempted to tear the glove from his right hand, but it stuck to the sweat on his wrist and he tore at it again and managed to free himself. "Bloody hell!"

The woman started up again. "Reverend Parsons woul..."

"Ha," the man laughed. "The Vicar? Take a look at the Reverend!" He turned and pointed at a body at the top of the pile, already turning crisp. Michael was able to make out a charred dog collar.

"Reverend Parsons! Oh God!" The woman swooned but regained her composure halfway through as another body landed on the fire, sending out a hiss of sparks.

"Stop! Stop this right now! I am the head of the Parish Council, you must listen to me!"

"The parish is almost completely inhabited by corpses, not much different to when people were alive at it was full of fucking old women, so I..."

"How dare you? How dare you say that? That is... I never thought the little boy who used to deliver my papers would turn out like this. If your mother were here she woul..."

"She is here," the man laughed. "She's at the bottom of the bloody pile, you snooty old bitch. Maybe we should put you on next!"

A large woman with a swollen face bustled forth from the crowd to offer her opinion. "Now, look! Look here everyone, Judith is the head of the Parish Council and the Women's Institute, and she's worked very hard at keeping the standards of Potsdon high, and I am sure you will all..."

The man who had been arguing decided he had heard enough, and punched this new woman in her piggish face. The first woman, Judith, let out a gasp and then a shriek. "Oh my God, Pauline! Oh you savage, burning bodies and

74

punching women! You absolute...you *bastard*!"

The crowd had been distracted from their bonfire and huddled around this new entertainment. A small boy held his mother's hand and laughed at the injured woman as she rolled on the floor, blood running from her nose. Michael did not know what he could do. Should he help, could he help?

Judith spun around, shrieking hysterically. She grabbed the nearest person by the collar, and sobbed into their face. "Oh my Lord, the savages! They are inhumane! Burning our friends!"

"Get off of me," cried Michael, who had happened to be the nearest person.

He decided it was time to leave and tried to pull the woman's hands away from him, but she only held on tighter and trailed after him as he turned to head back to his car. "Look, I, I'm not from here, this isn't my village. I can't help. They're right; they do need to burn the bodies. Now let me go."

The crowd gathered behind them now, jeering. The small boy, who had laughed at the large woman being punched, threw an empty drinks can after them. His mother scolded him whilst trying to suppress a shifty smile. The rest of the crowd joined in, throwing bottles, stones and sticks at the two departing figures. They did not care for accuracy and Michael became a victim of poor aim and impartial throwers.

The woman held on to Michael's jacket and would not let go, and he had no choice but to try to push her away, and after he did so, she fell to her knees in the grass. Michael ran to his car and around to the driver's side. He was leaving in a hurry once again. He slipped into the seat, started the engine and began to pull away, and just then the passenger door opened and Judith clambered inside. He must to remember to lock that door.

"What are you doing? Get out of my car!"

A stone flew into the passenger mirror; sending small shards of glass into the car. Another stone bounced off the bonnet, and yet another off the roof. Michael had no choice but to pick up speed and escape before both him and the woman were dragged out by the crowd, or his car was battered beyond repair by their projectiles. He drove as fast as the blocked road would allow and, within two minutes, both he and Judith had left Potsdon behind. Michael found himself on the road again; this time with a passenger.

Chapter Seven

They drove in silence, the woman sobbing gently into her shoulder as she stared out of the window. After a while, Michael stopped the car, got out and found the map book in the boot. He noticed the sky was darkening under heavy clouds that had not been there the last time he had checked, and had sprung upon him unwanted, like the woman in his passenger seat. What a failure that little expedition into the village had been. He had almost been killed by a shopkeeper and nearly fallen prey to crazed villagers, and now he had a strange woman in the passenger seat. What the hell was he going to do with her? Michael wondered.

He experienced a sudden moment of panic, thinking he had left the keys in the ignition and that the woman might casually shift across into the driver's seat and drive off, leaving him stranded there in the middle of nowhere. He flung his hands into his pockets and was relieved when he found the keys.

Michael returned his attention to the map and ate a slice of stale bread. Some of it was going mouldy, but he picked these bits off and flicked them away into the road. The map said he was going in the right direction, as far as he could tell. If he kept on this road and got onto the nearest motorway, he could continue south and eventually arrive at Dover. He would avoid small villages on the way and all would be fine.

He looked over the tins of food in the boot. There was still plenty left. He took out a tin of hotdog sausages and began to eat whilst he studied the map further. Then, the passenger door clicked open and the woman stepped out, hugging her arms around herself as though she were cold, even though it was still perfectly warm.

"Why have we stopped?" she asked, eyeing the food. "What are we eating?"

"I needed to check the map," Michael said, ignoring the question.

"Where do you want me to drop you off?"

"Drop me off? I'm coming with you. There is nowhere else to go." The woman looked around at the empty fields as the clouds darkened overhead. "Where are we going?"

"You can't come with me, I just..." Michael began but the woman cut in,

"Why can't I? Who are you to decide? I have as much right as anyone; I cannot go back, not back there..." With this her nose wrinkled into a sneer and she pointed her outstretched arm back towards the village.

"They will kill me, I'm sure of it! They are barbarians!"

Michael took a deep breath. This woman reminded him of every busybody he had ever known: his mother, his girlfriend's mother, his parent's friends, his grandparents, to name a few. So much of his life had been wasted by men and women with their inconsequential small talk; busy-bodies who were so self-absorbed that they thought their own unimportant lives were the most consequential and interesting things in the world. Judith was one of these people and Michael did not want to travel with her.

"Look Judith," he began, "this is *my* car and this is my food, so I am afraid you will just have to go and get your own car and food, go find your family, or that woman who just got punched, and go off with them instead."

Judith's face froze as though Michael had just slapped her. *"You* look. You are just a boy, whereas I am forty-eight. That means I have almost thirty-five years of experience over you. I think if anyone should be telling anyone what is going to happen, it should be me. The only people I have are in that

78

village and they have all gone bloody mad, even poor Pauline. As you were witness to my departure, you should have recognised that I had to leave in somewhat of a hurry, and did not have any time to pack any *food* or clothing. I do not run a car of my own, I never have. Besides, over the past few days I have been taking all my meals at Pauline's, she has such a lot of food, no wonder she's so portly..."

"Look," Michael cut in, "I don't really care. This is my car so..."

Judith cut back in, her voice hard as a week-old scone. "*Your* car? It's *your* car, is it? *Ha*! How does a *child* afford a Jaguar? Who did you steal it from? Did you think you could just take what you wanted now? I'll bet you did..." Michael rolled his eyes and rubbed his knuckles into his chin.

"It doesn't matter where I got this car from, does it? What does anything matter anymore?" He was shouting now and thought of driving away and leaving this woman behind.

Michael slammed the boot shut and rushed to open the driver's door. He got in and, as he fumbled for the key in his pocket, the woman climbed in beside him, glaring at him over the hand brake.

"Never try to leave me again."

Michael let out a sigh of dismay and started the car up, the wheels sending gravel shooting off into dust as the car sped away.

They drove past fields and woods and the sky grew darker. After a while, Michael could bear the silence no longer and, despite himself, urged for conversation. He had had no one to speak to since having left his grandfather behind and decided to put his dislike of this woman aside to see if she was capable of having some sort of conversation.

"So..." His voice sounded strange as it broke the silence and penetrated the atmosphere in the car. "Your name is Judith then?"

"No. Actually, my name is Mrs Allen," Judith said.

"Oh right, well nice to meet you Judith Allen, I'm Michael Taylor."

"Do not play games with me; I am not in the mood. Don't you think I ought to be driving? How old are you anyway? Do you even have a license?"

Michael laughed exhaustedly, "Look, we are in my car, I'm driving. I didn't steal this car, I found it and it's mine now, ok? I'm eighteen and I am old enough to drive, and yes, I do have a license."

"Eighteen...well I would never have imagined it from the way you behave, what do you supos..." Judith trailed off mid-sentence and sat as though dumbstruck, staring out at something through the windscreen.

"What do you suppose what?" Michael snapped.

Judith did not reply, her attention transfixed by something outside. Michael followed her gaze and almost lost control of the car.

In the field to the right of the road a tremendous furrow had been carved out of the soil, like the work of a giant plough. The great scar was over six-foot deep and as they slowly continued by, they came to the great plough, a huge piece of shorn and twisted white metal almost completely buried in the ground, but still standing over ten feet into the air.

"What the hell is that?" Michael whispered.

Over the next few miles, they came across hundreds more pieces of metal, of all shapes and sizes, strewn across the ground. Some were dug into the fields either side of the road, elevated at jaunty angles like drunken metallic scarecrows. Others littered the road like discarded toys, and Michael navigated around them with great care. Great craters had been scooped out of the ground where some of the pieces had landed, and the road was scarred and pitted.

A great triangular fin was embedded in the middle of the road, pointing back towards them, and as they passed it by, they were able to make out the words *British Airwa* in charred lettering, half obscured by burn marks and silver scratches.

"Oh, God...," Judith said.

"It's a plane," Michael said under his breath.

The ground was littered with half burnt suitcases and bags, some open, divulging their contents like the stomach of a dying soldier. The pieces of plane became more frequent and were grouped closer together, as though they had congregated in this way for protection, or some similar cause. It was nearly impossible for Michael to stay on the road and he had to drive half in the fields, the car rocking gently as they navigated the pieces of plane over uneven ground.

There it was: the body of the plane. Stripped of all wings, tails and engines, the main passenger tube lay shattered in the midst of the field to their right, still smoking gently. Blackened seats and bodies overflowed from the wreckage. The corpses were scattered over the fields like seeds in spring.

As they passed by, Michael and Judith could make out the great gashes and tears of the corpses closest to them. Some of the bodies were missing limbs and, as they drove onwards, they came across limbs that were missing bodies.

Michael had slowed down out of morbid curiosity, but he had seen more than enough now, and he put his foot down and they sped away from the scene of the disaster.

Despite their speed, it took them ten minutes to be completely free of the wreckage. Judith was sobbing into her shoulder and facing her window again. Michael did not know whether he should attempt to comfort her or how to do it. He did not really feel enough compassion towards her to want to make sure she was all right, plus she was an adult, so it should be him that was upset, he thought. He reached across a hand with the notion of touching her shoulder, but he changed his mind and withdrew it halfway.

"Hey...it's all right. There's nothing we can do for those people now. We, we've just got to take care of ourselves. We will get out of here, don't worry."

Judith raised her head from her wet shoulder and stared at the dashboard. "We heard something in the village when all this started. A great bang. It was loud, louder than anything I had ever heard. This was, how many days ago? Four? No. Five, five days ago. We all looked out from our houses. It was night time. Our electricity had already gone off. It was so dark, but there was this fire, burning, out in the fields a few miles away, and we looked out, Pauline and I. It was a windy night and we thought the wind carried the sound of screams, but of course it was just our imaginations.

Looking out over the fields at this fire I felt warm inside. Everyone had dropped down dead, for no reason. The ambulances had not come, no one came, no one cared about us all the way out here. We were alone. But that fire, it showed me there was something, some sign of life. It let me know I was not alone with the others. God was watching us. We had not been forgotten and I felt warm, knowing God had sent us this sign to say we were still in his thoughts and that he would help us."

"I knew then that it was a plane, but I did not want to admit it and taint the reassurance that the light brought me. We all knew, the people in my village, but no one said anything. But, it *is* a plane, it is real. People died in it, and we watched them burn."

She clasped a hand to her mouth; her voice was muffled behind it. "Just imagine, being aboard a plane, miles up in the air, as people are dropping dead around you."

Michael did imagine. The air hostesses were falling over, children were crying. The pilot was dead and the co-pilot was trying to revive him, perhaps thinking he had just passed out, or something like that. But the co-pilot could not control the plane on his own and they were falling out of the sky, and everyone was screaming, everyone was screaming.

Chapter Eight

The next half an hour crept by in slow motion. Neither Michael nor Judith spoke. The wheels turned and the car crept onwards. A blanket of darkness rapidly descended and it was only when the car jolted over something in the road that Michael thought to turn on the headlights. The fields turned into woods and soon they were driving through a dark tunnel of trees, the pale blue light from the moon kept away by the branches that reached over them and enclosed them in the darkness.

The soft crunch of twigs was the only music they listened to. Nothing came from the radio except an occasional crackle of white noise, as though the woods themselves were trying to speak to them. A set of bright white eyes shone at them from the darkness and then disappeared into the depths of the trees.

Michael rubbed his eyes and focused on a patch of road that was forever a few metres ahead. He could feel his eyes closing. Out of nowhere, a wooden sign at the side of the road became illuminated in the glare of the headlights. The rustic sign hung on motionless chains from a wooden post, and in the glow of the car's lights, Michael was able to read the words, *Uncle Harry's Family Restaurant.*

He slowed the car. Just before the sign was a patch of lighter darkness amongst the trees. Michael supposed this must be a turn-in. Without having to tell the car what to do, it turned off the road and down the lane. The headlights lead the way down a narrow mud path, which soon opened up into a gravel car park. There were no other cars. Michael could just about make out the shape of the restaurant beside the car park in the moon light. It was a converted barn, built from old stones, or new ones made to look old, he could not tell which.

Michael turned off the engine and the lights died. He sat for a minute becoming accustomed to the darkness, at first seeing nothing, and then slowly making out silver, moonlit shapes as his eyes adjusted to the moonlight. There were Victorian style street-lamps dotted around the car park but they were no longer working. Michael squinted and tried to see into the dark windows of the restaurant. Nothing seemed to be moving, but it was almost impossible to tell without a light inside in the restaurant.

Judith stirred in the passenger seat and yawned quietly beside him.

"What do you think?" Michael asked.

"Mmmh?" she replied drowsily.

"Ok. Stay here, I'm going to have a look around."

He did not wait for a reply. Making sure to take the keys with him, Michael slipped out into the darkness, locking the car behind him. Judith would be safe there.

Michael opened the boot and rummaged through his holdall. After a few seconds he found the torch he had taken from his kitchen. He paused and listened to the darkness for a few moments. All he could hear was silence, but he still did not dare to turn on the torch just yet.

The gravel crunched underfoot as he crept towards the barn. A children's playground stood motionless and silver in the moonlight to the right of the restaurant. Beyond that, he could just about make out more trees. Suddenly, something dug into his foot and he tripped, sliding through the gravel and grazing his hands. It was all he could do not to cry out. Michael's hand stung as though he had just touched them to a flame and a sharp pain throbbed through his foot. He shook with the effort of keeping silent, still afraid and paranoid that someone might lurk in the darkness.

After a moment, he got to his knees and found the torch. It

was lying next to what had tripped him up; a yellow plastic toy lorry. Michael was too tired now for all of this, and he picked up the toy and threw it into the playground where it clattered all the way down the slide. The noise split the darkness and echoed back from the surrounding wall of trees.

Michael's breath misted the glass of the restaurant window. Silhouettes of chairs and sofas, a counter, some bookshelves. There was no one inside. He found the unlocked door around the back of the building and stepped through it into a farm store. Michael listened for a moment to make sure he was alone. There were no sounds in the empty shop and, satisfied he was alone, he turned on the torch.

Rows of wicker baskets full of stuffed animals and shelves with row upon row of organic jam jars spread out in front of him. The shop smelt like potpourri. Signs amongst the produce informed him of their names: Grandma Mary's Organic Strawberry Compote, Auntie Mary's Tangy Pickle and Uncle Harry's Whole-wheat Luxury Loaves, beside a selection of mouldering bread.

Michael threaded his way slowly through the shop. At the counter were cake stands stacked with dried and crumbling lemon drizzle cakes, chocolate walnut cakes, Victoria sponges. He continued further into the store, the torch light sending shadows running up the walls. A smell of rotting meat hit him and he shone the torch around looking for the body. Instead, he found an archway with a sign above it directing him towards Uncle Harry's Award Winning Organic Sausages.

Michael passed the archway and went through a closed door into the restaurant itself. There was no one there, living or dead. A few plates of food had been abandoned on tables and the odd fly circled sleepily about them, disturbed by the torchlight. Michael wondered where the bodies were. There was no smell in the restaurant; nothing was rotting except the food.

Behind the counter, the till stood open and money spilt out

onto the floor. A discarded wallet lay on the counter next to a silent radio. There were fridges full of drinks behind the wooden counter and Michael squatted on his haunches and shone the torch over the glass front of the nearest fridge. All of the bottles and cans there were mineral waters or drinks with names like Organic Raspberry and Lemon Juice and Fresh Elderflower Cordial.

'At least I'm looking after myself,' Michael thought as he took out a glass bottle of orange and cranberry juice and drank it down in one, huddled up on the floor behind the counter, the torch at his side casting strange shadows onto the ceiling.

When he had finished, he left the empty bottle on the counter and looked out of the window. The Jaguar was still there, and he could just about make out Judith's silhouette in the passenger seat. The entrance track they had come down was obscured in a wall of trees. From where he stood, Michael could hardly differentiate it from the thicker blackness of the woods. No one would find them here.

Before he could let himself feel safe, Michael wanted to make sure he had checked the whole place. A door behind the counter led him into the kitchen. He pushed the door open and stepped through into pitch blackness. The torch revealed a world of metallic surfaces; a maze of fridges, cookers, fryers and work surfaces. The door to the restaurant eased itself shut behind him and he was alone in the kitchen.

A terrible smell of rotting fish hit his nostrils as he passed the hob. Michael shone the torch over it and saw a semi cooked and rotting slab of white fish in a pan. Plates of mouldering salad lay on the work surface. Forgotten knives and bottles of salad dressing were scattered about the surface. Something crunched underfoot and he looked down to discover he had trodden on a lettuce. The rotting vegetable was lying in a cold puddle of green juice and a few brown things scuttled away from the mess to hide under a nearby fridge.

Michael held his breath, trying not to inhale the stench of the rotting fish. He wanted to get out of the kitchen as quickly as possible, but his conscience would not let him leave without making sure it was empty. Something clattered to the floor on the other side of the central work counter, the noise cutting through the empty kitchen. Michael froze. There was the sound of something rattling slowly as it came to a stop, as though somebody had spun a coin.

Michael pulled out the kitchen knife that he still carried, tucked inside the waistband of his jeans. He held the torch up and scanned the area in the direction the noise had come from. Pots and pans hung from the ceiling, obscuring his view and distorting the light of the torch. Michael held himself taut, ready if something should jump out at him. As he manoeuvred around the counter, the torch cast eerie shadows of the hanging utensils which seemed to crawl along the wall after him.

He came to the corner of the counter and quickly stepped around, shining the light ahead of him to startle anything that was there. A rat the size of a small cat turned and ran, almost before Michael had noticed it. A plate lay on the ground, its food spilt across the floor. A hiss split the darkness and Michael jumped backwards, his torch illuminating the animal sitting on the counter, a sandwich clasped in its paws. The rat glared at Michael, hissing and barring its yellowed and pointed teeth.

"Go fuck yourself," Michael hissed in return, as he dropped the knife and grabbed a pan to launch at the rat. However, the rat was too fast, and dove into the darkness as the pan clattered off the far wall.

Michael bent to retrieve the knife and an exhausted laugh escaped him. He had turned to go back into the restaurant when he noticed another door at the edge of the darkness. It was a thick metallic door with a small window at head height. Michael shone the light through but could see nothing. A film of condensation obscured the glass. He put the knife into his pocket where he could get to it easily and, holding the torch in his teeth, he heaved open the heavy door.

A hiss escaped as he eased the door open and then a smell of rotting meat hit him like a fist in the stomach. He turned and vomited on the floor. More food for the rats.

The room was a freezer and shelves of packaged meats and fish and crates of vegetables lined the walls. Water dripped slowly onto the floor from the defrosting food and collected there in a large puddle tinged with red. Michael took a step back, only now realising that the floor of the freezer was lined with bodies. There were at least ten people stacked there, staring up at the ceiling with vacant eyes in vacant faces.

Michael leaned against the doorframe, took a deep breath and then exhaled slowly. A brown rat crawled from under the pile, dragging a piece of meat with it. A piece of meat wrapped in blue rags that matched the colour of the trousers on one of the bodies. Michael heaved a heavy cardboard package from a shelf and hurled it at the rat, which quickly scurried under the pile of bodies. The box landed where the rat had tried to make its escape with a sickening crunch and a satisfying yelp.

Michael stepped out of the freezer and shut the door, sealing the bodies inside. He felt drained and fatigue washed over him rapidly, but gently like an evening tide. Questions blew through his mind like plastic bags on the breeze; who had put the bodies in the freezer, and why? Where were they now, had they gone for help when this thing happened? Why had they not returned? He rubbed his temples gently, trying to slow the pace of his thoughts.

A large tin of tomato soup caught his eye and he carried it across to the stove. The fish smell assaulted him again and he threw the pan behind him onto the central counter where it slid and clattered out of view. Michael found a tin opener, opened the soup and poured its contents into a saucepan. The hob ran on gas that he could smell as he tested one of the knobs. Finally a bit of luck, he thought. Whoever left here last had had the sense to turn off the gas.

Michael searched the work surface for matches, but found none. He opened a drawer, sifted through kitchen utensils and found none there either. Then he spotted a box on the floor. He lit a ring and put the soup on to heat up before heading back outside.

Now that he knew the layout of the shop, he was able to find his way back through easily, and soon he stepped back out into the blue moonlit car park. He crunched up to the car and found Judith sleeping soundly inside, her head resting on the window. He tapped lightly against the glass with the bottom of the torch.

"Judith. Judith. Wake up. We can stay here. There's some food too," he called quietly.

Judith remained motionless, so Michael tapped harder and raised his voice. "Judith."

But it was no use, she was fast asleep. Michael scanned the car park and the play area. She would be fine there until morning. No one would find them here.

As he turned to go back inside, Michael felt calm for the first time in almost a week.

In the kitchen, the soup was simmering and Michael turned off the hob and carried the pan through to the restaurant, where he picked up a spoon, and collapsed onto a sofa. The soup smelled good as it steamed in front of him. He was going to enjoy this. But, before he could even lift the spoon to his mouth, he was sleeping soundly.

***

Judith was dreaming. Something about planes and bonfires. A bonfire on a plane? Pauline as a pig, roasting over a fire.

There was someone on the radio; a man speaking from faraway. "The answer is here."

A car on the curb. A little girl rolling from the bonnet, but it was the village fair and where were all the chairs going to go? Mr. Oldfield was drunk again. More radio: "near Lincoln and are fully equipped." Time for school. There was Reverend Parsons. Now gone above, but conversing with her presently. Those green eyes, shining. It had always been those eyes. "Judith". That smile. Acts 2:17-2:21. Remember His words, "I will show wonders in heaven above, and signs in the earth beneath: blood and fire and vapor of smoke. The sun shall be turned into darkness, and the moon into blood, before the coming of the great and awesome day of the Lord. And it shall come to pass – That whoever calls on the name of the Lord shall be saved." No, not today, it was the fair. And where was Emily? Where is this boy Michael? I wish he would hurry up. We're having a bonfire. "The answer is here."

Chapter Nine

When Judith woke, she did not know where she was. She sat up quickly and glanced around. Flames played through her mind. She felt claustrophobic in this strange car. Trapped. She fumbled with the door, but her hands were wet and clammy. The door opened but she could not get out. Something was holding her back; a great snake had coiled itself around her. She undid the seat belt and almost fell out of the car. She righted herself, slammed the door behind her and began walking round in brisk circles on the gravel.

As Judith paced about, she wiped her hands over and over on her blouse, mumbling quickly under her breath, as though she were trying to rush the words out and away, as though her tongue was tripping itself up.

"God have mercy on the souls of the departed and guide them through the gates of Heaven. Do not forget us here on Earth, and please guide us towards you. Amen."

She sat down on a low brick wall separating the car park from the small play area. Her back was to the slides and swings and other things used by happy children. She was sweating. It was always like this after she dreamt of her. She remembered that Reverend Parsons had appeared to her. They had could not have burnt him. Maybe it was even God himself speaking through him? Judith remembered his words.

"...whoever calls on the name of the Lord shall be saved."

She bowed her head and said another prayer, asking for God's protection.

A noise from behind startled her. A bird set flight in the distance, rising from the highest branches of a tree. Its wings made no more noise than the beating of a butterfly's. Judith watched the bird coast across the daybreak. The red sun was just rising, splitting the morning mist that lingered around the tree tops like a crown, red rays like embers smoldering warmth into the trees. A million shadows from a million blades of grass. Beads of dew burnt up like the darkness. But Judith saw none of this.

She was not exactly sure where she was. She could not be certain how long they had driven for the previous night. She looked around at the empty car park and the old-fashioned looking barn beside it. It looked as though the boy had left her. He had abandoned her as everybody else had. The car was still there though, but what could she do, she did not know how to drive a car. The old barn there looked like some sort of restaurant. Good. A cup of tea would help put things in perspective.

The door opened noiselessly and Judith stood in the empty shop. The smell of potpourri met her in the doorway. It brought back memories of Christmas as a girl. She moved cautiously through the quaint shop, stopping here and there to pick up a jar, or box of something, and read the quaint labels. There was a jar of pickles on a table and its label read Cousin Peter's Pickles. Just like the rhyme.

Judith put the jar down and suddenly became aware that she was trespassing. No one had invited her in there; she could not just come in and do as she pleased, just because of the situation she was in. She called out brightly. "Hello?"

She stepped back, startled by the sound of her own voice.

"Hello. It's Judith Allen. I was wondering if I could have a cup of tea?" She was answered by silence and decided to venture farther into the deserted shop.

A smell of rotting meat greeted her and she staggered backwards, holding her mouth. She thought she would faint and tried to steady herself on one of the tables, but blundered into it instead and sent jam jars crashing to the floor. The noise caused her to let out a shriek and she jumped away from the table, bumping into a shelf, sending handmade mugs to the floor.

Michael's eyes snapped open. He sat bolt upright and pulled out the knife. He stood up and kicked over the pan of soup without noticing. The noise had come from the shop. Michael edged towards the doorway. Whatever was in there, it sounded too big to be a rat. Whatever or whoever it was had better be careful, he was not afraid to defend himself, he was not afraid to...He pushed the door open and stepped through into the shop.

Judith was sitting on a table, sobbing. She did not look up as he came into the room. Michael let out his breath slowly, then coughed to get her attention. She appeared not to have heard him.

"Judith," he said, and she jumped to her feet with a start.

"Oh, it's you." She averted her face and wiped her eyes quickly on her blouse sleeve. "You have come back then?"

Her nose was running and she pulled a handkerchief from her other sleeve and cleared her nose loudly.

Michael stood awkwardly, scratching his hair. "I came back? What? I didn't go anywhere. Are you all right?"

Judith glowered at him reproaching. "Yes, I am fine. I just...I just startled myself, that's all." She tried to smile but did not quite manage it.

"Well, it's a good job you did come back Michael, because you would not last long out there on your own."

***

"It is stealing!" Judith held her hands to her face in despair.

"It's not stealing, Judith, no one is here. I told you, they are all dead in the freezer."

"So you claim, and no, I will not *have a look for myself*. Why on earth would anyone put dead peo... dead things in the freezer? And can you please put some clothes on? This is all

93

very inappropriate!"

Michael glanced up from the sink for a second, before dunking his head back into the water. He stood up, shaking his head and spraying water everywhere like a dog.

"This could be the only running water for miles, maybe the only running water in the country, and I can't have a wash? Relax Judith. We're lucky this place is so 'organically-eco-friendly' or whatever you call it. Who else stores recycled water?"

"Well, I will certainly not be having a wash. In this mess? I swear I saw a rat in here too!" Judith turned and stormed out of the kitchen.

Michael fingered water from his ear and shouted after her. "There are no rats in here Judith!"

The door closed behind her, leaving Michael in darkness. "Well, no big ones," he said as he toweled himself dry in the darkness.

When he emerged back out into the light of the restaurant, Judith was behind the counter, trying to boil the kettle. Michael threw his holdall onto the counter top, nearly knocking the radio to the floor. Judith looked up from the kettle, frowning.

"There's no electricity Judith. The kettle won't work. Maybe we can boil some water in a pan on the hob in there, there's still some gas."

Judith forgot the kettle and handed Michael a mug with a teabag in it. "Good, go and do that."

When Michael came back out of the kitchen with the pan of hot water, the solitary mug was still on the side and Judith was sitting in a chair, reading a magazine in the morning sun. Michael found another mug and teabag and poured two drinks which he carried across to Judith. She took the mug in silence and carried on reading. Michael read the cover of the magazine, Society Lady. They drank in silence.

After a few minutes Judith lowered the magazine. "Can you

please stop *slurping*?"

Michael wondered what he had done to deserve this woman.

"All right, but Judith, we really have to go; we have to get out of here, go on with the plan. *My* plan. We have to get south, see if we can get across the channel. There's no way north, we tried it, me and my family, but I think if..."

Judith put down the magazine. "Can you please be quiet? I have had a very stressful night. Terrible nightmares. Somebody speaking to me in my dreams, telling me 'the answer is here' or something along those lines, and then I received a message from God, calling upon me to ask for his assistance..."

Michael muttered under his breath. "Bloody hell..."

"Pardon?" Judith said as she shook the magazine in her hands. "All I want is to enjoy my magazine and cup of tea in peace. It's my Sunday morning tradition."

Michael rose out of his chair. "For God's sake, it isn't even Sunday!"

Judith sprang to her feet and advanced towards him full of fire and brimstone, the magazine clutched in one had.

"How dare you take the Lord's name in vain? On the Sabbath! You ought to be ashamed. He spoke to me and made my redemption clear. *I* will be saved, but *you* need to think long and hard about yourself if you think there is a place for you in God's kingdom!"

Michael stormed about the restaurant, stuffing anything of any use into his holdall. He knocked a chair over in his rush, but Judith did not seem to notice as she stood counting out change at the counter.

"Four-twenty for two cups of tea? Well, I never. Robbery..."

Soon the car was loaded and they were ready to go. The sun was already climbing up into the sky and the day was heating up. Judith sat in the passenger seat, offering a silent prayer. Michael rolled his eyes and imagined the day he could be rid of this woman. Maybe he would find someone to dump her on later today, perhaps in just a few hours' time. He could only dream.

Once the car was loaded Michael got in and turned the key in the ignition. Nothing happened. He tried it again. The car whined like an injured horse, but would not start. He tried again. Again, nothing happened.

"Fuck!"

He punched the steering wheel, accidentally catching his grazed hand. "Bastard!"

Judith looked at him with pity. "Swearing is not 'cool' you know, Michael" she sniffed. "What are we waiting for?"

Michael bit back his anger and spoke from between gritted teeth. "Well Judith, the car won't start for some reason. How about you stop all this religious stuff and focus on the real world, perhaps help make this car work? Or better yet, ask God to help us?"

Judith sighed. "Michael, the Lord is not a mechanic. When he spoke to me last night he said we shall be saved. He mentioned something about "the answer", and Lincoln too, which is odd because I have never been to..."

Michael interjected. "Oh shit, it's the battery. The light is on red. What were you doing last night Judith? Did you sleep with the lights on? The wipers? Were you listening to the radio all night? Did you have the radio on?"

"No, I certainly did not have the radio on, and I do not appreciate your tone Michael. There is nothing I would want to hear on the radio anyway."

The radio. Michael had a vague recollection of punching the radio and turning it on the previous evening. But there had been no signal, or at least no signal just then and there, but maybe here? Michael tried the key again. The car still would not start, but he pressed all each of the radio buttons desperately.

"Come on...C'mon." The radio light stayed off and not even a crackle of static came out. "Damn."

96

"What are you doing? How is this helping make the car work?"

Michael was not listening. Instead of answering Judith, he opened the car door and ran back into the restaurant. Judith was left sitting there in a state of bewilderment. The boy was having a breakdown. He had left her there all alone again. She got out of the car and called after him. "Michael, where are you going? Michael, wait for me."

She found him in the restaurant, crouched beside the counter, the radio held up to his face as he turned the dials. White noise crackled out. Michael clasped his hands around the radio and whispered a "thank you" to the ceiling. Thank God for batteries.

Judith came towards him, ready to shake him out of his delirium. "What on *earth*..."

"Shush!" Michael whispered as he turned the dials again, searching for the right station.

"This is no time for music." Judith said, shaking her head.

Michael shot her a look she was not used to people giving her. "Judith, shut up!"

Judith's mouth hung open. She blinked slowly a few times in shock, looking like someone had just thrown a cup of tea on her.

Before she was able to process Michael's words or think of a retort, the radio lurched into life and a man's voice spoke out. "...Whoever is out there. This is Ian Whitehead, MP. I have set up a refugee centre just outside of Lincoln, off the A15. This is the answer. There is food and water and we have emergency electrical generators. All are welcome. This is a safe place. We are working on your salvation. Come and join us, we are off the A15 near Lincoln and are fully equipped. This is elected MP Ian Whitehead. The answer is here. Whoever..."

Michael turned off the radio and smiled at Judith. "Change of plan."

97

Chapter Ten

"Make it work."

Michael ran a hand through his hair and exhaled slowly. "I'm not a mechanic Judith. There's nothing I can do."

He tried to think back to the things his father had told him about cars when he had been given his old rust-bucket on his eighteenth birthday. "I think we need to jumpstart the car, but..." he swept his arm over the car park, "there aren't any other cars around, and I didn't see any on the way in."

Judith called over from where she was sitting on the wall between the car park and playground. "Well, perhaps we passed one on the way. It was dark."

Michael rubbed his eyes. "We didn't."

"I beg your pardon?" Judith called, cupping a hand to her ear.

"I said, we didn't, Judith. We'll have to walk."

They sat in the playground on the roundabout, eating as much food as they could from what they would have to leave behind. The sun glinted off the silver slide and the bright greens, yellows and reds of the swing set. Judith shifted uncomfortably on the wooden seat of the roundabout as she tried to fish some peach slices from their syrupy tin. Michael was drinking from a tin of cold chicken soup as he studied the map he had spread out in front of him. Coloured lines interwove and threaded together to make a collage of the country. Michael could not taste the soup, his attention was focused entirely on the map, and he was too hungry to care what the thick sludge tasted like.

"I think it will take us maybe an hour and a half, could be

two if the roads are blocked. Of course, it all depends on if we can find a car. We're here right now." He pointed at the map, expecting Judith to look over, and when she did not, he looked up and saw her staring at the swings, as though deep in recollections, the peach tin forgotten beside her, the sharp edges glinting in the light.

Michael tried again to get her attention. "Judith…Judith, look, this is where we are."

She seemed to wake from a dream and glanced about as though unfamiliar with her surroundings. Before turning to check the map, Michael noticed her shoulders slowly rise and fall as a hand wiped something from her cheek. He pretended not to have noticed as he gestured to the map again.

"We're here Judith. We're going to have to walk for a while to find a car, but it shouldn't be too long. Are you ready?"

Judith ignored the map and picked up her tin of peaches. She began to look for any leftovers. "I think I will stay here for a while, I'm still quite hungry and it's so…nice here. Yes, very nice. If you go and find us a car you can come and pick me up, I will either be sat here or in the restaurant. I don't mind waiting."

Michael ground his teeth as he folded the map. He left the tin of soup where it was and stuck the map in his back pocket. "I'm going to the car to sort my things."

He looked at Judith, but she had returned to staring at nothing in particular. "I'll sort my things, then we're *both* going to find another car. Five minutes."

There was no response, so Michael left Judith in the playground and strode back to the car.

The boot opened with a click and Michael stood looking down at his worldly possessions. The gun was the main problem. So much had happened since the village yesterday that he had forgotten about it. The bonfire of corpses, the airplane wreckage, exploring this restaurant and now this news about some sort of help. It was a lot to think about.

Judith was another concern. She was constant white noise in the background, interrupting his train of thoughts. Michael glanced over at her now and saw her standing by the swing set, pushing a swing gently. The sound of the rusted chains floated back to Michael by the car. Judith and the gun. He had to decide what to do with them both. He could throw the gun away, but could not do the same to Judith, she seemed to be having some sort of breakdown, and he was being forced into the role of responsible adult, despite only just having turned eighteen.

The radio transmission repeated itself in Michael's head like a pop song. He was even beginning to mouth the words, "The answer is here..."

The answer was there. The answer to the Judith problem. There was nothing to say they had to stick together once they got to the camp, or whatever was at the other end of the radio waves. There would probably be thousands of people there, maybe even somebody Judith knew. Michael could leave her there and go across to France on his own. He had tolerated her for this long and would not be doing a bad thing if he left her when they got there. She would probably want to leave him. They might even bump into some other people on the road, and she might decide to leave him of her own accord and go off with them.

The gun was harder to reach a decision about. Michael thought again about the pros and cons of keeping it. The image of the dead man's boots flashed through his mind, followed by the image of Jim lying dead in his driveway. He had kept a knife though, despite having seen what they could do.

Maybe if Michael had not taken a knife with him, Steve would still have been alive, but then again, perhaps everyone who had survived was only living on borrowed time. Perhaps it did not really matter who was alive, Michael thought. Half the country was dead, if not more. Two-thirds, as an estimate, the television had said that first day, as his family huddled around the screen. That first day when there still had been television.

The holdall of clothes lay in the boot, along with the gun and three carrier bags full of food. From now on, Michael would need to travel light. He opened up the holdall and emptied its contents out into the boot. The gun just about fit inside, along with the satchel of bullets and Michael crammed in a few T-shirts and the torch, then zipped up the bag and slung it over his shoulder, leaving the rest of the things he had salvaged from his home behind. It had been a mistake to bring a jacket in this sweltering heat, he realised now, and he took it off and threw it into the boot. He could get another one in France.

He slung the holdall over his shoulder and took the three carrier bags of food from the boot and shouted across to the play area. "Judith, we're off!"

She did not seem to hear him at first, but when he repeated it she looked up and walked over, all sense of resistance gone. Michael handed her a plastic bag and after she had swapped it with him for a lighter one, they set off, back onto the road, leaving the Jaguar behind.

***

The sun was proud that day, the sort of sun that you can feel stroking your face and prickling your back. They walked onwards, further along the same road they had driven down the previous night, flanked by trees that funneled them down the road and shielded them from view.

They passed through patches of brilliant light and deep shadow in the shape of branches with thick leaves. The road was empty and, after an hour, they had not seen another person or vehicle. Rabbits hopped lazily across the road ahead of them and a drowsy peacefulness filled the air, bringing with it the rich smell of earth and bark.

They stopped intermittently to take breaks when Judith complained, Michael wanting to make better progress, but glad for a chance to relieve himself of the heavy bags for a moment. The first few times, Judith could not be persuaded to sit down on the grass or lean against a tree trunk, complaining of the dirt, but by the third break, she collapsed next to Michael without a word and accepted the drink he had taken from the restaurant for her.

After they had rested, they walked onwards with Judith always on the opposite side of the road to Michael, seemingly lost again in her own thoughts. Michael's own memories helped take his mind off the never ending heat and he thought first of the holidays with his family as a child, holidays in Yorkshire where his father would drive them to a deserted field that slipped down into woods and streams where Michael and his sister would explore in the cool water, walking along the smooth stones at the bottom as the water rushed through their toes whilst their parents lay in the sun with the sandwiches.

He thought of Her and the times they had spent together and, after remembering what had become of his family, the thought of Her was the only thing that made him keep walking. He smiled and brushed a hot tear from his cheek as he recalled an afternoon they had spent together in the woods near their homes, him trying to teach her how to climb trees, and her trying her best, not caring about the green bark marks on her new T-shirt. Her trying to push him into nettles in the shady grove of pine trees where the sunlight slanted down in knives, and him wrestling her back, and her smile as she told him how her friends raised their eyebrows when she told them about the things they did together.

Eventually, the woods sloped away on either side and they were walking along a ridge, looking down on wide expanses of corn fields on either side, interspersed here and there with vivid reds of poppies or the yellows of rape seed. They walked along here with Judith lagging behind and Michael setting the pace, waiting for her here and there, and spurring her on.

After another twenty minutes, a few trees began to litter the path again and the road became enclosed by hedgerows. They passed a few large houses, scattered along the road in their solitude. There were no cars standing outside and both Michael and Judith were reluctant to go into the properties to look for a garage, the memory of dead neighbors still fresh in Michael's mind. They walked on and looked away as they passed a coach that seemed to be growing out of a splintered tree by the roadside, unmoving people sitting wide-eyed as birds flew in and out of the shattered windows.

They left the houses behind and after a while, came upon a T-junction where a lonesome sign pointed them in the right direction. They pressed on, meeting no one and nothing. There were no cars, and the only thing that moved was the breeze that rippled the grass, and the flowers that drooped under the heavy rays of the sun.

They were tiring now as the sun beat down on them; their sweat-saturated clothes making every step feel like five. A sign beside a clump of trees told them of a village. As they reached the trees, Judith collapsed on to the grass verge, her concerns of dirty clothes now long forgotten. Michael shrugged the holdall off his shoulder and rubbed the red strap mark it had pressed into his skin. He sat down next to Judith, his arms aching from the weight of the tins in the carrier bags.

For a while, they sat in the silence, trying to catch their breaths under the shade of branches. There was one can of drink left in their supplies. Michael licked his dry lips. "Hey, it looks like we're down to our last drink. I don't know why the hell we didn't bring more."

Judith wiped sweat from her forehead. "Yes, I do not know either, and don't say hell. This horrible weather, this is England, why on earth is it so warm?"

Michael smiled and passed the can to Judith. "Here, it's

going to be warm and horrible, but you can have the first drink."

Judith reached out lazily for the drink, lacking the energy to move closer and take the can from Michael's outstretched hand, forcing him to shift nearer to her to pass the drink across.

As Judith drank, Michael took stock of where they were. Across the road lay the edges of a thick and dense wood, and, behind them, more trees. They were on the outskirts of the village and a crumbling footpath began a few meters further down the road and led into the village, before disappearing out of sight around a bend in the road hidden by the trees. A house stood on the far corner, set back from the road like a guardian of the village. Michael squinted against the sun, looking for a car in the driveway, but all he saw was an unkept front garden enclosed by an uneven wooden fence.

Judith handed the drink to Michael. He drank the few mouthfuls she had saved for him and then threw the can behind him into the trees. Judith said nothing.

"I think we should go look in that house across the road, there's bound to be some food and drink in there. I can't see a car, but you never know."

Michael began to rise, but immediately sat back down again, dizzy with the heat. "We'll go in a minute though, after we've had a rest, I'm..."

"Shhh!" Judith cut in sharply, her eyebrows furrowed in a look of deep concern, a finger clasped to her mouth as though Michael were a child she was telling to be quiet.

Michael sat silently but could hear nothing. "What is it?" he whispered, his voice hoarse from his dry throat.

"Shhh." Judith repeated. "Listen."

Michael cocked his head and listened to the breeze as it crept through the leaves of the trees. "I can't hear anything..."

Suddenly, the wind picked up and carried with it a man's voice, shouting through the trees.

104

"It sounds like it's coming from around the bend in the road there."

Judith stood up and brushed herself down. "Well, I don't like it. I think we should go back where we came from," she whispered.

Michael thought for a minute. "We can't go back now; we've been walking for hours."

He looked around, trying to assess their options. There was nowhere to go but back down the hot road, or onwards and around the corner. Whilst Michael deliberated, the shouting got louder, as though it were echoing from the trees themselves.

Michael stood up. "Right, I'll go see what's going on. Maybe someone is hurt, or it's someone who can help us. You stay here and try and keep out of sight."

Judith scratched at her neck. "Why do I have to stay here if it's someone who needs our help? Where do you expect me to hide?"

Michael looked around again and was unable to spot any good hiding places. "I don't know Judith, just stay here. Let me go look before we do anything else."

Michael stepped into the shadow of the trees, leaving the bags behind with Judith. Thin streams of light spilt through the roof of glowing leaves and dark shadows cut across the earth. He could not help but remember the dead dog he had found in the copse, and the man with him who had ended his own life. Michael shuddered and was glad he had left the rifle behind with Judith, so that there was no chance he would have to use it. He had the knife for protection if he needed it, and he patted the waistband of his jeans, checking it was still safely tucked away there.

Jim's singing began to play through his mind as his fingers felt the cool metal. '*Run rabbit run, rabbit run run run*'.

The words repeating over and over, getting louder and louder, until Michael thought they were a part of the shouting. It was becoming clearer as he made his way through the woods.

Michael ducked under a branch, a cobweb clinging to his face, and he halted for a moment, spluttering as he tried to wipe it away and out of his mouth. The soft earth tried to hold his shoes in its spongy grip and the dry twigs tried to warn of his approach as they snapped underfoot.

As he struggled, he kicked a stone by accident and it rattled away to ping against an empty and rusted beer can.

'Run rabbit run.'

Michael crouched now, sweating with heat and pressure as he crept forward towards the noise that seemed to echo from the trees.

He crept onwards and after a few minutes, he could make out the road through the trees ahead. He had managed to cut across the bend and was about to come out on the other side. The shouting was clear now, and as he maneuvered to the left of a tree, the source of the noise entered his field of vision. A man with a backpack grasped in one hand, stood in front of a four by four, his back to the vehicle as he waved something away with his other hand. Michael was no more than twenty feet away now, and he dropped to his stomach and crawled as close as he dared through the soft earth.

A second man stood beside the car, holding on to a small girl with one hand, and a cricket bat with the other. The girl stood crying as the men argued. Neither one seemed to pay any attention to her as she wiped her tears over her mud stained dress.

Michael crawled forwards until he had a clear view of the whole scene. The first man pointed towards the girl. "What kind of example are you setting here? She's going to think it is ok to wave cricket bats at people because she's seen her daddy doing it!"

The second man took a step towards the first, dragging the girl along like a doll. "You shut the hell up about my daughter!

What the fuck do you know about her, about us?"

Michael was close enough now to see the whites of this man's eyes and the spittle that flew from his red mouth. The girl sniffed and wiped a trail of snot from her nose. The music in Michael's head was drowned out now by the shouting.

The first man spoke again. "I'm not going to take you with me if you're going to wave that bat around! For God's sake. I mean, I don't even know who you are!"

"Don't know who *I* am? I don't know *you* from Adam. I'm keeping this bat; if you'd seen what they did to her mother, you would understand why. It was lucky I had my bat with me then, I tell you!"

The first man backed up towards the car, noticing the red stains on the wooden bat at the same time as Michael did.

The second man was speaking again. "Just give me the fucking keys; I'll drive us all somewhere safe. I'm just trying to protect my daughter, that's all."

The first man put down his backpack and took a slow step towards the other, both hands outstretched in front of him as a peace offering as he said quietly, "Look, I understand, but you cannot threaten people in order to protect others...If you would just put down the bat..."

An ant crawled across Michael's nose. He did not dare breathe to blow it away; instead, he dug his hands into the earth to try to resist scratching his nose and giving himself away. Once the ant had climbed down from his nose and ran off across the ground, Michael turned his attention back to the two men and the little girl.

The first man advanced slowly, his arms still outstretched. "Please, just calm down..." He laid a hand on the bat and tried to lower it, keeping his eyes averted from the second man's as he did so.

The second man let his bat be lowered slowly. He was unsure of what to do, until he saw the first man glance momentarily in the direction of his daughter. Then he brought the bat up suddenly, and with force, into the first man's chin. A hollow crack sent a tooth spinning away into the trees. "Looking at my daughter? You bastard, what the hell is your game?"

The first man stumbled against the car, his hands feeling clumsily for a door handle to steady himself against. He spluttered, but was unable to speak through a mouthful of blood. He could only put his hand up for protection, but it was the wrong thing to do and the second man swung the bat against his head with a soft *thlock* sound, followed by a thud as the first man's head bounced off the side of the vehicle and his body slid to the floor.

Michael was breathing like a race horse as he pressed his body against the soft ground. The second man stood over the body of the first. There was a gash along the side of the floored man's forehead which did not look so bad until sudden blood seeped through the wound and through the man's hair and down his cheek to flow over his skin into a sticky puddle on the floor which spread ever outwards from his head, slipping away with the man's life.

The girl screamed. Her hand had come loose from her father's and she turned and ran into the woods, thundering past just a few feet away from where Michael was lying. The second man peered down at the body, then raced off into the woods after his daughter. He dropped the bat.

"Holly, come back, Holly!" he called, as he ran after her, crashing into the undergrowth.

Michael pressed himself against the ground as hard as he could, until he thought he might suffocate there.

The sounds of the pursuit quickly receded into the distance and action took hold of Michael. He sprang to his feet and stumbled through the woods and out on to the road as if in a dream. He ran across to the injured man and crouched beside him.

Everything felt surreal as Michael pressed his hands against the wound on the side of the man's head. He could feel nothing; his hands were numb, as was his mind. He caught the man's blank stare and he gasped and fell backwards. Michael wiped his hands across his forehead, only just feeling the warm blood. He glanced at his hands and saw they were red with blood that ran down and along his wrists. He wiped them furiously on his trousers and turned his attention back to the injured man.

The man had not moved, and Michael did his best to feel for a pulse as his hands slipped over the man's blood-slicked neck. Michael could not find a pulse, and retched at the touch of the dead man's flesh, holding his hand to his mouth, and realizing too late that he had smeared blood across his lips. He spat and looked up suddenly, thinking he had heard a noise in the woods. The man with the cricket bat was returning.

Michael took quick stock of the situation, then thrust his hand into the dead man's trouser pocket, where he found the car keys.

Judith was worried. There had been silence now for a few minutes and Michael had not returned. Now there was the sound of a car starting up from around the corner and then the sound of an engine growing louder, as though it was coming her way. She stood up and tried to get behind the nearest tree, but before she could, a four by four rounded the bend and skidded to a stop in the road beside her.

Michael shouted at her from the vehicle. "Judith, hurry up, quickly, get the bags!" Judith reached for a single bag and Michael jumped out of the vehicle to collect the others, causing Judith to shriek as she saw the blood on his clothes.

"Be quiet!" Michael hissed, as a cry echoed from where the dead man lay.

"Hurry up Judith, get in, for God's sake!"

Judith did not argue as Michael took her by the arm and pushed her into the car. She sat in the passenger seat, almost used to being in a state of shock now. Michael's handprint shone in blood on her arm and she watched the way the red bled into the pink of her skin, like oil into water, as the car moved away.

Chapter Eleven

They drove back the way they had come and, after searching for a while, came across another road which by-passed the village. As they drove, Judith tried to ask Michael what had happened after he had stepped into the trees. Michael said nothing and, after a sharp "Huff," Judith abandoned her questioning. They returned to their usual state of mutual silence.

Cars, left crashed and abandoned, littered the road and hindered their progress. Michael was forced to weave in and out of the wreckage. Bodies were propped at unnatural angles in the vehicles and some lay on the road, after being thrown through the windscreens of crashed cars. Some were the bodies of those who had initially survived, but had been unlucky enough to be hit by other vehicles as they wandered along the road in shock.

To Michael, the bodies had become just shapes in the road. Judith sat with her eyes closed, mumbling to herself under her breath as Michael drove. Michael tried to ignore her, but with every murmur the bodies in the road became more vivid, as though Judith's voice was focusing his vision, until each body scorched his eyes in sharp clarity.

Michael shook his head and the shapes melted back into the blurred scenery. He reached to turn the radio on and was met by the emergency broadcast, "there is food and water..." Michael's eyes caught on the unfamiliar hand beside the radio; streaked in dried crimson, it lingered there at the end of his arm like someone else's appendage.

The image of the bodies became sharper again, Michael's

brow pricked with sweat and his breathing became heavy. He remembered the road too late and was not quick enough to avoid a collision.

The four by four struck the side of an abandoned van parked sideways across the carriageway. Both vehicles met with a jolt and Judith and Michael were thrust forward in their seats. There was the sound of glass headlights breaking and metal scraping against metal, but their car was large and powerful, and the speed they had been driving at meant the crash was more like a dodgems collision then a serious accident.

Michael sat back painfully and shook his head to shake away his momentary confusion. The radio was still playing. "… a safe place…"

In the background, but steadily becoming clearer, was the sound of Judith shouting. "What on earth are you doing? I told you I should drive, I cannot entrust my health to a child! Thank the Lord we are not dead! I think I have broken my arm, look at it, Michael, look."

Michael glanced sideways at Judith's arm, his sore neck preventing him from turning his head. The arm was bruised, but did not look swollen. It did not look the same as when he had broken his sister's arm when they were ten and seven, pushing her out of the apple tree in their garden.

"I thought you didn't know how to drive?" he said quietly.

"I beg your pardon?"

"I thought you had never learnt to drive?" Michael said, staring at the dashboard.

"I'm not sure what that has to do with anything," Judith said, as Michael undid his seatbelt. "Michael, where are you going? Michael, look at my arm. Well, are you not going to apologize?"

Michael looked over. "I'm sorry Judith. I don't think it's broken. I'll…I'll be back in a minute," he said dryly.

The door opened with a creak and Michael stepped out on

to weak legs, Judith calling after him over the sound of the radio. "Michael, where are you going? Michael!"

Michael walked wearily away from the car. "I'll be back in a minute, Judith."

He had to get rid of this woman soon; he could not concentrate with her around. After all that had happened to him, she was the final straw.

Michael walked away from the four by four to the edge of the road, climbing over a two car crash that blocked his way. He slid over the hot sun-warmed bonnets and jumped down onto the other side. A rusted metal barrier marked the side of the road and Michael climbed over this and stood staring out across the green fields that stretched as far as he could see, interspersed with telephone wires like giant's bones sticking up through the land, as far as the horizon, where a silvery haze marked the end of the world.

There was a ditch below and Michael clambered slowly down the grassy bank to the water. It was a clear brown and Michael began to wash the blood from his hands, watching the brown mix with the red and drip sparkling from his skin to ripple in the water.

The sun shone warmly on his face and dried his skin quickly after he had washed the last of the blood away. He felt like he could sit here for a while and not worry about Judith, not worry about everything or anything and just sleep. It would be nice to sleep in the sun, and Michael thought now that all he wanted to do was to find somewhere he could sleep beneath the sun, somewhere with enough food so he would not be hungry again, maybe he would grow a little fat and never have to worry about anything again. It was the simplest thing anyone could hope for.

Michael lay back in the grass between the weeds and massaged his eyes. He would sleep a while. No, he would not. He could not; something was interrupting his peaceful thoughts. Judith was calling his name. What the hell did she want, he wondered?

Michael twisted his head to try and see if he could see her, but instead, he saw, just a few metres along the dyke, a car resting upside down in the shallow water. A pool of brilliantly coloured oil lay unmoving on the surface of the water where more red mixed with brown.

When he got back to the car, Michael found Judith waiting in the passenger seat, cradling her arm. She saw him approach and began to say something, but then stopped and looked puzzled instead when he opened the back door.

"Well Michael, I am glad you have decided to let me drive, I am sure it cannot be that difficult, if even you can do it. Hopefully I will be more successful than you."

Michael took one of his remaining T-shirts from the holdall on the back seat. "You're not driving Judith. I thought your arm hurt, anyway? I'm going to make you a sling."

He went around to her side of the car and opened the door. Judith edged away across her seat. "Actually, I think I am all right now, it's feeling much better."

Michael scratched his cheek and held up the spare T-shirt. "It's not going to hurt you Judith; it will just support your arm. If it is broken it will help it heal."

Michael made the sling as Judith squirmed, almost jumping out of the car when he went to tie it around her neck. Afterwards, she looked happier and almost smiled at Michael, before checking herself.

Judith sat back comfortably in her seat as Michael climbed into the driver's side. "Yes, yes it does feel a little bit better. I suppose."

Michael smiled at her as he put the car into reverse. "Told you so."

The sky began to darken as they drove onward. Blue became dark blue and then the horizon became purple as the sun went from orange to red behind them, sending shadows racing ahead across the road.

114

Eventually, they could go no further as the road was blocked by abandoned cars which stretched away as far as they could see into the distance. They were not all crashed cars, instead, the row of vehicles had the appearance of an abandoned traffic jam. Some of the vehicles had bicycles or canoes attached to their roofs. Some towed caravans or jet-skis and most looked full of left-behind luggage.

"I think we're nearly there," Michael said. "We'll have to walk from here."

They got out and retrieved their things, Michael with two bags of food and his holdall, Judith struggling with the lightest bag of food, shrugging the shoulder of her injured arm, unused to the sling. They left the car behind, the doors open with the keys in the ignition. Whoever wanted it was welcome to it.

They walked down the side of the columns of cars and after a while, they were able to make out the shapes of people walking ahead of them, little groups here and there in the failing light. The notes of a song carried back down the line to them.

"This must nearly be it, Judith," Michael said. "We'll be safe."

He could just about make out her expression in the failing light, and she did not look as pleased as Michael had expected.

"What if there are more people there, like...like the ones in my village?" she asked.

Michael shrugged as the last of the sun's light disappeared behind them. "There will be people wherever we go Judith, we'll be ok."

There was music now, getting louder with each step. "Don't worry Judith," Michael added.

And then they came upon it. The camp that was to be the answer to all their problems lay before them; a huge bowl scraped out of the earth, filled with tents and thousands of people. Trees littered the space, hiding those below beneath their leafy boughs. The smell of cooking meat drifted up towards them as they stood on the brink of the basin and, in the purple evening, they could hear the sounds of laughter and music as a hundred glowing campfires pricked the twilight.

Chapter Twelve

They filtered slowly down into the great basin on the heels of the other groups of ragged refugees; no one speaking as they picked their way down the grassy bank, Michael taking Judith's good arm to help her keep her balance. The sky darkened above them, creating a deep blue lid which sealed them all in the bowl they ventured down into.

As they reached the bottom, they were funneled into a long queue that crept along into the camp. They were on a muddy track now, but most people let their bags drop to the floor, freeing their exhausted arms. Ahead of them, Michael saw children sitting in the mud, or leaning against the legs of adults.

A group of men and women in wheelchairs were being pushed through the mud. A crowd had gathered to help push them, but they were having as much luck as if they were trying to push a car across a sheet of ice, the wheelchairs skidding and sometimes crashing into the legs of those in front.

Others left the queue and walked a few metres to piss, in plain sight, women only making slightly more effort and using the nearest trees as shelter from the eyes of the queue.

They shuffled along obediently like the last drops of humanity being fed down a funnel into the camp. Michael had to keep bending to pick up his bags every few minutes, in order to move a few feet forward, whilst Judith stood rubbing her arm.

Michael felt uneasy in this queue, surrounded by strangers for the first time after what seemed like forever alone. Now he was surrounded by others, he was not sure which he preferred, or how he felt safer. Even with Judith for company he had felt alone. She was someone travelling in a parallel direction to him, but they were too dissimilar for their paths to ever properly cross. He had wanted to get rid of her at the first opportunity, but now he realised she was the only person he knew, and if he left her here, he would be alone once more, and he was not sure he was ready for that yet. Michael decided it would be best to keep her with him until he perhaps found somebody else who could help him, or at least until he got inside the camp and could see what the situation was.

"How's the arm?" he asked a vacant Judith.

She seemed to only just hear him, as though he had called her from far away, and she turned to him and seemed to notice him for the first time.

"Oh it is feeling a little bit better," she said, distractedly, almost automatically.

Michael had become used to her reclusive behaviour by now, but thought he should make an effort to see if she was all right, if he was to stay with her for a while longer. "Are you all right Judith?" he enquired.

She rubbed her arm. "Yes. Yes, I'm fine. I suppose it is just the shock of the past few days. I am not used to all of this travelling around."

She pulled her shawl tighter around her shoulders and strained her neck to try and see around the queue. "I suppose we will be sleeping in tents, then? I have never slept in a tent. A few times as a young girl, but I just could not stand it. All those insects crawling all over you in the middle of the night! No thank you!" she shuddered. "My John suggested it once, when he was still around, but I said I would rather a hotel."

Michael was surprised by this lapse in her defenses. Judith had let her guard down for a minute, and out of boredom, and the longing for conversation, Michael acted quickly. "John? Who was he?"

Judith smiled the whisper of a smile. It was the first time

118

Michael had seen her smile, and as she ran a hand through the stray strands of black hair that hung over her eyes, he thought for a moment he could see a younger woman in front of him. But her defenses were quickly restored.

"John was my husband."

She turned her eyes away from Michael, who became aware that no one around them was speaking, either lost in their own thoughts, or eavesdropping on Michael's conversation with Judith. He did not want to push her further on the topic, but felt it was only right to offer his condolences. "Oh, I'm sorry Judith...I didn't know."

She turned back to him, her guard restored. "Yes, it's ok. He did not die, well, as far as I know. We... well something happened and he could not go on living in Potsdon. We parted ways."

Michael thought he saw a faint tear cloud the corners of her eyes, but it was only a ghost and the next second she added sternly, "He was a fool," and that was the end of the conversation.

They waited in the queue. Michael did not want to check his watch. Things would happen when they did. He was not even sure if time existed anymore. Who or what was there to keep track of it now, he wondered? There was nowhere anyone had to be; no appointments, no jobs, no obligations. Things would happen when they happened.

A whistling broke his train of thought and ended his musings. It came from somewhere ahead and at first he thought it was the same song that Jim had sang forever ago. *'Run rabbit run'.*

After straining his ears, Michael decided it was something else, but what, he could not be sure.

He was tired now. The mud seemed to be sucking his shoes down. He was forever being dragged down by mud. He realised then how dirty his clothes were: his T-shirt was soaked in sweat and streaked in mud, leaves were stuck to his chest where he had had to lie low to the ground earlier on, and his jeans were encrusted with flecks of dirt. There was a certain smell characterizing the queue, penetrating through unwashed bodies and sweat soaked shirts. It was a smell that Michael had not noticed with limited human contact over the last two days, but now it was pungent and lingering. He felt grateful for his quick wash in the restaurant that morning and, as he looked over the queue, Michael wondered when these people had last had the chance to wash.

Michael looked over the queue once more and imagined that cleanliness was the last thing on everyone's minds. Men, women and children of all races and ethnicities, were gathered in patient obedience, waiting together for what was promised would save them. Some looked dead on their feet and ready to give up, whilst others appeared tense, alert and sharp; ready for anything to happen. An old man bent double over a walking stick stood alone in a pair of Wellington boots, casting his eyes around with a grim expression of determination etched into his cragged features. As well as those in wheelchairs, several people here and there throughout the queue were propped up on crutches, and there were several more slings as well as a few bandages tied around heads and necks, no doubt victims of injuries obtained the day the world had stopped.

The queue behind Michael was small, made up of no more than thirty stragglers. A child sat on a sledge tied to a middle aged man by a length of blue string. The child sat atop a small suitcase and played with plastic action figures, squinting as the light faded.

Eventually, the queue had moved enough to allow Michael and Judith to make out a ramshackle fence ahead of them. It was not a large fence, but a fence constructed quickly out of orange plastic fencing, of the type often used on road works. In the centre of the fence, at the point where the queue was being funneled to, was an archway, constructed from thin logs nailed together haphazardly. Hanging on either side of this wooden archway were two electric lamps, and, in their orange glow, Michael was able to make out a cloth sign, hanging over the centre of the archway. Written on this sign were the words, Camp Hope.

Michael raised an eyebrow. The name sounded like some American pilgrim settlement and it seemed to Michael there was a cheap Hollywood sentimentality to it, as though his life had turned into some sort of Disney film.

Judith had long been silent and the murmurings of the queue bubbled slowly along, below the surface of audibility. As they approached the gateway to the camp proper, a man in front turned round and scratched his beard, grinning happily. "Ha-ha, nearly there!"

He gestured behind Michael, sweeping his arm over the remainder of the queue. "Only in Britain, eh? Queuing at the apocalypse."

Michael smiled. Judith let out a gasp at the word 'apocalypse' and the man turned back around with a wink.

Michael picked up the bags again as the queue moved. He said Judith's name to get her attention, and then motioned with a nod to the bags he was struggling with, but Judith simply raised her eyebrows and nodded her own head at her arm resting in the sling he had made her.

Then it was their turn to pass through into the camp. The gateway was manned by a man and a woman who stood behind a mud covered desk. Both were wearing green high-visibility vests and fleeces, despite the heat that still lingered. They had name tags around their necks informing anyone who was interested that they were 'Official Camp Monitors' with their names beneath, but no picture, which Judith considered a flaw.

The thing that struck Michael immediately, was that both of them wore shotguns on straps around their torsos. He hoped they would not check his own bags and try to arrest him, or whatever they had the power to do once they discovered he had brought along a firearm of his own.

The man looked through them as they stepped up to the desk, then spoke in a voice that indicated how many long hours he had been there for. "Names."

Michael was unsure why they were asking, was there some sort of guest list for the camp, he wondered?

Judith stepped forward and was immediately restored to her Parish Council persona. "Mrs. Judith Allen" she said. She held out her hand, but neither of the monitors took it and she let it fall to her side, but kept her smile fixed.

The woman wrote Judith's name on a sheet of paper attached to a clipboard as the man turned his gaze to Michael. "Erm...Michael Taylor."

The woman wrote it down as the man took two bits of paper from a pile and handed one to each of them. "Okay, each of these tokens entitles you to three meals. Meal times are eight am, one pm and seven pm."

From another pile, the man took a green square of paper and handed it to them. "You are in tent area N."

Judith took the papers and thanked him, but the man remained impassive.

When Judith and Michael did not move, he raised his eyebrows and shouted, "Next!" and before the next people had even reached the table, he had called out, "Names" in a voice that sounded like it had been repeating the same questions for days.

They gateway soon disappeared behind them as they passed through into the camp. Ahead and all around them stretched a collage of tents, from small red one-man tents to some almost marquee-like in size. The tents were rammed together, creating alleyways of guy-ropes amongst walls of bright colours, now seemingly dull in the beginnings of the night. The moonlight shone down to illuminate the scene and cast jagged angles of tent shadows across canvas walls and what little empty ground there was. The whole bazaar of tents appeared to be held together by endless tangles of rope, like spiders' webs, and it looked as though if one rope were cut, the whole camp might come crashing down.

Two spotlights guarded the edges of the camp, raised high above the ground by what looked through the darkness like two small cranes. Michael remembered the generators the radio transmission had promised. One of the spotlights was away across the crooked sea of tents and illuminated a makeshift wooden stage, which appeared to have been hastily constructed at the far side of the basin.

Beside the stage were several large tents with more people wearing high-visibility vests milling around outside. Michael could not see if they had shotguns or not. Next to these tents was a large marquee. Michael could see some of those who had arrived just ahead of them stood, gesturing angrily, to some of the vested-guards, the paper slips of the meal vouchers waving in their hands. Michael looked at his watch and saw it was after nine, long past the last meal time. The late comers would be hungry until morning.

Judith did not take any of this in, but stood and scanned the mass of tents. "Well?" she asked.

Now they were supposed to share the same tent, Michael was beginning to regret sticking with her. "Well, what?"

Judith sighed as she folded her arms across her chest, shaking her head at Michael as though what she wanted was obvious. "Well, take me to my tent Michael."

He was too tired to argue.

Together, they made their way through the crowds of people half illuminated by spotlights, and half hidden in shadow. There were hundreds of people, some strolling around in the early night, some sitting playing guitars under trees or around campfires. The sound of a trumpet cut through the thrum of acoustic guitars, screeching against them in protest. A group of people in the distance were trying to split up a fight and a man somewhere behind them was calling a girl's name over and over again. The ground was littered with empty beer cans and bottles and plastic bags and tin cans and every now and then, a used condom.

Each area of tents had its own sign painted on cardboard and nailed to a wooden post, but there was no sign of *Tent Area N*. Some of the signs had fallen and in the dark it was only possible to read those still standing when a camp fire flared up and lit up the face of the sign for a second. The spotlights did not penetrate this far, they only touched the edge of the camp and left the middle shrouded in a pool of mystery and darkness, lit only by the silver light of the moon mixed with the red glow of campfires. Away from the moon's eerie silver light and the dancing flames of the fires, the shadows were held deeper in their darkness.

Just as finding their tent began to appear hopeless, Michael spotted a sign with a single *N* painted on it, standing beside a long tent flying a Jolly Roger flag. He pointed the sign out to Judith who gave no sign of acknowledgement and instead looked as though she was about to drop down dead. They made their way across, tripping over guy-ropes and trying to ignore the hostile remarks and glares of the strangers whose tents they kicked in doing so.

Every now and then, they would pass by a disposable barbeque with a small group gathered around it, to cook whatever meat they had which still smelt as if it might be ok to eat. Once, as they passed such a group, a young woman sprinted into the middle of the crowd and snatched a piece of half cooked chicken from the grill. Ignoring her burns, she raced away, pursued by one of the group who soon fell into a tent and returned, defeated.

They wound their way over towards the *N* sign. A young boy with a dirt covered face appeared from amongst the dark maze of tents, took hold of Judith's shawl and tugged on it sharply. "Have you seen my mummy?"

Before Judith could stammer out an answer, a man stepped out of the darkness behind them and shouted to the boy, "Come here," and the pair of them were lost into the sea of tents.

They reached the sign which was roughly planted in amongst a crowd of tents, nearly all of which seemed to be occupied. Neither Judith nor Michael knew where they were supposed to be, and when Judith tried to stop someone to ask, they ignored her and carried on walking. Michael opened a few tents to see if anyone was home. In the first one a child slept and Michael backed out and zipped it back up. The second contained a skinny white boy wriggling about on top of a black girl. Michael stared in surprise for a second, until the girl kicked him in the face and yelled, "Fuck off pervert!"

Judith caught up to him but did not ask what had happened.

They stumbled around from tent to tent. They were both growing weary and Michael's nose was sore. He was beginning to think they would have to sleep under a tree when a woman called out to them from the mouth of a large green tent. "Hey there!"

She was young, maybe in her mid-thirties and Michael thought she had a friendly face, but why he thought that, he did not know.

"Hey," The woman repeated. "Do you guys need somewhere to stay?"

Michael was about to answer, when Judith cut in.

"Why, yes we do, that would be wonderful. Judith Allen," she said as she bent down beside the tent's entrance and extended her hand to the woman. Judith certainly was not fussy about taking up an offer, Michael thought. The woman climbed out of the tent and shook her hand.

"Hi Judith, I'm Mary," she said, before turning to Michael. He quickly looked her over, deciding she was definitely mid-thirties. She looked like the practical sort, dressed in hiking boots and combat trousers and a dark T-shirt covering a blue long-sleeved top.

"I'm Michael," Michael said as she shook Mary's outstretched hand.

"Well Judith and Michael, it's nice to meet you. You are both welcome to come and stay with us for however long we'll be here. However long that will be...It's just me and my little boy, Terry. He's only six and he's a bit grumpy sometimes, but I'm sure he won't bother you nice people."

"That's splendid!" Judith exclaimed. "We don't mind about youngsters at all," she said as she began to climb into the tent, her muddy shoes disappearing after her.

Mary smiled and indicated that Michael should follow.

He bent down and began to undo his trainers, but Mary stopped him. "Oh no, no, there's really no need. A bit of mud doesn't matter. And besides..." Here she looked about, as though expecting to see someone or something lurking behind one of the tents. "There have been stories of people's shoes being stolen from outside tents, so best keep them inside!"

She smiled a "but-everything's-fine" smile, then disappeared inside the tent. Michael followed and almost fell over trying to bring all the bags inside; it seemed Judith had forgotten about them again.

Once inside, Michael could see nothing except for a few sparks of a lighter in the darkness and then, suddenly, there was a small flame which flickered over Mary as she used it to light a candle she had melted to a dish in the middle of the tent. The candle caught and a soft light painted the shadows of giants against the walls.

The floor was spread with thin blankets over the ground sheet and was comfortable after a day of walking and queuing. Judith and Mary were sitting one to a corner. The tent was cramped and Michael put his bag in the only free space there was and sat down resting on it. He had to keep his feet tucked under him, otherwise they would almost be in Mary's lap.

What actually *was* in her lap was a sleeping blond-haired boy wrapped in a blanket, who stirred as Michael sat down. The boy began to cry out. "Mum, mum!"

"It's ok," Mary said as she stroked the boy's hair. "They're just new friends."

Without warning, Michael's eyes began to well up and there was a lump in his throat at this display of maternal affection. He remembered nights as a child when he had woken up thinking he was in a strange place and had called for his own mother. She was not here for him now though, and no one he had known ever would be.

Michael kept his face hidden for a few minutes, pretending to do something with his hair as he attempted to stop the quiver of his bottom lip. Judith wasted no time in making introductions, grabbing one of the carrier bags they had carried with them and emptying it out on the floor by the candle, the last of their tins bouncing off one another and rolling about the tent.

"Well Mary," she said, "we were just about to eat. Won't you join us? What would you like?"

Cheeky bitch, thought Michael. Those were his tins, that his grandfather had given him. Michael had carried them all the way here too; only half an hour ago Judith had refused to carry one of the bags. Mary and her son were welcome to their food, but Michael resented the way Judith offered the tins to them one by one, as though she herself had grown the damn food.

"Beans?" she offered Mary, showing her the tin.

"Oh, please," Mary replied, as she gently shook Terry awake. "Terry, Tezzle, come on baby, we are going to have some food."

Terry stirred and did not seem to want to wake up, but when he saw the tins in front of him and realised that food was an actual possibility, he sat bolt upright and grinned.

"What would you like dear?" Judith said to him in a

toddler's voice that made Michael nauseous. "How about some sardines?"

Michael laughed. "Judith, no one likes sardines, especially not a six year-old, give him that tin of spaghetti shapes, he'll love them" he said, giving Terry a wink which the boy did his best to return, but could not quite master.

"Michael! Will you please be quiet, I will find something suitable for Terry, do not worry."

Michael was about to snap and tell her she could go fuck off and find her own food when Mary cut in. "Michael, I'm sure your mum knows what she's doing."

Michael coughed and Judith spat out a sardine tail.

"He is not my..."

"She isn't my mum, bloody hell!" Michael cried, as Mary scowled at him.

Terry shouted "Bloody hell!" and Michael laughed loudly.

Just then someone brushed against the tent outside, scraping their fingers along the canvas.

"Shh!" Mary whispered, wrapping her hand over Terry's mouth. She said it with such force that Judith and Michael both froze and remained silent. Mary stared at the side of the tent and they remained silent for what seemed like five minutes before she removed her hand slowly from Terry's mouth and said in a low whisper, "It isn't safe here, sometimes. People have been attacked for their..." She trailed off and covered Terry's ears. He tried to squirm away for a moment, then complacently began to tuck into some spaghetti shapes with his fingers, after Michael passed him an open tin.

Mary continued. "It isn't safe here. All sorts goes on. I've only been here a few days, but it's a bit scary. The food vouchers they give you are not enough for anyone. It's for three meals all together, not three meals a day. I've tried to save some of mine for him. Some people have had their vouchers stolen. Some people with their own food have been attacked for it!"

"Yeah, we saw someone steal some meat from a barbeque just now," Michael began.

Judith interrupted him. "Well, do not worry Mary, we are here now. I am sure the three of us and little Terry will be ok. The Lord will watch over us. In fact, we should pray now."

Mary shot Michael a glance as if to ask, '*Really?*' Michael smiled and rolled his eyes as if to say, '*Yeah, tell me about it*'.

Judith took Michael's hand and Michael took Mary's. It was his first female contact in what seemed like months (he did not, could not, count Judith) and he tried to remove all impure thoughts from his mind. Terry was focused on his spaghetti and did not seem like he wanted to be involved in any prayers, but after a look from his mother, he did as he was told and held out a hand to her and Judith.

Judith began to pray. "Our father, who art in heaven...."

Michael's thoughts drifted and he tried to remember the last time he had prayed before a meal. He could not recall. The only thing he could think of to do with prayers and mealtimes was The Last Supper, and he hoped this would not be theirs.

Chapter Thirteen

Michael awoke suddenly and in a state of alarm. He was being attacked from all angles: someone was digging into his side, shoulders, back, stomach and legs with blunt objects. There was something grinding into his ribs. He could feel it rubbing between the bones.

He sat up in the stale morning air of the tent and ducked his head under the low roof. Judith, Mary and Terry slept on, wedged together amongst bags and shoes as the June sun quickly turned the air thick and warm, the tent walls sagging inwards like a surrendered lung that could breathe no more of the heavy air.

Michael knelt as he struggled with the zip, kicking someone in the process. It was impossible to find the zip when you wanted it. When you needed the toilet in the middle of the night, there was nothing you could do, you were trapped forever. He found it, and quickly drew it back around the circular doorway. There was another zip to be done but this one was on the opposite side of the door. Michael found it after a time, and pulled it open so fiercely that the whole tent shook, causing Terry to murmur in his sleep.

Michael burst out into the morning air, walked a few feet, then sat down sweating on a small patch of grass between a confusion of tents. A few people were moving around, but he was hidden here, down amongst the canvas walls. He looked at his watch. It was only six a.m. His days were starting earlier and earlier. He was wide awake though, and did not relish the thought of climbing back into the sticky tent to wedge himself between Judith and Mary.

Michael smiled, and waves of nostalgia washed over him. He remembered camping with Her in an older time, the two of them and another couple in a field of sheep. Competitions at night over who could have the loudest sex in their little tents. It had been a great week. They had cooked breakfast as the grey sky shone overhead and sheltered together in the afternoons as the horizontal rains strove to carry their tent away.

There did not seem to be any hint of rain now. Or sex. The sky was a brilliant blue. A blue that Michael had begun to associate with the end of the world. Where were the rolling thunderstorms and earthquakes that films had promised? Why was the only time England was having nice weather when there was no one around to enjoy it, he wondered?

Michael lay back against a tent wall and yawned. This could possibly be the first day of the rest of his life. After days of wandering the country, of sitting at home with his family, not knowing what would happen to them, here at last was some sort of an answer. But why had it taken them so long to set this place up? If they had done it four days earlier, there was a good chance his family would have been there as well.

It felt like a long time had passed since he had lost them. The memory of that day did not seem real, or perhaps it was too real. It was a fact, something that had happened that he was now removed from. He felt the same way about Her, but knew she was different.

Michael's thoughts were rudely interrupted as an elbow jabbed at him from inside the tent, accompanied by a shout of, "Oy, fuck off!"

Michael crawled away, back to Mary's tent, and sat cross-legged, waiting, but for what, he did not know.

A chicken appeared from around a corner and clucked and pecked its way closer to Michael, seemingly unthreatened by his presence. Michael began to salivate. A hunger which he had not noticed before was suddenly upon him, and he felt as though the bottom of his stomach had dropped away and his body was crying out for something to fill the empty space.

In his mind, he pictured a cartoon where Sylvester looked at Tweety Pie, imagining her roasting over an open fire. Michael licked his lips. He still had a knife there in his jeans, and was sure that the blade was keen enough to slit a chicken's throat.

The chicken clucked ever closer, bristling its feathers every now and then, and spreading its wings out, as though it were sneezing. It pecked at the ground with its mud-yellow beak and its black beads of eyes were focused only on where they could find worms in the soft morning soil.

Michael drew out his knife slowly. He shuffled forward on his backside, quietly, he thought, slow like a tiger.

There were other animals out to catch their breakfast that morning. A herd of children came storming through the valley of tents crying "Here chicken" and "Get chicken-licken!" They were upon the bird before it had chance to run, trying to grab it with their fat little hands, whilst it hopped about lamely, spluttering into momentary flight, before landing and eventually making its escape, running down a gap between two tents, too narrow for the children to follow. The chicken disappeared, head down and running for its life. The children ran on looking for some other distraction and vanished amongst the tents.

All over the valley, people were dragging themselves wearily from their tents, stretching and exhaling their stale breaths into the heat of the morning. Those that had a change of clothes put them on, others put their sweat and dirt covered clothes back on. An old woman changed her underwear, turning it inside out to the jeers of a group of young boys.

Men and women took children up the grassy sides of the basin to find an empty bush, but none remained, only bushes someone had found before them, which were now strewn with toilet roll and tampons and sometimes condoms. Children

132

and their parents pissed in plain view on the sides of the basin, not bothering with the bushes, and a muddy river of urine formed on one side and bubbled down the hill to gather around the foot of a tree on the edge of the camp, turning the ground into marsh land.

A dog barked from somewhere and banged against tents as it ran wildly through the alleyways of brightly coloured canvas walls. Its eyes shone brightly and its ears were flat as it fled from a middle aged woman with a carving knife, who yelled over and over "I have a child! I have a child!"

A man's voice rang out calling "Chinaski! Here boy! Chinaski!"

The dog made it to the edge of the tent city and bounded away up the hill into the mist of the pissers, and vanished amongst the soiled bushes. The woman fell on a guy rope and the knife slit the side of a tent and came to rest in an old man's shoulder. An uproar filled the camp.

Terry poked his head out of his tent and saw Michael sat cross legged in the sun. There was the older boy, quite still and with his eyes closed. Terry snuck stealthily out of the tent, his bare feet making no noise in the wet grass as he approached, getting ever closer, until he could see the hairs on Michael's back and then, suddenly, he was directly behind him and with a gigantic war cry, he leapt upon Michael's shoulders.

The cry startled Michael, as did the impact upon his back and in one movement he grabbed Terry's arm and threw him onto the grass in front of him, and then dived upon him, bringing his knife to rest inches from the boy's throat, before realising who the little sack of skin and bones he had pinned to the ground was.

"Terry! Bloody hell mate. Are you all right?"

He sat back and got off the boy, quickly sliding the knife away into his waistband. Terry laughed and sprang up. "I got you Michael, I got you!"

Michael leaned backwards on his elbows. "You did mate,

well done, you little ninja."

"When's breakfast, Michael?" Terry asked, rubbing his stomach absent mindedly. Mary's head appeared from the tent. "Terry! Leave poor Michael alone, come here!"

Michael looked over to Mary and realised he could see partly down her top. "Morning Mary. He's all right, we're just playing. Shall we all go to breakfast?"

Mary squinted as the bright sun hit her eyes. "Well Michael, I'm not sure if me and Terry will come, you know after what I told you yesterday...the tickets..."

Michael stood up and took Terry's hand. "That's no problem, I'm sure I can share with Terry, and Judith can bring you something back. I'm not that hungry anyway."

Mary was about to say. "Oh no, I couldn't possibly" but as she opened her mouth to speak, she was interrupted by the roaring of Terry's empty stomach.

"That would be really nice of you Michael." Mary smiled as Michael felt his own stomach rumble from hunger.

After waiting for Judith to wake up and do what little she could with her hair and have a stretch and then find her breakfast ticket, the three of them set off amongst the tents towards the food marquee, where a huge crowd was already forming. Mary had stayed behind to watch over their belongings and Michael held Terry's hand and told him a story about a pirate who had lived in a tent.

Judith walked beside them in the silent state that Michael had grown accustomed to. She wore her cardigan even though Michael could see sweat prickling her brow.

Just as Michael came to a particularly gruesome part of his pirate tale, Judith took Terry's other hand and pulled him out of Michael's grip.

"That is quite enough," she said. "You are going to scare him."

Terry seemed not to agree and stuck his tongue out at Judith who, fortunately for Terry, did not notice. She appeared

134

to be preoccupied with something and her head spun from side to side, as though she were searching for something. At last, she turned to Michael and asked quietly, "Michael, where is... where are... where is the bathroom?"

He laughed and gestured around them at the people still relieving themselves on the side of the basin. "We're in it Judith."

Judith said nothing but, "Hmm," and tightened her grip on Terry's hand, half dragging him along now.

They walked on a few more feet, weaving their way amongst the tents. All the while, Judith shifted uncomfortably, sweating in her cardigan. "It's so warm today! Where are the showers Michael?"

"I don't know if there are any, Judith. Everyone could do with one, I know, but I'm not sure washing is anyone's priority right now."

Judith fished about in her cardigan pocket with her spare hand and brought out a soiled tissue. She looked at it for a moment and, deciding she had nothing better, used it to wipe the sweat from her brow with an uncomfortable shudder.

They made their way clear of the tents and joined the end of the queue at the marquee. Hundreds of people were already lined up and the heat in amongst the hungry masses was almost unbearable. Michael lifted Terry up and sat him on his shoulders to try and save him from it, but he was heavier than he looked and Michael soon had to put him down again. The crowd slid along as though on a conveyor belt as small groups disappeared into the marquee at a painfully slow rate. The entrance was guarded by two more people in high visibility vests, but as far as Michael could see, only one of them carried a shotgun, and the other was armed with a baton of some kind.

Judith looked more uncomfortable than ever and, after waiting twenty minutes, she stepped out of the queue. "Michael, I have to, erm...I have to go. I will be back shortly"

Before Michael could reply, Judith had left the crowd and her narrow legs carried her around the back of the white marquee. Terry did not ask where she had gone.

Suddenly, a girl ahead of them in the queue was sick on to her own shoes. Michael did not know whether she was ill or she was just so hungry that she had vomited. He had felt that way some mornings after a night out. There were no noises of disgust or laughter, and most people seemed not to notice the girl had been sick at all. Terry had noticed though, and he asked Michael what was wrong with the lady. Michael said he did not know and Terry fell silent again.

A woman in front of them turned around to face Michael. "It's the food," she whispered. "The food they serve is awful. It's enough to make anyone ill."

Before Michael could ask her more, she had turned her back to him again.

They were nearing the entrance to the big marquee when Judith re-appeared. She looked happier now and there were almost the beginnings of a smile on her lips as she strode up to Terry and Michael, hoping to rejoin her place in the queue.

"I see we are almost there! Thank the Lord, I'm starving!" she said as she slid into the crowd beside Michael.

A voice rang out from behind them. "Oi, excuse me love? What's your game? We've been queuing for half an hour here. There's a bloody line, you know!"

They turned to face a large woman in shorts and a pink T-shirt who held a young child in her arms. Michael could not tell whether the child was a boy or girl.

Judith put on her Parish Council persona as she addressed the woman. "Oh, I am sorry. My name's Judith, Judith Allen. I'm not "pushing in", I am simply rejoining my friends, you see. I have been queuing."

The woman rocked her head from side to side. "I do not give a fuck what your name is love, you're pushing in." She put the child down and it merged into a crowd of more children of around the same age that the woman seemed to have collected around her legs.

"Here, Kev! Kevin!" the woman shouted.

A man came up from behind her and flicked a cigarette out of the queue with a snap of his wrist.

"What the fuck is up love?" he asked in a Mancunian drawl.

"This snotty cow here's pushed in front, that's what!" the woman answered, fired up now, and out for justice.

Judith stepped forward and offered her explanation again. "Sir, as I was saying to your wife..."

"Wife! Ha ha, fuck off, she's not me wife, love," Kev laughed, his stomach shaking.

"Nah, is she fuck! Anyway, fuck off to the back, there's a good lass!"

Judith stood indignantly as she tried to form a few words. Before she could say anything, Michael took her by the arm (her bad arm mysteriously having healed overnight) and pulled her back a step or two.

"Excuse me mate," he began. "I know what it looks like but she was in the queue with us, she just left for a slash. This is her lad here." He nodded at a confused Terry. "You don't want to separate him from his mum do you? It's just one more person."

Before Kev could reply, the woman cut back in, this time almost screaming at Michael. "I do not give a fuck. The lot of you can fuck off to the back of the queue! I've got kids to feed here! Kev!"

At this prompt Kev, weighed back in to the debate. "Yeah, fuck off, all of you, and now, before something happens!"

Those nearest to them in the queue had formed into a ring of spectators, and those a few places away were straining over the heads of others to see what was going on.

Just as Michael thought a fight was about to erupt, a new voice entered the furor and Michael was relieved to see one of the vested guards standing beside them.

"What's the problem here?" he asked calmly, his baton resting against his leg.

"There's no problem mate, everything's under control," Kev said, an undercurrent of unpredictability in his voice. The guard stood a moment and looked over Michael and Judith, and then Kev and the woman, apparently deciding what to do.

"Sir," he said, addressing Kev, "I'll have to ask you to step out of the queue."

The woman started up again. "It's not fucking Kev mate, it's those two pricks there!" she shouted, spraying those nearest her with spittle.

The guard ignored her and took Kev by the elbow.

"Oy fuck off mate!" Kev yelled. He turned to swing for the guard, but before the punch could connect, the guard hit him squarely in the stomach, causing him to double up.

The guard took him by the arm and threw him to the ground beside the queue. "I will fucking say what goes on here!" the guard shouted.

Kev sat up in a daze and tried to stand as the guard swung his baton into his face. There was a crack as the baton connected with Kev's nose, and a stream of red sprayed the mud.

The woman stepped forward, shrieking. "Keep your hands off Kev!"

The guard raised his baton at her threateningly and she fell quiet again.

The guard walked off and the woman rushed out to cradle Kev's head, their children running after her. Judith shuffled from one foot to the other in embarrassment and Michael put his arm around Terry, who looked like he might be about to cry. The whole queue had fallen silent.

When they finally made their way to the marquee entrance, there was another problem. They only had tickets for two people and the guards would not let three of them in with only two tickets. Earlier, Michael would have argued against this, but now he was not sure how they would react. Both of the guards looked fed up and Michael thought they might as well beat him up for entertainment, as listen to his argument. He pointed out a grassy mound to Terry and told him to go and wait there, and not move until they came out again. Terry trotted off obediently as Michael and Judith stepped into the heat of the tent.

It was stifling inside and smelt strongly of grass. The cream canvas walls were stained green and brown from the mud and grass people had flicked about the place as they trudged across the soft ground. They had each given their tickets to a third guard on the door, and had been given a paper bowl and plastic cup in return. They joined a small queue at a line of desks behind which stood a row of people in dirty aprons, sweat dripping from their brows and wet patches forming under their arms.

Judith and Michael shuffled along in the close air of the tent and when it was their turn, one of the helpers behind the desk handed them a stale piece of baguette each. They shuffled along to the next person who dipped a ladle into a cauldron he had burning over a small fire, and ladled them each a grey mess of porridge into their bowls. The third person took their cups and filled them with water from a large keg, and then they stepped outside again into the bright morning light.

They quickly found Terry where Michael had told him to wait, and they sat down beside him on the grassy mound. Michael took a swig of his water and almost spat it out again. It tasted of chemicals, but it was the only water he had, and he quickly swallowed half of it down, then gave the rest to Terry. Michael expected him to complain about the taste, but Terry drank it down without a word and then scrunched up the plastic cup. Judith had got stuck into her bread and porridge, using the stale bread to scoop up the grey porridge. She seemed to have forgotten she was meant to be saving some for

Mary. Michael took a bite of dry bread and then poured as much porridge as he could stomach into his mouth to help him chew.

He handed the bowl to Terry and said around a mushy mouthful. "'ere Tez, 'elp 'urself."

Terry understood and went to work on the food, again with no complaints, his cheeks bulging like a fat little hamster, flecks of porridge covering his freckled face.

Each time Judith took a gulp of water she grimaced and shook her head theatrically. She swallowed it down eventually and turned to the remaining porridge. She did not seem to know whether to scoop it up in her long fingers or drink that down too. Her fingers were poised over the bowl when she evidently decided it was more ladylike to drink the remaining porridge, and she raised the bowl to her lips.

Michael coughed, but Judith did not get the hint. "Judith, what about Mary?"

Judith looked at him over the top of her bowl and the gulping noises coming from her gullet stopped. She lowered the bowl and looked at what little porridge she had left. "Oh yes...of course... I almost forgot," she said, as though a little fly that had gone away had returned to bite her.

Just then, a commotion broke out at the marquee. What remained of the queue seemed to be trying to rush into the tent, and the guards were pushing them back. The third guard had sprinted out from inside and all three were swinging batons indiscriminately as they forced the crowd back.

"The breakfast is closed!" The man who had hit Kev yelled. "The breakfast time period has passed. Please make your way back to your tents!"

The crowd surged forward and there were cries off "Fuck off!" and, "For God's sake, we're starving here!"

Michael, Judith and Terry sat motionless, watching the situation develop. The crowd surged forward as one, young and old, black and white, and it looked as though they might

140

succeed in rushing into the marquee when suddenly a crack pierced the atmosphere and sent a chill through the morning heat. The second guard held a shotgun above his head. The crowd paused momentarily and some backed away. The more determined amongst them held their ground and seemed ready to attempt another surge, when a second shot rang out, echoed and amplified by the marquee, causing them all to jump backwards in surprise.

The guard who had dealt with Kev shouted again. "Breakfast is now closed. Go. Back. To. Your. Tents."

The guard with the shotgun was reloading as Michael took Terry's hand and ran with him back into the maze of tents, Judith hurrying along behind, trying not to spill her porridge.

***

As they neared the tent, Mary ran out to meet them, almost falling over in her flip flops in her hurry. Terry ran off ahead and she snatched him up, and whispered his name over and over into his ear. She looked up with wet eyes as Michael and Judith reached them.

"I was so scared! What the hell was all that?"

"The guards," Michael said, gesturing behind them to the direction they had come from. "It looks like everyone's getting a bit restless."

"They're savages!" Judith cried. "I thought we had escaped all of this, Michael. Wherever we go there are young men acting like animals. There is violence for violence sake."

Mary's look of concern deepened and Michael quickly changed the subject. "We brought you some food Mary. Terry had some of mine. It's not much but..."

Judith stepped forward and put her arm around Mary, who still held Terry, and offered them both her leftover porridge.

"It is not much," she said brightly, "but we have to share with Terry so he grows big and strong. Your mother too Terry, we must not forget her,' Judith said, ruffling the child's hair. "She must have something to eat, so that she has the energy to deal with you."

Michael laughed out of the corner of his mouth. Maybe he could leave Judith behind after all.

Chapter Fourteen

After the excitement of the morning, camp life returned to a gentle lull as life simmered away beneath the summer sun. Now there was nowhere to go and nothing to do until the next meal. This sort of schedule had filled Michael's days since finishing college, but now he did not feel as ready as he once had to sit around in the sun all day. He wondered what She might suggest if she had been there and this had been a normal day; perhaps a trip to the park or a drive to the beach. Those days were so far gone that they seemed like memories from someone else's life that Michael was intruding upon, as he lay outside the tent staring at the sky.

He ground his teeth restlessly. He could not spend the whole day there, listening to Judith snoring in the stale heat of the tent and Mary reading the same book to Terry over and over again.

Michael sprang up and yawned like a disturbed cat. "Mary, I think I'm going to go have a walk round, do you two want to come?"

"Yes!" Terry cried, jumping up and copying Michael's yawn.

"Terry, sit down!" Mary shouted, pulling the boy back down by his arm. Terry began to shout in protest and Mary tried to quiet him as she addressed an embarrassed Michael.

"Terry needs a sleep. He's always behaving like this and he is going to get a slap if he's not careful!" she warned, directing the last part at Terry who simply stuck his tongue out at her.

"It's all right Mary," Michael said, "I'll look after him."

Mary became suddenly serious, as though the sun had just slipped behind a cloud in the middle of a summer's afternoon.

"I know you will Michael, but I think he would be best off here. With me."

"All right, well I'll see you both later then," Michael said and he turned to set off on his walk.

"Michael!" Mary called, and he turned back to her. "Keep your eyes peeled! I've heard people say that that woman is here, the one from that show where they're all on that island!"

Michael did not have a clue who Mary was talking about. "Oh right..."

"You know the one, the one with the hair. If you see her, get me an autograph." Mary grinned.

"Yeah. Yeah sure, definitely," Michael said as he walked away, confused.

Michael set off amongst the tents. He had been worried for a minute about leaving the gun behind in Mary's tent. He had almost forgotten it, hidden in his holdall at the bottom of the pile of bags and clothes. He thought it was unlikely that anyone would find it there; Judith was too lazy to look for anything unless she thought there might be food (and she knew there was no food anywhere) and even if Terry found it, it looked like Mary was never going to take her eyes off him, so there would be no danger of him getting hurt.

Michael wound through the rainbow maze of tents, slowly making his way to a small area of open grass that lay behind them, at the foot of the sloping hill that led up and out of the basin. The sun had disappeared somewhere and the sky was a warm grey, hiding the heat in its somber palette. Michael walked on. Groups of people sat around outside tents. An old woman was sunbathing topless, her face hidden by a huge sun hat. Children ran around everywhere.

An old man argued animatedly with a younger man, shoving his finger into his chest. "It's the goddamn Russians!"

The young man huffed and shouted back. "Bollocks! It's the North Koreans, if it's anyone!"

Michael walked on, guitar song assaulting his ears from all

directions. It seemed as though guitar players had been exempt from the apocalypse. A torrent of minor keys and songs about lost lovers drowned each other out and became a single, droning piece of background music. There was no sound of the trumpet today.

Michael's ears were not the only sense being assaulted. From somewhere came the smell of frying onions, carried on the wind like a whisper of the Promised Land. It was the best thing Michael had ever smelt in his entire life and he inhaled deeply, until he could almost taste the onions lying against his tongue. He followed his nose and began to run after the smell.

He jumped over sleeping dogs that quickly woke and ran after him, following their noses to the smell, until a troupe of canines followed him as he cleared the tents and came upon, in the empty grass, a burger van with a queue of a hundred people. Michael's momentum almost carried him over as he stopped dead, so great was his surprise. A burger van at the end of the world, in the middle of this basin. How had they even got it down here, he wondered?

The van was battered and old and covered in red and green writing, its menu faded. Inside, a fat man in a vest and a pair of shorts sweated from every orifice whilst he scrapped at the onions and burgers and hot-dogs on the grill. Flies buzzed around a young girl in a tank top who pulled stale bread buns from their packaging and warm bottles of Sprite from the dead fridge. The man swore at her under his breath, urging her to go faster, faster! The crowd stood patiently, all one hundred of them standing in pools of sweat, waiting under the sun for a taste of meat.

The man inside the van called out, as if he needed to attract a larger crowd.

"Burgers, hot-dogs! Come and get them! Only twenty pounds each! Drinks, Drinks only five pounds! Just five pounds for a refreshing can of Fanta!"

Michael wished he had taken some scratch cards from the

newsagents, it seemed as though money might have a use after all, although it appeared that prices were ridiculously inflated. The people in the queue seemed happy to pay these ridiculous prices, in fact, the prospect of hot food seemed to bring a little bit of joviality to their day as families laughed and parents ruffled their children's hair.

Michael could see the happy face of the fat man in the worn burger van from where he stood. The sight of all these happy bastards just made Michael's stomach rumble even more, and he sat down disheartened in the grass, watching his crowd of dogs running about the legs of the huge, hungry animal that was the burger queue.

The dogs were kicked away and sent scattering off in all directions before circling back for another pass.

A Labrador amongst the pack of canines suddenly turned its head at the call of "Jasper! Jasper!" from the direction of the tents.

Jasper was visibly torn between the hope of meat, and the command of his master, eventually he relented and ran back to his owner, tongue lolling hungrily. Jasper had not got far when he ran across the path of three men, the first of whom kicked him hard in the stomach and sent him whining away with his head hung low.

Two of the three men were guards in their uniform of high-visibility jackets and shotguns. They walked along with their heads held high, their eyes hidden behind cheap aviators. In between them, a thin man panted along in an expensive suit. The man's hair was graying and slicked back but seemed to be wilting in the heat and he was forced to keep brushing it back with his fingers every few seconds to maintain his slick hairstyle. His cheeks were red and flushed.

As he approached, Michael saw that his first impression of him as a thin man had been wrong. The man was, in fact, rather large and seemed to have been forced into a suit that was two sizes too small for him, and he now appeared to be in the process of being squeezed out of his suit like toothpaste from the tube. His face alone was thin, but there was an excess of skin around his jaw and his hairless jowls rubbed against his stained collar as he marched along. His tie was secured tight against his Adam's apple and each time the man went to brush his hair he seemed to be resisting the temptation to loosen the tie and undo a button on his suit jacket, but his resolve held fast and his buttons remained fastened. Style over function.

The man had clearly tried to polish his shoes, but all he had succeeded in doing was rubbing mud around them, so that they now appeared to be made from brown leather, instead of black.

The trio strode to the front of the burger queue, seemingly oblivious to the people waiting in line.

The fat man behind the counter greeted them with a wide smile and spread his arms.

"Ah, Mr. Whitehead! What would you like?" he cried, leaning forward and trying to shake the hand of the suited man. One of the guards poked him with the butt of a shotgun, and he leaned back inside the van, laughing nervously. "How about burgers for everyone? Two each? A drink."

He turned to the girl working beside him and sent spittle flying into her face as he shouted. "Kelly! Get some fresh buns out! No, not those ones, *fresh* buns, dig around at the bottom. Ha ha," he laughed nervously, turning back to the man in the suit.

The three men were served their food and walked away without thanking the fat man. Michael did not see any money change hands.

So, that was Ian Whitehead. The man who had promised to save them all did not look like his idea of a saviour, Michael thought. He shifted position so he could watch the trio walk off and noticed someone else was watching them.

A middle aged man in blue jeans and a navy jumper was

crouched on the balls of his feet at the point where the tents became grass. Michael could not make out much of the man, but could see an angular jaw line and a mess of black hair which was beginning to fade to grey.

Michael turned his attention back to the trio. When they had passed him by, the man stood up slowly and spat on the ground in their direction. He brushed himself down and turned to walk off somewhere when he noticed Michael staring at him. Michael quickly looked away, but was slow enough to catch the nod that the man sent his way. Then the man disappeared back between the tents with long, purposeful strides.

Michael was intrigued. He had a feeling that he and this man were on the same page. The queue at the burger van had not offered a single objection when the suited man had walked right to the front and received a free burger, but this other man had not been a part of the crowd. The man seemed to be thinking for himself and, after Michael had seen the man's reaction to Whitehead, his own sense that things were not right there began to awaken and quickly jumped to the forefront of his mind.

His musings were interrupted by a shout from the direction of the burger van. The fat man was loudly urging Kelly to change the gas cylinder that powered the van. "Just hurry up and do it! We have all these hungry people here Kelly! Bloody hell girl!"

Michael watched as Kelly struggled to move a gas cylinder away from the van and then fell over in the grass as she tried to drag another one into place. She stood up; her stomach covered in mud and kicked the cylinder, which echoed with a hollow clang.

She hopped around holding her foot, cursing at the skies. "Fuck! My fucking foot! This one's empty too you fat cunt. We don't have any more gas. So sort it out yourself!"

And with that, she hopped off, clutching her foot and

falling over every few steps as she shouted insults back at the burger man.

The burger man looked worried. He rubbed his hands together and cleared his throat to address the queue, which had now turned into a crowd in front of the burger van. "Ladies and Gentlemen, it appears we have run out of gas and therefore, we will be unable to provide you with any more burgers today. Be sure to get here early tomorrow for a tasty breakfast hotdog, though!"

But the crowd was not so easily placated. A woman's voice shouted out. "We have been queuing for twenty minutes!"

A man joined in. "My kids are starving here mister, give them some food, at least."

Hands began to grab at what was left on the grill and there were cries as people burnt themselves on the hot surfaces. A child began to cry. The crowd was united in its indignation and the burger man's pleas were drowned out in the uproar.

Snatches of "please," and, "tomorrow, tomor...," reached Michael's ears as the crowd surged against the van. A few people even tried to climb through the window.

The burger man was defending himself now, hitting people with a red hot spatula, whilst desperately trying to pull the shutter down over the window. A skinny boy was wedged half in and half out of the window, stopping the burger man from closing the shutter.

The van began to rock back and forth from the force of the crowd surging against its side, and suddenly, the inevitable happened and the whole operation tipped backwards, rocked in the air for a moment, and then landed with a thud on its side in the soft ground. The boy disappeared through the shutter which fell shut behind him and there were screams from inside as hot grease and food were flung about and cutlery and boxes of napkins found new homes. The crowd drew back and slowly dispersed, and Michael stood up and moved on.

Not everyone that occupied this patch of grass behind the tents had been concerned with the goings on at the burger van. Here and there, people were sitting around selling things on blankets spread out in front of them. Old trinkets, earrings, hats, children's toys, tins of food, old books. Some people had little tables set out, and were sat resting on deck chairs behind them, some drinking from thermo-flasks as though they were at work down the market. Michael wandered amongst the little stalls. He was not the only one wandering about, and he certainly was not the only disinterested face in the milling crowd. They moved like zombies, aimlessly and slowly, taking in every detail in bored observance. The trinkets were relics of a past life and each was something abstract, now removed from all meaning in this new land.

The sky grew darker and the heat became a constant and oppressive weight, slowing Michael's progress through the crowd. He was thirsty and hoped it was nearly lunch time. His eyes were beginning to sting as though he were hungover. A familiar smell drifted past him and he turned to see a group of teenagers smoking with a young child, all of them too high to care what was happening, just waiting under the grey sky for something to happen. As was everybody else.

The stale air was suddenly cut by a high, crackling voice that boomed through the basin and then echoed back from the grass walls. The voice was familiar to Michael, but he could not place it at first. A stab of excitement ran through his heart. He had heard this voice before, was it someone he knew, he wondered? Then he heard the words of the propaganda slogan that had drawn him here and he knew who was speaking.

"The answer is here."

It was Whitehead, the man whose voice that had spoken to them over the radio. The man whose voice had interrupted Judith's dreams.

Everyone around Michael stopped what they were doing

and turned in the direction of the voice. It seemed to be coming from the direction of the food marquee, and Michael guessed, the stage that he had seen beside the marquee. As one, people began to move and soon a crowd was weaving its way amongst tents like a platoon of soldiers stepping through the jungle.

They arrived as one to find a crowd already gathered in front of the stage, and as more people arrived behind them, Michael was pushed forwards until his crotch was pressed up against somebody's back. Michael glanced around in the crowd and noticed two of the wheelchair-bound men he had seen yesterday. He doubted they could see much. He was having trouble himself, and had to stand onto his tiptoes in order to see the action on the stage. Towards the front of the crowd, he spotted Terry, sitting, he guessed, on Mary's shoulders. Next to them was Judith, eagerly craning her neck above the crowd to get a glimpse of the stage.

There he was again. Ian Whitehead MP, stood before them all, a microphone held in his hand and a grin stretched across his face. The microphone was plugged into an amplifier which led to two large speakers and, as he moved forward to address the crowd, the microphone wire was stretched taunt and he had to step back to stop it being pulled out of its socket.

Whitehead brushed off this lapse in sophistication with practiced ease and, with a final smile, began his address. "Good day everyone! Welcome! For those of you who do not know me, my name is Ian Whitehead and I am the locally elected MP. Welcome to Camp Hope."

Here he paused for effect, and then stared at the floor for a few seconds to signify a dramatic change of tone. When he returned his gaze to the crowd, his voice was laced with concern. "It has been a week since this catastrophe struck our great nation. A week of confusion, a week of anger, and a week... a week of asking why? But let me tell you this, when we find out why, when we find those responsible for this assault on all of us, there shall be no end to our wrath. We shall have our retribution!"

Here there were scattered shouts of approval from the crowd. Whitehead raised his voice and continued. "Do not think that your government has abandoned you. I have it from the highest authority that they are working on your salvation from a bunker below the streets of London. Soon, we shall return your lives to normal so that we can strive, hand in hand, to rebuild this great nation of ours, and I truly believe that out of the fires of this great tragedy, we shall rise ever stronger!"

More cheers now.

"Rest assured, none of us shall stop until we have done everything we can for you!"

A shout of "Bullshit!" split the air and Whitehead glanced uneasily to one side. He recovered his flow as one of the guards shifted from one foot to the other.

"Please, all of you are safe here under our protect..."

A woman's voice now. "My daughter was raped last night!"

There were more shouts of outrage and gasps from the crowd.

Whitehead swallowed and continued. "My dear madam, I am terribly sorry to hear about such a terrible incident, please know that my staff," he gestured with a slightly shaky arm to the guard at the side of the stage, "are doing all they can to make this camp a safe place. We will not stand for any undesirable elements here!"

Whitehead's voice quivered on the last word and he quickly wiped away the beginnings of a bead of sweat from one side of his face. "Furthermore, I would like to thank you all for your continued patience, and I would like to personally assure you that it will not be long until you are all safely back in your own homes, and we can all resume our lives. As far as I am concerned..."

No one ever found out what he was concerned about

because, just then, another voice cut the air. It was a warm southern accent, its origins indistinguishable except that it was a product of education. The voice made itself heard with ease and calmly drowned out Whitehead's strained protests.

The voice asked simply, "What about the food?" and, as Whitehead began to hedge in anticipation of a response forming in his mind, the voice spoke again. "How can you look after us when there isn't even any food for us?"

Michael searched the crowd and saw the same man who he had seen watching Whitehead walk away from the burger van. The man stood tall amongst the crowd and waited patiently for an answer to his question, his eyes fixed firmly on Whitehead, not allowing him to wriggle out of a response.

The crowd had turned to face him and mothers nodded agreement as men murmured amongst themselves, and then began to shout, "Yeah!" and "Yes! Where is the food?"

Whitehead looked flustered now and took a step back. He went to speak into the microphone, but feedback echoed through instead, and those nearest the stage cringed at the uncomfortable noise, covering their ears. The guard who stood beside Whitehead looked about uneasily, and was quickly joined by two others, who ran up from behind the stage.

Whitehead looked down at the mob of people and knew he had lost the attention of the crowd.

Ever the politician, Whitehead put a brave face on the beginnings of disaster, and addressed them once more. "Ladies and Gentlemen, I would like to thank you for your time and to ask you to do your best to stay strong in these hard times, just as I know our government is doing for us as I speak."

By the time he finished the sentence, there no one was left to listen to him and his words fell like ashes blown by the wind as the backs of the crowd walked away.

***

Lunch came and went. By then, Michael had managed to find Judith, Mary and Terry, and they all queued up again in the midst of more unrest and arguing within the queue. There were more guards at the marquee this time and they patrolled up and down the length of the queue. Those who did not hold shotguns brandished batons, and one even carried a sawn away table leg. The meal was little more than they had had for breakfast. Again Michael gave the majority of his food to Terry who ate quickly and asked for more. Mary gave most of her share of Judith's meal to Terry as well and tried not to look hungry herself.

After the meal, Michael fell asleep beside the tent. The sun had disappeared behind clouds and the sky was darkening. A warmth still hung in the air and Michael lay undisturbed. He dreamed about nothing in particular, shades of colours, rather than images. He had a vague feeling the ground was turning beneath him, that he was being swept away into the slow movement, but he felt no need to hold on and he did not care where he was being taken. The colours in his sleeping mind became dark blue with flashes of black and suddenly, the earth slipped from beneath him and he felt himself falling.

Michael landed with a thud and found himself grasping at dry grass, tearing the roots from the ground. Above him, the sky was working its way towards the dark blue of his dreams. A constant moaning, a heavy breathing as though of someone sobbing to themselves overpowered his senses and, half asleep, Michael tried to cover his ears and close his eyes to force the sound away, before he realised that he was awake and these noises were real. The darkness of his dream spilled over into his conscious state and reality did not seem to offer any brightness.

Michael sat up and could see no one around. Apart for the noise of the sobbing, the camp seemed eerily quiet. The crying was coming from inside Mary's tent and Michael opened the zip slowly. He lifted the canvas door and peered into the gloomy tent. Judith was huddled in a corner, her body shaking slowly with every sob. She held something in her hand which Michael could not see.

He wanted to leave her to her thoughts and moved to back out of the tent, but fumbled as he did so, and Judith glanced up quickly. She hid the item in her hand behind her before Michael had a chance to see what it was.

"Michael, I... I," she began between sobs which she was unable to suppress.

"Judith, are you all right?" Michael asked, still half in, and half out of the tent, feeling like he had intruded on a deeply private moment. "I mean, what's the matter?" he continued.

Judith tried to smile at him, her face creased beyond all recognition, the muscles clearly unused to smiling. "I am sorry Michael, it's..."

She started to cry again, almost uncontrollably until, after a few moments, the sobs subsided and Judith was able to speak clearly again. "A girl is missing," she said. Her guard was back up and she appeared to have returned to her usual emotionless state.

Cramp was beginning to set in as Michael remained kneeling in the doorway. He shifted his weight from one knee to the other. "What do you mean, a girl is missing?"

He waited a moment for an answer, but Judith had become unresponsive. "When did she go missing?" Michael asked, not knowing what else to say.

Judith wiped her eyes. "Oh I don't know, it was sometime today. I was just having a stroll earlier and I came across this woman... she, she was just howling with grief. I sat down to comfort her and she told me her daughter had disappeared from the camp."

"Well..." Michael began, but, before he could say more, he was interrupted by Judith. "I told her we would find her. It is not right for a mother to be separated from her daughter. But, I cannot, I could not find her, and now a little girl is wandering around all alone. What if something happens to her, Michael?"

Michael did his best to sound comforting. "I'm sure she will be all right. Someone is bound to see her wandering around and look after her. I'm sure she will be back with her mum soon."

This did not seem to be of any comfort to Judith.

"Maybe," he continued, "maybe, erm, God will help find her. Maybe if you...pray? That might help?"

Michael did not know if this was the right thing to say, but he remembered Judith's prayers the previous evening and hoped it would give her some comfort to think she could do something.

"That will not help," Judith said as she stared at Michael with stony eyes.

"God does not want to help lost children," she said, as though it was a fact she had become resigned to.

Michael looked about the dim tent for inspiration, then ran a hand through his hair. "Ok, well, I'll go see if I can find her then. You...you stay here and rest."

Judith stared silently at her knees and did not acknowledge him.

"Judith," she raised her head slowly, "it'll be ok," Michael said, backing out of the tent quickly, zipping the door behind him.

He stood up and shivered, despite the warmth of the evening. He did not think Judith could act any stranger, but now she was beginning to scare him. He began to walk in no particular direction through the camp. He did not believe he would find the girl, in this camp it would be like looking for a needle in a hay stack. Someone would find her; she would be fine, he was sure of it.

The sky had turned almost completely dark blue, despite it still being early evening and not yet even seven o'clock. All around the camp, people were milling about, most portraying

156

an expression that indicated a lethargic resignation to the helplessness of their collective situation. It was a resignation that Michael was beginning to feel himself. He saw no point to being there in the camp. If the people stayed there, then everyone would surely starve. Whitehead did not seem to have any answers, just empty promises.

Michael's clothes were filthy and when he touched his face and hair, they felt slick with grease. He had been hungry since he had arrived in the camp and had had to gouge another notch in his belt with the kitchen knife in order to hold his jeans up. Shortly, it would be dinner time and he would eat hardly enough to even register, and what food he did have, he would share with Terry. Tomorrow he would have no food tokens left, and then his options would be severely limited, it was likely he would have to leave the camp, with or without Judith. He had been held up for far too long when he should have been traveling to France. He could have been there by now, away from this broken country and this disaster.

He walked onwards with no destination in mind, lost in his thoughts. He found himself climbing the side of the basin, past the bushes filled with used toilet roll and nappies and discarded chicken bones, moving up towards a tree that stood right on the lip of the valley and leaned forward, as though trying to stretch its boughs across to the other side.

If Michael had been more observant, he would have noticed the lethargy of the camp slowly brewing into something else. This new feeling spread on the tongues of those below him and was whispered into the ears of the nearest man, woman or child. Some of them shook their heads in response and returned to their business. Others, the majority even, nodded, and their empty lethargic expressions flickered into anger and determination. Husbands rummaged through their belongings for knives, whilst teenagers foraged for fallen boughs then, once they were prepared, they dropped back into a trance-like state, waiting for the next stage to begin.

Michael only realised he had made his way to the tree when the leaves of the lower boughs brushed against his face. He sat down at the base of the trunk absentmindedly, his thoughts still focused on how he could get out of the camp. He did not suppose it would be as easy as just collecting his things together and walking out. This basin had scooped them all up and had trapped them down there.

It was unnaturally dark now for the middle of June as Michael sat beneath the tree, observing the people below lighting their fires, which flared into life like stars in the universe of the basin.

"Hello," a voice said from somewhere, and Michael almost jumped to his feet, not expecting to meet anyone up here, away from the camp.

Michael caught his breath and searched for the source of the voice. In the failing light, he was able to make out the man he had seen earlier near the burger van. He was standing not more than four feet away from Michael, beneath the boughs of the tree, and, like everyone else, he looked tired and dirty. There was a tattiness to his clothes, his blue jumper was coming unthreaded at the bottom and his jeans were wearing thin at the knees. They were not tatty in the same way that Michael's clothes were tatty and muddy after the toils of the last few days, instead, the man's clothes looked worn in and comfortable.

"May I sit down?" he asked hesitatingly, keeping his distance from Michael.

"Erm, yes, please do," Michael said, moving over as though, to make room for him against the base of the tree.

The man sat down beside Michael and offered his hand. "I'm David, David Marshall."

Up close, he seemed older than Michael had first thought. A crop of messy black hair shot through with grey tumbled down over his ears and almost to his eyebrows. His jaw was defined and Michael could imagine he had being good looking twenty years ago. An even covering of short grey hair covered his chin and Michael rubbed his hand across his own chin subconsciously, feeling the start of a thin and scraggy beard.

He shook David's hand. "Michael, Michael Taylor."

The man nodded, then smiled and brought out a hip-flask from a pocket. He unscrewed the lid and took a long swig. He lowered the flask, giving no indication of what the liquid inside might be, and then he wiped his lips on the back of his hand and offered it across to Michael, who took it eagerly. Someone had once told him to never turn down a free drink.

Michael raised the flask to his lips, tilted it towards David and took a swallow. It was whiskey, and even the small drop he took seemed to fill him with fire. His throat burned, sore as it was from a lack of food, and as soon as the liquid hit his stomach, Michael felt a warmth spread through him and the superficial perception of his senses sharpening.

He handed the flask back to David, slightly tipsy after days of a poor diet and no alcohol. David took the flask from him and smiled. It was not the patronizing smile the middle-aged often reserve for the young's attempts at maturity, but a different kind of smile. There was something sad about it, perhaps a regret for the future that Michael may never know.

They leaned back against the tree as more and more people began to mill about restlessly below them. Michael thought he saw Mary chasing Terry through a crowd and was about to call down to them, when he suddenly decided he did not care whether it was them or not. He had gotten stuck with Mary and Terry and Judith and was becoming weighed down with responsibilities for other people, when he should be travelling lightly so that he could escape this place without any complications.

Michael stared out over the camp and could sense David doing the same beside him. After a minute, David spoke, his voice filling the empty evening air. "What do you think of all this Michael?"

Michael scanned the horizon, beyond the far lip of the basin he could see for maybe a few meters, and then his eyesight failed him in the premature evening darkness. His whole world was in this depression in the earth.

"I don't know what to think about it," Michael answered, "How are we supposed to feel after everything that has happened recently?"

David nodded. "Indeed, indeed. Never before has anything like this befallen the human race. Yet here we are, forced to confront this scenario, poised on the verge of extinction, with no idea how, or what, to feel about it."

He took another drink from the flask and passed it over to Michael. "Where did you come from Michael? Are you alone?"

Michael swallowed the whiskey, and began to feel a little drunk now. He thought about the events that had led him to the camp. Everything before he had found himself alone in his house felt far removed from the reality of his life at that moment, like some half remembered plot from a novel he had read a long time ago.

"I'm not sure if I'm alone. My...my family was killed."

Michael was surprised at how effortlessly he could speak those words, the memories of their deaths just another image he had stored away for later.

"We tried to get out of the country, on a boat to the continent and...they died. After that, I decided that I would head down to Dover and try to get across to France, and that's what I've been trying to do these past few days."

"France is a fine idea," David said. "I think that's the best option available to us now. There's not much here. How many people are you travelling with?"

Michael chewed his lip. "Well, I suppose I've been collecting people since I set off. There's this woman, Judith," he began, pausing to take another swig of the whiskey, before passing it back to David. Michael's hunger was forgotten, stomach rumblings replaced by the warmth of the whiskey.

"This woman, Judith has attached herself to me, but I suppose having her around is better than having no one. It's strange," he said. "I thought she was uptight and emotionless, but earlier, I caught her crying over a little girl who is missing. I'm supposed to be looking for her now, but I'm sure someone will find her down there."

David looked away for a second and scratched his head. He turned back to stare over the basin below and took another swig of whiskey. "I suppose the girl is just one of many who have gone missing in this thing. At least she didn't die when the others did, days ago. She will be fine, I'm sure her mother will find her."

There was silence for a few moments as a warm wind skirted the top of the basin and rustled the branches of the trees above them.

"Did you...lose anyone?" Michael asked tentatively, feeling as though he was verging on intrusion.

David shook his head. "No," he said. "I had already lost everyone, through one thing or another."

Michael shifted uncomfortably against the tree trunk, fearing he had over stepped the mark. "I'm sorry," he said, trying to put an end to the conversation, but David did not seem to want to hide anything.

"It's ok; it's not your fault. I had a wife once, Mia, and a daughter, Jessica. I loved her too much. In the end it did not work out, and they both left me. I haven't seen either of them for five years. Jessica would have been twelve on the eleventh of November. I think they're doing ok, although maybe not now, who knows. It's hard to keep in touch with people."

Michael was not sure whether David meant it was hard to keep in touch now, or had been in general. Everyone in the country was sharing some form of grief, but to Michael, David's story seemed more powerful in its isolation. His family had left him willfully, not as victims of whatever it was that had stripped so many others of their families. David's family had had names and lives, whereas everyone who had died in the past week seemed to be part of the same thing, a statistic, a percentage of the same disaster. Even Michael's family were a part of this collective, and he found strange comfort in knowing they were not alone in their deaths, and that he was not alone in having lost people.

Before Michael could let himself feel worse for asking too many questions, David continued. "I am sorry Michael, as if things weren't depressing enough."

He scratched his chin in thought. "What was it you did before all this, Michael? In your past life?"

Michael laughed, scratching his own chin as though the answer could be found there. "I was about to go to university. To Durham, to study literature. It seems stupid now, after all the work I put in to get there, for it to suddenly mean nothing. There's no point in anyone studying anything anymore, I suppose."

David suddenly sprung up to crouch on the balls of his feet. "There's always a reason to study, Michael. What would be the point in everything mankind has achieved if now this has happened, we just gave up on education and progress? It's only through these things we can hope for a future. We can't return to living like apes, just because we are without electricity and fresh water. These conditions affect millions all over the world every day. We're essentially refugees from a natural disaster. It's not quite the apocalypse. We're no different to the millions fleeing a war zone or a volcanic eruption, it just happens that we're on an island and have become cut off from the rest of the world, but that's not to say we won't reconnect. When we do, we will have learnt something from all of this, and that is the most important thing, what we carry with us. It is through our studying and a hope to better understand our world that we can adapt," he

162

finished. David leaned back and took a long drink of the whiskey, emptying the flask.

Michael sat quietly, in one sentence he had revealed himself as the inexperienced teenager he felt he surely was.

David remained crouched on the balls of his feet, now facing Michael. "But, Durham though. Congratulations. I used to be a lecturer, not at anywhere as prestigious as Durham, but it was a good job, while it lasted. History though. Although, I do have a passion for literature. Perhaps we can have a chat about Vonnegut or Dostoyevsky sometime, eh?"

Michael nodded; Dostoyevsky was a bridge he had yet to cross.

At that moment, a shout echoed from below, cutting their conversation short. David stood up and Michael shuffled forward and peered down into the basin. The cry was repeated and they spotted the source of the noise, a group of men and women standing in a circle, shouting to one another, as though hyping themselves up before a sports match.

The sky was tipping into darkness now and the last traces of sun were covered by thick clouds, casting the basin into deep blue shadows.

David checked at his watch. "We best get down there. It's almost time."

Michael stood up, taking in the growing activity below them. "Time for what?" David stood beside him. "You don't know? We're standing up for ourselves Michael! No more of this political bullshit, we are going to fight back at dinner time as a unified army of the people. Tonight everyone eats as much as they want. That parasite Whitehead can't rule over us, no one elected him, and to be honest, I don't have much respect for those bastards who are elected."

They slipped and stumbled down the hillside in the growing darkness, crashing through bushes and almost falling into the midst of a group of women gathered around a fire on the edge of the tent site. Even more fires had been lit now, and it looked to Michael as though there was a fire burning for each person in the campsite as the smell of smoke filled the air.

All around people were chanting. "Food and freedom!"

Some tents had been pulled down and discarded and others were hastily being packed away in the last of the sunlight.

The two of them pushed their way through the crowd, Michael trying to make his way towards Mary's tent. He suddenly felt David was not there and looking around, saw him being carried in the flow of a crowd which surged towards the food marquee.

"Michael," he shouted over the collective noise of the crowd, "get your bag and I'll meet you at the entrance soon!" and then David was gone, washed away amongst the mass of people.

Michael pushed onwards, past groups of determined looking youths. An old woman marched with the crowd, waving her walking stick above her head wildly, as though she had never needed it, and it was merely there to clobber someone with. A few people hid in their tents, poking their heads out to watch the mob as it clambered over the tent city and filled the air with shouts and war cries. A young woman in a wheelchair had become stuck in the mud and as she hopelessly tried to wheel herself after the crowd, an old man appeared and tried to pull her chair in the opposite direction.

"No!" she yelled, "Let me go with them too!"

"But, Rose..." the man began, but Michael was moving too quickly to hear the rest of their conversation.

It took him a few minutes to find Mary's tent. It was even more difficult to find his way around now that some of the poles with the letters denoting the different zones had been torn down to use as weapons. Suddenly, the floodlights came on, and everything became a hundred times brighter.

A voice, unmistakably that of Ian Whitehead, filtered through the P.A. system and spread over the camp like

164

wartime propaganda. "Everyone calm down, we are doing all we can to help you. I realise that some of you have issues but we can discuss them personally..."

Michael stopped listening and, seconds later, the sound of gunfire replaced the voice. He could not tell whether it was coming over the P.A. or if it was simply loud enough to carry over the basin and drown out the drone of Whitehead. The shots started slowly, at first there was one, then a few seconds silence, and then another, until gradually, they became more and more frequent. It sounded like a number of shotguns were firing together, as fast as they could, trying to drown out the shouts of the people. Michael felt sober now, and panic that he might not be able to find Judith, Mary and Terry took over.

He came across Judith suddenly. She was standing outside Mary's tent, her head darting from side to side, her eyes wide with horror as something exploded in the direction of the stage and marquee. The orange light that billowed into the evening sky illuminated her dazed expression.

Michael took hold of her hand, squeezing it. "Judith, Judith, listen to me!"

Judith snapped out of her trance and came back to Earth. She was a long way from the crying wreck she had been only two days earlier when they had been chased from her village, Michael thought. "Michael, what on earth is happening?"

"I think everyone is rebelling Judith, about the food, about not having any food and being trapped here. We have to go."

He dove into the tent and grabbed his holdall. He could tell by the bag's weight that the gun was still there.

"But this place is safe. They are looking after us here," Judith protested.

"They're not Judith, we aren't safe. This place was no good. We have to go." He glanced around the nearby tents. "Where are Mary and Terry?"

There was no longer any question whether Michael would take them all with him; he knew he had to try to help them

165

all.

"They've already left, Michael. They set off somewhere a few hours ago. To find food, I think. Terry was crying so much about being hungry." A tear rolled down Judith's cheek.

"Okay, well they're gone, then. But we're still here and we have to go, right now."

Judith gathered a jacket from the tent, one that must have belonged to Mary, because Judith had brought no luggage, and they set off as quickly as they could through the tents, some of which were burning now, a toxic smell of burning plastic seeping into the evening air as the fire spread from tent to tent.

Michael led the way, Judith holding on to his arm a little too tightly, as though she was blind and he was her only lifeline out of the camp. They made their way through the maze of burning tents and passed by the blazing marquee. Silhouettes grappled with each other in the glare of the fire. A group of women kicked at a man lying prone on the ground in a high visibility jacket. A lone shotgun rang out once and was silent.

They clambered through overturned water barrels and boxes of food, leaking their contents into the mud. A whole pack of people gathered hungrily around the boxes, shoving each other as they reached for stale bread and bags of crisps no one knew had been available to them at the camp, likely stolen from Whitehead's private stash of food.

There was no sign of the man himself, and Michael supposed he had run when the trouble had kicked off. The guards had failed to keep control and were now either dead or far away over the hill. The crowd had worked itself into a frenzy and was now insatiable in its appetite for destruction. All around them people were fighting over anything and everything, as the crowd turned upon itself.

Michael and Judith ran into the shadows of the camp entrance as one of the floodlights came crashing down behind them with a sound like a screaming pig. The floodlight crashed through the stage and sent hot shards of bulbs in every direction. Neither Judith nor Michael looked back. They were almost away when a man jumped out at them in the dark. He was a short man and spun a baseball bat in one hand, but before he could say or do anything, Michael pulled the kitchen knife from his belt and thrust it in the man's direction, hissing at him as he did so, and the man jumped backwards and disappeared back into the darkness.

The force of Michael's jab caused him to slip in the mud. He fell and landed on his back, holding on to the knife. His left arm flailed as he fell and a sharp jolt shot along his arm as his watch smashed against a rock. Michael pulled himself up, slid the knife back into his jeans and grabbed the holdall from where it had fallen. Then he took Judith by the arm and dragged her along, and a moment later they passed through the gate and emerged into the total darkness outside the camp.

A voice whispered his name and on instinct Michael spun towards the noise. He reached for the knife again, but saw only David crouching behind a bush.

David smiled, picked up a bag and took Michael by the arm, pulling him and Judith along, away from the camp and up the muddy side of the basin. "Come on," he said, glancing back at the chaos behind them. "We have to go. We'll be all right now."

The three of them climbed up the wet sides of the hollow, none of them looking back at the rioting behind them and the fire that spread from tent to tent, the orange glow from the basin painting the night sky for miles in all directions.

Chapter Fifteen

Michael awoke to a cool breeze on his face and a gentle rhythmic vibration beneath him. He opened his eyes slowly, leisurely. He watched the blue sky pass by above him as the car drove onwards. In the front seats, Judith and David were breaking the ice.

"No, I finished school at sixteen. Higher education just was not an option in those days, really," Judith said.

"Oh really?" David turned his attention from the road and fixed Judith with a smile. "And how old are you, if you don't mind me asking?"

"Oh well," Judith adjusted her position in the passenger seat, "I'm forty-eight actually." She tried for a joke. "I know I might not look it."

David continued smiling at her; it was the sort of smile that seemed genuine in any scenario. "Quite. Quite. Well, Judith, I'm fifty and I had a chance to go to college, but maybe there were more options for me, down in London."

"Oh yes, I'm sure," Judith cut in quickly. "I grew up in a small village, you see, and when you finished secondary school, that was it. I had to help my mother about the house." She lowered her voice. "My father passed when I was fairly young," she said, as though whispering something about a child.

"Oh, I am sorry. I hope it wasn't a painful death," David said, his attention back on the road.

"Heart attack. Well, anyway. Tell me about your job, I would have loved to have been a teacher, given the chance."

"Well," David began, pausing as he maneuvered the car

around a dead cow in the road. "Well, I was a University lecturer, actually. It's a bit different from being a school teacher, but yes, it was a fantastic job and..."

"And you moved up north with it I assume?" Judith cut in, the scent of other people's more interesting lives fresh in her nostrils.

"Well actually no," David continued. "I separated from my wife, and...came up here. It was quite a difficult break up."

"Oh you poor lamb," Judith said, with genuine sadness in her voice.

From where he laid, with one eye half open, Michael thought it looked like she might burst into tears.

"My husband and I are also separated. He is a rotten fellow though, good for nothing. I was glad to see the back of him in the end. It must be terrible for you though, were there any children involved?" Judith asked David.

"I had a daughter," David said, tightening his grip on the steering wheel. "A beautiful little girl. I wasn't allowed to see her after her mother and I separated. She really was a little angel."

"Oh my!" Judith was actually crying now, tears rolling down her cheeks. "Oh excuse me!"

"That's ok, don't apologise." David took a hand away from the wheel and placed it on her shoulder, rubbing it slowly.

Bored with this small talk, Michael decided to try and get back to sleep. His neck was aching from the way he had slept, so he shifted his position, his back to the conversation in the front. He closed his eyes and tried to sleep, but was only met with the events of the previous night. He remembered scrambling up the mud slope in the rapidly darkening night, Judith hanging form his arm, almost having to be pulled along. The gun in the holdall constantly banged against his leg. At the top of the hill, David had led them on to the road and across to the other side of the abandoned cars. They ran then, as fast as circumstance would allow. Predictably, Judith

169

could not go far and they had to stop, sweating, hidden behind a people-carrier trapped in the never ending column of traffic.

People began to pour from the basin, looking like they were emerging from hell as the glow of the fire illuminated the pit beneath them. The rioters had destroyed their camp and now had nowhere to go. The fire was spreading and burning everything in its path and no one could stay and sleep in the ash pit it would leave behind.

Wild-eyed, the rioters ran down the road. Most stopped and looked up and down the road, in search of some other option, but it was impossible to see more than a few metres in either direction. Then they left, families, men carrying women, women and men carrying children, old men and women carrying each other.

For every one who emerged from the fiery basin carrying the fire in their eyes, there were two who came up on to the road looking terrified. All were covered in mud and no one seemed to know what to do. Some simply sat by the side of the road and waited for something, but for what, even they did not know.

The rest of the refugees quickly dispersed, some going either way up or down the road, others crossing the road and disappearing into the dark uncharted fields that lay there. A few managed to find a car in the queue with keys in and drove slowly off into the night, forced to drive next to the road rather than on it, in order to avoid the torrent of people and the unmoving cars.

Michael, Judith and David knelt behind the people-carrier until most of the crowd had gone, watching from their hiding place. As they waited, David noticed what looked like a picnic hamper inside the dark car. When the coast was clear, he tried the car's doors and found them all to be locked.

"Michael," he said, pointing to the hamper on the backseat. "Can you get us in there?"

Michael smiled; glad to finally be free of the basin. "Of course," he said with renewed confidence.

He shattered the window in a single attempt, using the butt of the rifle, which he still kept concealed in his bag. Judith jumped back at the sound of the breaking glass.

"Jesus!" David cried, a smile across his face. "What the hell have you got in that bag?"

Judith winced at his use of "Jesus" and "hell", but the other two did not notice, all their attention was focused on what might be in the hamper. Michael put the holdall down on the ground and reached in through the broken window, opening the door from the inside.

Inside the hamper they found a few stale sandwiches, some tins of fish, stale sausage rolls and enough cans of lemonade for three each, as well as some chocolate bars. It was a feast they ate quickly and greedily, all three of them crammed into the backseat of the car, the broken glass swept out onto the road.

All three had sat back with stomach cramps afterwards, and the pain was so bad Michael wished he had not eaten anything. No one remarked or perhaps even noticed that it was odd a family would pack a small picnic instead of all the food they could carry, but these were strange times.

After the cramps had diminished David declared, "We'll sleep in here tonight and tomorrow take another car, one with all of its windows intact, and then we will work out what we are going to do about getting across to France, eh Michael?"

Michael nodded and Judith said nothing. It was the first time she had heard of this plan to get across to the continent but, as far as Michael could tell, she had no opinion on it either way, and seemed happy to go along with them, wherever they went.

Michael had swept the remaining splinters of glass from the backseat and as soon as the last shard was gone, Judith climbed in, offering only an exhausted, "Good night."

She left Michael and David to sleep in the two front seats, which they did as soon as their eyes closed.

In the morning, there had been a terrible stench of ash and smoke and scorched grass. The smell combined with the thick morning air, stirred up by the strong new sun and made staying near the basin unbearable. All three of them had woken early and then they had set off to find another car. Finding one had not been difficult in amongst the hundreds of abandoned vehicles which lined the road, and soon they had set off, David driving them southwards as Michael stretched himself out in the back and went back to sleep.

Sleep was not forthcoming now, though, and Michael decided to give up on it. He sat up and stretched as well as he could in the cramped car.

David momentarily interrupted his conversation with Judith to say, "Good morning Michael," before carrying on.

David did not appear bothered by Judith's company; it seemed to Michael that he was happy to speak to anyone. *He must have been lonely before*, Michael thought.

"Yes," David said. "So I left there when this thing happened and I have been wandering around ever since, trying to find a solution, and of course, that's when I heard about this place on the radio, and so here I am."

"I see," said Judith, sounding very much like she did not follow. "Where exactly was 'there' again? The place you left behind?"

"Oh, did I not say? Well before this I was in Hull."

"Hull?" Michael's ears perked up. "You were in Hull, David?"

David glanced back over his shoulder, looking slightly concerned at Michael's apparent state of alarm. "Yes, Hull. Why, what's wrong?"

"It's just," Michael began, "it's just well...did you try to take the ferry from Hull?"

"I couldn't," David said, glancing at Michael in the rear-view mirror. "I got there a few days after this, this thing, whatever it is that has happened, happened, and the ports were closed. I heard it was bad though."

"It was," Michael said quietly. "I lived near there and went with my family to try and escape and...well...the crowd went crazy and the soldiers just started shooting at everyone. My parents were killed...my sister too, I was lucky to get out." Michael said the words, and afterwards, felt drained, as he though had let a little part of himself slip away.

David's eyes offered genuine sympathy in the rear-view mirror. "I'm sorry Michael."

"It's all right...thank you."

Michael wanted to change the subject now and grasped at the straws of stories he had heard about Hull in the days after the disaster. "The prison in Hull got broken open, when...when everyone died. I think there were prisoners there when I...lost my family. I think they were trying to get on to the ferries and that's why the soldiers started shooting, but obviously, well...a lot of other people got caught up in it."

When David spoke he sounded nervous, as though afraid of saying the wrong thing and upsetting Michael. "I heard that too. That the prison got broken into, I mean. I heard they were able to get out because one of the prisoners was able to get a key off the body of a guard."

David swerved around a trio of women, marching sullenly onwards in the road. "A lot of scores must have been settled that day, with enemies locked up behind bars and no guards around to protect them, and no police to be called either. I imagine those that had done the worst crimes had a terrible time. Probably tortured."

Judith shuddered and opened her mouth, and then closed it again without saying anything.

David continued. "Of course, as you say, many did escape. We had a bit of...trouble with them, looting and the like, that's part of the reason I left Hull. I didn't really know what

173

to do before that. You soon realise it's time to leave when there are convicted criminals roaming free, though."

"Wait!" Judith shouted suddenly, causing Michael and David to almost jump out of their seats. They had both almost forgotten she was even in the car. David slowed the vehicle to a crawl.

"What is that?" Judith asked, pointing at something ahead by the side of the road.

David and Michael strained their necks to try and see what she was trying to show them.

"I don't know Judith; I think it's an elm tree. Michael, would you say that's an elm tree?" David asked, his tongue poking his cheek.

Michael squinted against the sun. "I'm not too sure. It could be an oak actually, do you see the way the leaves are?"

"Oh you could be right, Michael, you could be right," David said, leaning across Judith to get a better look.

Judith squirmed and rolled her eyes as David leaned across her. "I am not talking about a tree, thank you very much. What is *that* over there? Behind the tree?"

"Oh," David said whilst Michael laughed. "Michael, what *is* that?" he asked.

As they approached, the scene became clearer. In a leafy shade to the side of the quiet road, a ten foot cross, constructed from planks of splintered wood, had been erected. Gathered around it was an assortment of caravans, no more than three in total, interspersed with a few tents here and there.

Judith was in danger of smiling as they neared the cross. She wound her window down and shouted to the small group of people milling around outside, "Yoo-hoo!" and waved her arm wildly in an awkward flapping movement.

The campers smiled and waved back. Strains of a song floated on the breeze and in through the car window.

David turned, looked Michael directly in the eyes and said

ominously, "Hymns."

Michael shook his head and repeated it back. "Hymns."

A world of understanding passed between the two.

"Stop the car!" Judith cried.

"I really don't think we have time Judith. We're making good progress, and it might be best to keep going just in case we..." David bumbled.

"Stop the car!" Judith cried again, ignoring his excuses.

David shrugged his eyebrows at Michael in the rear-view mirror. There was no avoiding it, and so they pulled over beside the caravans. The people gathered around the cross rose and came to meet them, smiling from ear to ear, some holding hands, some with their arms wide open, welcoming the new sheep to their flock.

Chapter Sixteen

"Welcome, welcome!" an old man with a neat white beard beamed at them, grasping their hands, one by one in his, shaking them as he stared into their eyes, as though searching for something there.

"Welcome!" he repeated, as he took each new pair of hands. "Please join us. Please sit. Do, please, just there. That's it."

The three newcomers were seated on the grass. The caravans and a camper van enclosed them on three sides and the road and their car lay behind them. Around the little camp, clean clothes hung from the branches of bushes and a dog rested lazily in the mid-morning sun. Behind the caravans was a small copse of trees, their branches casting shadows across the ground and scraping along the roofs of the temporary homes as they swayed to and fro in the slight breeze.

Beneath the great cross were the remains of a campfire. A metal pot was suspended above white embers, held over a pit, dug into the soft earth. Something was cooking in the pot and Michael breathed in the smell, trying to inhale as much as possible. Four chickens stood close by the cooking pot, pecking at the ground absent-mindedly, each tied to a young sapling by one of their legs. David tapped Michael on the shoulder, nodded towards the chickens, then at the steaming pot and gave him a thumbs up.

Three other men were sat beside the remains of the fire and the old man who had welcomed them sat down now as well.

"Susan," he called to a middle aged woman who emerged from the nearest caravan. "Bring our guests some soup." He smiled at the group and then, as if just remembering something, called after Susan. "Oh, and a cup of tea!"

The cross they had seen from the road towered above them, acting as a marker to attract people to the camp. Judith constantly glanced up at it, the traces of a smile on her face.

Michael looked up at the towering symbol and saw it had been constructed from two fallen tree trunks, held together with rope. He was surprised this group had been able to construct it. Susan looked almost fifty and the four men looked like they were comfortably in their sixties.

The man who had greeted them followed Michael's gaze. "Ah yes, it is impressive, isn't it? A reminder that Jesus Christ is always with us, even in such turbulent times. It took us a long time to erect but, with the power of God, we got it up in the end."

Michael smiled, unsure what to say. "Hmm, it's, erm...nice," were the words which eventually found their way out of his mouth.

"My name is Matthew," the man said and he gestured to the other men seated beside the embers one by one, "and this is Mark, Luke and John."

"Pardon me?" David laughed, before he could stop himself.

"Yes?" Matthew asked, genuine concern wrinkling his brow.

"What...a coincidence," David recovered.

He was saved by an unwitting Judith. "Oh, Matthew, thank you so much for receiving us like this, what a wonderful camp you have. One feels safe here."

"All of God's children are welcome my sister. Pray, what are your names?" asked John, or maybe Luke.

Michael could not be sure who was who. All four of the men were of a similar age, all wore grey or white beards and, in their combat trousers, shirts, fishing jackets and walking boots, they looked more like they had just come in from a fishing trip than survived what may well have been the end of the world.

Michael noticed more fish on the side of their caravans, the type Christians use to display their faith and let people know they are good people.

They finished the introductions and Susan brought them each a steaming bowl of soup and a mug of hot tea. She sat down silently beside them and Michael was not surprised to see her dressed the same way as the men. The soup smelt delicious and Michael took up his spoon, anticipating large chunks of chicken. Instead he was disappointed to find a slice of carrot floating in the watery soup. He held the spoon halfway to his lips.

David looked across at Michael and raised his eyebrows. "I suppose the chicken's had a lucky escape?"

"I'm sorry?" Matthew said, not entirely understanding.

Judith was unusually quick on the uptake. "Oh, ignore him Matthew, this soup is delicious."

"Ah," Matthew smiled, "you'd rather have chicken soup, eh? Well, I'm afraid we don't eat God's creatures."

Michael laughed and soup almost came out of his nose, burning his nostril. "Shit!" he cried, taking a drink of the tea, hoping it would somehow cool his nose. The tea was not what he was expecting, however, and tasted like watery grass. He spat it out quickly.

He sat back wiping his face, greeted by silence all around, except for David's quiet chuckling. Michael scratched the back of his head in embarrassment. "Went up my nose...I'm sorry. Do you have any water?"

Susan stood up obediently and brought him a cup of warm water. It tasted of disinfectant, with a slight bubblegum aftertaste. Michael thought it best not to complain.

Judith was busy recounting their travels thus far to the horrified faces of the group, as Michael and David slurped noisily on their soup. When Judith had finished speaking, Matthew sat back and shook his head.

John spoke with an indiscernible boarding school accent. "How awful. How many sheep have lost their way? We need

178

to let them know the church is still here for them and always will be. We have survived centuries of turmoil, and it will take more than these recent events to stop us spreading the word of God."

"Hear, hear!" the others mumbled.

John continued. "The earth has been cleansed of all undesirables, and now we are left to ride the Ark like Noah, until the seas of turmoil have receded and order is once again restored to our land by the almighty Jesus. The second coming is upon us."

Michael sat wide-eyed, not sure he was actually hearing these words. The word *batshit* was another word that came to his mind.

"The second coming of Jesus?" David asked in a voice that suggested someone had just told him Jesus was stood behind him. "Why doesn't Santa come as well and rescue us all in his sleigh?"

Michael tried his best to suppress a laugh and Judith looked shocked, as though someone had said something rude in front of guests at a dinner party she was hosting.

Matthew spoke again. "I can see you are not a believer David. That is sad. You will be condemned like the criminals, homosexuals and other non-believers."

John or maybe Luke spoke again. "Like the Jews, Muslims, Hindus and all others who worship a false God. This is His land only, and there is no room for any others! He has washed his lands free of the taint of deceit and now we are ready to begin a new Christian nation."

Even Judith did not know what to say to this. David was about to argue, but realised it was probably pointless against people with such firmly misplaced beliefs.

It was Michael who spoke first, jumping to his feet. "Well, thank you so much for your hospitality, but we really must be on our way. We'll be sure to mention your message to anyone we meet. Thank you."

Taking the cue, David stood up slowly, but Judith remained seated.

"Oh, must you go? It's always a shame to lose fellow Christians," John asked.

"But not Muslims or Jews, eh?" David said under his breath, just quietly enough for Matthew to not hear.

"Well, good luck and may God look after you," Matthew said, rising with them, and taking their hands one by one.

"Judith..." Michael called.

Judith seemed to snap out of her thoughts and stood up with them, as if only just realising they were leaving.

They walked quickly to their car, followed in each step by Matthew, still beaming at them, and wishing them a happy journey. They got into the car quickly, Judith somewhat hesitantly, looking slightly confused as to why they were leaving. Michael sat in the front this time and Judith in the back. They pulled away quickly, Matthew still calling well wishes after them. Michael closed the window, despite the heat, and soon the cross disappeared in their rearview mirror.

"Batshit," Michael said. "The whole world has gone batshit."

Chapter Seventeen

Hours passed as the landscape slipped past the windows, changing from fields to woods to hills to small towns. They kept to A-roads, but even this meant slow progress. Every new road was cluttered with vehicles. Some crawled along the roads, uncanny reflections of their own vehicle, but most of the cars they came across had been abandoned, and it was clear any motorway would be impassible.

Judith dozed in the backseat, waking from time to time to rub her neck and point out some quaint piece of scenery. David engaged Michael in a conversation about what he hoped to do in the future. Discussion petered out when they passed a car overturned inside a field, unmoving shapes visible through broken glass.

David took to whistling a tune Michael did not recognise, repeating it over and over again.

David noticed the confusion on Michael's face and explained. "An old nursery rhyme I used to sing to my daughter."

As the sun burnt its evening glow into the rearview mirror, Michael began to hum his own song, stopping when he realised it was Jim's song.

A decaying Jim, his shirt caked in dry blood appeared before him, reclining across the bonnet, and began to sing along. Michael closed his eyes and rubbed his palms into his temples, as if massaging away the vision, and when he opened his eyes again, there was only the road ahead of him.

After a while, signs by the roadside proclaimed a town ahead.

"We'll have to get some fuel," David said, nodding to the fuel gauge which Michael saw was dangerously in the red.

They turned off the road into a small retail park they came upon on the outskirts of the town. They drove slowly, winding between the occasional abandoned car until they came to a garage. The place looked as if it had been abandoned for years, not days.

The only sign of recent activity was a lorry parked in one of the bays, a figure in blue overalls slumped on the floor inside an open cab door.

David parked the car and got out. Michael stretched in his seat, opened his door and swung his legs out stiffly. He took a few steps, seemingly having lost the power to bend his knees. He recovered the ability to walk and looked around. There was a shop and he decided to go and see if there was anything to eat in there. He thought about the last petrol station and kept a hand close to his knife. However, there was no sign of any danger and he was surprised by how quiet the place seemed.

"Is there any fuel?" he asked David across the roof of the car.

"There seems to be a bit," David answered, shaking the tube that linked the nozzle to the machine. "We might have to get a length of pipe and suck some out of that lorry."

"Let's hope not," Michael said, the taste of petrol in his mouth already. "I'm going to look in the shop. Want anything?"

"Surprise me," David called.

Michael turned towards the shop but remembered Judith and leaned to tap on her window. She looked startled and it took her a few seconds to work out how to lower the window.

"Anything from the shop, Judith?" Michael asked, his voice betraying how tired he was of her.

"Oh," Judith weighed up the options, biting her bottom lip. "Perhaps a sandwich."

Michael nodded and took a few steps away from the car

before returning. "Judith, I'm not sure a sandwich will be in the best condition by now."

She could not decide on anything, and the shop had little left inside. Michael took a selection of chocolate bars and shared them out as he climbed back into the car.

"Let's have the Twix, Judith," David said, twisting around in his seat, eagerly.

"You most certainly cannot," Judith spat around a mouthful of the chocolate bar. Michael laughed silently as David turned back around. "Milky Way it is then."

"Petrol?" Michael asked.

"Yeah, there was a full can just the other side of the lorry. I suppose someone came to get some for his lawnmower, or something, but forgot about it when he saw that guy drop out of the lorry cab."

There was the sound of Judith choking on a mouthful of chocolate, but further comment was unforthcoming.

They drove slowly through the retail park, past dull brown and grey garden centres, discount clothes shops and furniture stores. Brittle weeds poked through the tarmac and had overrun the flower beds. Rows of small thorny bushes decorated the car park, which still contained the odd car.

"Supermarket," Michael said, pointing and spitting out chocolate as he spoke. They drove over, avoiding bodies beside cars and the odd shopping trolley that had been let loose to wander the car park forever in the wind.

They parked as close to the Supermarket as possible and stepped inside the entrance. Judith wandered off to try and free a trolley from a chained row just inside the entrance. She looked around, as if searching for something, and patted her pockets, before pulling out her purse and beginning to rummage through it.

Michael took hold of an abandoned trolley near the door and threw out the four bags it contained.

"Judith," he said and motioned inside with a nod.

"Yes Michael?" she answered with visible irritation. "I would like my own trolley, for my own purchases, thank you very much."

"Ok, well...we'll see you in there then."

A set of automatic doors parted for them. As Michael and David stepped inside, they were met by the loud hum of electric lights. The bright artificial light was almost blinding after dark nights and camp fires.

David scratched his head. "Maybe that power station we passed a few miles back."

Michael wore a blank expression "Erm..."

"It must be powering this area. I'm amazed it hasn't run out yet...although, if it's powering the whole town, it can't have much juice left. We best be quick," David said, casting about as though the source of the power might be somewhere inside the supermarket.

Judith blustered through the doors behind them, almost running into their heels with her own trolley, which she had eventually managed to free. The supermarket was her domain, shopping for bargains her forte, and she wasted no time in setting off down the aisles, apparently not surprised there was still electricity.

David and Michael hesitated in the entrance.

"Do you think, if the electricity is still working, we might be able to find a computer here and find out what's going on in the rest of the world?" Michael asked, uncertainly.

David scratched the stubble on his jaw and shook his head slowly. "No, I don't think so. I imagine the internet will be down. It makes sense if the phone lines aren't working. Don't worry, we will be safe and sound in France soon enough."

Judith was slipping out of sight ahead of them, and they started after her, like parents afraid of losing a child. They passed a fridge of week-old sandwiches, green mould eating them inside their wrappings. The last ever editions of newspapers littered the floor, headlines declaring This Is The

End and, on a tabloid, The Answers Are Blowing In The Wind.

They passed by without reading them. They had been witness to the panic first hand on that day of disaster, when the television and radio screamed warnings and hearsay at them. A few days later, everything fell silent, and they were left alone with no fresh news, except for what they could see with their own eyes, which was more than anyone had ever wanted to see.

Bodies and trolleys lined the aisles and a smell of sour milk or rotting meat made them gag as they passed, trying to keep their eyes focused straight ahead. Judith's progress had been halted by the bodies, and she stood wiping her eyes near the body of a small girl, her hair spread across the floor like seaweed floating in the ocean. David touched Judith gently on the elbow and she wiped her eyes and fell in beside them.

A sound of music reached them from somewhere amongst the aisles. They followed the sound, keeping quiet, Michael and David exchanging glances, telling each other to stay alert. They did not take anything from the shelves and Michael left his trolley behind as the music got louder. Judith did the same, and suddenly, they could hear voices, laughing and shouting, seemingly coming from the next aisle. They stepped over more bodies, but these ones were covered, their faces hidden by jackets which still had price tags on, and must have come from somewhere in the supermarket.

The sound of something smashing competed against the voices and music, and as they rounded the alcohol aisle, they could see the source of the commotion. A boy in his late teens stood drinking whiskey from the bottle. He took one bottle, opened it, took a sip, and then threw the bottle behind him to shatter against the far shelf, before selecting another bottle and doing the same.

He stopped when he saw them, and opened his mouth to say hello. Instead, he coughed, then stood back against the shelf like a child who had been caught doing something he shouldn't, and thinks he can avoid punishment by acting good once he has been caught.

Further along the aisle were three or four more teenagers of roughly the same age. They had made a comfortable area from a huge pile of clothes, which appeared to have been collected from another part of the store, and parts of their bodies emerged here and there amongst the jackets and jumpers, so that Michael could not be sure how many of them there were. A boy reclined on top of the pile, fiddling with the CD player next to him and a girl lay beside him, staring at the ceiling.

"I can smell it again," she said, "Spray it again."

"Just a minute, for fuck's sake," the boy said.

"What's it going to be then, eh?" he asked no one in particular as he finished what he was doing with the CD player. A blast of classical music replaced the rap they had been listening to. Michael thought it might be Beethoven, but classical music had never been his strong point.

The boy, satisfied, put aside the CD player and picked up two cans of deodorant, which he sprayed until the air became thick with mist, and figures jumped out of the pile of clothes, gagging and coughing, with cries of "Fucking hell Ben!"

Michael, David and Judith approached them, stepping over empty food wrappers and half-eaten cakes and scraps of meat. Michael slipped on a doughnut but steadied himself before the teenagers could see him. They noticed them suddenly, and a second girl turned off the music.

"Hi," David said in his friendliest teaching voice. "How long have you guys been here, if you don't mind me asking?"

The boy who had sprayed the aerosol stepped forward. "Look mate, we haven't stolen anything ok? There's no food anywhere, we had to come in here. You can't do anything to us, we had no choice."

The girl who had turned off the music grabbed his arm and pulled him towards her. "Shut up Ben. They're not the police," she said, before turning her attention to the newcomers. "We've been here three days. We came out of the city, our families were gone and we had nowhere else to go. Everyone stopped here on the way out of town; you can see how much of the food has gone. We thought we would be safe here, especially as everyone else left town, headed south I think."

Michael was about to suggest that they should head south as well, but David spoke first. "All right, that seems like a good plan. It'd be best if you kids stayed here out of the way, until things have blown over. But," and here David turned to point to the boy behind them, struggling to hold himself up against the shelving, "be careful, you need to remain alert. Don't waste food either."

Michael felt his cheeks turn hot with embarrassment at David's words; he was torn between wanting to have fun with people his own age, or being sensible and sticking with David and Judith. He had been robbed of any chance to enjoy this new world, from the minute he had been left alone, everything he had done had been geared towards survival, but here was this group of friends who had spent the time gorging themselves on the best food and getting drunk, whilst Michael had spent nights sleeping in restaurants and fields, putting up with Judith's complaints.

The boy called Ben pulled himself up from the pile of clothing and stepped towards them, his pride damaged by the girl speaking over him. "All right mate, we're not stupid, we've been okay so far. Don't think we've not had to be smart."

David held out his hands as though he were trying to calm a dog. "Okay, I know. I wanted to make sure you'd all be all right, but it looks like you're doing fine. We're just going to take some food, I'm sure you can spare some, and then we'll be on our way."

Before Ben could speak again, a small girl ran up behind the group of teenagers, almost tripping up over the hem of her oversized and jam-stained dress which trailed on the ground behind her, mimicry of a wedding gown.

"Lucy, Lucy!" she cried, and the girl who had spoken to them turned and took her by the hand.

David took a step back.

The teenager began scrubbing at the younger girl's face, kneeling down beside her and spitting on a handkerchief, causing the little girl to wrinkle her face in protest. "Annabel!" The older girl chastised, "I told you not to wander off. What's this blue stuff around your mouth?"

The younger girl squirmed and tried to wriggle free. "I don't know," she said with a secretive smile.

"Oh how adorable! Hello Annabel," Judith said in a voice that implied she was not sure whether the girl was a human, or someone's pet rabbit.

"How old are you?" Judith asked, bending down to Annabel's level.

Annabel was not interested in this woman, instead she stuck out her tongue and, after managing to free herself of Lucy's grip, she disappeared back down the aisle, laughing to herself as she went.

The rest of the teenagers had returned to their comfortable pile of clothes and had lost all interest in the newcomers.

"Sorry about her," Lucy said.

"That's fine," Michael said. "We'll just do our shopping now and then be off."

The girl nodded, then sat down next to the others and Judith, Michael and David returned to their trolleys.

***

The classical music started up again and turned the high ceilings of the supermarket into the epic vaults of a cathedral. Michael and David raced their trolleys through the aisles, tipping food in without discrimination, opening packets of biscuits and shoving them into their mouths, as though they had never tasted them before. They drank from cans of soft drink as though they were the last ones in the world, gulping them down, their eyes watering as belches erupted from their throats.

At the deli counter, they almost wept for what could have been. The cooked meat and dishes of curries and other foreign delicacies were now dried out and crusted with flies. Michael's stomach contorted in pain at the sight of such good food having gone to waste.

In the freezer aisle, Judith found bodies placed in the compartments, hard as ice and resting atop packs of oven chips. She decided to leave the frozen food. She did, however, take a pot of vanilla ice-cream which, after making sure no one could see, she dug into with her fingers and ate hungrily, the entire tub in one go, ice cream running down her chin.

When they had finished, the three of them headed to the exit, each with a trolley overflowing with food. The packets of biscuits and chocolate bars made Michael feel slightly better about not staying behind to get drunk with the other teenagers.

As they passed the toilets, David let go of his trolley and said, "I might just have a quick sit down."

Michael laughed. "I might just join you."

Judith looked disgusted, but after the two of them had disappeared into the men's room, she darted into the women's.

The bathrooms were clean. Michael was surprised, expecting, for some reason, to see them trashed. He tried the taps but no water came out.

"No need," David shouted from inside a cubicle. "There are bottles of mineral water in here."

Michael took the next cubicle and found there were indeed a few two litre bottles of mineral water. He had always felt calm in bathrooms, he had no idea why. Maybe it was the cool white tiles, or perhaps the privacy. At primary school, whenever he had felt he would be in trouble for something, he had always gone to the toilet and tried to work out plausible lies to tell to any teacher that might accuse him.

After he had covered the seat in toilet roll and sat down, Michael felt a huge weight drop from him. He felt, for the first time in a few days, that everything might be all right. He stayed there for a few minutes, reading the graffiti on the walls, trying not to laugh at the noises coming from David's cubicle. When he was finished, Michael poured water from the bottles into the bowl to flush the toilet and took another bottle to the sink to wash his hands.

David shouted to him from inside his cubicle. "I might be a few more minutes here, mate. Why don't you go load the car?"

David slid the keys under the door. Michael hesitated to pick them up, but decided he could always wash his hands again. He headed outside. Judith was nowhere to be seen but the three trolleys remained unmoved.

Michael took the nearest one and wheeled it outside. The car was where they had left it and, after checking his holdall with the rifle inside was still hidden in a foot-well, and after working out how to open the boot, Michael began to load the shopping into the car, throwing the loose packets in one by one.

He reached back to grab another packet from the trolley when something hard swiped his hand away. Confused, Michael turned around and found himself confronted by a cricket bat being shoved into his throat, his Adam's apple feeling like it was being jammed to the back of his neck. Michael stumbled backwards and only just stopped himself from falling into the boot by clutching the sides of the car. He regained his composure and noticed for the first time the person who wielded the weapon.

A slender golden arm held the bat, the hairs raised from the skin and glowing in the evening sunlight. The arm led to a thin shoulder which just about held a white vest in place, a faded pink bra strap showing underneath. The neck was golden as well, and when it swallowed, it seemed to Michael to happen in slow motion, every movement and muscle perfectly defined. Her jaw was pointed, but soft and the eyes were hidden behind a pair of dark Ray Bans. The hair was as golden as summer sunlight on a field of wheat, and was tied back beneath a brown straw hat, stray strands lying against the smooth skin of her face.

Michael was in love. He tightened his grip on the sides of the boot, afraid his legs would give way beneath him. His stomach was trying to climb out of his mouth, pushing against the cricket bat that blocked its passage.

The girl's lips were symmetrical and perfect, and the skin above the top lip was dotted with freckles like icing sugar on top of a sponge cake. When she spoke, Michael thought he had passed out for a minute. The words came out like music and if Michael has been able to pull himself out of his lust, he would have noticed an indiscernible southern accent.

"Are you fucking stupid?" she asked again, forcing the cricket bat further into his throat. "I said, give me the keys and I'll be on my way."

Michael tried to push the bat away, but she held it firmly where it was. He tried again, and managed to push it back a little, and they found a compromise where he could speak.

"Tell me your name," he croaked, his voice coming out high and cracked.

"What does my fucking name matter? I want your car and your food, not to be your best mate."

Michael laughed. He had to show this girl he was a worthy adversary, if he was to have any chance of romancing her.

"Look at all these cars," he said, pulling himself forwards to sit on the edge of the boot so he could casually gesture around the car park with an outstretched arm.

"There's a supermarket full of food right there," he said, pointing with his other arm.

The girl had taken a step back and had lowered the bat. She

held it at waist height now, ready to hit him if he tried anything. "Look, I just want to get out of this shit hole, so can I please just have the keys to the car?"

Michael wanted to rub the sore marks on his throat, but did not want to show weakness in front of this girl. Instead, he coughed into his hand then said, "I'm Michael."

The girl took off her sunglasses to reveal eyes that were the same green as the colour of sunlight illuminating a leaf as you lay beneath a tree on a summer's day.

"Where are you heading?" Michael continued. "We're going south, why don't you just come along with us? There's enough room, more than enough food...it'd be better than going off on your own."

The girl rubbed her eyes with the hand that held the sunglasses. The other still grasped the cricket bat, which she lowered to her side and leaned upon. She said nothing and replaced her glasses.

"I'm Michael," he repeated, his hand outstretched.

"You've already said that," she said, ignoring the hand. She was silent for a moment before she spoke. "I'm Zanna."

"Zanna?"

"Zanna, yes, Zanna, that's what I said isn't it?" she said irritably.

"Nice to meet you," Michael said, but Zanna was ignoring him.

She put the bat down beside a leather jacket she had left on the floor, and began to help herself to food from the trolley.

Michael glanced over to where David and Judith stood leaning on their trolleys in the entranceway. David was chuckling to himself and winked when he saw Michael looking over.

Michael headed across to them. He almost turned to tell Zanna that he would be back in a minute, but realised that she probably would not care.

David laughed as Michael reached them. "Smooth work,

young man. Smooth work."

Michael shook his head. "Shut up David."

David laughed again.

Judith watched the girl eat like a hungry cat. "She's beautiful. Who is she Michael?"

"Zanna, apparently. Her name is Zanna," he said, regarding her along with the others.

"We've had some good finds today," David said, scanning the darkening sky. "Why don't we stay here tonight and carry on tomorrow morning, see if Zanna wants to come with us?"

"Sounds like a plan," Michael said, his heart and loins directing all his thoughts towards this girl who had appeared from nowhere to threaten him with a cricket bat, and who now stood shoveling food into her mouth by the car, looking like the most beautiful thing Michael had ever seen.

Chapter Eighteen

"If you want some space, all you have to do is say the word," David said, handing a bottle of shampoo across to Michael.

Michael squirted shampoo into his hands and massaged his scalp for a long time. An aroma of mint filled his nostrils and his scalp tingled. "Don't worry, don't worry. It's under control."

They stood naked in the bathroom, having their first proper wash in a week. They had taken shower gel and shampoo from the shelves and took it in turns to pour bottles of water over each other to rinse the lather away.

When they were finished, they dried with new towels, slipped into new pairs of jeans over new underwear, and Michael pulled on a new white T-shirt. They had each taken a bag from the shelves and packed it with a few more items of clothing for the journey.

Michael sprayed deodorant on himself for the first time in a week and was amazed at how different he smelled now that he was clean. He knelt and pulled his old Converse on, as David stood bare-chested, shaving in front of the mirror. Michael's shoes were looking the worse for wear, caked in mud and grime, but he did not want to throw them away. They were one of the only things he had left from home.

He stood beside David, noticing a few white scars on his torso. David caught his eyes in the mirror. "Battle scars."

David said nothing more and Michael turned his attention to his own reflection. He had not properly examined himself since the first night he had spent alone on his bathroom floor. His face looked gaunt and the eyes floated amidst deep bags.

His sparse facial hair was growing into a meager little moustache/goatee combination that looked like the pelt of some injured animal, and Michael decided it had to go and, as he shaved, his thoughts drifted more than once to Zanna.

Once he had finished, Michael stood and regarded his reflection again.

"Very dapper," David said, his face still covered in shaving foam.

Michael thought the reflection looked older, his skin seemed tired and wrinkles had appeared across his brow and around his mouth, prematurely ageing him in a matter of days.

They left the bathroom refreshed and in high spirits. and Michael began to make his way through a packet of Party Rings as they waited for the two women to emerge from the bathroom.

Zanna came out first, dressed as she had been outside, in dirty Converse, tight jeans and a white vest. The vest clung to her not-fully dry stomach, and patches of wet skin showed through the damp material. She held her bruised black leather jacket over her shoulder and clasped the cricket bat in her free hand. Her straw hat balanced on top of wet hair. A water-darkened strand fell loose and brushed against her cheek, and it cost Michael a considerable amount of restraint not to reach out and tuck it away.

She sat down beside them on a plastic chair, and leaned forward on her cricket bat.

"I think she might be a while," she said, pulling out an almost empty packet of cigarettes and a Zippo lighter.

"Do either of you smoke?" she asked, offering the packet as a token of peace.

"No thanks," Michael said, rubbing his newly smooth chin in the hope Zanna might notice he had shaved.

"I used to smoke," David said, shaking his head, "but I've given them up. Although, perhaps now is the time to let ourselves do exactly what we like, if this really is the end."

"That's what I thought," Zanna said, shaking a cigarette loose from the pack. "I never really smoked before, but it's helped me to relax this past week."

Michael gripped the seat and a tremor crept through his right leg as Zanna brought the cigarette to her mouth in slow motion. He could not take this much longer.

A short while later, Judith came bustling out of the bathroom. She had chosen a selection of clothes from the supermarket's shelves and discarded her old outfit in favour of a pair of brown trousers, a pink T-shirt and a cream cardigan.

Michael was surprised to see her smiling as she called across to them. "Hello! Are you all nice and refreshed? I'm feeling lovely. It's amazing what a nice wash can do for you, isn't it!"

Zanna flicked the spent cigarette butt across the floor, "Is this what you've had to put up with all this time?" she asked, turning to Michael with a look of mock pity.

"You don't know the half of it," he said. "She's calmed down a lot now."

***

They made a bed like the one the teenagers had constructed, pulling clothes from the shelves and spreading them across the floor. Michael and David set about moving any nearby bodies, whilst Judith had cornered Zanna who smiled politely as Judith held up different items of clothing for her approval.

"Isn't this lovely and soft, Zanna? It's just like this jumper I used to have a few years ago."

"Hmm," Zanna replied as she dumped more clothes on to their pile of bedding.

"Oh, this is fun. It's like we're shopping together, isn't it? I always wanted to have a teenage daughter," Judith said as she busied herself with a long, flowery skirt.

Michael and David worked silently. There were many bodies to be moved if they were going to be comfortable. They each had tied a T-shirt around their mouths and noses, but they did little to keep out the stench of the rotting bodies and Michael had to fight to stop himself being sick. One of the teenage boys wandered over, munching on a bag of crisps. He watched them for a few minutes and then, once he had finished his crisps, he helped them move the last body out of the way.

"How long are you staying for?" he asked, wiping his hands on his jeans.

"Just tonight," Michael answered.

"Okay," said the boy. "I'll tell the others to keep the noise down and give you some peace."

"Very kind of you," David said, but the boy had already turned his back to them and was heading back to his friends.

Judith fell asleep as soon as she laid down. She seemed to Michael to be constantly resting, yet always tired, spending most of her time asleep, as though in preparation for death.

David stretched himself out and made a huge display of yawning. "Well, I'm knackered. Probably go straight to sleep. Early start tomorrow, kids. Goodnight!"

He gave Michael a last wink, rolled over, and was silent. Judith was snoring like a trooper, the noise a kind of hollow rattle in her throat. Michael sat beside Zanna, sharing a packet of digestives, embarrassed by David's lack of subtlety. It reminded him a lot of his father and, like his father, he knew David would be lying there, listening to every word that passed between himself and Zanna.

"Do you want to go for a walk?" he asked, aware of how absurd it sounded asking someone if they wanted to go for a walk in a supermarket.

"Ok," she said, "I can't stand that bloody snoring anyway."

They headed to the alcohol. The teenagers laughed and passed bottles between them at the other end of the aisle.

Zanna and Michael ignored them, browsing the shelves.

"Dark rum is what we need," Zanna said.

"You're right," Michael replied, as if he knew anything about rum.

"Hey!" a boy's voice shouted from the mass of bodies and clothing on the floor. "Why don't you come and have a drink with us, love? There's plenty of room for sleeping too."

The whole pile of teenagers erupted in hysterics.

Michael was about to shout an unimaginative *Fuck off* but Zanna got in first. "You little boys wouldn't know what to do with me. I'm sure you'll find a lovely girl your own age once you've hit puberty."

They left them behind to laughter and shouts of, "You sure? We'll be waiting for you if you change your mind!"

They made their way through the empty supermarket, stepping over bodies and around trolleys.

"I wonder what time it is," Zanna said, taking the first hit from the rum then offering it to Michael. "It feels like a casino or something in here. No clocks, no windows. It feels like it's late though."

Michael took a drink and nodded. He glanced at his useless wristwatch, the face shattered, shards of glass engrained with mud from his fall. He could see a watch on the wrist of a body slumped behind the checkout, her hand still holding a loaf of bread in front of a scanner which still beeped repeatedly.

"It's strange, isn't it? It's almost like time doesn't exist anymore," he said.

They sat down on a checkout conveyor belt, helping themselves to chocolate and sweets from a rack next to them. Michael looked around the empty store, feeling the warm rum slide down his throat. He laughed.

"What's so funny?" Zanna asked, touching her face subconsciously. "Chocolate?' she asked, wiping her mouth with her sleeve.

She had nothing there, but Michael leaned forward and ran

his thumb across her cheek, pretending to wipe something away. He sat back and an awkward jolt of silence passed between them.

Michael laughed again, trying to take the conversation back a few seconds. "No," he said. "You're fine. I was just thinking, I always wanted to somehow find myself locked in a supermarket overnight. Drink all the booze, eat loads of cakes. I thought it would be amazing."

Zanna nodded. "Dawn of the Dead style, eh?"

Michael grinned. "Exactly. The original though. But, yeah, I never could imagine a scenario where you'd get away with staying in a supermarket. Now I suppose we know…"

His mood suddenly dipped and he was reminded of Her. Michael felt guilty being there, drinking rum with this other girl. It had only been a week ago that he had told Her he loved her. Now, he was sitting with Zanna, feeling like he wanted to lay in bed with her all day, or hang out all night and drink and listen to music. Together they could run through the empty streets, or watch the sun or moon and stars from a roof top whilst they pitched empty bottles out into the night. He wondered if there was any place for romantic nonsense like that in this ruined country. If there was, he would not be able to be a part of it, in a few days he would be in France, and then he had no idea what might happen.

"What do you think caused… all of this?" Zanna asked quietly, passing the bottle back to him.

Michael had not even realised that Zanna had taken the bottle from him. "I don't know. Does anyone? They said something about whatever it was being carried on the wind, but, if it were some sort of terrorist attack, surely we all would have died. If it was some, airborne virus, or something, why didn't we all catch it?"

Zanna rubbed her eyes, and then brought them up to meet Michael's gaze. He took a quick hit of the rum to give himself a reason to look away, afraid of what eye contact might mean.

"I've heard all sorts on my way down here," Zanna said after a moment. "Muslims did it, Hindus did it, Buddhists, Catholics. It's the wrath of God or Allah, or whatever. Someone even said it was a pagan witch's curse and pagans would come out of hiding all around the country, emerging from the forests after centuries of silence to take over." She raised her eyebrows and forced out a quiet laugh.

Michael gave an uneasy smile. "You haven't told me about yourself," he said, changing the subject.

"In the two hours we've known each other?" she asked sarcastically. "My name's Zanna. I'm twenty. I'm a student, or maybe, was a student. At Newcastle. Study/studied Philosophy. Second year."

Michael lay back on the conveyor belt, propping himself up on an elbow so he could still see her. "Well, twenty-year-old Zanna from Newcastle, I'm Michael, eighteen years old. About to start, or was about to start, at Durham. My...friend...was actually supposed to start at Newcastle this September. You might have met her..." He paused and blinked something away.

"I was going to study literature," he added, more to stop tears escaping, than because he thought Zanna would be interested.

"Oh right, maybe I would have met her," Zanna replied, disinterested.

"So...philosophy. If two people take a bottle of rum from a supermarket and there's no one around to see them, does their conscience make a sound?"

Zanna rolled her eyes. "Very good, that was almost a joke. I get it, tree in the woods? There's a little bit more to philosophy than that."

She jumped down from the counter and began to walk away. Michael hopped down and hurried to catch up with her.

"Well, eighteen-year-old Michael, how fascinating you are. One thing though, I'm not from Newcastle." She stopped and looked him dead in the eye, an expression of teasing outrage on her face. "Do I sound like a fucking Geordie?"

They continued walking.

"I suppose not," Michael said, slightly embarrassed due to her obviously southern accent. "What are you doing then? I mean, where are you headed, what's your plan?"

"I'm heading to London, where I am from. I want to see if my family is still alive. If they're still there. I've hitchhiked from Newcastle this far. Had a few scrapes, hence the cricket bat."

She turned to him and with a look that Michael would have said bordered on flirtatious and said, "I haven't decided if you lot are shady characters yet. So be careful, otherwise I might have to give you a whack with this bat."

Michael was feeling cocky now that the rum was swimming inside him. "*Another* whack don't you mean? Not that I felt the first one."

"That was a tickle," Zanna said. "Next time I won't be nice."

Before Michael could reply, there was a loud whirring noise, as if from a piece of dying machinery. The lights above them flickered once, twice, then dimmed momentarily, before dying altogether, dowsing the store in darkness.

Michael stood still in the blackness and felt Zanna's body pressing against his in some instinctive act of shelter. He reached his arm out slowly and put it on her waist.

They stood like this for what seemed like a few minutes, until their eyesight adjusted to the dim gloom. It felt as though all the rules had changed now that the lights were off; like it was non-uniform day at school. If Michael was going to kiss her, it should be now.

He leaned forward, but Zanna, perhaps not noticing, took his hand in hers and pulled him onwards. "Well, it couldn't last forever. Come on; let's get back to the others."

They walked back in silence, Zanna letting his hand drop

after a minute as she unscrewed the lid of the rum.

When they reached their pile of coats and trousers and T-shirts and dresses that was to serve as their bed for the night, they found David's snores mixed with Judith's. They worked in a sort of harmony; one filling the silence between the other's rasping snuffles. Michael lay down next to David, leaving a space for Zanna to the other side of him.

"Well, goodnight," she said in a voice that sounded like it should be followed by a kiss.

She stood beside the nest of clothing and, in the darkness, Michael could see her peel off her leather jacket. He saw the shape of the vest and how it hung over her breasts. She turned her back to him and fiddled with her belt buckle. Glancing back over her shoulder, she caught Michael trying hard not to stare.

"Close your fucking eyes," she hissed.

Michael rolled onto his back, pretending to have his eyes clamped shut, whilst peeping out from under a single eyelid. Zanna let her jeans fall down, and they seemed to take forever to slide to the bottom of her long, cream legs. She stepped out of them and Michael caught a glimpse of bright white underwear that seemed to shine in the darkness. It was too much for Michael to take and he clamped his eyes shut. Zanna lay down quickly and pulled some clothing on top of her, turning her back to Michael.

Michael lay for a while, staring at what he could make out of Zanna's back in the darkness, wondering if she was asleep, and if anyone would notice if he was to sneak off to the bathroom.

Gradually, sleep took hold of him too and he dreamt of Zanna sliding on top of him, kissing his neck, whilst Jim stood in the background, bleeding onto the floor. Much more blood now then there ever had been. Jim's hands covered, his sideburns stained red. He grinned at Michael and suddenly, Zanna was gone and replaced by Judith. Michael tried to push her away, but was not able to and then he was pushing the darkness away as Jim sang a song that shared the tune of *Run Rabbit Run* but had different words that he could not make out.

Michael woke suddenly, damp with cold sweat. It was still dark, and he could not tell if he had been asleep for hours or just minutes. He was facing towards David now and noticed, in the darkness, an empty bottle of whiskey lay between them, half hidden beneath a jacket. Michael turned back on to his other side and could just about make out the shape of Zanna's body, her shoulders rising and falling rhythmically; peacefully, like the tides of the ocean lapping at a moonlit shore.

Michael tried to sleep, tossing and turning, fragments of the dream playing through his mind. He could not close his eyes without seeing Jim, but he was unable to keep his eyes open without seeing Zanna, or Her, and sometimes Michael was not sure who the girl he saw was. He lay still for half an hour, willing himself to sleep, and just as he was drifting off, a rustling sound caught his attention and he turned slowly and deliberately to see what it was.

Two dark shapes were making their way slowly towards them in the blackness. As they approached, Michael could smell the deodorant the teenagers had sprayed earlier, and was able to make out the face of the one they had called Ben. Beside him, was the boy who had been drinking the whiskey that afternoon. They moved almost silently, sneaking upon the sleeping forms like Jack's hunters stalking a pig.

They tiptoed past Michael, not noticing as his hand moved slowly under his blanket of jackets, searching for the knife he carried tucked down the back of his jeans. They paused over Zanna's sleeping body and Ben poked the other boy in the ribs, laughing silently.

They lowered their faces, like dogs sniffing at food. They were almost close enough to kiss her when, suddenly, the sleeping form sprang upwards, kicking Ben in the stomach,

203

sending him stumbling back into the other boy. Zanna sat bolt upright, her cricket bat extended towards the two boys. They backed up against the other side of the aisle, holding their arms up in defense.

"Fuck off, you little pricks," Zanna whispered through gritted teeth.

Neither David nor Judith had stirred during the commotion. Ben made as if to say something, but stopped as Michael sat up, the knife held loosely in his hand, as though he had forgotten it was there.

"You heard her. Fuck right off," he whispered.

The boys backed away, saying nothing, not daring to turn their backs on the pair until they were a safe distance away, and then they disappeared, merging back into the inky blackness.

Zanna turned towards Michael, her gaze momentarily resting on the knife in his hand before she looked up and met his eyes.

"Thanks," she said, with something more than thanks in her voice. Something that Michael could not place.

"Ok," he said, the sound a small noise that was forgotten as soon as it happened.

Zanna sank back down to her bed and Michael did the same. This time sleep came easily.

Michael awoke again briefly in the night and was surprised to find David gone. "Must be at the toilet," he mumbled aloud to himself and fell back into sleep.

Early the next day, Michael woke to the sound of the others gathering up their things. Zanna and David stood fully dressed, gathering a few last bags of food and clothing whilst Judith struggled to put her new shoes on.

"Oh they are a lot of trouble, these shoes," she said to no one in particular.

Now that the electricity was gone, the shop was drenched in a gloomy grayness; light from the doorway filtering in up to a point, before merging into the collection of dark aisles and grey shadows that made up the rest of the store.

"Get up you lazy bastard," David said, and he winced at the volume of his own words.

Michael looked at Zanna. He was not able to get up just yet. "Big night last night, David?" Michael asked from his bed.

"What?" David asked, his face creasing in pain.

Michael nodded to the whiskey bottle that still poked out from the makeshift bed.

"Oh," David said, his expression relaxing somewhat. "Just a few quiet nips."

They trudged outside and loaded the bags into the car.

"So," David said, addressing the group. "Zanna's told me she wants to go to London. I have no objections to making a quick detour there, how about you two?"

Michael shook his head and Judith seemed to perk up like a child offered a trip to Disneyland. "London! I haven't been there in twenty years. Pauline and I went once on a W.I. coach trip. Michael, you remember Pauline, well..."

Judith was interrupted by a shout from the entranceway. Lucy, the girl they had spoken to the day before, ran outside, shielding her eyes against the morning sun. Michael noticed her eyes were tinged with red as though she had spent the night crying.

"Have, have any of you seen Annabel?" she asked, trying to keep her voice calm, but betraying a hint of panic. "I woke up and she was gone. I don't know where she is."

"No, sorry love, we haven't. I'm sure she's not gone far," David said.

"Oh no," Judith said, looking as though she might burst into tears, reminding Michael of how upset she had been when a girl had gone missing in the camp.

"We'll help you find her," Zanna said, starting towards the entrance.

But help was not necessary as, just then, Ben emerged from

the store, dragging a silent and un-protesting Annabel behind him. She too looked as if she had been crying, but now her face was blank and expressionless, as though she were not a real girl, but only a doll.

"Where the hell have you been?" Lucy asked, roughly dragging Annabel back into the store by her arm.

They disappeared back into the murky shop. Ben lingered for a moment until Zanna shot him a dry smirk. He looked away quickly and shuffled back inside after the girls.

David opened the driver's door. "Well, now that's all cleared up, shall we get going?"

Chapter Nineteen

They wound southwards, still making slow progress, picking their way tediously between lorries and motorbikes and cars with no owners. Occasionally, they spotted other vehicles labouring forward ahead of them, their roofs glinting in the sun as they trudged onwards like metallic beetles.

By the sides of the road, or hidden away in fields, they spotted camps of people, families or groups, their tents wilting under the sun. Occasional lanterns lit the windows of the small towns and villages they passed through, and the people stood, sharing food or drink amongst themselves, beside the road.

The four in the car did not acknowledge them anymore. They made no stops and did not wave to those they passed. Even Judith faced them with a blank expression, as though staring through a looking glass at a strange and foreign civilization.

London appeared before them like a mirage, stretching across the horizon, a collection of crooked spires glimmering silver in the distance. The sky was darkening under rain clouds and they moved on, the headlights cutting through the gloom. Michael drove now, with Zanna sitting beside him, smoking the last of her cigarettes and flicking ash out of the window.

"Nearly there," he said in a voice that was barely above a whisper.

Zanna did not answer or acknowledge him, nervous in the knowledge that soon she would be home and she would know for certain what she had known inside of her for the past week.

Ten miles outside of the city limits, they came upon abandoned tanks and jeeps, littering both lanes of the road. Michael slowed the car as he searched for a way through. The abandoned cars of those who had tried to leave the city were backed up for miles behind the military vehicles, blocking both lanes. Where the people had gone to now, no one could say.

"It looks like we're stuck," Michael admitted, stopping the car entirely.

Judith leaned forward in her seat. "What do you mean we're stuck? The military can help us now, surely."

David stretched and yawned before leaning across Judith and peering out of her window. "No Judith, I don't think they'd be any help. Not from what I've heard."

His eyes met Michael's in the rear-view mirror. Michael glanced away and tried to stop the scenes of gunfire and panic playing through in his mind.

Zanna massaged the bridge of her nose between a thumb and forefinger. "We'll have to walk the last part. At least until we can find another car on the other side of this mess," she said.

"Agreed," David nodded.

A thick splotch of rain landed heavily on the windscreen with a loud tap that startled them all. The raindrop slid lazily down the glass, minuscule particles of dirt swimming inside of it. Another landed next to it, and then another.

"Let's go now then, and find somewhere dry to sleep tonight," Michael said.

They piled out of the car before Judith knew what was happening. David leaned in to give her a hand and picked out Michael's holdall from the foot-well. He weighed the bag in his hand for a moment and frowned at the shape that, with only a little imagination, described the outline of a rifle. Michael stood idly, unsure what to do or say. David threw him the bag along with a quizzical look, as Zanna shouted to them, her body half buried in the boot.

"Come on, for God's sake. I'm getting fucking soaked."

"Please don't say that, Zanna," Judith called above the sound of the quickening rain as she wrapped her cardigan tightly around herself.

Rainwater collected in a puddle on the rim of Zanna's hat and dripped slowly down onto her nose, creating a curtain of water in front of her eyes.

"Sorry Judith, for...whatever," Zanna said, shoving a bag of food into the woman's hands.

Judith looked surprised and suddenly remembered her injured arm, letting the bag hang loosely. "Michael..." she began, about to protest.

"Just grab food, we'll leave the rest," David shouted over the metallic clang of the rain on the roofs of the cars and tanks that blocked their path.

"I suppose we were being quite vain bringing new clothes, optimistic too, we're not out of the fire yet..." David said.

Bags in hand, they ran through the quickening rain, sliding over car bonnets and under tank turrets, stepping over forgotten suitcases.

Michael led the way, stopping to give Zanna a hand over a car. She struggled over with her cricket bat and a shopping bag full of food. She was too cold and wet now to remember she that was proud and did not need any help.

David helped Judith along behind them, and suddenly slipped, his shopping bag splitting, sending packets and tins bouncing off across the rain-slicked road.

A boom of thunder from somewhere in the distance drowned out his curse. A flash of lightning followed in quick succession, indicating the storm was over the city itself.

The sky was now darkening rapidly, and in the distance, they could see the towers of London turning into dark silhouettes against the blues and reds of the sky. The buildings seemed to absorb all colour, as though they were missing from the horizon and had been replaced by a black nothingness. The only light to give shape to the buildings was the occasional glow of flames that surged here and there amongst the buildings of the distant city. Fuzzy orange warmth licked at the towers and flames reached up to the sky to merge with the deepening shades of red and blue.

Michael grasped Zanna's hand now as she ran to keep up with him. David and Judith were almost imperceptible shapes behind curtains of rain. Michael's eyes flickered from one side of the road to the other, searching rapidly for some shelter. He could see nothing amongst the empty cars or in the narrow trees that flanked the road and enclosed them under their long arms.

"There!" Zanna shouted suddenly.

She took hold of Michael's arm and dragged him towards the trees, but to what, Michael could not tell.

"There isn't anything there," he cried, his voice lost beneath a crack of thunder.

They stumbled through the mud, Zanna leading him along and then suddenly, the rain ceased.

They were inside a tent, hidden in the shadows of the trees, its dark green walls hiding it from the road. They stood together in the entrance, catching their breaths and feeling the cold water run down their backs. They let their bags drop to the floor. Two more figures ran into the back of them and shoved them forward, further into the tent.

A light appeared in mid-air and illuminated Zanna's face. Water ran down the skin in rivulets and a haze of smudged black eye-shadow made the green eyes burn even more fiercely in the protective light.

The light moved and became a larger, unnatural orb that suddenly filled the room. The smaller light disappeared back into Zanna's pocket and she took the electric lamp and hung it from a hook in the ceiling above a small round table.

The four of them stood panting inside the tent. It was large and spacious, an army tent, lined with cots and boxes and chairs. David shook himself like a dog and picked up a camouflage jacket off a chair beside a table.

"Nice of them to leave us supplies," he said, taking off his jumper and shirt, and hanging them from one of the ceiling poles.

Zanna glanced at the scars on his bare and wet chest but David did not notice as he quickly wrapped the jacket around himself.

"We'll have to get out of these clothes or we'll all catch a cold," David said.

Judith sneezed as if on cue.

David glanced at Michael, remembering how the boy's family had been killed. "We might not want to wear army uniforms, but it's the only option to keep warm."

They searched the tent, opening boxes and pulling out tins of food and first aid kits, boxes of bullets and maps with red pen lines across them. An SA80 rifle lay in the corner, and it was an unspoken rule that no one mentioned it; they each wanted to feel safe there beneath the taunt canvas and the machine gun fire of the rain.

After a short search, they came across jumpers and jackets, green or camouflage and made of itchy wool. Michael stripped off his jacket and T-shirt and slowly pulled his military jumper on, trying to catch Zanna looking at him. If she had been, he missed her. She was still to mention his freshly shaved face.

Michael expected her to turn her back to him to change but instead she threw off her soaking hat into a corner, peeled off her jacket and pulled her vest over her head, her chest stretching as she did so. Michael could just about make out her nipples through the bra, standing to military attention in the cold.

Michael looked away with embarrassment as Zanna pulled a jumper on, and then imagined he had caught David glancing over at her. However, David was too busy hanging up everyone's clothes. As Zanna passed her wet vest and jacket over to him, Michael swore he saw her hand linger on David's. If it had, David did not notice as he shook out the vest, then hung it up.

The three of them turned their backs whilst Judith took off her wet outfit and dressed again in the oversized army clothes. Michael stared at the dark green of the tent wall and, in the stifling warmth of the thunderstorm and glow of the lantern, he felt suddenly exhausted. His thoughts turned instantly to Her, and he had to grip the table, and squeeze until his knuckles turned white, in his attempt to regain control of his emotions.

As Judith coughed and struggled behind them, Michael's bottom lip began to quiver, and there was nothing he could do to stop it.

A hand touched his as he stared at the canvas wall and the feeling of another person's skin offered in compassion was almost too much. He knew the hand was Zanna's, and suddenly, her perfume or natural scent filled his nostrils. It was a sweet odour of white chocolate, and as soon as Michael smelled it, the lamplight began to burn brighter and his lip suddenly stopped quivering. He squeezed her hand once and felt her squeeze his in return, a conversation between skin; no need for words.

Judith's voice brought Michael back into the room. "You may turn around now."

They did, and watched as she bustled about the tent, closing the door and tying it firmly shut, tidying the crates and boxes into neat piles, then throwing a spare jacket over the rifle in the corner.

Michael thought of his own rifle and whether or not it would be wet from the rain. He decided to try to dry it once everyone was asleep. It had become his rifle now. Owning this rifle was no stranger than any other scenario he had found himself in during the course of the past week. He had killed a man in that time, and this thought was ever-present in a corner of his mind as just another fact, a piece of information processed and stored away until it was time to bring it out again and perhaps attach some meaning to it; to try to understand what everything meant.

The rain fell unabated and beat a permanent tattoo against the tent, enclosing them in their own world, far removed from anything and anyone that lingered outside in the night. The branches of trees scraped gently across the roof, the low boughs stroking against the tent; a further layer of protection and obstruction from the rest of the world.

Judith continued to bluster busily about the tent, the rain seemingly having seeped down into her and re-invigorated her bones. The others sat under the lamp around the makeshift table.

"This is a bit better than the last tent, eh?" Michael laughed, and in response to Zanna's confused look, her eyes appearing wide and panda-like in her smudged makeup, they told her of their time at the refugee camp and how they had come to meet each other. She nodded along, unsurprised, and with stories of her own that she would never tell anyone.

"Ah ha!" Judith cried, and with a triumphant smile, she pulled a pan and gas stove from behind an empty crate. "I will cook tonight," she beamed. "It's about time I made myself useful."

"Have you been drinking Judith?" David asked, winking at Zanna who was sitting beside him.

Michael clenched his fist, his sudden jealousy returning. If anyone was going to make jokes about Judith, it should be him, Michael huffed internally, he had basically looked after her for almost a week, he reasoned to himself.

Michael's bad mood soon subsided as Judith busied him with washing out cups and cleaning tin plates using a scavenged bottle of water, whilst she set Zanna to work clearing the small table. While this was happening, Judith

213

emptied packets and tins into a large saucepan and up-ended a tin of meatballs into a pan over the gas stove. Immediately, the meatballs began to sizzle and Michael's mouth began to water.

"Bloody hell!" David cried. "Judith, you're our saviour!"

Judith blushed. She began to ask him not to blaspheme when David took her by the hand and pulled her into a waltz, dragging her around the tent as he belted out a tune, the electric lamp painting energetic shadows against the walls.

Michael and Zanna sat beside each other atop stack of crates, shaking with laughter. Watching Judith try to push David away, Michael wondered if he should grab Zanna's hand and pull her onto the impromptu dance floor. He glanced at her and she flashed him a smile that cut him like a knife, then she turned her attentions back to the odd, dancing couple.

Later, as they sat down to the meal, David pulled out a bottle of red wine from one of the bags he had taken from the car, and began to fill their tin cups. Judith put a hand over her glass and coughed into her other hand.

She cleared her throat and began to speak solemnly. "The Lord has been merciful to us today and has provided us with this bounty, so we now offer our prayers to the one and only Lord God and his son, Jesus Christ."

There followed a murmur of *"Amen"*, and the eating began in earnest, and the piping hot food was shovelled into hungry mouths with no regard for the temperature. Meatballs, noodles and tomatoes combined to create the best food any of them had ever eaten. The wine continued to fill their glasses and seemed to make everyone drunker than they had ever been; the entire meal enthused with their relief at this brief respite from the new realities of the world outside.

As Michael, David and Zanna laughed and joked, Judith coughed into her hand beside them. The spark, which had animated her earlier on, seemed to have dwindled to almost nothing. She became quieter and quieter until eventually she declared she would retire. After a round of applause and thanks for the meal, Judith crawled into a cot in the corner of the tent, and the sound of her rasping breathing and occasional coughs combined with the rain to become the background music to the merriment of the others.

The conversation and laughter eventually faltered with the last of the wine, then died out and allowed the noises of Judith's laboured breathing to fill the tent, the sounds an ever-present reminder of their situation. David stood up and silently nodded at Zanna and Michael in turn, before going off to find his own cot, walking on unsteady feet across the tent. Almost immediately, the sound of snoring mingled with Judith's wheezing and the patter of the rain.

Zanna and Michael sat opposite each other, both drowning in the oversized military jumpers. Michael could not help but notice the smooth curves of Zanna's chest outlined beneath the heavy material. Zanna leaned forward on the table and without warning, she began to sob silently, tears mixing with the black smudges around her eyes, sending black streams crawling down her cheeks.

Michael dragged his chair around the table to sit next to her, and pulled her towards him. She nestled her head in his chest and in that moment, Michael never wanted to let her go.

"They're dead," she whispered.

The wine had slowed Michael, and he took a second to think of what he should say to her. Before he had chance to say anything, Zanna seemed to recover from her momentary lapse, and she looked up at him with dry eyes, her jaw muscles twitching as she concentrated all of her energy into maintaining a brave face once again. "I know my parents are dead."

Michael wiped away the dark tears that still lingered on the soft cheeks, his thumb turning black.

"I'm sure they're ok. We don't know anything yet," he said quietly.

Zanna fell silent. She stood, separating herself from

Michael as she walked away and climbed into a spare cot. She lay down and turned her back to him.

Michael was too drunk and tired to linger on this apparent rebuttal. He sighed and stood to turn out the electric lamp, and, in the near pitch-blackness, he found a cot of his own and crawled into bed.

He had forgotten to check if the rifle needed cleaning after the rainfall, and fell immediately into a deep sleep, the sound of Judith's coughing filling the hallways of his empty dreams.

Hours went by. Judith and David's snoring hummed along gently, and the rain outside raged down upon them in a last surge of power, and then fell silent. At some point in the middle of this dark and lonely night, Michael woke again, aware of a movement in the tent. He opened his eyes slowly, his sleep-encrusted lashes sticking together at first. Before him, illuminated in a silver and mystical light, stood Zanna.

She was dressed only in the large wool jumper and in the dim light, Michael was able to make out the triangle of her underwear where the jumper brushed against her thighs. He did not know where this light had come from, for all he could tell, it radiated from inside Zanna herself. She bent over him, celestial and almost translucent in the glow.

Wordlessly, she brought her face close to his, until her lips parted slowly and pressed gently against his own. She held the kiss for a second, and then withdrew, silently. Michael resisted the urge to pull her into his cot and bury his lips on hers, her neck, in between her breasts, her thighs, every inch of her incandescent skin.

She stood over him for another moment and then, with a half-smile, she whispered, "thank you...for earlier," and before he could respond, she turned and padded back to her own cot, as silent and mercurial as a midnight doe in the depths of the forest.

Chapter Twenty

Michael awoke with the first colours of dawn painting the tent a pale grey. He sat up and remembered Zanna's kiss in the night, as if recalling a dream. The grey light became the ashy remnants of her silver glow. Michael glanced towards her cot, where the blanket hid a motionless figure. The peace of the morning was interrupted by Judith's rasping breathing, which filled the tent and seemed to grow louder and louder, until even David's choking snores were almost drowned out.

Michael peeled back the blanket and swung his legs over the side of the cot. He moved silently to where his clothes hung from the ceiling poles and took down his T-shirt. He pulled off the thick green jumper and threw it aside, before furiously scratching himself where the rough fibres had rubbed against his skin in the night. His jeans still felt damp and Michael regretted having slept in them, but there was nothing he could do about it, there were no other trousers to change into.

Outside, the ground was damp and the air smelled fresh. There was a quiet sense of calm, as though the storm had been a raging argument, and now the country could relax again in the aftermath. Between the trees, it was easy to make out the shapes of London on the horizon. The previous night the buildings had looked as though the colour had been burnt out of them but, as the sun spread a pale pink light over the morning, the buildings of London seemed simply drained, grey shapes that resembled buildings in form only.

Michael stretched his arms above his head and walked a few steps to the edge of the road, rainwater dripping from leaves disturbed by his passage.

He yawned, undid his fly and began urinating into the road. His mind was on nothing in particular when a noise along the road shook him from his morning haze. Michael finished quickly and zipped up his fly. He scanned the road in each direction, but could see nothing. As he was about to head back to the tent, he caught a flash of red in the corner of his eye. Turning, he was met by a rust coloured fox trotting slowly across the road.

The fox saw him at the same moment and, for a second, their eyes met, before the animal dismissed him with a dip of its head and disappeared into the trees on the opposite side of the road.

When he returned to the tent, Michael found the others in the various stages of getting up; ready to start a new day on the road. It was a mechanical process now, done without thought or emotion. There was no time for lie-ins or complaint; a new day meant it was time to wake up, pack the bags and step onto the road. A new day meant moving a step closer to civilisation.

Zanna was awake now and sitting on her cot. She looked up as Michael came back into the tent, but there was no recollection of the previous night in her eyes, and before Michael could think of anything to say to her, she stood up and began searching about for her discarded hat.

Judith lay curled up in her cot, coughing into her hand, as David knelt beside her. A kettle whistled on the gas stove and David went over and poured the steaming water into a tin cup. An aroma of coffee filled the air as David walked back and handed the mug to Judith. She sat up a little and drank slowly, blowing the liquid between sips. Michael noticed her sallow complexion for the first time as sweat beaded her brow. Judith's skin seemed to have grown tight around her face in the night and her eyes appeared to have become sunken and buried, so that now they peered out from a web of crow's feet

218

and dark bags.

David stepped close to Michael and said quietly, "I don't know what's wrong with her, but she could do with a doctor."

Michael nodded. "She's been quiet the whole time I've been with her, but this is the first time I've noticed her looking ill."

David scratched his morning stubble. "She looked fine when we left the camp, it must have come on quickly in the last day, maybe with all the rain."

Zanna finally located her hat, sniffed it, wrinkled her nose, and then sent the hat spinning to the other side of the tent, where it disappeared behind a box.

"Damp," she said. "Probably going to go mouldy. I liked that hat."

She realised no one was listening to her and noticed for the first time the two figures gathered around the thin woman in her bed.

She tapped Michael on the shoulder. "She needs a doctor."

"I know," Michael replied. "We were just discussing it. She's always seemed a bit weak, but she's never been this bad."

Zanna looked over at Judith who lay still, sipping her drink, unaware of the three pairs of eyes on her.

"She looks malnourished," Zanna said. "She could have hepatitis or maybe typhoid, maybe something else, you'd have to do some tests, take some blood."

David nodded. "We've all been around a lot of dead bodies, they're not the most hygienic things, especially with all this heat we've had."

Zanna shook her head. "The number of diseases passed on by contact with corpses following natural disasters is negligible. The diseases can't survive more than a few days on a dead body. It's more likely that she's ate or drank something she shouldn't have."

Michael and David stared at her, trying to hide how impressed they were. Zanna's eyes dropped to the ground for a second and then came back up to dart shyly between the two curious pairs.

"My parents are... my parents were...well they're doctors," she said, embarrassed by how much hope she had betrayed by speaking as if she knew her parents were still alive.

Michael and David said nothing.

"I used to ask them questions all the time, read their medical journals," she continued. "They were quite disappointed when I chose to study philosophy." The corners of her mouth creased in a melancholy smile. "Dad was always annoyed, but I think Mum was coming round to the idea of having a philosopher in the family."

Michael smiled at her and then quickly glanced away.

David rustled his feet awkwardly. "I'm sure they will be able to help us, then. They must be busy though, there's got to be a lot of work on for them at the minute," he said.

Zanna smiled her sad smile again and Michael's heart sank to the pit of his stomach.

"If we can find them, I'm sure they'll want to help," she said.

Michael reached out a hand and squeezed her arm gently, just like he had seen people do in films. "Don't worry," he said, "we'll find them."

***

Four figures set out along the grey road, weaving their way slowly between and over the vehicles that blocked their paths. They did not bother going back for the bags they had left behind, or those they had lost the previous night, certain everything would have been ruined by the storm.

Everything now was about pressing onwards. As the sun rose, it glinted off the ever-distant buildings and cast lengthening shadows which chased after the four shapes that moved purposefully along the road, like mice searching out food. They walked, spread across the road, in a horizontal line, checking each car they came to, but finding most to be unmovable and of no use, wedged into the rows of unmoving traffic.

They moved through the black puddles with a tireless persistence, despite them each fighting against a weariness that felt like it started in their bones and spread through their bodies, poisoning each of their organs and limbs so that with each step their legs became heavier.

Judith had refused to leave Michael's side and now clung to him, forcing him to almost drag her along the road. Her body was an inconvenience as he made his way between the obstacles in the road, but her weight was almost unnoticeable. With his arm around her waist, Michael could feel that the slim woman, whom he had met only days ago, had rapidly lost weight. Her bony body dug into his left side whilst the holdall swung on his right shoulder, the metallic bones of the rifle banging against his ribs. Judith's coughing increased, so that every few steps she sprayed Michael's cheek with a warm dampness. Michael took his hand off the holdall strap for a second and pulled his T-shirt up over his mouth and nose.

They came to a wall of sandbags and Michael hoisted Judith over. She stumbled as he set her down on the other side, and Michael caught her roughly under the arms and pulled her upright. Judith regained her balance and turned to Michael, as though noticing him for the first time.

Her eyes looked distant and far away; the deep bags making it appear as if she were looking at him from the other end of a long tunnel. "Oh, hello, who are you?"

She looked around distractedly and a mask of fear came over her face.

"Where is Emily?" she demanded.

Michael still held her under her arms. "It's me Judith, Michael. Come on, we have to get into the city."

She suddenly noticed his hands gripping her, and pushed him sharply away, raising her voice as she did so. "Get your hands off of me! I will tell Reverend Parsons!"

Again, she glanced worriedly around her. "Where's Emily?" she demanded, almost pleadingly. "She is not allowed to play around cars."

"Ok Judith, ok," Michael answered, trying to calm her with his hands outstretched, just as he had once seen a man do before another man had killed him with a bat.

"Ok Judith, I'll go look for...for Emily. You just sit here."

Michael took Judith gently by the hand, led her to the nearest car and sat her down on the bonnet.

"What time's the bonfire?" she asked.

Michael opened his mouth and then closed it again. She had gone insane, he thought. He had been forced to put up with her all this time, and now she had gone insane.

"I'll be right back," he said as slipped away towards the others.

"They've stopped," David said as he came towards Zanna through the rows of empty vehicles.

Zanna pushed her sunglasses back onto her forehead. What little light there was burned her eyes and, as she squinted in the direction David pointed, she saw Michael making his way over to them.

"Is she ok, Michael?" David called as the boy came across to them.

Michael shook his head and exhaled slowly. "Not exactly." He paused, unsure of how to word what he had to say. "She...I think she's gone crazy."

"Ah," David said.

Zanna stood on her tiptoes and caught a glimpse of Judith resting across in the next lane. "Normally," she said, "I'd say with people like her, it's just a matter of time before they go crazy. Spending their lives keeping everything cooped up and always trying to fit in. But, in this case, I'd say she is very ill and is probably hallucinating, so we need to get her to my parent's, soon as."

"Agreed," David said. "I saw a car just over there that we might be able to maneuver out of this jam and drive down the verge, until we can get back on the road."

The small car poked out of the queue of traffic, its doors wide-open, dank puddles collected in the foot-wells.

"Looks good," Michael said. "Keys?"

David poked his head in the driver's side door and slammed his fist on the roof. "Shit. No luck, I'm afraid."

Zanna glanced in quickly from the passenger's side. "Michael, give me your knife," she said.

"What?"

"The knife, Michael, the knife, give it to me."

"Why?" he began.

Zanna rolled her eyes. "Because I said so. It's not just choosing philosophy over medicine that pissed my parents off," she said, holding out her hand. "Now, give."

Michael took out the knife from the back of his jeans and handed it across to her. She took it and slid across the wet bonnet, before ducking inside the car on the driver's side. There came a sound of scratching and banging.

David looked from one of them to the other, shaking his head. "That's it. I'm a dinosaur. I'm out of touch with you kids, you with your knives, her with her car theft!"

In response, the car choked, stuttered and then coughed into life. Once it had cleared its throat, a healthy hum rumbled from under the bonnet. Zanna re-emerged and tossed the knife nonchalantly to Michael. He panicked and stepped back quickly, but somehow managed to catch the knife in one hand without slicing his fingers off.

Zanna raised her eyebrows. "Are you quite ready, Michael?"

David took the steering wheel and Michael and Zanna pushed from behind, and the car slowly emerged from the queue. David turned the wheel so the front end shot out into the muddy verge. Quickly, Zanna and Michael switched ends and pushed the car back onto the road, before it began to sink into the mud. Pushing and shoving, they managed to force the car through a three-point turn until it faced back towards the way it had come.

When they were ready, Michael and Zanna went back to get Judith. She had not moved and was coughing violently into her hand. She looked up lethargically as they approached.

"Oh, are we ready?" she asked, addressing the question to no one in particular.

They took an arm each and quickly maneuvered her towards the waiting car.

With Zanna in the back, wiping a hand over Judith's forehead, and Michael in the passenger seat, the car lurched slowly forward. David drove aggressively, with one side of the car ploughing through the mud beside the road, and the other side scraping against the cars that blocked the way. The car pushed onwards, whining, as David gathered speed in low gear.

After ten minutes of this, the mud verge became a footpath and the car shot forwards as both wheels touched concrete. The way ahead was clear enough to make relatively quick progress, and the car rolled towards London under the crimson of the rising sun.

In the backseat, Judith sat up; fighting against Zanna's restraining arms, pointing ahead to where black smoke still rose from the dark buildings.

"The good book mentions signs in the earth... blood and fire and vapor of smoke," she said as they crept past the blackened remains of a car.

"Blood, fire and vapor of smoke," she repeated, as though her words were a prophecy of things to come.

Chapter Twenty-One

"Let me drive," Zanna said as the car penetrated London and was quickly absorbed by the city.

David glanced across to Michael in the passenger seat. "There's a girl here who wants to drive."

Michael stuck pushed his tongue around his mouth and raised his eyebrows, as though deep in thought.

"I'm all for equality," he decided.

"Stop fucking messing around!" Zanna yelled from the backseat. "Judith isn't looking too good here, and I am the only one who knows where we're going."

David stopped the car in the middle of the road. There was no need to pull over. "I suppose you're right. I haven't been to London in ten years."

Michael had a sudden idea. "Your family. David, we have to look for them too, they could still be here."

David stared into the steering wheel. "They're gone."

"How do you know? We may as well look, I mean..."

David turned towards Michael, his hands turning white as they gripped the wheel. "They're gone," he repeated with a finality that settled any argument.

Michael sat back, his head resting against the window, unsure of what to say. Zanna saved him the trouble of having to think of anything as she wrenched open David's door and stood there, glaring at him. "David, get the fuck out!"

Her voice shook David back to the present and he stumbled quickly out of the car, wilting under her glare.

Zanna drove as though pursued by wild horses, swinging the car into every corner. Michael braced himself against the

225

window, but it was impossible to avoid suffering a few bruises.

In the backseat, David cradled a weak Judith in his lap. "For God's sake Zanna! Try and get us all there alive."

She took the next corner faster still. David shot out a hand to hold on to the seat in front, but said nothing.

"I'm trying to keep us all alive," Zanna said through red lips clamped tightly over white teeth.

Beside her in the passenger seat, Michael noticed how a vein in her neck throbbed a sea green under her almost translucent skin.

Outside the car, the capital grew up around them. Michael had never been there before, nor had he imagined his first visit would be in this sort of situation.

Rows of council flats stood next to hotels and restaurants of black steel and glass. Bars and pubs of cream coloured stone with gold lettering mingled in with corner shops and takeaways. They passed more shops with shutters that had been ripped off and hung loosely, the windows smashed. Piles of food, clothes, white goods, lay scattered across the pavements and broken shards of window glass had been powdered under foot, rejecting the sunlight in rainbow colours as though the streets were dusted with jewels.

They drove past Regent's Park, now home to tens of thousands of people living in a city of tents. They were people who had been forced from their homes in the city, for whatever reason, and had nowhere else to go, and no one to go with. They were the people who had traveled up, down and across the country to the capital, because the answer to this disaster must lay there, there must be some form of help in the heart of England. They were young men and women, just moved to London, their eyes wide enough to take in all of the sights without seeing, the promise of jobs and futures now shattered, no way to tell if their families still survived in far flung corners of the country. They were the homeless people whose position had, if anything, improved; amongst the newly

226

homeless refugees, they were old hands, the experienced leaders, teaching those who came in suits how best to keep away a chill at night, in return for a little bit of food; money had never been of much use to them.

The buildings they passed wore a residue of smoke. Some had been gutted by fire, the blank windows staring out like black, empty eyes. Signs of rioting and looting were everywhere. Buildings had been barricaded shut with tables, desks and chair legs nailed across the doors. They passed one house where a middle-aged couple hung from a third floor window, hurling books and crockery at a gang of men and women who were trying to breach the doorway, hammering at the barricade with bats and crowbars.

The roads were littered with cars, vans and motorbikes, and around every corner was another pile up that needed to be carefully maneuvered. A delivery van had crashed into a Chinese takeaway, its back doors flung open, its cargo of boxes spread across the road. An army of cats was feasting on the moldering food.

A little further on, they were forced to maneuver a collapsed scaffolding rig; metal bones that half hung from a building and lay half sprawled across the ground, slowly peeling away from the side of the building like a scab. A red double-decker bus lay wedged on its side where the scaffolding should have gripped the building. A bank had been burnt down and singed twenty-pound notes blew across the road and stuck to the wet windscreen of the car. Through the windscreen wipers and sodden banknotes, they caught sight of a lone tower in the distance. It stood simmering gently as orange fire glowed in wounded patches, like fungus growing on a tree. A huge stream of black smoke rose steadily from the gaping holes.

"The Gherkin," David said under his breath.

Judith moaned steadily from the backseat, her voice a constant presence, like the swell of waves in a nighttime ocean.

David wiped sweat from her brow with his hand, but new beads appeared almost instantly.

"Zanna," David said calmly.

In the driver's seat Zanna gripped the wheel intently, her green eyes searching the road, taking in each and every danger whilst her hands moved automatically from gear stick to steering wheel, the muscles of her legs flexing as they drifted from clutch to brake pedal.

"Zanna," David repeated.

There was no need for him to tell her to slow down again because, just then, the car jolted to a sudden stop, throwing each of them forwards in their seats. Michael sat back slowly, rubbing his head with his fingertips where it had connected with the dashboard.

Zanna calmly turned off the ignition. "We're here," she said.

They were in a leafy square. As he did not know the city, Michael had no idea which area they were in, but the buildings surrounding them seemed somewhere in between rich and poor. A light breeze blew rubbish across the wet street, plastic bags and wet newspapers clinging to trees in the middle of the square. Through these trees and bushes, Michael could make out a red slide and a yellow set of swings, creaking back and forth slowly in the wind. A low green fence surrounded the garden. Cars lined the side of the road, as though their owners were home and might appear any second. Only shards of broken glass and two cars, which blocked the road ahead and seemed to be growing together in a heap of twisted and stretched metal, showed any sign that anything out of the ordinary had happened in the quiet square.

"This is where you live?" Michael asked.

Zanna seemed not to hear him; she sat wide-eyed, exhaling slowly, her breath clouding the window.

"Zanna," Michael repeated. "Do you live here?"

Zanna seemed to have only just noticed as though she was

returning from the other side of some imperceptible barrier, and Michael's voice had struggled to reach her.

"Yes," she said. "I mean, no, I don't live here. My parents, my parents worked here." She gestured vaguely out the window and sat back in her seat.

Michael turned and glanced back at David, who shrugged as he cradled Judith in his lap.

Michael lowered his voice and leaned towards Zanna. "Zanna, I know it's difficult, but, whether your parents are...there or not, we have to help Judith somehow."

She turned her face to him, golden strands of hair floating beside her cheeks. In her wet emerald eyes, Michael saw a fear that made him want to take her hand and lead her somewhere far, far away, never to return.

"Zanna... ok?" he asked.

She blinked and a tear rolled down her cheek as she tried to smile.

"David, will you stay here with Judith? I...I don't want to move her if, if there's no help here."

David smiled at her and in his warmest teaching voice he said. "Of course I will, go do what you have to."

Zanna opened the door and swung her legs out. "Michael," she said over her shoulder, "will you come with me? Just in case?"

"Of course I will," he said, the words catching in his throat.

They got out of the car together, leaving David and Judith behind. Zanna reached into the backseat, took out her cricket bat, then set off, with determined steps, down the street.

Michael followed behind, unsure how close he should get, or what would be the right thing to say to her. He remembered the emptiness and uncertainty he had felt when he had returned home after witnessing the death of his family; he had felt like an un-tethered balloon, floating aimlessly in the sky. Now, Zanna might be about to feel the same.

She stopped in front of a house in the middle of the row, a

few houses down from where she had stopped the car. A brass sign attached to the wall read Bradbury Rehabilitation Clinic.

Zanna gripped the cricket bat, her knuckles cracking. "My parents worked with addicts, they always said it was the best way they could help anyone."

Michael smiled, waiting for her to go inside.

"You're coming with me, aren't you?" she asked, sudden panic in her eyes.

Michael squeezed her arm. "Always."

They made their way up the steps, steps that seemed to stretch on forever, neat steps with little green weeds poking through the cracks. Zanna paused on the threshold. Bars covered a window of green glass, and nothing could be seen through it. There was a buzzer beside the door, but there was no need to use it, as the door stood ajar.

"I'm right here Zanna. Whatever we find, we'll be ok."

She turned to him, smiling weakly, and tucked a few strands of hair behind her ears, as though making herself presentable, and then pushed the door open. They stepped into a murky corridor, light falling into the space from open doors on either side.

"Their offices were after the waiting room," Zanna said pointing along the corridor with the bat.

Leaflets were strewn across the floor and a strong smell of vomit hit them as they passed one of the doors leading off the corridor. From behind a closed door came the smell of decomposing meat. Zanna swallowed audibly and her hand shook as she held the bat out in front of her. Michael walked along behind her with his hand on her shoulder, like a blind man being led to safety.

A rattling, clinking sound as though of someone rummaging through a cupboard drifted down the corridor and grew louder as they stepped into the waiting room. Zanna nodded towards a desk enclosed behind a wire mesh window, with the word Pharmacy printed above it on a neat white sign.

Behind the wire mesh, Michael could see rows and rows of bottles and boxes on white shelves.

"We can get in around here," Zanna whispered, and she began to lead them around a corner of the room, where Michael presumed was a door that led behind the reception desk.

The rattling noise suddenly stopped, and Zanna froze where she was, the cricket bat raised before her. Michael put his arm on her shoulder and tried to pull her back behind him, but she would not move. He slipped past her, his hand reaching for the knife he carried.

As he approached the corner, a chair appeared in mid-air. It was a red plastic chair and looked like it had come from the waiting room. It hung horizontally in the air now, and, at the end of two of its four bent legs, a pair of thick brown arms hung on tightly. The chair grew suddenly bigger and then it connected with Michael's nose, sending him reeling backwards as pain shot up into his head and electricity screamed behind his eyes. He lay sprawled on the floor, unable to move as syrupy red blood ran freely from his nostrils and over his cheeks and chin.

"That will teach you to sneak about, thief!" a woman's voice boomed.

On the other end of the chair (now lowered) appeared a robust woman of West Indian descent, dressed in a wide blue nurse's uniform, a white blouse pushing her breasts tightly out in front of her. The woman stood over Michael on stocky legs and raised the chair again, the ropey sinews of her forearms bulging. Suddenly she stopped, as though unable to move, and the chair clattered to the floor, inches from Michael's head.

"Lord," she said with a slight West Indian accent. "Good Lord, is that you girl?" Zanna let her bat drop to the ground, mirroring the woman's actions.

"Come here girl!" the woman said with eyes wide with wonder, and she pulled Zanna towards her, the girl's head disappearing in the woman's straining bosom as the thick arms closed around her narrow back. They stood as one figure, shaking silently together, their movements in harmony.

Michael lay with his eyes screwed up in pain. He reached a hand slowly to his face and gingerly stroked his nose with a finger. Shards of pain drove deep into his head. Even his teeth felt like they might jump out of his gums. He pushed himself into a sitting position with his grazed elbows and saw a pool of blood collecting around him on the floor. There was too much to be his, and when he noticed most of it was already dried, he scuttled away as quickly as he could. He took out the knife, ripped a sleeve from his T-shirt, and held it to his nose, wincing at the pressure.

As Michael's rag turned pink, the women broke their embrace and stood regarding each other with damp cheeks and red eyes.

"Jesus girl," the woman began. "I thought you'd be dead. Good Lord!"

Zanna tried to smile as the woman took her lightly by the hand and led her over to the red waiting room chairs, where they sat facing each other.

"Salema, what, why are you still here?" Zanna asked quietly.

The woman let out a long sigh and shook her heavy head slowly from side to side. "I don't know girl, be honest with you. I don't know. When this *thing*, this disaster," she shook her palms towards the heavens, "when it happened, well I decided to stay, to help the poor souls here, Lord knows they don't have much help at the best of time. So, so I stayed and..." She trailed off slowly and her eyes became a picture of compassion, aware of what she would have to tell Zanna.

"They're dead aren't they?" Zanna said calmly.

Salema reached out a warm hand and gripped the girl's shoulder.

"They're dead," Zanna repeated. "Answer me."

"Hush girl, hush," Salema said softly. "When the thing

happened, it, it took your poor mother, Zanna," she paused; expecting tears or anger, but Zanna remained impassive as she waited for her to continue.

"It took your mother, and of course everything was confusion. Your father, he tried to call you, he tried so hard, but he couldn't reach you. Nobody could reach anybody. "She's a smart girl," your father said, "I raised her smart and she'll know what to do," he said. Said he could feel it in his bones that you would be ok."

Zanna shook with silent tears and as Michael watched, he felt something warm mingle with the sticky blood on his face.

Salema continued. "So your father, he decided to stay here, he said there was nothing he could do, for, for his girls now, but he could help his patients. We...we buried your mother in the square, under the oak tree, you know the one. Well, it was mayhem. Your father and me, we stayed here, and the next day, well some of the patients came back, some didn't. Most o' those who did, it had tipped over the edge, and well one man, he try to break into the pharmacy, but your father stopped him. This man had a knife though and..." Salema's voice quivered and she blew angry tears from her lips.

"The man, he stabbed your father Zanna, and I rushed at the man, I don't know what I was thinking, but somehow I got the knife and, oh Lord, I killed that wretched soul!"

Michael's stomach leapt into the back of his throat and he stood and stumbled away quickly, swaying as though drunk, as he crashed through a door into an empty room. He knelt and vomited a thin watery stream, blood mixing with his vomit, a tang of metal and sour milk in his mouth.

His blood was the same colour as the sunset over the fields the night Jim had appeared singing 'Run Rabbit Run'.

In the waiting room, Salema continued, both women oblivious to Michael, both reliving Salema's story, Zanna's imagination filling in all the details. She watched her father die in front of her, his life slowly bleeding out of him.

"There's nothing I could have done girl, nothing..." Salema said, a hand on either of Zanna's arms, shaking her gently.

"It's ok Salema, it's ok..." Zanna repeated until Salema stopped shaking her and her heavy arms fell lifeless by her side.

Zanna took one of her large hands in hers. "I know you did all you could. Thank you."

Salema wiped her eyes and nodded to herself. She sniffed and let out a low cough. "Thank you child, you know I did what I could. Afterwards..." she paused as Michael returned and stood in the doorway, leaning against the frame, his white T-shirt tie-dyed red.

Zanna nodded for Salema to continue. "I buried him next to your mother. He always complained about her spending her lunches under that tree, but I think he would have wanted to be next to her. Then, well I didn't know what to do, I had to stay here. I had blood on my hands and some o' the patients kept coming back. Your father, and I know your mother too, just wanted to help people and, with them gone, I thought it best I carry on, so I been here looking after people, but no one's come now for two days and, to tell the truth, I'm about to leave."

"We've got someone you can help," Michael said from the doorway.

His voice came out thick and clammy and he sniffed and turned to spit a glob of bloody phlegm into the corridor. "Our friend, Judith, we don't know what's wrong with her, but she's quite ill, can you take a look?"

Salema rose from her seat, a hand resting on Zanna's shoulder. "Seems you've made some friends girl. This one looks a bit young, but maybe a few years he'll be all right, eh?"

There was no trace of laughter in her voice and neither Zanna nor Michael gave any sort of reaction.

"I'll help your friend," Salema said. "If I can."

Michael felt dizzy and he gripped the brass handrail loosely as he descended the steps.

David jumped out as he neared the car. "Bloody hell, Michael. What happened?"

"Just a misunderstanding," Michael called. "Help me get Judith inside."

David clapped a hand on his shoulder. "Are you ok?"

Michael nodded.

"Her parents?"

Michael shook his head.

They carried Judith between them, each with one of her arms draped over their shoulders. Judith could only manage minuscule steps, but together they managed to get her inside and down the corridor. Salema was waiting for them in the reception area, but Zanna was nowhere to be seen.

"Come on through to the back room," Salema said, and they followed her through to the room, where they laid Judith down on the examining bed.

David sat down on a desk cluttered with open textbooks and Michael went to a sink in the corner of the room and began to wipe the blood from his face with dry paper towels.

Salema listened to Judith's heartbeat and then shone a small torch in her eyes. All the while Judith kept trying to sit up, Salema gently forcing her back down with a hand on her shoulder.

"What's your name dear?" Salema asked.

"Judith, Judith Allen," she replied quickly. "What is going on?"

"Nothing to worry about, just a checkup," Salema said.

Judith lay still on the black leather bed and seemed to sink back into her own world again.

"I'm sorry I hit you," Salema said as she probed around in Judith's mouth. It took Michael a second to realise she was speaking to him. He lowered a paper towel from his nose.

"Oh, well...don't worry; I suppose you had no idea who I was."

"Still don't," Salema replied, "but if Zanna trusts you, then you must be ok. I only hit you because, well, you heard me tell Zanna about her father. Some of the patients here don't want help as much as they want to take all the drugs they can get. It's a blessing they've stopped turning up, really."

Salema rummaged in a drawer and took out a syringe and a small bottle of clear liquid. She drew the liquid into the syringe, let a few drops drip from the end and then injected it into Judith's arm, just inside her right elbow.

"Will she be ok?" David asked, standing up and taking a step towards the bed.

"She'll be ok, no need to stand up, Mr."

"My name's David," he said as he sat back down.

Michael waited for Salema to continue, but she didn't.

"I'm Michael by the way. What do you think is wrong with her?"

"Hmmm," Salema mumbled. "Nothing much, she's dehydrated. She needs food and drink; she's looking a bit frail. When did she last have a good meal?"

David and Michael both tried to remember.

"Last night," David said after a minute.

"Well," Salema continued, "she needs to be eating well, and regularly. I can stand a bit of hunger, maybe do me good, but she's skinny, she needs to be eating. Nothing much I can do, I'd like to put her on a drip, but you'd have to go to the hospital for that. I've given her an injection, some salts," she smiled at Michael and David, "things that are good for her. I'll give her some vitamin tablets; you could all do with them, I imagine. Other than that, she needs to rest a while and eat. You can all stay at my house tonight, it's not too far, little bit further without the tube, you understand, but I imagine you didn't walk all the way here, so we'll take your car. I'll do what I can for her today, but tomorrow I'm leaving."

"Thank you," David said, standing up.

"Thanks, Salema," Michael said as he scrunched up the

bloodied paper towels and threw them into a bin.

He winced as he twitched his nose. "I think this makes up for my nose." There was no trace of humour in his voice and no one laughed.

***

The sun had begun to slide behind the chimneys of the houses in the square and in its last hour, it seemed to shine brighter, deepening into a gold that shone from the wet pavement. The gate to the garden was directly opposite the clinic and, when Michael pushed it open, its creak was a whisper in the calm evening. A path led through the small garden and once he was beneath the trees, Michael was surrounded by the rich smell of damp earth. He passed the little playground and continued to where he could make out a large oak tree in the centre of the garden.

A sparrow stabbed at something in the grass ahead and flew off as Michael approached. He stopped walking and stood observing the girl beneath the oak tree. Her hair was brilliant gold, as though the last of the sun radiated from her, filling Michael's fingertips and toes with a warmth he had not felt since sunlight had radiated from another girl on a summer's day, forever ago.

The girl who stood with her head bowed in front of him could easily have been Her, or Zanna, Michael was not sure anymore. The two mounds of freshly dug earth could have been his parents, his sister. He should have buried them. He would bury them, beneath a tree like this. The boughs of the oak would keep them safe there, a living, protective head stone that would endure in their memory.

As if she had known somewhere inside her that he was there, and as if she were able to look inside him and know his thoughts, Zanna said, "Did you get a chance to bury them? Your parents?"

"No," Michael said, talking a few steps closer until he stood beside her.

A smell of some sort of flowers mingled with the smell of the rain on the leaves of the oak tree. "I will though, I will. When this is done."

They stood beside each other, two sets of eyes on the two mounds at their feet.

"They would have liked to be buried here," she said. "My parents, I mean."

"I'm sorry," Michael said. He did not touch her for fear that whatever it was that radiated from her might peer deep inside of him and know the way his muscles contracted and the blood flowed through his veins, and what he could feel in his bones.

"It's ok," she said. "I'm sorry too. For your parents...' She paused as another sparrow hopped lethargically across the mounds of earth at their feet.

"I'm sorry for everyone."

The breeze returned and shook the branches above them. A few loose leaves drifted down and settled lazily upon the graves. One day these mounds would be gone, grown over and forgotten. Even the oak tree would fall eventually, the buildings too, and then the last people, and then none of this would matter, Michael thought to himself. Zanna's fingers stroked his hand and a thousand nerve endings caught fire in his palm. She let out a single quiet laugh and Michael's chest contracted and forced the air from his lungs.

"It's my birthday tomorrow," she said. "Twenty one."

Chapter Twenty-Two

Steam coiled slowly and steadily skywards from the wet streets of London, taking in every sight as it rose over doorways and above archways and statues and pillars, until it cooled, condensed and grouped together to be blown along on the breeze to another place that was hard to imagine for those below.

Figures lay slumped in the same wet streets. The pale morning sun woke the rats that slept, burrowed inside of the warm and rotting carcasses, and they began to scurry away down the alleyways and drains, chasing after the receding darkness. The streets were silent except for the steady hum of a car alarm that had screeched out its message like a crow for the past two days. Finally, like a dying tape, it slowed, the sound becoming grotesquely distorted in its final moments, the last call stretched out for what seemed like eternity until silence crept over it and the sound was instantly forgotten, as though it had never occurred.

In another part of the city tower blocks rose, charcoal-coloured from the concrete streets. A man stood in a window, yellow light filtering though the curtains which he had half drawn aside. He stood in his underwear, proud over the empty city below. A beep of an electric clock told him the time and he shook his head irritably. He turned his back to the window, his frame illuminated in silhouette. Amongst the cigarette burns of the worn and bare carpet lay two discarded and empty blankets. The man raised a hand to his face and nails combed the greasy grey stubble.

A second form stirred restlessly on the sofa, and a thin cry escaped her lips, as though she were in the midst of a bad dream. The man walked across to the sofa and held a bottle of water to the woman's lips. Without waking she drank and then rolled over.

The man placed a hand to her head. "Ssh," he whispered. "Ssh."

Elsewhere in the city, two shapes rode steadily along on stolen bicycles. A crow sat watching them from a streetlight, then hopped from its perch and flapped lazily after them, until it decided they were too big to be food.

Milky light filtered in through a pane of smooth and clear glass. Golden letters spelt something out in an arch across the windowpane, but what they said was no longer important. Dust motes cast long shadows, like spiders creeping across the smooth wooden floor. A mouse crouched perfectly still amongst the shadows and the dust and cocked its head slightly to one side, as though straining to hear something; as though it could sense something as imperceptible as the way the air on the opposite side of the glass moved apart, like a curtain, as something passed through. The mouse was certain and darted away to a corner of the room, its claws leaving tiny scratches in the wooden floor.

A slight shadow flickered across the same floor, like a moth fluttering around a candle. A spider's web appeared in the middle of the window, a tiny network of lines that grew and spread, interconnecting. The lines spread like icy fingers over the warm glass and then, as though molten, the center of the glass web bubbled and expanded and stretched out into the gloomy and dusty room. The glass had been pierced and something heavy pushed its way through, like a pin through a balloon, and clattered and rolled across the wooden floor, sending the mouse into further flight.

After this first object came a million clear shards like drops of rain, spreading through the air like diamond shrapnel, and then the golden lettering dropped from its place, and the

240

whole window fell and folded in upon itself like waves smashing against the rocks. The tiny diamonds and flecks of gold cut through the dust that coated the wooden floor, and for a millisecond, the air was a multitude of colours, the weak milky light reflected in a thousand angles, and then, in the next millisecond, everything fell and lay still and silent across the wooden floor, as though they had never known flight.

Michael stepped over the few shards of glass still held in place in the window. First one foot and then the other and he was inside the shop.

"You can open your eyes now," he called through the empty window. Outside, Zanna lifted her palms away from her eyes, her lips stretched in a grin that revealed her glittering teeth.

"I had a word with the owner, and he's agreed to let us have the shop to ourselves for a bit," Michael said, as he helped Zanna over the shards of the shattered window.

Glass crunched under her Converse as she stepped into the shop. "Oh Michael, you shouldn't have. What a simply wonderful present," she cried in her best received pronunciation, her tongue poking her cheek

Her lips darted quickly to Michael's cheek, then were gone again, gone with her into the gloomy depths of the dress shop. Michael stood for a moment, poking the broken brick with his toes, then crunched off over the shattered glass, following after her.

Outside, the sun rose higher and inside the shop the milky light became brighter; illuminating the colours of the dresses which hung on walls and rails. Michael wandered through the shop after Zanna, losing sight of her ahead as she explored the maze of fabric. When he caught up with her, he found her stood before a lone dress the colour of ivy that hung in solitude, demanding attention like something from a fairytale.

Zanna stroked the fabric. "This could be the one," she said, searching for a price tag. She held the tag between two fingers and then pulled it off in one swift movement. "It's definitely the one."

She turned to Michael. "What do you think?"

"Don't ask me," he said, "I never was good at shopping with girls. I, I like the colour though, I think it'll go nicely with... your hair."

Zanna raised her eyebrows and wrinkled her nose at the compliment. "Well, we'll see. Turn around pervert."

Michael did as he was told. Behind him, he heard Zanna's heavy leather jacket drop to the floor. He heard her struggle with her shoes, swearing under her breath. He heard her unbutton her jeans. He ached with the urge to turn around and pull her to him and be absorbed into her. He dug his fingers into his palms so hard that he thought he might draw blood.

He scanned the shop for a distraction and caught a glimpse of her reflected in a mirror, half hidden amongst the crowd of dresses. A golden back flexed as two slender and perfect arms raised the dress above a head of golden hair and pulled it down over the soft curve where her back melted into white cotton.

The reflection turned to face him and Michael quickly shook his head away. He took a deep breath in an attempt to calm his runaway heartbeat.

"Well, have a look then," Zanna called.

He turned reluctantly towards her, hoping she might not notice in the still gloomy shop. The dress hung to her, holding her proudly as though she were carved from stone, her figure too perfect to be natural. Beneath a smooth stomach, the green material flowed loosely about her thighs and as she stepped forward the dress swayed and rose slightly, revealing a freckle hidden on her right inner thigh.

She stood before him, barefoot in the dust. Michael stood dumbly, unable to find words or even remember what language he was looking for them in.

"Do you hate it?" Zanna asked, her smile faltering slightly, her hands reaching behind her back to where the zip was.

"No!" Michael cried. "I mean, no, don't take it off, you look beautiful," he said, his attention fixed on the wall behind her shoulder.

Zanna's smile held firm as she tucked her legs under her and bent to pick up her jacket. She stood up and swung the jacket over her shoulder, her Converse in hand.

"Michael, come here," she said.

"What?" he asked, his voice little more than a whisper.

His feet took him forwards, unsure where to stop. Zanna pulled him towards her and brought her mouth close to his neck. Her lips parted at his ear.

"You're such a wet blanket," she whispered in a voice that made him lightheaded, and then she skipped away, laughter echoing back over her shoulder as she disappeared into the maze of dresses.

Michael stood for a few moments and then trudged after her.

***

Inside the tower block, time ticked slowly onwards. The man sat by the window as the light outside changed from grey to pink to red to a sallow yellow; the sun's movements in unison with those of the clock that had slipped into double figures some time ago. Occasionally, the man rose and looked out of the window, over the maze of the estate. He was able to make out figures moving below, but they were too far away for him to tell whether they spoke to each other or what they said.

The woman on the sofa slept peacefully. At one point in the grey dawn, a woman had entered the room carrying a suitcase in her broad hand. She smiled at the man and then knelt down by the woman on the sofa and injected her with something. She straightened up and emptied a brown paper bag onto a coffee table in the middle of the room. A collection of plastic pill bottles jumbled out.

243

"Make sure she takes one, two of these a day. They're antibiotics and vitamins." The man nodded. Then the woman picked up her suitcase, walked to the door and nodded at the man who had followed her halfway across the room.

"Make sure she gets some food," she said and then she stepped through the doorway. As an afterthought she added, "Look after Zanna."

Then Salema was gone.

Afterwards, David paced the room, intermittently checking on Judith. He read the label of each pill bottle twice and lined them up along the table. He began to remember his old life in London, far away from somewhere like this. He started to remember the time since he had last seen his wife, his daughter. Maybe they were alive. It didn't matter to him though; he knew they would be better off with him dead. He would not look for them. He clenched his fists, where the hell were those kids? It was always kids causing problems.

He grew restless and began pulling out drawers and moving furniture around until he found what he was looking for. He drank what was left in the bottle in one go. He felt better now; fierce. Judith stirred but did not wake. She would be all right if her left her for a minute.

David slipped out the door and pulled it gently shut behind him, so that if anyone walked past they would not think of going in. The corridor was pitch black except for where light bled in from the open doorways that led into other flats. He picked his way carefully along the corridor, unsteady in the darkness and with the drink in him.

He found the staircase. With his left hand on the wall, he took one step after another, round, round in the darkness until the wall suddenly ended, and he staggered, blinking, into a bright corridor.

David walked steadily onwards, out of the estate. He searched about for somewhere to get food for Judith. A corner shop appeared to the right; the shutters smashed and caved in.

David approached warily, straining his eyes to try to see into the shop. Black figures moved in the darkness, like dogs suddenly woken and alert. David walked on; he was not fierce. Sometimes he had had to be, but now he was tired.

He walked onwards through empty streets that were never built to be so quiet. He passed by people every now and then but most looked away when he tried to make eye contact. Some smiled helplessly and opened their mouths as if to speak, but they did not, and passed by without a sound, blown along on the wind.

"They know," David thought to himself. "They know." He could feel himself becoming fierce again and the next people he passed lowered their heads, dug their hands deeper into their pockets and hurried along.

He had not passed a person for twenty minutes when he spotted a small supermarket ahead, its doors wedged open with a trolley. David clambered over the trolley and picked up a basket. A rich blend of rotting aromas met him inside the shop.

Bodies lay scattered across the aisles, and David clasped his shirt firmly over his mouth and nose as he negotiated his way past. The smell seeped in through the fabric and his stomach churned until the sickly taste of whiskey came back to his mouth. Clouds of fruit flies rose from a sickly sweet pile of rotting fruit that David had to run past as something rose in this throat.

He turned down the next aisle and stopped suddenly. Slowly, he began to retrace his steps. The dog looked half-dead; ribs showed through patches of mottled yellow and brown fur and fresh, raw, wounds criss-crossed its muzzle. The dog looked as though it had had to fight to survive. It crouched there, gnawing on a chunk of meat wrapped around a bone, unaware of David's presence. Its teeth scrapped against the bone as it ate, and the hairs on David's arms stood on end.

Suddenly, as though catching a scent on the wind, the dog

stopped its gnawing and glanced sharply in David's direction, its neck cracking with the speed of its movement. David ran, but his leg caught on the body of a child on the floor, and he fell and landed tangled up with the corpse.

The dog was a foot away when David's hand closed around some sort of bottle. He grasped the bottle neck tightly and swung the weapon up to meet the animal's head, with such force that the bottle shattered and the dog fell limply to the ground as shards of glass and red wine fell on David like a blood red rain.

He pushed the child's body quickly to the side and stood reeling, the whiskey in his system moving his head separately to his body. The reek of wine was nauseating and he swallowed quickly; once, twice, three times to stop himself from vomiting. The dog lay on its side, shards of glass protruding from its face, its tongue flapping slowly as a puddle of blood dribbled from its mouth. Its legs kicked lifelessly across the floor, the long nails scraping like nails on a chalkboard.

David took what little was left un-spoilt from the shop and ran, shaking, along the streets. His legs guided him back to Judith but his mind was not on the journey.

He passed by a primary school, children dead in the playground, no parents to pick them up. He reeled away from the scene and stumbled across the road, rolling drunkenly across a car bonnet, and dropping some of the food. He pressed onwards and found himself in a park. There was a small fountain that was still working, the clear water rising in streams and falling in slow curtains.

David stopped and stared at the way the water was being pumped round and round. He stripped off his sodden shirt and dropped the carrier bags to the floor, before clambering into the water and letting himself slip under the surface. The water swirled around him and small bubbles like the breath of tiny fish tickled his skin. He saw his daughter appear towards him from the depths and she smiled at him with her beautiful smile. He reached out his hand to hers, and then his head crowned the water, and he emerged back into the weak sunlight, rivulets of water running down his face and chest. He was breathing heavily now, but his head was clear.

David brushed the heavy wet hair back from his face and climbed slowly out of the fountain.

"I've been gone too long" he said to himself, and, leaving the soiled shirt where it was, he picked up the bags of food and set off back to Judith.

He found the estate easily enough and was surprised to find Judith sitting up on the sofa as he entered the flat. She squinted at the dim doorway and then recoiled at the shirtless man standing there.

Seeing the look of confusion on her face brought David back to reality. "Judith, it's me, David."

She squinted at him and spoke as though remembering something that happened a long time ago. "David? Oh, yes...where have you been?"

She glanced wearily about the room, as though unsure of where she was, before deciding that maybe she did recognise the place and had perhaps just forgotten. "I woke up alone David."

David came into the room and sat down opposite her. A stale reek of whiskey filled the air. "I've brought you some food Judith, you're a bit poorly. You need to eat."

Judith strained her neck to get a better look at the bags. "Oh, ok then. Is Emily here? She will be hungry too."

David scratched his head, and scanned the empty room for an answer, before speaking slowly. "No, Emily isn't here at the minute Judith...

She'll be back soon though, and so will Michael and Zanna."

Judith's face sank into confusion, as though she were hearing two new names. "Oh," she said, as she settled back into the folds of the sofa. "Oh, ok."

Chapter Twenty-Three

A drop of sweat fell on to silver handlebars, distorting the reflection of the graying sky above. Michael peddled onwards, blowing warm air over his sweat soaked face. The designer shirt he had stolen earlier stuck to his back in a wet mess. Balancing the handlebars with one hand, he wiped the hair back from where it stuck to his brow.

Zanna cycled silently on beside him, her green dress billowing behind her, looking as though she had been lifted directly from the pages of a catalogue, and was only there to sell dresses or bicycles. Michael saw her cycling along sunny French lanes, tall poplars rising on either side of her, the sound of the sea breaking calmly in the near-distance.

Amongst the grime-covered streets of London, the smells of decaying bins, week-old corpses, and the acidic, ashy smell of chemical fires, Zanna was as foreign as the sun in the depths of winter. Against the hopeless dreariness of what the city had become, Zanna in her billowing green was nature and vitality. As the walls of the city closed around them, and roads led the pair back on themselves in endless circles, it seemed this force of nature would never have the chance to grow.

The pair had not spoken for an hour, and tension had risen between them like storm clouds as the humidity rises. Michael could sense that behind Zanna's eyes the storm was about to break, but he knew that the relief it would bring would be beautiful. He had long since given up asking her where they were and believed that despite her increasingly frustrated expression and outbursts of swearing, she would get them back to the others.

Zanna glanced up at the grey blanket overhead and brought her bike to a sharp stop, as though suddenly struck by an epiphany. Michael, caught unawares, struggled to stop in time and caught himself painfully on the handlebars. The warm sweat that lay like a second skin over his body suddenly turned to ice, and for a second, he thought he might faint. He bent forward, pushing warm air between his lips, as though trying to blow the pain away. The feeling passed like a cloud over the sun and Michael sat back on the seat, feeling foolish and hoping Zanna had not witnessed his injury.

She hadn't. Zanna stood, serene in her birthday dress, without a single mark of fatigue to be found on her forehead. They had come to a crossroads and as Zanna turned her head slowly from side to side, biting her lips and Michael noticed the way her bottom lip turned pale under the pressure of the white teeth before the blood rushed back, like a burst of solar flare.

Behind them, the sun sent its own flames glinting over towers and buildings. A dull glow smoldering on ash-choked windows and smoke stained steel. Before them, a row of buildings, reduced to orange embers, throbbed like a dying heartbeat.

"This way," Zanna said, as though speaking to herself.

They cycled onwards, everything unfamiliar to Michael, except a few streets he thought he recognised from films. Films and television programmes had formed his concept of London, but now he was here, his reality was far more unbelievable than anything he had seen on a screen. Michael had almost become accustomed to seeing bodies in the streets. He had tried to forget what they were; forget about his family, his friends, and all of the people he had once known; people like Jim. He told himself it was the usual state of affairs that roads should be blocked by cars and debris, that all of the shop windows had been smashed in, that the streets should be so quiet, and that his stomach should constantly twist and turn of its own accord.

"I know where we are," Zanna called, looking back over her shoulder. "We're about twenty minutes away."

It was hard for Michael to make out her expression in the dusk light, but he was sure that in her voice he caught a note of relief. They passed a roundabout with a towering statue in the middle, now hung with streamers and toilet roll and pictures of missing people; pleas for help that no one was around to read. In the broken streets, they had seen no one all day, as though the people who were left were afraid of the sunlight, and hid deep inside the buildings that had escaped being gutted by fire.

They would not have been able to hide from the sunlight in the tunnels of the Underground because, suddenly stretching across the road, was a mighty tear in the pavement that sank down to reveal the empty tracks of the Tube. A mighty gouge had been ripped out of the belly of London, the skin punctured by a train that had somehow burst through the surface and now lay sideways, half in and half out of the crater, disappearing into a building at the side of the road like a great white snake sliding leisurely into its den.

The crater was immense and seemed to have spread like a tumor, eating everything it came across. Cars balanced on the far side of the toothless gap and, down in the pit, more vehicles were tangled in the coils of the train. Splashes of red painted the windows of the vehicles, and the feeling in Michael's chest would not let him pretend that the shapes he could see were not bodies.

Zanna's bike fell to the floor with a soundless clatter and her legs took her to the edge of the pit. Michael swung a shaking leg over his bike and let it fall behind him as he walked slowly towards her.

Zanna looked like a woman about to jump from a tall building, hoping for something better to meet her in the air and take her somewhere else. Michael expected her to be upset, but when he reached her, she stood calmly, staring down into the crater, as though it was a painting in a gallery that she was yet to make her mind up about.

"I'm sorry," Michael heard himself saying.

He did not know why he had said it, and it had seeped through his lips without him even knowing what he was sorry for. Zanna turned to him, her eyes dry, but alert and searching. Her mouth quivered as though angry words were struggling to form there. Michael took her hand in his and Zanna opened her mouth quickly as though gasping for breath. Every fibre of Michael's body was burning with the need to be close to her, as though if they could just connect, a current would flow through them and right the world's wrongs.

Without thinking, he pulled her towards him, her body firm but unresisting, her lips parting slowly to receive his. Their fingers ran through soft strands of hair as their arms enclosed each other's bodies, pulling each other as close as they could. In that moment, Michael felt as though he could never be close enough to this miraculous girl. As suddenly as it had happened, they fell apart and stood facing one another, struggling to catch their breaths. Michael saw the tears in Zanna's eyes and could not help but mirror her emotions. They stared into each other for what could have been a second, or an hour, and between them passed a lifetime of understanding.

A cry split the silence. A savage call of "Whoop! Whoop!" boomed along the streets in stark contrast to the deathly silences of the afternoon.

Zanna, startled by the noise, stepped backwards instinctively and stumbled on the edge of the chasm, sending an avalanche of rocks to chase each other down into the depths. Michael moved quickly and caught Zanna's arm as she wavered on the edge of oblivion. He pulled her to safety as the cry echoed from the buildings around them.

"Woop woop!" came the cry again, like the hunting call of some tribe, like television's idea of Red Indians on their way to scalp cowboys.

Reality returned to them, bringing an undercurrent of fear.

"Zanna," Michael said.

She was unresponsive and he shook her arm lightly.

"Zanna! Do you know the way home?" he asked, searching her eyes for an answer.

They were the same sharp eyes that Michael had first seen from the other end of a cricket bat, and he knew that she was back with him.

"Yes. Let's go," Zanna said.

The cries continued and were joined by wolf-whistles and howls from among the encroaching darkness. A fire sprung up in a window across the chasm, and three black shadows were silhouetted in the light. Something arched from the window and was suspended in the flicker of the flames, before it fell and landed with a clang, somewhere in the depths of the pit.

They set off on the bikes, burning through the streets with new energy, pursued by the catcalls and cries of savages. Half-imagined figures moved in the shadows behind the wrecked cars and chased after them on giant's legs. Fires sprung up in windows and alleyways, and the flames cast the shadows into further darkness. Silhouettes moved in windows and doorways, some turning to watch the two young people as they rode quickly through the streets. Others threw whatever was to hand after them, without really knowing why they did so.

Michael and Zanna flew along, winding amongst the people who spilled out into the streets, emerging from the buildings to a new nocturnal life. They weaved in and out of the wandering souls, like pigs running through the jungle with hunters hot on their trail. The winding, never-ending streets became sinister in the darkness, the people the personification of the dark soul of the city.

Michael pedaled onwards with all of his thoughts focused on the green material that billowed like a flag in front of him, spreading like the wings of some mighty bird guiding him home. Then, out of the darkness rose the very tower blocks they had left that morning, rising like granite statues against the deepening blue and crimson of the sky.

Chapter Twenty-Four

They navigated the gray tunnels and alleyways of the estate, leaving their bikes behind and running hand in hand to the tower. Shapes moved in the darkness; figures distorted by the glare of the fires that had suddenly sprung up, throwing orbs of light across the concrete landscape.

Once inside the tower, they made their way slowly from floor to floor, the small yellow bulb of Zanna's lighter guiding them. Scratches of graffiti shone in the dull light, like hieroglyphics in a tomb.

"How far up do we have to go?" Michael whispered into the darkness.

"We're on the seventh," Zanna's voice replied from nowhere and everywhere. They fumbled onwards, feeling the shapes of the steps in the darkness with their toes.

A third voice met them from the blackness above, an old voice, frail but unafraid. "Hello?" it asked, reverberating down the stairwell and echoing from the walls, as if the tower itself was speaking to them.

"Shh!" Michael hissed, pushing Zanna back against the wall.

"Get off me," she whispered.

She pushed past him, leaving Michael momentarily fixed to the spot as the light disappeared around a corner ahead. Michael hesitated for a second, and then stumbled blindly up the stairs and after her as the light was swallowed by the darkness.

Michael's foot caught on something and the cold edge of a concrete step sawed into his shin and sent him flailing forwards into the darkness. He lay sprawled across the cold stairs, his hands and back burning with a hundred grazes. He sat up, reached down to feel his knee, wet with blood, and then scrambled up the steps towards the light, on all fours, clawing and grabbing at the concrete like an animal.

The light grew nearer and Michael pulled himself to his feet. The yellow glow flickered and ballooned and doubled in strength to reveal an old man, with deep wrinkles and a narrow nose, holding a candle. He stood as an antiquated sentinel, a centuries-old guardian of the tower. Time had made him a part of his surroundings, as though he too was made of concrete. The candle shook slowly in a hand that looked like the talon of some ancient bird, flecked with drops of dried and drying wax.

Zanna stepped from beside the man and took Michael by his scuffed hand, pulling him roughly up the remaining stairs to where they stood.

The old man's lips cracked like old paint as they drew back into a toothy grin. Michael did his best to smile back in the darkness, but wondered if the old man could even see him. The man took a step to the side and, reaching out his free hand, he opened a door that appeared out of the blackness behind him. Candle light flooded into the stairwell from the doorway.

Michael peered into the new corridor and saw candles rising like stalagmites from the cold floor, throwing eerie columns of shadow against the walls, transforming the passage into some long-forgotten cave.

The man turned and smiled again at Zanna and Michael, and then reached his head into the corridor.

"Anya," he called softly, and this time warmness replaced the frailty in his voice. "Anya, come here."

The light grew stronger around the doorway and a small girl appeared in a dirty white dress, carrying a candle at arm's length in front of her, like a gift.

"Anya, these are some new friends, come on. We're going to their flat."

Zanna led the way up the remaining stairs, the old man behind her, Anya following obediently behind him, with Michael bringing up the rear. They moved in a bubble of light, protected from the darkness. They reached the seventh floor and the light overflowed into the corridor and sprinted to try to reach the dark lengths, but fell flat before it made it, leaving the far depths of the floor in a deeper darkness.

As Zanna led them along to Salema's flat, the old man turned to Michael and held out a wax-splattered hand. "Hello young man, my name is Harold."

Michael thought his voice was like the rustle of leaves in autumn.

"And who might you be?" Harold asked.

"I'm Michael," he said, shaking the ancient hand. "Do you want me to take that candle for you?"

The man winked at him. "Oh no, I'm quite all right."

Zanna opened the door and they stepped through into Salema's flat. Moonlight shone through the open window and turned everything a spectral shade of grey. Someone had lit a hundred tea lights that were scattered about the room on tables and bookshelves and windowsills, as though venerating the uncountable dead.

"Come in," Zanna said to the new guests. "Please, sit down. I'll find you some food."

She disappeared through a beaded curtain into the kitchen and a sound of clattering and rummaging could be heard. David was nowhere to be seen, and it was only when Judith rose, groaning, from under covers on the sofa, that Michael realised someone else was in the room. The figure rising, as if from the grave, startled him and he instinctively reached for the knife in his waistband, before he realised there was no danger.

Harold set his candle amongst the tea lights on the coffee

table and sat down in a deep armchair, scooping Anya up into his arms with surprising strength. The child, Michael thought, could have been no more than six years-old, but she was stocky and looked as if she had the makings of a heavy girl.

"Hmm, Michael, Michael is that you?" came Judith's voice from the sofa where she had propped herself up against a bed of cushions.

Michael went across to her and, for the first time, felt complete compassion towards this woman. Her skin was dry and leathery in the grey moonlight and her cheeks were hollow, as though she had endured a famine since he had last seen her, just that morning.

"I'm cold Michael," Judith said through clattering teeth.

"Ok, Judith, I'll cover you up," Michael said, and pulled a sheet over her, wrapping it around her shoulders, which felt slight and boney beneath her shawl.

"Thank you," Judith whispered, and she smiled at him with a genuineness that, up until this point, Michael had yet to encounter in her.

"Just try to rest, Judith," he said softly as he reached out a hand to touch her brow.

Michael brought his hand away quickly, surprised at the heat. It felt as though someone had lit a fire behind her forehead that was trying to consume her. He found a half-full water bottle on the floor beside the sofa and held it up to her lips.

"Here, Judith, drink this, it will help."

"I couldn't Michael, I'm full of water."

Michael began to pour the water slowly into her mouth until the bottle was empty. "It'll help," he repeated.

"Michael," she said, suddenly grasping his hand in hers, "you're an angel."

Michael smiled, and, unsure what to say, stood up and walked over to the window.

Harold and Anya were sitting motionless in the chair. The

silence in the room was cut only by the clatter that still echoed from the kitchen. Harold looked about uneasily and spoke.

"Hello, I'm Harold, and this is my granddaughter, Anya." He smiled enthusiastically at Judith, but she had fallen back into fevered dreams and broken mumblings were the only reply she could give.

Michael walked over to shake Anya's hand. "Hello Anya, nice to meet you. How old are you?"

She smiled and fidgeted in Harold's lap.

"Don't be shy girl," Harold said, his voice cracking as he laughed. "Speak up."

"I'm six," Anya said in a voice that was little more than a whisper.

"Six? Wow," Michael offered. He could not think of anything more to say to the child.

At that moment, Zanna emerged from the kitchen carrying a plate piled with sandwiches.

"Cheese sandwiches," she said to everyone, but no one in particular. "I'm afraid the bread's a little stale, but we have plenty of water to wash it down with, so help yourselves."

Zanna offered the plate to Harold and his narrow fingers sprung quickly into action, collecting a mound of sandwiches that he stacked neatly beside him on the chair arm.

"Thank you ever so much, we've just been eating tinned tuna haven't we Anya?" Anya stared miserably at the floor and did not answer.

"Have a sandwich Anya," Harold offered.

"I don't like cheese!" Anya shouted, her voice erupting like thunder out of a clear sky.

"Anya..." Zanna began, but Judith, whose tone seemed to suggest she had miraculously recovered from her illness, cut her off.

"Emily! Eat your sandwich and let's not have any more misbehaving."

Zanna and Michael shared a wide-eyed glance. Anya began

to eat her sandwich, too confused to argue.

Harold had not seemed to notice what had happened and began to tell them about his life as Judith fell back into restless turmoil on the sofa.

"I've lived in these flats since I was thirty, in nineteen seventy-four. They'd just built them then and my wife and I, God rest her soul, we loved the idea of living in a fancy new place. Of course, it didn't last long, and by the eighties we were having all sorts of trouble with youths. Blacks and yellows."

Harold covered Anya's ears and lowered his voice conspiringly. "Her mother married a spade, that's why, well, she's brown. Of course, he soon cleared off, and her mother with him. Some say it's not my business to raise a little brown girl, but they can be damned!"

He rose slightly from the chair, almost dislodging Anya, who had to cling to his trousers to stop herself falling to the floor. "Yes, she is my flesh and blood, and we've been doing a fine job of looking after each other since all this, this... business happened, haven't we my dear? Hmm?"

Anya was not paying attention as she slowly and steadily worked her way through Harold's stack of sandwiches.

Michael began to wonder where David was. Surely he should be here, looking after Judith? She was delirious; she seemed almost crazy. Why had David left her? Perhaps they should have told them they were sneaking out that morning. They had not planned to be gone so long, though. Michael had just wanted Zanna to have a good time on her birthday.

His ponderings didn't get much further because, just then, the door swung open and a shape resembling David leaned loosely against the doorframe. He trod heavily into the room, as though dragging invisible chains behind him, and left the door wide open, the coldness of the corridor trailing in after him.

David shuffled into the room with the detached

259

concentration of the drunk, and stood gripping the back of Judith's sofa, veins bulging in his forearms. His hair was slicked back, as though wet, but he looked dirty and his face was a mess of red cuts and grey stubble.

Harold had stopped speaking and Anya nestled herself into the old man's body for protection. David scanned the room, looking as though he was about to erupt into a fit of anger and then, suddenly, like the change of a tide, the anger washed from his face.

"Hello there," he said to the corner where Harold's chair sat. "I'm David."

David smiled and looked about the room, skimming everyone's faces. His eyes finally came to rest on Michael.

"Michael, can I have a word please?" he said, before walking steadily out of the room and into the kitchen.

Michael rose to follow him. As he passed Zanna, her hand brushed his arm. Michael met her eyes and, without speaking, told her everything would be ok. Zanna smiled thinly and let go of his arm.

Michael made his way through the small kitchen and out into the corridor on the other side. There were only a few tea lights here, resting on shelves, like islands of light in a dark sea. There were two other doors in the corridor and one stood open. A glimmer of silver moonlight spilled into the corridor. Michael entered the bedroom to find David sitting on the edge of the bed, his head in his hands. Michael leaned against a dresser in a corner of the room. David seemed not to have noticed his presence.

"David," he said quietly. "Are you all right?"

David sighed slowly, his head still in his hands. After a moment, he raised his head slowly and met Michael's eyes. In the gloom of the bedroom, Michael saw that although the eyes stared into his own, they were not looking at him. Whatever was behind those eyes was miles away.

"Why are you all scratched and cut up?" Michael asked, his

voice returning to its normal volume, scaring him in the uncomfortable silence of the room.

"Where have you been?" David asked flatly.

"Yeah, I'm sorry...it's Zanna's birthday. We thought we'd go out and get something for her. You know, a present. We should have told you, I know, but you and Judith were both fast asleep. We didn't plan to get back so late, you wouldn't believe how lost we got," he laughed nervously. "I got this shirt; it's about ruined now, though. I've been sweating in it all day."

David sat back, straightening his back and Michael thought he could hear the bones sliding over one another.

"Things like that don't matter Michael, clothes...money. Especially not now that all this shit has happened. What matters is staying together."

Michael could smell the whiskey, the sweet scent rising like warm water around him. He could almost taste it in the air as David spoke.

"I know none of that matters, David, but I just thought it would be nice for her birthday."

David smiled a rickety smile that hung unnaturally, like a broken children's toy that someone had put back together the wrong way.

"You thought you could get some sex. You thought you could just leave the two old bastards behind and go and fuck your young girl."

The words stung Michael like a sharp slap to the face. "Hang on! It's not like that. We're not trying to leave you behind. Or Judith, we just thought it wouldn't matter if we were out for a few hours. Her parents are dead for God's sake!"

David continued, ignoring what Michael said. "And then you bring those two back? That old man and that, that girl."

David roughly massaged his temples with his fingertips, as though trying to squash an insect that crawled beneath his skin.

"I want them gone Michael," he said, as though chastising one of his students who had just received their last warning.

"What are you talking about David? Why can't they stay? They've done nothing wrong? We have food!"

David rose suddenly and stood swaying on shaking legs. He felt fierce again.

"I want them gone!" he shouted, and the silence that followed was absolute.

In the lounge, a chorus of "Happy Birthday to you..." began, the sound quietly and faintly trickling down the corridor, like a music box that has begun to wind down.

David paced the room, rubbing his hands together and shaking his head. Michael spat on the floor in disgust.

"I trusted you," Michael said through gritted teeth. "I thought you'd help us all, but you're nothing but a useless alcoholic."

David laughed. "Oh, I'm plenty more besides."

"I saw you, you know," Michael continued, "in the supermarket, I woke up in the night and you were gone, and all that was left was an empty whiskey bottle. That's why you don't want to look for your family isn't it, David? They don't want you."

David turned and took a step towards Michael, a fist half raised in front of him. Michael stepped back into the dresser, which shook as ornaments, and photo frames fell over.

David stopped and seemed to regain his composure. A flush of colour washed through his cheeks in the grey light. "Do not talk about my family."

The words were almost a plea, and, for the first time, Michael could see how pathetic the man in front of him really was.

"I'm sorry," he said as David sat back down on the bed.

"You know Michael, you really should fuck Zanna; she wants you to by the way. I can tell. But then, I always did think girls were interested when they weren't, so maybe I'm not the best person to listen to."

David laughed at a joke that Michael did not understand.

"David, come on, why don't you sleep it off? We've got some cheese sandwiches if you want one?"

Like a light switch, David's mood changed again and his face distorted into a sneer.

"Ah yes, Michael, good idea. You're the boss!"

Michael rolled his eyes and turned to leave the room when David reached under the bed and pulled out the rifle Michael had been carrying with him for so long.

"If you aren't the boss, why would you have this? It's the Wild West out there Michael, we're on a new frontier! Are you going to shoot some Indians with it?"

Michael did not have the energy to accuse David of going through his things, or to ask for the rifle back, instead he simply said, "I don't want to kill anyone."

David smiled. "Good, I couldn't see you hurting anyone, Michael, you're too lacking in direction for that. You should use it to hunt rabbits."

Immediately '*Run Rabbit Run*' began to play on loop in Michael's mind and he almost had to shout to hear his voice over the song.

"What did you say?" he asked animatedly.

David smiled a slow smile, but said nothing. Michael walked to the doorway.

"Michael!" David shouted. "Don't forget this!"

He flung the rifle clumsily towards Michael, forcing him to drop to one knee to catch it, half-afraid that it would accidentally go off. Michael stood up, held the rifle to his chest, and walked out of the room, closing the door behind him.

***

The rifle shone a dull bronze in the candle light. Michael

held it as though it were some relic from his past, half-remembered, but a past that was his, nonetheless. He no longer felt like the scared boy who had taken it from a corpse in a field. Now, Michael knew that taking the rifle had been the right decision, but it was one he wished he hadn't made, because he knew that not too far in the future would be a time when he would have to use it.

He stood for a moment in the calm of the kitchen amongst dirty crockery, a picture of Salema and what could have been her family on the wall, looking out with eyes full of life. Dead flies lay in breadcrumbs on the sideboard. The linoleum floor was dotted with sporadic cigarette burns, and an ashtray balancing on a shelf was piled high with long cold butts.

Michael leaned on the rifle and stared at the picture of Salema's family, but he could not see them. All he could see was a picture of six people; a family smiling on a holiday in Cornwall, a picture he had long since lost. They too were part of an old life, and when Michael thought of them, it was as if remembering a dusty box of toys from his childhood. Even when he thought of Her, the memories did not feel real, as though everything that had happened with Her, with his family too, had happened to a stranger whose life Michael could half remember.

Michael hid the rifle in the cupboard under the sink. He knew it wasn't a great hiding place, and that David could find it if he wanted to, but it was better to leave it there than to take it out into the lounge in front of the others. Michael passed through the beaded curtain and sent it clacking around him as he stepped into the lounge. Harold and Zanna were sitting in silence, watching Judith, who seemed to have regained her strength and was sitting upright on the sofa next to Anya.

Michael crossed the room to the window, catching Judith's attention.

"Michael, Michael, I want you to meet Emily!" she called.

Michael turned from the window slowly. Zanna shook her head at him. Harold was leaning forward in his chair, grinning as though eager to participate in the conversation. Anya sat quietly beside Judith, ignoring the woman's hand that stroked through her hair.

"Pardon me?" Michael asked.

A slight frown crossed Judith's brow, but was quickly swept away.

"This is my daughter Michael. Emily, say hello!"

Anya sat dumbly; unaware Judith was speaking to her, until Judith squeezed her lightly on the shoulder. The girl glanced over at Harold who nodded happily back at her.

"Hello," she managed in a voice in-between a sob and a murmur.

"Hello...Emily," Michael replied.

He turned back to the window before he was dragged further into the madness.

Outside, the sky had deepened to a charcoal grey. From high above the street, Michael could no longer hear the '*Woop woops*' that had chased them back to the tower. He began to wonder if he had imagined them, and realised that he wasn't sure of anything anymore. Maybe Anya actually was Judith's daughter, Emily. What did any of it matter?

From there, Michael could see no future for any of them. David had seemingly had a breakdown, as had Judith. Harold was a senile old man, and Anya a helpless little girl. Zanna's family was dead, and so was his. There was nothing and no one for any of them, but each other, and it looked as if their group was on the brink of collapse.

From amongst the grey shapes of the estate, something rose. A bright whistling light gliding up into the night air. The light was held for a moment by the cool darkness, before erupting into a flash of brilliant red, a flower that hung in the sky, and then fell to earth as fiery rain. A firework shot up, followed by another across to the right. As far as Michael could see, all across the city, fireworks rose in a cacophony of colours and screeches. The colours exploded like a thousand cannons over the city and the whistling as they shot skyward was like the screams of the city's dead as they flew towards the heavens.

Michael felt a hand on his shoulder and moved aside to let Zanna peer out of the window. He knew it was her without looking. He didn't even need to recognize the sweet smell of her skin, it was as though she touched some sort of extra sense that told Michael she was nearby, giving his body time to adjust accordingly, for his muscles to tighten and his stomach to contort as his mouth became dry.

"Fireworks," Zanna said quietly, like a child seeing them for the first time, but somehow knowing what they were.

"I remember them," she said, and Michael knew that she too felt his sense of disconnection, and that as long as she felt that way, as long as he wasn't alone, they'd both be all right.

Something caught Michael's eye in the streets below and pulled him roughly back to reality. A shadow moved slowly through the deeper, stationary, shadows of the estate. It climbed over burnt-out cars and jumped over bins and the bodies that littered the ground like leaves. Fireworks erupted nearby and shards of green and gold painted the scene below. The festive light illuminated this dark shadow amongst the thick smoke. It was a boy, skinny and dressed only in ragged trousers, like some savage orphan. In the few seconds that the firework shone above, Michael imagined he saw the boy's face streaked with soot and tears, eyes shining dimly from the black mask. Finger nails cracked and dirty, and elbows raw and bleeding. Michael felt the wound on his knee throb suddenly, and the small grazes on his hands and arms jumped into life, sending shivers of pain across his body.

Zanna caught Michael's wince, but rather than let her know he was in pain, Michael pointed to the boy down below, his finger squeaking against the glass.

"Look, a boy. A lost boy," he said.

Zanna drew herself nearer to the window. Her nose brushed it gently and her breath clouded glass.

"I can't see him," she said.

More fireworks exploded and shone blue light into the room. Michael knew that if any of them were to continue living, they'd have to act or they would fizzle out, just like the lights in the sky. He took hold of Zanna's wrist and pulled her away from the window so she faced him.

"We have to do something," he said quietly. "Salema's left, like she said she would, on to better things. Judith's gone mad and David; he's had some sort of breakdown; he's not the same person he was before. I don't trust him."

Michael wanted to tell her that together they could leave them all behind. Together they could run away somewhere, far from everyone else, far from cities and roads and people. They could live and be free, and there would be no one to ever tell them what to do.

As soon as the words formed in his mind, Michael felt sick. There was no way they could leave the others behind. Now, more than ever, they needed them. He turned away from the window and found that his grip on Zanna's wrist had slipped down to her hand. She grasped his firmly in return, as though it was a rope and she was in danger of falling.

Fireworks exploded directly outside the window and the room shone with red fire. Michael felt a sharp burning in his chest, as though the light was real fire and, suddenly, all of his thoughts were focused back in the room. Everything had changed in that flash of light. Judith sat alone on the sofa, rocking softly and crying into her palms, which she held clasped to her eyes.

"Emily! Oh Emily, come back dear!" Judith sobbed between tremors that shook her thin shoulders.

Immediately, Zanna was at her side and Judith began crying into the folds of Zanna's emerald dress as the younger girl rested a leather-jacketed arm around her shoulders.

Anya was nowhere to be seen, and neither was Harold.

"I'll find her," Michael shouted above the crackling of fireworks and Judith's sobs.

He moved towards the kitchen just as Harold emerged through the beaded curtain. Harold looked adrift, as though he too had just woken up, and wondered where it was that he now found himself.

"Anya's gone," he said in a voice that suggested he did not want to worry anyone. "Anya's gone," he repeated, and he smiled at Michael who took him by the arm and led him back to his chair, helping the old man to sink back into the cushions.

"She was frightened by the fireworks and ran off and, and now I don't know where she is," Harold said in the voice of a school boy trying to eradicate any blame as he confessed to the Head teacher.

"It's ok," Michael said, "I'll find her."

Before Harold could reply, Michael was gone, crashing into the kitchen with a force that snapped the curtain and sent coloured beads flying about the room like ball bearings. Michael marched down the dim corridor. The bathroom door appeared, still closed, to his left and he barged his shoulder against it, sending the door flying into the room. The door swung open, crashing against the bathroom mirror that fell in a hundred silver shards into the sink. The room was empty.

The bedroom door was open and Michael burst in with a hand on his knife. But as he had guessed, this room was also empty. There was no sign of David and there was nowhere else Anya could go.

Back in the kitchen, Michael took the rifle from under the sink and pulled back the bolt to check there was still a round in the chamber. He could not remember where he had left the satchel of bullets, but it did not matter, one would be enough.

Beads scattered across the floor ahead of him as he emerged

back into the lounge.

Zanna glanced up from where she knelt beside Judith.

"Anya's with David. I'll go bring her back. Stay here with these two," Michael said, the rifle in his arms.

Zanna eyed the rifle, but betrayed no sign of surprise. Instead, her face had hardened into a mask of determination.

"Go get her back. Be quick."

Harold sat motionless in the shadows of his chair whilst Judith continued to sob as she rocked back and forth.

"Find Emily," Zanna repeated under her breath.

"I will," Michael said, and then he was gone, disappearing into the corridor.

Chapter Twenty-Five

The darkness of the corridor was almost absolute, save for the lights of the fireworks that flared briefly through open doorways, like flashing Christmas lights. Michael moved quickly but methodically. David and Anya were not in the corridor. He hurried from door to door and stood for a second outside each, listening. He heard nothing along the corridor, and no lights shone from under the doors.

Michael entered the dark column of stairs and began slowly to descend the tower, with one hand on the wall and one gripping the stock of the rifle. The pain in his shin throbbed and reminded him to watch his step, but there was no time to be careful and he took the steps two at a time, almost falling over when the stairs leveled out on the sixth floor landing. The candles still burned in the corridor and a veil lifted in Michael's mind and he knew that the sixth floor was where they would be.

Michael stepped out into the light, swinging the rifle out in front of him. He stood for a second, the rifle held waist high. Shadows danced in front of him and for that first second, anything might have been David. Then the lights settled and everything came into focus, and Michael stood alone in the corridor. He moved along slowly, on the balls of his feet, like a cat hunting a rat.

A faint blue light shone from under a door just ahead of him and he made his way silently towards it. Two dim voices could be heard, and Michael pressed his ear flat against the wood to listen to what they were saying. The voices did not sound like a man and a child, more like two men, but Michael could not afford to be wrong.

He held the rifle in one hand and slowly turned the cold doorknob. A resistance told him the door was locked. He took a step back and, holding the rifle in both hands, ran shoulder first into the door. It crashed open and sent him stumbling into the room. Michael glanced about quickly. A light shone into the room from the far end. Michael regained his balance and swung the rifle around to confront the light source.

Two men dressed in camouflage scrambled under sleeping bags and rucksacks, searching for something. One, half-kneeling, found an SA80 rifle and had it half raised towards Michael, as Michael took a step forward and raised his own rifle at the man's chest. The man lowered the gun and the second man backed up slowly to sit against the wall.

"Don't fucking shoot us!" the second man called.

"Shhh!" Michael hissed, and immediately both men fell silent.

They were soldiers, and from what Michael could see, it looked as if they had been hiding out in the room for some time. A battery-powered camp light shone a shallow pool of blue light on the floor. In the centre of their mess of bags and blankets, a small fire burnt on a metal tray. A pan full of baked beans bubbled in the heat, and empty tin cans surrounded the fire. The men looked young and could not have been much older than Michael. Their faces were stained with dirt, their hair cropped close, and there was a few days' worth of stubble on their cheeks.

The first soldier put his rifle down and tried to stand. Michael pointed the rifle at his head and the soldier hovered for a moment, halfway between sitting and standing, before he sat back down and slid over to where the second soldier leaned against the wall.

"Don't shoot us!" the first soldier said, echoing the words of the second.

"Be quiet," Michael said with calm contempt.

He glanced at the SA80 lying out of reach on the floor and, as if someone had pressed play on the film reel of his memories, he saw again the day he had lost his parents, and remembered again the way the soldiers had opened fire on the crowd.

Michael shook his head violently in an attempt to shake the images away. The soldiers glanced at each other. The first had tears in his eyes as he chewed his grime-covered bottom lip.

"Don't fucking shoot us mate," the second soldier pleaded, in a strong cockney accent that made Michael think of gangster films.

He shook his head again and lowered the rifle to his waist. "I'm looking for a man, and a little girl. The girl's black. Have you seen them?" he asked.

The soldiers shook their heads vigorously from side to side.

"Nah mate. Nah, we ain't seen no one."

"Honest!" Their voices clamored over each other to be heard.

"Are you lying?" Michael asked calmly.

"No mate!" the first soldier shouted.

"Be fucking quiet," Michael said through gritted teeth.

He turned to leave, but again, the images of gunfire and bullets passing through living flesh flashed behind his forehead. Michael turned back to the soldiers who drew themselves nervously back against the wall. They sat there silently, their faces shaking with the effort of grinding their teeth, in case the wrong words slipped out.

"Why are you here?" Michael asked.

Neither man answered.

"I said, why are you here?" Michael repeated.

"We, we got cut off from the rest of our unit," the second soldier answered in a tone that verged on begging.

"We had to hide," the first soldier added.

"They would have killed us. The people. None of this is our fault, you know!" He tried to stand but Michael took another step forward and the soldier sank to the floor like an empty sack.

Michael lowered his voice and leaned towards them, keeping the rifle out of their reach. "It wasn't my family's fault either, was it? Thanks to you fucks, they're dead now. Do you like shooting unarmed people? Mothers and children?"

Michael spat the words at them and with each one, the soldiers' faces became a paler shade of white.

The first soldier nodded along, as though understanding exactly what had happened; as if he had been there a week ago, hundreds of miles north, when so many people had died.

"The people were angry," he said, his voice squeezed out between tears now. "Everywhere, they blamed us, we were trying to help. They tried to overthrow us, to kill *us,* as if all this was *our* fault."

He glanced around the room, as if searching for something, and then his eyes met Michael's. "It's *nobody's fault.*'

Michael straightened up again. He looked at the cowering soldiers and their small pan of beans that had begun to burn. He spat on the floor and looked them in the eyes, each in turn.

"Get out of here," he said, and immediately they both sprang to their feet, the beans forgotten.

The first soldier reached for his rifle, but Michael shook his head. The soldier nodded and reached out a hand to drag the other man along with him. Michael stepped aside and they slid past him like ghosts and disappeared into the corridor.

***

The corridor was as empty as it had ever been. Candles flickered and light ducked along the walls, sweeping great shadows across the damp stained roof, the mildewed patterns like the vaulted ceilings of cathedrals, painted with angels and saints and Latin phrases offering salvation or damnation.

The next door Michael tried was locked, as was the next. A candle flicked and the light dimmed before returning with a renewed brightness, and with it, Michael heard a man's voice singing softly.

"Half a pound of tuppenny rice, half a pound of treacle..."

The song seeped from behind the next door. Michael hesitated outside, knowing what he would see when he went in, knowing he had known it all along, but had chosen to ignore the signs. He touched the door handle. It was warm and turned easily in his hand. The door opened into a dark room. The singing was louder now, but as soft as the candle light that flickered from the next room. Michael made his way slowly towards the light.

"Every night when I get home, the monkey's on the table."

The singing voice almost sounded like that of a child. The voice cracked and quivered, as though on the verge of tears, and Michael knew it belonged to David.

"Pop goes the weasel!"

There was no laugh to greet the rhyme, only a soft sniveling punctuated by slow and wheezing intakes of breath. Michael stepped from the darkness into the light of the room. Anya stood before him, her back to him, her dirty dress discarded on the floor. Her brown skin shone like chocolate in the lone candle light.

David was kneeling in front of her, fully clothed apart from his shirt that had been torn half open. An empty whisky bottle lay by his side, and he knelt in the broken glass of a second bottle, his trousers dark with blood at the knees. One hand lay on his thigh and the other stroked Anya's bare shoulder. With each brush of his hand, Anya shuddered and drew her arms tighter about herself.

Michael felt a sudden urge to vomit, to cry, to run from the room. He felt as though he was adrift in the ocean as waves crashed down upon him. It was all he could do to stand and, as a cold sweat coated his skin, his insides twisted themselves into knots.

David looked up at him slowly. With his free hand, he shakily wiped a film of sweat from his brow. He tried to smile but the muscles around his mouth would not work properly, and the smile capsized into a half grimace. His eyes were rimmed with red rings and beads of sweat, whisky and saliva glistened like rubies amongst his stubble.

"Take your hand off her," Michael said, his voice distant, as though he were shouting from under the waves that drowned him.

David stared at him with wide eyes that seemed to be searching Michael for a hint of their old friendship. He opened his mouth slowly, but was cut off before he could speak.

"You heard me!" Michael barked.

David closed his mouth slowly, as though confused, and let his hand drop from Anya's shoulder.

"Anya, get behind me," Michael said firmly.

The girl stood, rooted to the spot in her bare feet. Her knees buckled and she began to wet herself. Michael took her by her other shoulder, the one that David had not touched. She did not wince at Michael's touch as he had thought she might, and she let herself be dragged behind him.

Michael took his hand from Anya and steadied the rifle at David. He could feel Anya's small hands grasp the back pockets of his jeans, as though she was holding up a shield.

A flurry of fireworks erupted outside and Michael and David both glanced sideways out of the dirt stained window. Michael could not see the colours anymore.

"You know," David began in a voice that was not his. "You know, they used to let fireworks off on the estates when they had a new batch of drugs in. To let the buyers know. I wonder what they're letting them off for now. Celebrating the end of the world, perhaps?"

Michael wanted to scream. He wanted David to be quiet.

He wanted to rush to him and smash the butt of the rifle into his nose until he saw blood shoot out and heard cartilage grind against bone. He did nothing, however, and David remained motionless, on his knees with his hands clasped in front of him.

"I thought I was all right, Michael," he said.

David stared into Michael's eyes and regained the ability to smile for a second, before his lips began to shake uncontrollably.

"It's not fair," David said and he scratched furiously at his stubble until Michael though he would draw blood.

"It's not fair that people like me survived this thing when good people died," David said as his nails raked his chin.

"You might not survive it yet," Michael said, the rifle heavy in his hands.

David seemed not to hear him and carried on, still scratching at his face, as if trying to uncover something there that might redeem him.

"I thought I was all right. I was safe, other people were safe. I hadn't drunk in three years, I was doing well, but then, *this* happened." David waved his arms about him like a preacher channeling the power of God. "What the hell happened? I found myself one of the only ones left. The guards were being killed... the others were coming for me, so I ran."

"Prison," Michael said flatly, asserting what he had already guessed.

David moved his head slowly up and down. Blood had come to his cheek, but he still scratched.

"Stop it," Michael said, but David was not listening.

The fireworks continued to erupt in constant showers of light outside of the window.

"I was afraid. Not for myself, but for what I might do," David said, and suddenly he convulsed, as though shook with some powerful force from within. He buried his head in his hands and his nails clawed at his forehead. "My daughter!" he cried, drawing blood.

The fireworks became a cacophony of light and noise outside, their colours bleeding into the room. Anya's grip became tighter and tighter on Michael's pockets and the rifle became heavy in his hands, the barrel hovering inches from David's chest.

"I'm sorry Michael, I've let you down. I only wanted to help you. I hope I did, in some way?" David's red eyes swam imploringly, searching for a sign of forgiveness.

He began to drag his blood soaked knees slowly across the floor towards where Michael stood with a terrified Anya clutching his legs. David's arms were outstretched, as though for an embrace, and tears washed down his face, mingling with blood, as sobs shook his chest.

"We don't need your help," Michael said.

Fireworks exploded outside the window, shaking the glass as the rifle jumped in Michael's hands. A crack and a cacophonous bang reverberated around the room, and Michael was not sure where either noise had come from. David fell back, winded by the bullet, as the fireworks burnt red light into the room, and blood sprayed against the wall and hung in the air in a mist.

David laid back, his body reclining over his bent knees, his arms outstretched by his side. A smell of hot metal and singed meat filled Michael's nostrils and he stood for a second watching watery blood bubble from the hole in David's chest, listening to the wet gurgling coming from his throat. Now it was David who was drowning.

Outside, the red light faded back to darkness and the room slipped back into the glow of the single candle that had almost burnt down to the ground.

Michael felt Anya's grip on his legs as she stood frozen behind him. With the rifle in one hand, he reached down and collected her stained dress that was now flecked with red. He turned to face her and knelt silently beside the girl. Her eyes were screwed up so tightly that Michael thought she might never open them again. He laid the rifle down and raised Anya's unresisting arms over her head. He pulled her dress awkwardly over her head, but still she did not resist. Neither did she resist when, with the rifle in one hand, Michael scooped her into his chest and stood and carried her from the room.

He carried her back down the corridor in a daze, stepping around candles automatically and only half registering the smoke that drifted lazily from beneath the door of the soldier's room. Anya held onto him tightly and silently, a mute gift he was taking to those upstairs.

When he stepped back into Salema's flat he let Anya down gently and she stood not knowing what to do for a second, until Judith took her by the arms and pulled her to the sofa.

Judith held the girl against her as she sobbed. "Emily. Oh, my Emily!"

Harold had risen from his chair, but paused halfway towards them, embarrassed and unsure of how to retrieve his granddaughter from this woman.

Judith pulled Anya's face to her chest. "Oh, Emily, I knew you were all right. Thank God! I told you not to play near the road!"

Zanna took Michael away from the sofa, her expression somewhere between concern and relief.

She stared at him for a moment, then threw her arms around him and pressed her cheek to his. She pulled away slowly and Michael was surprised to see something wet and red glistening on her face.

He reached and wiped his hand over Zanna's soft cheek. "You're bleeding," he said.

Zanna said nothing, and when Michael raised his hand to his own face, he brought it away sticky with David's blood.

"Is she all right?" Zanna asked quietly, gripping Michael's arms tightly, desperately.

"I don't know," he answered in exhaustion. "I did all I could..."

"Of course you did, of course," Zanna said, stroking his hair back from his brow. "Of course you did."

Judith had sat Anya down next to her on the couch and Harold hovered nervously beside them as Judith fingered Anya's dress. "Goodness! You've had an accident, look how dirty your dress is! I told you never to run off. I told you, I told you not to go near the road. Your father will be very angry!"

Judith began to pull up Anya's dress as she glanced about the room. "Pauline!" she shouted. "Pauline, fetch some hot soapy water, Emily has had an accident."

"The building's on fire," Michael said calmly into Zanna's ear.

Zanna squeezed his hand. "I've got our things together," she said without surprise.

An explosion outside bathed the room in green light. Zanna strode purposefully over to Judith and pulled down Anya's dress.

"Judith," she said, with quiet authority. "We can't change Emily here, all her clothes are downstairs, come on, we'll go get them."

Judith shook her head slowly and looked around the room, as if seeing it for the first time. Her cheeks seemed to have become hollower and the bags beneath her eyes had deepened by several shades since Anya had gone missing.

Zanna took Judith's hand. "Come on, you take Emily's hand, we're all going." She squeezed Judith's hand gently. "There you are, come on. Pauline is downstairs, waiting."

"Is she?" Judith asked excitedly, "and Paul as well?"

Zanna exhaled slowly. "Yes, Paul too. Everyone's downstairs. Come on," she said, trying to sound as cheerful as possible.

Michael placed a hand on Harold's shoulder. "Harold, I'm

afraid we're going to have to leave. It isn't safe here anymore."

Harold nodded slowly, but did not take his eyes off Judith and Anya.

"She's harmless. Don't worry; she would never let anything happen to her," Michael said.

Harold smiled and his dry lips drew back like stage curtains to reveal rows of yellow teeth. "I know son, I know."

He shook Michael's hand from his shoulder and grasped it in both of his leathery palms. "Thank you Michael," he said, gripping tightly. "Thank you for bringing her back."

Chapter Twenty-Six

They hurried down the staircase, Michael leading the way, the rifle clasped unconsciously in his hand. Harold followed him, his long fingers stretching out behind him to grasp Anya's hand. Judith held the girl's other hand and Anya hurried down the stairs in an attempt to get away from this strange woman. Zanna brought up the rear, a single bag slung over her shoulder, her cricket bat swinging by her side like an extension of her arm.

The candles of the sixth floor corridor had melted into shapeless masses, wax bubbling across the floor like melted fat. The fire had spread from the soldier's abandoned room to the corridor and, as they passed the orange glow of that floor, a wave of heat struck the group, sending Harold into the spasms of a coughing fit. There was no time to stop and allow him to recover and, as they blundered slowly downwards, half blind in the darkness, his coughing became more and more intense, until it sounded like some creature was clawing its way up his throat as Harold wheezed in protest.

Zanna's lighter flickered and died in Michael's hand as they reached the ground floor. A glare of moonlight lit the open door ahead and Michael threw the useless lighter aside. They paused for a second. Harold slid to the ground, a hand held to his throat as he gasped in deep lungfuls of air. Anya ran to him and shook his shoulders, silent tears sliding down her cheeks. Judith, who still held Anya's hand, found herself dragged along by the child.

She knelt beside Harold and, unsure what to do, began to rub his shoulder and whisper. "There, there. There, there."

281

Slowly, the coughing subsided, faltered, and then stopped, and Harold struggled to his feet, wiping something from his eyes.

"It's all right Anya, I'm ok. I'll be fine," he promised his granddaughter, ruffling her hair.

The party huddled in the doorway and Zanna shuffled forwards beside Michael. In the grey forecourt of the tower blocks, fireworks were being released skywards by the shapes of men, women, teenagers and children. They were old, young, black and white and wore hoods and hats or nothing at all on their heads. From the doorway, Michael saw their faces turned skywards to the colourful explosions that had replaced the sky above. They stood huddled in small groups amongst the burnt-out cars, the sofas, smashed television sets, and all of the debris of people's lives that had flown from the high windows of the towers.

They laughed, drank and smoked as they crowded around their fires, but this was no bonfire-night party. A current of mistrust and apprehension intermingled with the smoke that polluted the air. Metal bars, baseball bats and knives glinted in the dull glow of the fires and the moon and the coloured explosions that lit the blackness above them.

"We can sneak past them and get to the tunnel," Zanna said, pointing to the dark concrete underpass that stood across the forecourt and was the only way out of the estate.

Michael looked again at the people gathered around the fires; they were ordinary people, trying to survive, just as they were, but something inside had made Michael distrustful, something had changed over the past week and if it had ever been possible to tell good people from bad people, now it was impossible.

The fire limped from floor to floor above them, the heat following in their footsteps, down the funnel of the stairs. Michael wiped a bead of sweat from above his eye. The smell of burning wood and plastic burned his nostrils. Anya sat silently and rigidly like a doll in Harold's lap, as he coughed sharply into his hand. Judith was gazing straight ahead, drenched in sweat. They were all waiting for either Michael or Zanna to tell them what to do.

"We'll have to try," Michael said, turning to Zanna.

She nodded and slid the bag from her shoulder. She reached inside and brought out the satchel of rifle shells.

"I...I brought the bullets," she said, holding the satchel out for Michael to take it from her. Michael glanced at the rifle in his hands, as if surprised to find he still held it.

"No. No one else is getting shot." He was determined, but he still could not let the rifle go; it was as if his hands had cramped around it.

"We need it," Zanna said as she slipped a golden bullet from the satchel and pressed it against Michael's fingers.

Michael was silent for a moment, then he took the bullet, pulled the bolt back, slid the bullet into the barrel and loaded the rifle.

They turned to the others. Judith whispered to Anya.

Harold had stopped coughing and appeared bright and alert. "I've recovered my breath. Let's bloody go. Don't mind these estate yobs, we'll be fine."

Michael nodded. Zanna shoved the satchel back into her bag and swung it over her shoulder.

She picked up her cricket bat and turned to Judith. "Judith, come on, let's go," she said, taking her hand.

An explosion sounded from somewhere above them and flaming wood, cushions, bricks, pots and pans fell through the sky, scattering the crowd below.

"Let's go!" Michael shouted.

He grasped Zanna's hand, and then all five of them ran out into the forecourt, ducking behind burnt-out cars and sofas, as though dodging bullets. The crowds had abandoned their fires as they ran from the falling debris. Nobody tried to stop the people that had just emerged from the tower, or even noticed them.

Further explosions echoed behind them as gas met flame inside the tower. Michael glanced back to see the tower transformed into a raging inferno, flames glaring like bright eyes in the windows of each floor. A steady rain of burning debris fell down towards them, like a sudden blizzard of fire.

A hand tugged on Michael's shoulder and over the melee, he thought he heard Zanna calling his name. The group came to a halt and crouched behind an old fridge, taking cover as strips of burning wood clattered about them.

Zanna glanced back in the direction they had come from. "Harold! Fuck. It's Harold!" she shouted over the roar of flames.

Michael turned and looked back in the direction she was pointing. There was Harold, limping towards them, a hand clutched to his chest.

He shuffled towards them, his steps ungainly, stumbling along like a half-swatted fly.

He raised a withered hand and gestured for them to go on, but Zanna shook her head fiercely and screamed encouragement. "Come on Harold, hurry!"

He quickened his pace and had almost reached them, when a flying splinter of wood caught him across his cheek. Blood flowed freely from the wound and down the old man's neck.

"Granddad!" Anya cried, her first words since Michael had brought her back.

Anya tried to run towards her grandfather, struggling against Judith's desperate grip. "Emily! Behave! Emily!"

Harold sank slowly to the floor, resting against the shell of a car. He smiled and gave them a thumbs up as blood ran into his mouth. He signaled again for them to carry on without him, waving them away as though trying to brush away a pest. Michael rose to go and fetch him, but stopped suddenly as two figures in green camouflage emerged from the smoke, and ran and hid behind Harold's car. The soldiers crouched for a moment and then ran on, their SA80s cradled in their arms.

"Oi! Army!" a voice boomed from somewhere, and then another voice, and yet another, joined in the shouting.

Bottles and bricks began to fly overhead and crash around the soldiers.

"Granddad!" Anya shouted again.

Judith held her tightly, but the little girl whipped back her head and caught Judith sharply in the nose. In her surprise, Judith let go of Anya as hot blood began to dribble from her nose. Anya got to her feet and, before anyone could stop her, she was running across the concrete towards Harold.

The crowd had become a mob again. They had found unity in their hate for the soldiers and were heedless to the dangers of the burning tower that still spat out burning debris. Fireworks shot by Michael's face, scorching his cheek. The missiles spun dizzily past the soldiers and hit the far wall of the forecourt in an eruption of brilliant blues and silver.

The two soldiers had nowhere to go. Realising they were trapped, they began to fire sporadic bursts at the crowd. The bullets found targets, and those that were missed were showered with blood, as those beside them fell to the ground. The crowd threw missile after missile, advancing relentlessly towards the two cowering shapes that hid behind a smouldering table. The soldiers cowered behind their makeshift shelter and, knowing all was lost, they switched their rifles to automatic and fired blindly over their heads.

One bullet hit a little girl in the chest and when it came out the other side of her, it took her arm with it, dousing her dress in blood. She fell down limply in a pile of stolen life. From where he lay sprawled against the burned car, Harold screamed in anguish, as though his ribcage had been prized open and everything he had ever treasured had been torn from inside of him. The sound was lost in the roar of the crowd, and faded into nothingness like the last cries of a deer, trapped and dying alone in a great expanse of winter wilderness.

Harold was lost to them now, out of sight and out of their minds as their senses were overwhelmed by the carnage around them. Judith struggled against Zanna's grip, the last of her strength pushing her frail body free of Zanna's arms. She stumbled to her feet and ran with the crowd towards the soldiers, screaming something imperceptible. Zanna tried to chase after her, but Michael pulled her roughly back down next to him as the crowd surged around them in a stampede.

Judith charged valiantly towards the soldiers, flames shining in her eyes, her arms raised above her head as she screamed Emily's name like a battle cry. A firework came from the depths of the crowd behind her, and when it pierced the small of her back Judith froze in surprise. She managed to remain standing for a moment, clutching her side in confusion as red crackles of light erupted around her, and danced up her legs to set fire to her clothes.

Judith turned, as though searching for something and her eyes met Michael's for the last time. The look on her face was once again the same Judith Michael recognised. He knew she was asking herself what had happened to her life, and the world, and how God had led her to die in this estate in London.

Judith stood transfixed, staring at Michael as a bullet burst through her shoulder, the impact forcing her back a few steps. A second bullet passed through her waist and a thin glob of blood dribbled from her mouth to her chin. She collapsed slowly to the ground and lay in a crumpled pile whilst the soldiers fired indiscriminately into the charging crowd, until the click of their empty rifles signaled their own deaths.

Michael put his hand over Zanna's eyes but she batted it away, pulled him to his feet, and led him sprinting towards the tunnel.

As the tower burned above them, the crowd crashed into the soldiers and beat and stabbed and burnt them, until they were satisfied in their vengeance. The bodies of the dead and dying lay stretched out amongst guttering fireworks, smoke, and piles of charred debris and fire.

Chapter Twenty-Seven

The night passed as a dull nothingness, penetrated now and again by the sharp gleam of the stars that passed overhead. As Michael slept, he was aware of a movement, a change being undertaken, but whether geographical, psychological or metaphysical, he did not know. The night continued in such a manner and once, waking in utter darkness, he felt strangely weightless, as though suspended underwater or held in some uncanny grip. Later, a soft light warmed the darkness and Zanna's face appeared momentarily in a frame of golden hair, before quickly receding back into the night.

Hours or minutes later, Michael became aware of a diffusion of pale grey light, diluting the remnants of the darkness. He awoke to find himself being pulled backwards, hands hooked beneath his arms. A sense of falling shot through him and then, half a second later, he landed on his hands and knees and felt the soft, wet ground beneath him.

A voice told him to stand. He did, and found himself beside a car in a field of long grass. The tide of sleep pulled at him again, as death pulls at a man lingering on the border of this world and the next. He must have succumbed, because the next thing he was aware of was being dragged up a wet slope. At the apex of the hill stood a wall of unnaturally bright colour.

Michael willed his stiff legs to move as he forced his way upwards. However, there was some problem in communication between his mind and limbs, and his legs would not do as he commanded. A sudden spasm of pain rushed up his legs as the cuts on his shins came back to life, and Michael stumbled and fell against the muddy slope.

Hands gripped his shoulders and dragged him to the top of the hill. Michael closed his eyes again, and then opened them, and found he was sitting against the strange wall of colour, which now appeared to be bright red. He sat for a moment, his breathing laboured, only half-aware of his surroundings. He reached out a hand and touched the coloured wall. It felt something like wood, and when he brought his hand away, he was surprised to find a thin splinter protruding from his palm.

When Michael awoke again, it was with complete clarity. He was acutely aware of his surroundings, his senses overcompensating, as though he had just emerged, gasping, from under a great depth of water. There was a pain in his hand and, as he raised it to his face, Michael realised he was lying on his back. He had no memory of the splinter and gave little thought to it as he pulled it out with his teeth, then spat it away. His back was stiff and there was a musty aroma of damp wood and dust.

He sat up slowly, the muscles of his back protesting as they slid back into more natural positions. The grey and black lights of his half-dreams had been replaced by a steady white brightness. As far as Michael could tell, he was in some sort of tube, lined on each side by what looked like old bus seats. He pulled himself to his feet and found he had to duck beneath a low, curved ceiling. Square windows lined the walls. The white light dimmed, and he was able to make out an empty vista of dark green grass, met on the horizon by a continuous sheet of grey.

The floor was wooden and creaked underfoot as Michael made his way along the passage. No one had been there for some time. Cobwebs hung from the chairs and around the window fittings that had leaked puddles of water onto the mildewing seats. The seats themselves looked as though they had been eaten away by sets of tiny teeth, and dry mouse droppings littered the floor. Michael stepped around the mess and over the dried and dusty carcass of a pigeon or dove. There was a door to the left, old and heavy, which Michael managed to open on his second attempt.

He stood for a moment, stretching in the doorway, breathing in the smell of the wet grass. The view from there was no different to what he had been able to see through the windows. Everything around him was enveloped by a grey nothingness, and Michael felt that if he were to step out into this empty limbo, to walk to meet the grey horizon, he would be at peace.

He stepped down from the doorway and turned to see where he had slept. It was an old steam train that stood on rusting tracks and had been painted in reds, yellows, and greens, as some long forgotten tourist attraction. Only a handful of rotting carriages remained, and when Michael walked to the rear of the train, he found the decaying tracks disappeared beneath the grass after only a few metres.

There was no sign of how the train had ever come to be there, and Michael supposed that other than himself and Zanna, no one would ever see it again.

"It's strange isn't it?" Zanna's voice said, as if from inside his head. "It's like it's lost out here," she said, appearing suddenly beside him.

Michael nodded slowly, rubbing his sleep-stiff neck as he took a last look at the train. "It feels like we're lost out here," he said, and the sight of Zanna, her skin ever luminous in the pale light, made him remember how her face had appeared to him through the darkness of the night. He knew that as long as she was with him he could never be truly lost.

"Let's get to somewhere else," he said. "I don't think this train is going to take us anywhere."

"Come on then," Zanna called as she led the way back down the slope towards the car. "Don't fall over this time, because I won't save you again," she shouted over her shoulder.

Michael's mouth began to form the word *'What?'* but it

died on his lips as the green of Zanna's dress slipped away down the hill.

***

Soon they were on the road again, traveling between rows of hedges and beneath archways of trees. They had left behind the arteries of motorways and the veins of main roads in the night, and had bled out into obscure country roads that took them winding and climbing across wide-open country, punctuated by far-off villages and fields inhabited by sheep that climbed high amongst sheer cliffs.

The roads wound upwards and the grey of the horizon closed in around them, until they found themselves crawling along in a suffocating mist, unaware of where the road ended and where some deadly precipice was waiting beside the narrow pass that cut through the hills.

The fog drew close and brought with it a renewed sense of despair. As Zanna drove, Michael could not shake from his head the images of a little girl standing scared and naked, an old man bleeding in an apocalyptic wasteland, and Judith, tortured in body and mind, leading a charge to the death.

In Michael's wearied mind, David blurred into Jim, and more than once, Michael had sat bolt upright in his seat at the sight of him standing, bloody, by the side of the road, 'Run rabbit, run' surrounding him like the fog.

Sleep for Michael was as far away as his family. They too appeared in his waking dreams, but only as shades of colours, which never held an exact hue long enough for him to capture the image, and remember the way his dad's eyes or his sister's nose had looked. He could not help but cry out, and only Zanna's cool hand on his cheek could subdue him for a moment or two, until the hallucinations began again.

All the while, he felt a sense of having forgotten someone who had once been integral to him, but this was quickly replaced by a feeling of guilt at the touch of Zanna's hand.

***

They left the hills behind and descended into a valley full of the deep green of leaves and rich browns of earth and bark. A narrow and winding road descended slowly towards a bridge that crossed over a thin river. Towards the bottom of the descent, a car stood sideways in the road, blocking their descent, partially protruding over the wooded slope that rolled down to the river. A branch lay across the car's bonnet and the unmoving shapes of a driver and passenger were slumped in the front seats.

Zanna edged their own car forwards into the back of the car, sending it tumbling down the slope, crushing plants as it went, before diving into the shallow river and coming to rest, half-submerged, in the middle of the river.

The air was cool and refreshing in the valley, and Michael opened the window and gulped down deep lungfuls, relieved after the claustrophobia of the fog. They crossed the bridge slowly, creaking past a man's body that still clasped a fishing rod. The remains of a dog lay chained to the railing beside him.

On the far side of the bridge lay a small village green. A few houses of old stone bordered the forlorn square of grass, in the middle of which stood a bench and an old red phone box. A bicycle lay abandoned in the middle of the road, but there were no cars or bodies around, as far as either Michael or Zanna could see.

Zanna brought the car to a stop outside what looked to be a post office or corner shop, the wooden lattice window displaying prices of envelopes, stuffed bears and magazines.

"I'm going to see if there's any food in there," Zanna said as Michael struggled with his door handle.

Zanna reached across and touched his shoulder. "Stay here,"

she said, and leaned across and kissed him on the cheek.

Then she was gone. The shape of her lips on Michael's skin was a patch of warmth that spread over his face and through his body, and made him think that everything might be all right.

Gravel crunched underfoot as Zanna made her way to the doorway of the shop. Something moved in her periphery and she swung her cricket bat sharply in that direction. A tabby cat dropped from a wall and bounded away between two bushes. The rest of the valley was quiet and still, without even a slight wind to disturb the trees overhead.

The shop door was locked, so Zanna swung the cricket bat through the glass, slid her arm through the hole, and unlocked the door from the inside.

Four minutes later, she threw the bat into the backseat, tiny shards of glass protruding from the wood. Michael looked up expectantly as she slid into the seat beside him. She shook her head slowly from side to side and started the car.

"There's nothing in there. It looks like everyone has left." She said as the car rolled forwards once more. Michael took a last look at the flowering gardens, proud stone houses and neat pathways, as they made their way out of the village.

"Why would you want to leave here?" he murmured into his shoulder, but he knew the answer was that nowhere had been left untouched by the disaster, the plague, the unexplained event that was responsible for the deaths of almost everyone he had known.

Sometime later, they found themselves rising steadily out of the valley. Huge cliffs of grey rose before them and they were forced into a deep tunnel, like an almighty crack in the earth. Moss grew up the sides of the cliffs and here and there, a goat pulled at the leaves of some stunted tree. Fallen rocks lay scattered across the road and their progress was slow and arduous.

The visions that had haunted Michael had subsided for the

most part, but had now been replaced by the bright explosions of fireworks that erupted ahead of the car, as though some ghostly prospector was trying to blast their way through the cliffs.

The car began to slow and shudder as it lurched forward, shaking them in their seats.

"Shit." Zanna punched the dashboard.

"Petrol?" Michael asked.

Zanna blew strands of hair from her eyes and nodded slowly.

"Lovely day for a walk," she said through clenched lips.

Michael stepped out of the car and suddenly found the ground beneath him to be unstable. He leaned against the car as the rock walls swam about him, before beginning to sharpen slowly into focus. Zanna came around the side of the car, swinging an arm into her leather jacket, cricket bat in hand.

"Are you ready?" she asked.

Michael took a breath as his surroundings came into calm focus. "Yes," he said, and he began to walk off down the road.

"Michael!" Zanna called.

He turned back to her and saw she was holding the rifle. A sudden flash of red mist passed before his eyes, and Michael saw again the way David's body had folded back on itself from the shock of the bullet. Something inside crushed his chest and a cold pool of sweat collected at the base of Michael's spine.

"I don't want it," he called. "We don't need it."

Zanna placed the rifle on top of the car beside her cricket bat and came towards Michael. She placed her hands lightly on his shoulders and pressed her forehead against his. Michael could hear the blood pounding in his ears.

"Everything that has already happened, is done. Everything we have done, we have had good reason to. Now, right here in the present, we might need this gun. We've come too far; we need to protect ourselves. I hope we won't have to use it, but isn't it better to have it and not need it, than need it and not have it?" she asked.

The green eyes stared into his and calmed the waves that crashed inside his chest. The racing of the blood in his ears faded like the receding tides and Michael was able to hear, and think, clearly once again.

Practicality returned, and with it, came a determination to survive.

"I'm sorry," Michael said quietly. "I'm all right now, don't worry. We'll sort this out, together."

He walked past Zanna, took up the rifle and the bag of spare bullets, and slung them over his shoulder.

The car soon vanished behind them as they wound onwards amongst the cliffs. The air was cool and the sun's rays were weak, as though they struggled to penetrate the rocky chasm. They walked onwards, resolutely placing one blistered foot in front of the other, Zanna in her emerald dress and jacket, dragging her cricket bat behind her, and Michael with his sweat and blood encrusted shirt open to the waist, the bag of bullets hanging by his side and the rifle balanced across his shoulders.

The visions had left Michael, and now all he could see was the grey and browns of the rocks that surrounded them, and the green shape of Zanna, Mother Nature in this sterile place, leading him to some sort of salvation.

After a while, the rumbling of their stomachs could have passed for an avalanche, and they stopped and sat breathing heavily by the side of the empty road. Michael put the gun down and leaned back against a smooth rock. His stomach gurgled and he thought he would be sick.

"I'm famished," he said.

Zanna pulled him roughly forwards so that he was sitting upright. "You're not. We're fine. We ate last night."

She was right, but the memory of stale cheese sandwiches

seemed faraway to Michael, but then, so did everything that had happened over the past week. If his feet did not burn so much, his knee did not throb so sharply, and his head did not swim with such vivid images, Michael might have thought it had all been a dream.

Zanna stretched her arms out in front of her, then ran her hands through her tangled hair. Her lips were cracked and dry and there was blood at the corner of her mouth. Her brow was slick with sweat and her face dirty with ash, mud, and dirt. Her dress was torn, muddy and dusty, and her jacket was frayed at the elbows. Zanna did not seem to register any of this. She did not appear tired to Michael, only determined, as though she was sure of something that Michael did not know.

"We're all right," Michael said after a minute.

He struggled to his feet and bent to help Zanna up, but she batted his hand away and sprung to her feet of her own accord.

They wound their way onwards, enclosed by the grey walls that reared above them. They rounded a corner and then stopped, listening. They stood straining their ears, trying to capture a vague and distant sound. The sound came again and Michael's stomach twisted in anticipation. He shared a glance with Zanna and, without speaking, they had reached an agreement and set off at a trot in the direction of the noise.

The noise of the cows came from above and wound through the rocks like strangled and distorted horns. Michael and Zanna ran beside the rocky wall until they were able to find an incline shallow enough for them to scramble up and, after a minute, they reached the summit, leaving the road twenty feet below them.

They crawled over the edge, elbows and knees scraped and raw. They had arrived on the top of the world. Before them, the ground sank down into a pit where rocks jutted out like giant's teeth, exposed to the world through thousands of years of wind and snow and rain.

The cows stood lazily chewing the grass at the bottom of the pit, or wandering slowly up a shallow slope to where Zanna and Michael found themselves. Beyond the cow-pit, the air stretched out emptily, until it was met many miles away by the tips of hills, green, grey, and brown in the distance. All around them was blue sky and patches of cream clouds.

Now that the reek of cow shit was in his nostrils, Michael began to doubt what they had decided.

"We're just going to do it?" he whispered. "Shoot one of them. Skin it. Take out all its, organs and...and parts and cook it?"

Zanna nodded, the determination in her expression betraying her hunger. "Aren't you hungry?" she asked. A grumbling that could have come from either of their stomachs answered the question.

They crawled on their bellies, peered down into the rocky pit, and watched the cows shuffling about. A pile of fresh manure lay nearby and flies buzzed close to Michael's mouth, making his tongue feel furry and his skin itch.

Zanna placed a hand calmly on his back. "You'll scare them away."

A smaller cow, which might have been a calf, (Michael knew nothing about cows) had separated itself from the herd and wandered amongst the long grass on the lip of the pit, not more than ten feet from where Zanna and Michael lay. Zanna pointed across Michael, towards the cow and Michael nodded irritably.

He rolled onto his back and fumbled in the satchel that held the bullets. He found one, brought the rifle up to his chest, then remembered it was already loaded and put the spare bullet back in the satchel. Zanna squinted at him as if to ask what he was doing, and he turned onto his side, ignoring her.

Michael's hands felt too large and his fingers too thick. Eventually, he was able to pull the bolt back and check the round in the chamber. It was fine. There was nothing stopping him. He slid the bolt back into place and the rifle was ready to fire.

He took a deep breath and glanced back at Zanna lying beside him. She nodded and arched her eyebrows, as though telling him to hurry up.

Michael crawled around to face the lone cow. He brought the rifle up into position and aimed along the sights. A larger cow came up, stood beside the smaller one, and nudged it with its head for a second, before wandering away again. A lump formed in Michael's throat. He tried to swallow it back down, but was unable to. He aimed along the sights again. Something dried and red shone dully on the metal. Whether it was the blood of the man who Michael had found, or the blood of David, was impossible to say.

A greasy film of sweat appeared on Michael's brow and he glanced awkwardly over his shoulder to where Zanna lay beside him, her green dress one with the grass. She nodded again, this time accompanied by a gentle smile, and Michael was calm again.

He turned back to the cow. It had moved slightly and Michael had to shuffle through the grass to get back into a good position. He raised the rifle. The sights found the cow and his finger found the trigger. Michael aimed at the centre of its body; to make sure he could not miss. He took a breath and stroked the trigger and his finger slipped away, slick with sweat. He took another breath and gripped the rifle to him, tightly.

Michael tried not to think about the bullet ripping through the skin and muscle of the cow, or how he would cut it apart with his knife or how David's eyes had frozen when the bullet had hit him.

'*Run rabbit run*' began to play in his mind. Michael gripped the trigger again, ready and determined to fire, but at that moment, a dark shape descended in front of his face, blocking his vision and forcing the barrel of the rifle into the ground. Something hard and cold scratched Michael's temple, and he turned his head slowly to find the double barrels of a shotgun tickling his face.

There was a man at the other end of the shotgun, and he raised the weapon slightly, keeping his foot pressed down firmly on the rifle in Michael's hands. Michael let go of the rifle and spread his arms out slowly at his side.

The man kicked Michael's rifle away and stepped back slowly. "I don't think you'll be shooting my cows today, will you now?"

Chapter Twenty-Eight

The man reached down and pulled Michael to his feet. "It's much better if I do it. Save you making a mess of it. Besides, shoot that cow here, and you'll scare the rest. I can't have my livestock running off now."

From beneath them a cow snorted, as if in agreement.

"I'm sorry," Michael said, unsure of what to do.

The man nodded a head of grey hair. The shotgun was held loosely by his side. "Pick up your rifle and dust the mud off it. Try not to shoot anything. Then follow me," the man said. "Bring her too" he said, jabbing his elbow in Zanna's direction. Then he walked calmly over to where the calf stood.

Michael bent and retrieved the rifle.

Zanna stood beside him, watching the grey-haired man. "What do you think?" she asked quietly.

"I think if he was going to do anything to us, he would have done it already," Michael said as he glanced about the rocky top of the world. "Where the hell did he come from?"

"I don't know," Zanna said. "He surprised me too."

Michael watched the man lead the calf across the grassy plateau. The man was old and thin, but the cow did not resist and allowed itself to be led away from the herd.

"We have the rifle," Michael said, "if we need it."

They followed him across the grassy ridge, climbing over rocks that protruded from the earth, shoulder bones of the hills. Their fatigue had been replaced by intrigue, but as quickly as they hurried, they were unable to catch the man, who strode nimbly across the uneven ground.

He led them downhill, the cow still following behind him.

After a few minutes, they descended into pine trees and the rich smell of damp earth and pine needles. A red pickup truck stood in a clearing at the bottom of the descent and the man waited for them beside it. As they approached, he slipped a noose around the cow's neck and tied the other end around a tree.

Once he had finished, he held his hand out in greeting. "The name's Robert, but you can call me Bob. Or Robert. I don't really care. It's all the same to me."

Michael nodded and stood his rifle against the truck. "I'm Michael."

Robert nodded and held his hand out to Zanna.

"Zanna," she said. "Do you live around here?"

The man began to fiddle with something and then the back of the truck swung open. "You'll see soon enough. Nice to meet you both, by the way. Michael, give me a hand with this."

Robert reached into the back of the truck and dragged out a sheet of metal. After some instruction, Michael helped him set it up as a ramp into the truck, and then Robert walked over and untied the calf.

"Sometimes they don't want to go, so we might have to scare him in," Robert said.

He led the cow to the ramp but it turned and grunted at them and tried to barge its way back to where it had come from.

"Get that side, Zanna! Michael, close him in. Come on now!"

After pushing, shouting and pulling, they managed to get the cow up into the back of the truck. They quickly shut it in and shoved the metal ramp in after it.

"Right, hop in," Robert said and nodded to where the cow stood moaning in the back, its head peering over the side of the truck.

Zanna and Michael stared at the cow for a moment.

"You're not country people are you? Get in, he won't bite. Try and stay away from his legs, though."

They rode through the trees, Zanna and Michael sitting in the back of the truck, each holding on to the other for balance. The cow shifted its weight from one hoof to another and snorted to itself.

The pickup drove onwards, climbing up a dirt road before crossing a grassy field. A small house could be seen in the distance and, after a while, the pickup stopped beside it. Robert got out of the truck and opened the back and Zanna and Michael jumped down. They had similar trouble getting the cow out of the truck, and Michael had to climb around it and slap the animal's shoulders whilst Robert pulled it backwards down the ramp. Zanna stood watching them, wiping the mud from the rifle barrel with the hem of her dress.

When the cow was down, Robert led it around to the side of the house where he tied it to a post. Michael and Zanna followed along behind. Dried blood was splattered against the side of the house and the ground beneath where the cow stood was a mess of blood, faeces and churned earth. Fragments of bone and dried tissue, like strips of leather, littered the slaughter spot. The calf was becoming unsettled by these surroundings and began to huff and blow air from its nostrils, stamping its feet as it strained against its tethers.

A woman came from inside the house and stood beside Michael and Zanna.

"These are some young uns I caught trying to shoot our cows," Robert said.

The woman smiled. "We'll have to shoot them too then," she said.

Zanna gripped the rifle and Michael remembered the knife he still carried.

"Calm down," the woman said. "You can't take everything seriously. I'm his wife. Maureen." She offered them both a

302

hand.

Robert broke the barrel of the shotgun and checked the shells as the cow bucked against the wall. "Right," he said, "anyone of a nervous disposition, now's the time to avert those eyes."

He raised the gun to where the cow's skull met its neck, and then there was a crack as the cow's face shot forward to splatter against the wall. The lifeless body buckled under its own weight and slumped to the ground. The rope slipped over the stump of the neck, and the smell of burnt gristle filled the air.

Michael coughed into his hand and felt his legs go weak. Zanna grabbed him and held him upright.

"Whoa, whoa," Maureen said. "I think we have a fainter."

Robert nodded as he once again broke the barrel of the shotgun and picked out the used shell. "Better take them inside, get them a drink."

He threw away the empty shell and glanced to where Zanna still held Michael upright. "You two go with Maureen and get some rest. In a few hours we'll have some broth. Looks like you could do with some bread and a sit-down before that though."

***

The shirt was itchy around Michael's neck and too tight. Michael pulled at the collar as Zanna entered the room. She stood before him, dressed in a blue dress and a jumper that was slightly too big for her. Candle light flickered against the walls where pictures and paintings hung in crowded comfort. The table was set before them and the smell of beef stew seeped in from the kitchen. For two hours, the smell of the cooking meat had driven them crazy with desire, and the bread they had eaten upon their arrival had done nothing to diminish their ravenous hunger.

Robert entered the room, dressed in old jeans and a

checked shirt. His grey hair had been brushed back with water and he had shaved for the occasion.

"Sit down, sit down," he said distractedly as he hunted about for something in a cupboard beside the table. "Maureen," he called into the kitchen.

"It's in the sideboard," she called back.

Robert disappeared into a corner of the room for a few seconds, and then re-emerged from the shadows with a bottle of red wine. "So it was," he said.

"Take your places," Maureen said as she emerged from the kitchen, carrying a steaming pot that she set down on the table beside them. Robert moved about the table, filling each glass with wine that shone a dull red in the candle light.

Maureen moved about, ladling the steaming broth, rich with carrots and leeks and potatoes, into bowls, whilst Robert handed out chunks of bread. Maureen filled the last bowl and untied an apron from around her waist. She threw the apron into the shadows and took a seat.

Robert raised his glass. "To new friends in strange times."

The table echoed with the toast. They all took a sip and lowered their glasses.

"What are you all waiting for?" Maureen asked, a spoon halfway to her mouth. "Tuck in."

Zanna and Michael ate quickly, spooning the burning stew into their mouths, drinking the wine quickly to stop the heat. Michael could feel everything getting better as each mouthful warmed his insides. The cow was forgotten and all that existed for him were the tender strips of meat and the beautiful flavours of the stew. Maureen and Robert looked on approvingly as the broth disappeared in front of the two newcomers, and when their bowls were empty, Maureen rose to refill them.

When the pot was empty, the four figures in the candlelight sat back contentedly, finishing the last of their wine.

"Thank you so much," Zanna began.

"I'm sorry we tried to steal your cow," Michael continued.

Robert raised his palms to them. "Slow down, relax, and let the food digest. You're very welcome. It's a good job you didn't kill my cow, I doubt you could have done as good a job as Maureen does cooking it."

He reached over and took her hand in his. Michael saw this and longed to take another hand in his. He did not think of Her, or even remember her, but he did not dare look at Zanna for the next few moments.

Outside, a thousand stars smoldered above them, silver light shining through the window.

"They're up there," Maureen said, breaking the silence. "Everyone we've lost is up there. Parents, friends, everyone."

Zanna and Michael were silent.

"You don't think so?" Maureen continued. "I'm not talking heaven. I'm talking stars. We're, all of us, made of stars. Made of explosions and bits of this flung into bits of that. And when we die, that's what we'll all go back to being again."

The candles flickered and shadows stroked the walls. Zanna took a sip of wine and, as she lowered the glass, a drop of red, like blood, ran over her bottom lip. Her tongue slipped out and touched it and then it was gone. Michael felt the stars burning inside of him.

"We won't ask you where you come from, or what you've been through, because your stories are the stories of the whole country, at least, those who are still out there. Besides, it's none of our business," Robert said, picking up where his wife had left off. "I can say though, that you're both welcome to stay here as long as you need to. Until this thing gets sorted out."

Maureen nodded her agreement, and the candlelight emphasised the soft creases at the corners of her eyes. "We've enough here for two guests. Lord knows we don't get many visitors living up in these craggy hills. You can work to earn your places, though, and there's a lot to be done, mind."

"Thank you," Michael began, "but we were planning on trying to get across to France, at least I was..." He trailed off, aware that Zanna had only wanted to go as far as London.

Something touched his knee under the table as Zanna spoke. "Yes, that's right. Thank you so much for the offer, though, but there are things we have to do there," she said with a glance in Michael's direction that he couldn't quite read.

"You think things are all right there?" Robert asked.

Michael sat up in his chair, suddenly alarmed. "What have you heard?" he asked, expecting the worst.

"Nothing," Robert said. "Nothing at all. Radio silence. I just thought you might know whether this thing was an international occurrence, or not."

"We haven't heard anything," Zanna said, and Michael's heart shook as her fingers knitted into his under the table.

Robert's chair creaked as he leaned forward. "I wouldn't be surprised if they were in the same situation," he said.

"This sort of thing has to be worldwide. It's not surprising, the amount of rubbish we pump into the atmosphere and dump into the sea, the animals we've driven to extinction and forests we've destroyed. It's not surprising the planet would want to get rid of us. The Ice Age did a good job of it before, but we crept back, surviving epidemics and pandemics, multiplying and spreading across the surface of the planet. Punching holes in the atmosphere and throwing bombs at each other so we can become richer. Human beings are the most selfish race this planet has ever known, and it's all because we've outsmarted everything else. Still, we couldn't stop this thing, that's how smart we really are. We're nothing in the grand scheme of things," he said, pointing to the stars that shone through the window. "Human life is but a twinkle in the eye of the universe. Our lives can be snatched away as easily as they're given."

Michael's head swam with images of stars exploding in the

voids of space, supernovas and red giants. He saw oceans devouring the land, cow's heads exploding and towers burning. He saw Jim, David, Steve, Judith, Harold, Anya, and his family. His fingernails scratched at the table and his shirt tightened around his throat.

He rose from the table and stood clawing at the tight material at his neck, as the candle light climbed the walls. Zanna was speaking to him, her arms outstretched. Robert dashed towards him, but Michael fell backwards and the world that swam about him washed over him in blackness.

Chapter Twenty-Nine

Michael awoke in a strange room and found himself to be lying down. He tried to get up, but his elbows gave way beneath him and he sank back down to sleep. The next time his eyes opened, an orange light filled the room and the warmth of the light lulled him back to sleep once more. He dreamed of climbing endless hills as Zanna ran ahead towards a golden cow which shook its head at him, sadly.

He found himself in conversation with Judith, listening as she told him about the finer points of embroidery. Suddenly, he was in bed, sweating beneath a heavy patchwork quilt. He slept again and, when he awoke, Maureen was sitting beside him, sponging his brow with a cold cloth and whispering, "Hush, hush. Hush, hush."

Michael tried his best to smile, but the effort exhausted him and sent him back into sleep. He saw his sister there. He was pushing her on the swing in their garden, but the ropes snapped and she fell to the floor. When she got up again, she had turned into a rabbit and ran off into the fields across the road from where they had lived.

'*Run Rabbit, Run*'.

Michael awoke to find Zanna, her skin shining golden and her hair burning amber, the glow of her skin warming his face like the springtime sun. She brought a spoon to his lips, and when he opened his mouth, some sort of warm liquid slipped down his throat like honey.

He slept again, and in his dreams, he had shouted her name and darted out a hand to stop her falling from a cliff face. He awoke to find himself in a dark room, Zanna sitting beside the bed, a candle guttering in a mound of wax, illuminating her sleeping figure.

When he was able to stay awake for any length of time, Zanna brought him plates of solid food that he hardly touched at first, but soon devoured as his appetite began to return. The taste of cooked meat was like heaven after all the days spent eating stale bread and chocolate, and Michael felt every mouthful giving him more strength.

One day, a few days after his appetite had returned, Zanna came in to clear his plate away and, finding him awake, sat down on the edge of the bed beside him.

"How are you feeling?" she asked, one hand resting on his knee.

"I'm all right. I just felt a bit under the weather," Michael said, smiling in an attempt to look healthy.

Zanna nodded slowly.

"I didn't faint," Michael added quickly, earning a smile from Zanna.

"You were just exhausted," she said. "Don't worry about it. We've been through a lot." She let her hand rest on his cheek for a moment.

"Thank you for looking after me," Michael said, feeling the cool palm on his face. "How has it been, here, with Robert and Maureen?"

"They're lovely. I've been helping them with jobs around the house. They're not worried about this thing. It's as if nothing has happened here. Well, apart from us turning up. It's like we're hidden here, away from everything." Her hand drifted back to Michael's knee as she stared vacantly out the window. "It's like we're safe here."

***

Michael slept peacefully for the first time in days, but awoke suddenly in the middle of the night. He was not panicked; he felt relaxed and knew exactly where he was. Something was burning in his chest and he pulled his T-shirt off and sat upright in the bed. He sat for a moment, as though expecting something. The curtains were closed and the room was dowsed in the depths of night. The door creaked open at the foot of the bed, and a slender shape slipped through the crack and shut the door silently behind it.

Zanna stood for a moment, illuminated in her own light that always seemed to radiate from within. Her hair fell about her shoulders and her green dress clung to her. Michael was certain she could hear his heart racing inside his chest. Zanna hesitated a moment, seeing Michael awake, and then she padded towards the bed on bare feet, pulling the dress over her head as she did. The dress slipped up her body, over thighs and golden hair, over a flat stomach and smooth breasts, and then it was a crumpled pile on the floor. She crawled silently onto the bed and slowly made her way to Michael, her nipples brushing against the quilt.

Michael reached out and pulled her towards him, a soft gasp escaping her lips as her mouth met his. She slid under the covers and he pulled her as close to him as was humanly possible. Their tongues found each other and their mouths drank in every inch of their bodies. The two shapes moved in silence beneath the heavy sheet as they sank into each other, trying to press the way their hearts felt into the other through the touch of skin on skin. Michael's fingers combed Zanna's hair as she arched her back and they each grasped the other towards them, as though they were all they had in the world.

***

The weeks slipped past, the days shortened into autumn and before they knew where the time had gone, the first chills of winter were upon the land. Michael and Zanna lived a simple life; they rose early and saw to the livestock, or helped

310

Maureen in the vegetable garden, or helped to fix things around the house or in the fields. Maureen and Robert kept out of their way as much as they could, and there was little talk of what and where they all had been before Zanna and Michael had appeared. After a while, it seemed as though nothing else had ever existed.

It was easy then, for Michael to forget the visions that had plagued his mind and, since he had arisen from his incapacitation in bed, there had been little to trouble him.

As the seasons changed, Michael and Zanna discarded their worn, old clothes in favour of those borrowed from Robert and Maureen.

Robert and Maureen were silently aware of the relationship developing between the two youngsters and knowing smiles would pass between them at the dinner table when Michael and Zanna began to argue, or eventually made up. The midnight visits to each other's rooms continued and sometimes, they would meet in the middle, blundering and stifling laughter in the dark corridor.

Shortly after they had decided to stay, Zanna ceased carrying her cricket bat around and it stood discarded in a dusty corner of the house. Michael had forgotten where his rifle was, but there was never a use for it, except when Robert took him and Zanna on the occasional pigeon hunt in the woods. Michael still carried his knife, but now he used it for cutting rope or skinning animals, which he did with a steady hand, his unsteady stomach of yesterday settled.

Michael brought the knife out now and cut back a clump of thistles. He threw them away and straightened up, rubbing his hands together.

Robert threw a large stone across to him. "Getting cold, eh? Put that one between those two, pound it in hard. That's it."

They were miles out from the house, repairing a dry stone wall that sheep had escaped through. Packs of wild dogs had started wandering the hills and, forced out from the cities and towns, they scrounged for food in the wilderness and took down anything they could find. For a month now, Robert had been finding the carcasses of sheep and cattle beside canine tracks in the mud. There was nothing they could do about it but pen the sheep in and shoot anything that ran on four legs and hunted their animals.

One evening, walking alone, Michael had come across a lone dog, limping and whining, dragging a bloody leg behind it. Michael considered crushing its skull with a rock, but it was getting dark, the evening was cold and he had grown to resent the dogs for the trouble they had put them through, so he left the animal to suffer and went home. He hardly slept, overcome with guilt, and even Zanna's caresses could not settle him. He had gone back to the same spot at first light to try to help the animal, but instead, found its carcass torn and spread about the tracks of a multitude of dogs.

Michael shivered again as the sun sank slowly behind the horizon, its light pale now, each day only breathing a little life into the earth. Robert passed him another stone that Michael struggled to fit into place on the wall.

He forced it in and it slipped, grazing his hand. "Shit," he said, sucking blood from the wound.

"All right?" Robert asked. He looked about at the darkening evening and the lines of purple on the horizon. "Get yourself back Michael. I'll handle it."

"I'm fine," Michael replied.

"I know," Robert said. "All the same, it's getting cold and there's no reason for us both to be out here."

Michael set off back along the fields, the cold numbing his grazed hand. He thrust both hands into his pockets. It was a long walk back, but the thought of seeing Zanna made him hurry. The sky was deepening into grey, shot with strips of deep blue and purple. The silhouettes of a thousand birds moved in unison across the sky, heading south to warmer climates.

312

Michael watched them move as one, until they flew out of sight behind a range of hills. He turned to walk down through the woods when another movement caught his eye, and he looked up to see a single bird flying in the opposite direction. It was nearer to him than the others had been, and looked to be a dove, but it could just as easily have been a wood pigeon.

The bird flew on, heading towards what? Michael did not know. He wondered why this bird had not left; why it did not migrate with the others. Another image of a dove appeared in his mind and he stood for a moment, trying to remember where it came from. His mind took him back to that morning, standing in his kitchen, months but more like years ago, as he watched a dove take flight across his garden.

A sudden surge of grief rose inside of him. Not for the people he had lost, or the things he had done, but for himself, for that boy who had stood in his kitchen and made a plan of action, and had thought he was doing some good. What had happened to that boy? Michael felt embarrassed remembering him now. He had not known it at that time, but everything he had done there had been for Her, and somewhere along the way he had lost sight of that and had become complacent here.

Michael walked onwards and tried to shake the feeling that had settled upon his shoulders as the darkness closed in about him and the cold seeped into his wound and crawled up his arm.

He ran back to the house and clattered through the doorway, breathing heavily. Zanna looked across from where she stood chopping vegetables, and her eyes met Michaels, asking what was wrong. Michael brought his bloody hand from his pocket and shook it back to life.

"Cut my hand," he offered in response to Zanna's inquisitive glance. "It's freezing out there too," he said as he stamped about the hallway.

That evening there was a tension in the air that drove the

dinner along at an uncomfortable velocity.

As soon as the last of the food was gone, Robert rose and took Maureen by the hand. "Come away to bed, darling. Leave the washing; it'll keep for the morning."

They left the room and then Michael rose as well. "I think I'll go to bed too. It's been a long day."

Zanna followed him into his room. Michael sat down on the bed and began to take off his muddy trousers whilst Zanna pulled off her heavy jumper. She took off her trousers and crawled next to Michael in an oversized T-shirt.

She began to nuzzle her head into his neck, but he was unresponsive and lay stiffly beside her. She began to kiss his cheek, but Michael pulled away and turned to face the wall. Zanna pulled him back around towards her.

"What's the matter?" she asked. "Don't say, nothing."

Michael stared at the ceiling. "It's just my hand. It's aching a bit," he said, but before he had finished, Zanna had interrupted.

"Bullshit. What is it?" She looked about the room. "Is it me? Are you tired of me, or this place? Both?"

Michael said nothing.

Zanna sat upright in the bed and rubbed her temples with her fingers. "Why were you heading to France, Michael? Who's there?"

Michael sat up beside her, took her hands away from her head, and pulled her towards him. She was unresisting, but now her body seemed stiff against his.

"It's a girl," Zanna said without emotion.

"I'm sorry," Michael began. "It's not that I love her more than you, it's just...I set out to find her, and I haven't and I'm not sure if I've betrayed myself, or her, by giving up."

He rubbed his eyes with his free hand. "Christ, I don't even know if she's alive. She was on holiday when this whole thing happened, I haven't heard from her since. Well, I suppose no one has heard from anyone."

Zanna shuffled where she sat, and the space between them widened. "I understand," she said. "We've all been trying to pretend everything's been all right here, and really..."

"But it has. It *has* been all right, these past few months. It's been some of the best times I've had, ever. With you, here. It's been so simple and straightforward." Michael said.

"Let's go to France," Zanna said, her grip tight on his arm. "But promise me I can come with you."

Michael pulled her to him again and pushed his lips against her cheek.

When they parted he said, "Of course. Of course."

The cold crept into his hand again and he pulled the blankets tightly around them.

"I'm glad you want to come," he said, half-smiling in the moonlight.

"I'm glad you want me to come," Zanna said, and Michael knew she meant it. "It's too cold to try anything now though. We'll have to wait out the winter," Zanna said.

She lay down beside him and their bodies became a single warm shape.

***

Days passed and nothing was said between them about their discussion, and though Michael often thought about it, his desire to leave, and perhaps see Her again, sank back inside of him as life returned to a form of normality. There was much work to do as winter approached, and Michael and Zanna were so weary at the end of each day that they were happy just to collapse silently into bed together.

Some days later, it became unusually warm; as though the sun were beaming down with all of the energy it had kept hidden over the past month. Michael had been helping Maureen fix the fence that enclosed the house. By midday they had finished, and Michael set off for the stream on the edge of the farm, hoping to sit and enjoy the rare sun for a while. He made his way leisurely across the fields and over fences and after a while, the sound of running water met his ears.

Michael approached the stream and something golden caught his eye. He trotted towards Zanna who turned to meet him with a smile.

"What a nice surprise," he said with a wink as he sat down beside her.

"It's such a nice day, I had to come and sit here for a while. I was shooting rabbits with Robert, but I told him I would be right back and dashed off. That was about an hour ago, so I suppose he'll have given up on me by now," Zanna said, brushing her hair out of her eyes.

Michael smiled and put his arm around her. They sat beside each other in silence for a while, as twigs and the odd dried leaf floated past on the crystal blue water. The sun was warm against Michael's neck and, after a while, he slept.

When he awoke the sun had retreated behind clouds and the air was cold. His surroundings were hazy at first, but a sound quickly shook him awake. The sound was half scream, half sob. He sat up and saw Zanna was gone.

He ran towards the water and found her sitting limply against a log. "Hey, hey, what's wrong?" Michael asked as he put his arm around cold shoulders.

Zanna said nothing. She stretched out a pale hand and pointed to the water. Michael followed her gesture and saw, trapped below the surface by the roots of a tree, a bloated and decomposing corpse. Rags of clothing washed grey by the current swirled about it, and a nose rubbed to the bone was all that emerged above the water.

Michael pulled Zanna up the bank, her legs dragging and stumbling.

She clung to him, bitterly wiping tears from her eyes. "You were right," she said, angry at a situation that neither of them could control.

"You were right, we can't stay here. We've been pretending everything is all right, but it isn't. It never will be here. We need to leave."

As the sun dipped behind the horizon, they sat down on a dry stone wall overlooking the wide expanse of neighboring hills, by now familiar to them. The shock of the body had worn away from them both, but a residual sense of reality remained.

"It's not fair to the others, Judith and the people who have died," Michael said quietly. "If we stay here, we may as well have died with them. We have to keep looking for somewhere, safe, untouched."

Zanna's hand was cold in his. "We gave up too easily. We tried, we needed a rest, but we should have left here earlier."

Michael nodded slowly. "No one is coming to help us here. Not the UN, not the British Government, nobody, it's been months. Something has happened, something unexplainable, and we've been left to deal with it." He stared out at the hills, and he knew what was beyond them was no different to what was there. "Since there's no help, it's up to us to look after ourselves," he said.

That night, two figures met in the corridor of the house, but they did not laugh or creep back to peel each other's clothes away, instead, they crept to the kitchen and lit a lamp.

They searched methodically through drawers and cupboards until Zanna whispered, "Got it."

They spread the map on the dining room table, the lamp pinning down a corner.

"It looks like we're here," Zanna said.

She pointed at the map and then her finger traced a line to the sea. "This is the way we should go. How far do you think that is? Six miles?"

"It must be about that," Michael whispered. "It's definitely walkable."

Their eyes met over the dimly-lit table, and a current of excitement and trepidation passed between them.

Chapter Thirty

The following morning, a frost shone on the ground and the air was bitter in Michael's lungs. They had decided to leave that night, no matter what. They could stall no more. They had decided to either find civilization in Europe, or keep looking until they at least found more people. There had been no more mention of Her, and Michael knew that finding Her would change nothing between him and Zanna.

The day passed torturously slowly for them, as do all days of anticipation. Throughout the morning, they spoke little as they busied themselves gathering firewood and carrying it back to the house. At midday they rested for a while, sitting beside the great pile of wood. Maureen came from inside, bringing with her two mugs of soup.

She nodded at the pile approvingly. "You're a great help, you two. I'm glad you dropped in on us."

Michael smiled and rubbed his calloused hands together. "Yeah, so am I. It's been great chopping wood all day."

Maureen laughed whilst Zanna shot him a dirty look. "Ignore him. Thank you Maureen, it was kind of you to take us in. I don't know what we would have done otherwise."

Maureen nodded and turned to go back inside. "Well, that's all right. Don't get sentimental now, there's plenty more wood to be chopped. We're almost ready for winter though."

They worked hard the rest of the day, trying to somehow repay the kindness of the past few months in a day's work. By the time it got dark, the wood pile almost reached the roof of the house and Robert had to come outside and shout them in to dinner, before they would leave their work.

Michael had grown accustomed to real food again. The stews and roasted meat of Maureen's kitchen was now his staple diet, but on this last night, he remembered the first night and how close to collapse both himself and Zanna had been when they wolfed down their first bowls of beef stew.

When they had finished eating, Michael coughed gently until there was silence about the table. "I just wanted to say, to Robert and Maureen, thank you so much for looking after us. Zanna said it earlier, (and here he took her hand under the table) we don't know what we would have done if we hadn't met you, so thank you so much."

Maureen stood up and began to clear dishes. "Nonsense, no need to thank us."

Robert nodded in agreement as he rolled his sleeves down. "Aye, think nothing of it," he said. "One day you two can do the same for us, eh?"

Michael could have sworn he caught Robert glance suspiciously between him and Zanna.

***

Michael awoke naturally when the full moon was halfway across his open window. He sat up and slowly tiptoed across to the cupboard, where he searched for his jeans and the shirt he had stolen on Zanna's birthday. He slipped easily into his old, familiar clothes and then slipped his knife into the back of his jeans. There was a creak at the door and Zanna entered.

For a moment, Michael could not speak as she stood before him in her green dress, her black leather jacket hanging open.

"You look beautiful," Michael whispered and he pulled her towards him.

In the kitchen they took the map book out again and studied the route they would take. Then they took a few tins from the cupboard, leaving the majority, unable to steal from hosts who had shown so much kindness. They slipped the tins into an old rucksack that hung beside the door. In a corner nearby stood Zanna's cricket bat. She hesitated, not knowing whether she should take it or not.

Michael came up behind her and slipped his arms around her waist. "No weapons," he whispered in her ear.

She pushed her body back against him. "I think you're right."

They gathered up the rucksack and the map, and were about to open the door and step out into the night when the door to the corridor opened, and Robert stepped through into the kitchen, candle in hand.

They stood motionless, unsure of what to do or say, feeling like midnight thieves caught in the act.

Michael opened his mouth to speak, but Robert raised a finger to his lips for silence. "You'll wake the old lady," he whispered. "She can sleep through a hurricane, but still, if she finds out I'm in on this, I'll have hell to pay," he said with a wink. "Got everything you need? I don't think you have, that's why I made this up for you," Robert said as he pulled a second rucksack from a cupboard and threw it to Michael, who stumbled to catch it and was surprised by its weight. "Maureen's baked a lot of cakes recently," Robert continued. "God knows I can't eat them all myself, so I thought of you two. There are blankets too."

"How did you know?" Zanna asked.

Robert smiled. "Come on, two young kids? You're not wanting to stay around here forever. There are questions that need answering, and maybe those answers are out there. Maureen and I are too old to care. We're fine here, as you've seen. Don't worry, we both knew you wouldn't be with us forever."

"Robert, we're so grateful for what you've done for us. Without you we..." Michael began.

"All right, all right," Robert whispered, holding up his hands for quiet.

"So you've said Michael. I know you're grateful. We're grateful for you two as well; all the work you've done has been fantastic. I had my doubts about this winter, but we're so far ahead of schedule with what needs to be done, I know we'll be fine. Now, come on, where can I drive you to?" he said, slipping on his coat.

"No it's fine," Zanna whispered. "You've done enough."

"Horseshit," Robert replied, searching for his keys. "I take it you're heading for the coast? Across to France? Well the nearest beach is fifteen miles away, and there's no way I'm letting you walk that. Now, come on."

***

The farmhouse disappeared behind them, bathed in the red taillights of the pickup truck. The three passengers sat pressed together in the cab as they dipped down hills and through woods, the truck shaking gently over uneven ground. The blue night turned to grey dawn as the truck emerged through a copse of trees and joined a road that swept them along towards the coast.

As always, they encountered the odd vehicle abandoned along the road, but Michael still could not help but feel that this place was hidden away, and had avoided the full horror of what had happened elsewhere. This corner of the country was perhaps the safest corner there was, but it was still not enough for them.

The grey lanes of the road were bordered by icy fields and frost covered hedges. After a while, the soft lapping of the sea washed against their ears and Michael was suddenly overcome with nostalgia, remembering the holidays spent amongst pebble beaches and lukewarm seas with his family. Zanna squeezed his knee and he stared out of the window for a few minutes, before turning back to her and forcing a smile.

Then the ocean was all they could see, stretching out ahead

of them, grey in the weak light of dawn. As Michael looked over the fogged expanse of water, he knew the seas would never change, and their tides would lap against the shores of the places men called home long after the last man had left.

Robert stopped the truck at the top of a rocky slope that slipped down to the beach. The engine hummed for a moment, and then stopped.

Robert killed the yellow headlights and immediately the grey morning sprung up around them. "There's a fog," he said. "But as soon as the sun rises, it'll burn through that. You'll need a boat of course."

Zanna and Michael glanced at each other, suddenly embarrassed they had not thought that far ahead.

"We thought if we came to the beach, we would find one," Michael said sheepishly. Robert laughed. "*The* beach? Do you know how many beaches there are along this coast? Luckily, I thought ahead. Do you see that little shed by the water's edge?"

Michael and Zanna strained in their seats and could just about make out a small wooden cabin in the fog.

"Well, Greene keeps his motorboat down there. He always keeps the key in a cup under his desk. There should just about be enough fuel to get you to across to the continent. When the sun rises, keep it on your right side; you'll make it there soon enough. It should cut through the fog before midday, and then you'll see where you're going easily enough," Robert said.

"Thank you," Michael said, and they were the only words they needed.

Two figures slipped from the truck into the cold morning air.

"Good luck!" Robert called after them, and then they began a slow descent down the scree to the beach below.

Robert turned the headlights on again to light the way for them, but soon they had passed beyond the reach of the yellow lights. There came the sound of a vehicle reversing and driving away, and then they were alone once more.

They made their way slowly down to the beach, hand in hand, shivering in the deep cold of the morning. A loose rock slipped underfoot and sent them tumbling down the pile to land on the sand, aching and bleeding from knees and elbows.

Michael jumped up and stumbled across to Zanna. "Are you all right? Zanna?"

He shook her lightly and she pushed him away, standing up and wiping a thin trail of blood from her scalp as she did so.

"I'm fine," she shivered, and Michael held her to him for a moment. "I'm fine," she smiled.

Their feet sank one by one into the soft blackness of the dawn sand. They ran in ungainly strides, hand in hand towards the shed, the icy breeze seeping into their lungs. The shed was old, the wood was damp, and it took little effort for them to break through the door, shoulder first. They stood inside and stamped their feet for a few moments, trying to regain some warmth.

The boat bobbed in the water beside them, tied loosely by a rusting chain. They stood hand in hand and took in the small boat.

"It looks all right," Zanna said, a note of optimism in her voice.

"Yeah, I'm sure it will be fine. It's a bit small, but we won't be in it for long," Michael said, eyeing the boat's flaking paint.

"No."

"Where's this key?" Michael said as he began to search the barely furnished shed.

"Under the desk."

And there it was, exactly where Robert had told them it would be, inside a cracked and chipped mug that Michael let drop into the water.

"This is it," he said.

Outside, the fog had begun to lift and the sea was

becoming a pale blue as the sun rose from its nighttime rest.

"Now seems as good a time as ever," Zanna said. "The sooner we leave, the sooner we'll get there."

"Yeah," Michael said. "No time like the present."

They turned and held each other for a moment and, once again, Michael became lost in those green eyes. He did not think they would ever lose the effect they had on him, even if he and Zanna lived to be one hundred together.

"I'm glad I met you," Michael said.

Zanna smiled, nodded, and squeezed his hand. "I'm glad I met you too, Michael Taylor."

They placed the rucksacks gently into the boat, and then Michael held Zanna's hand as she stepped into the swaying vessel. Michael stepped in gingerly beside her. There was a second key beside the engine key, and Michael used it to unlock the padlock that held the mooring chain in place. A slight current lifted the boat and drew them away from the platform. Michael let the rusty links of the chain coil through his hand and sink down into the green water.

Michael slipped the first key into the boat's motor, turned it and then began to pull back the ripcord, as though he were starting a lawnmower. The engine spluttered, coughed, and then petered out on the first attempt. He tried again and achieved a similar result. Zanna slid towards him, the boat rocking slightly, and together they ripped back the cord, once, twice, and on the third time, the engine whined into life and the boat crept forwards into the watery expanse.

Zanna took a blanket from one of the rucksacks and lay back against Michael, wrapping it about them against the morning cold. The sun rose rapidly and the fog was clearing. Soon, Michael would be able to see where they were going. Already he could make out the shape of some sunken ship, its hull rising, half-submerged, like a great grey whale. He maneuvered the rudder, so that they would avoid the ruin, and settled back, the warm shape of Zanna resting against him.

There were no birds in the sky as they lay there, in silence, but the clouds moved above them and the sun was rising. The sea washed past them, the waves breaking against the shores of England, before being dragged back out to sea once more. The fog was attempting to clear and a brightness began to diffuse throughout the sky. From behind the clouds, the sun shone down on the small boat, covered them in its rays, and made them golden.

Fantastic Books
Great Authors

Meet our authors and discover our exciting range:

- Gripping Thrillers
- Cosy Mysteries
- Romantic Chick-Lit
- Fascinating Historicals
- Exciting Fantasy
- Young Adult and Children's Adventures

Visit us at:
www.crookedcatbooks.com

Join us on facebook:
www.facebook.com/crookedcatpublishing

7819749R00196

Printed in Great Britain
by Amazon.co.uk, Ltd.,
Marston Gate.